SCORCHER

SCORCHER

ROZ SOUTHEY

ROBERT HALE

First published in 2018 by
Robert Hale, an imprint of
The Crowood Press Ltd,
Ramsbury, Marlborough
Wiltshire SN8 2HR

www.crowood.com

© Roz Southey 2018

All rights reserved. No part of this publication may be reproduced or transmitted in any form or by any means, electronic or mechanical, including photocopy, recording or any information storage and retrieval system, without permission in writing from the publishers.

British Library Cataloguing-in-Publication Data
A catalogue record for this book is available from the British Library.

ISBN 978 0 7198 2801 0

The right of Roz Southey to be identified as author of this work has been asserted by her in accordance with the Copyright, Designs and Patents Act 1988.

Typeset by Chapter One Book Production, Knebworth

Printed and bound in India by Replika Press Pvt Ltd

DEDICATION

To C. F., for inspiring in me a love of bike racing.

AUTHOR'S NOTE

The modern bicycle was 'invented' in Paris in the late 1860s but the British took to it at once, so much so that the first known bicycle race in Paris in 1768 was won by a Briton, James Moore. Less than six months later, bicycle races were being held all over Britain, despite the poor state of many roads and the rudimentary (not to say, non-existent) comfort of the first bicycles. There was a good reason they were nicknamed 'bone-shakers' …

In the north-west counties of England, Cumberland and Westmorland, the bicycle was adopted with enthusiasm and by the 1890s a large number of bicycle clubs were in existence, including at least three in the county town of Carlisle, close to the Scottish border – clubs that were divided along political lines. Thirty miles south on the Cumberland coast, in the fishing town of Maryport, the Wheelers were one of the most successful clubs in the area.

Rivalry, between clubs and between individuals, was intense and the many races of the cycling season keenly contested. Most of the racers were from the middle and working classes – miners, shop assistants, clerks and even hairdressers …

But not, of course, women.

1

'THERE ARE SO many things one would wish to achieve,' said Charles Albert Frederick Wetherall, leaning back in the chair and narrowly avoiding having one of his ears cut off by Eppie's scissors. 'Before, that is, I – er ...' He paused and after a moment, added delicately, 'Before one leaves this vale of tears and departs for a better world.'

'Indubitably,' Eppie murmured, readjusting his aim and snipping judiciously at the area around the councillor's balding patch.

Beyond the shop window, emblazoned with the backwards letters of his own name – EDWARD EPFORD, HAIRDRESSER – a cyclist scorched down the street, nose to the handlebars, back horizontal, legs pedalling furiously. Eppie sighed. Plainly one of those who think all you have to do to win a race is to dash off at top speed as soon as the gun sounded. Of course that way you do get half a lap ahead of everyone else in no time at all. Then your legs run out on you and you end up trailing in dead last. Speed isn't everything. A little bit of guile goes a long way.

Eppie flattered himself he was good at guile of all sorts, particularly the flattering unctuous variety, though he wasn't proud of the fact. But agreeing with the customer was one of those traits a hairdresser needs in bucketsful. What on earth was making Wetherall think of mortality? He couldn't have been much more than fifty, and as hale and hearty as anyone Eppie had seen in a long time. Though fate can take a surprising turn now and again. Maybe something had happened on his trip to upset him. London apparently did that to people.

'Admirable,' he said, as Wetherall outlined all the good deeds he was doing as Chairman of the local Conservative Association. 'Most admirable.'

What on earth was the fellow going on about? If he carried on this way, Eppie would be here half the afternoon and never get to the tea-rooms. Wetherall did realize Eppie always closed on a Wednesday afternoon, didn't he? So he could go and train.

And other things.

'In order to do great deeds,' Wetherall mused, 'one has to take big risks.'

Eppie had heard about Wetherall's risk-taking – and his penchant for always managing to bet on the wrong horse. Literally.

'Without, however, compromising one's principles.'

Did politicians have principles? Wetherall was reputed to have a principle against spending money, though Eppie had always found he paid his bills promptly. Wetherall, unusually, was remarkably conscientious about such things. Not many men were as scrupulous in money matters. Though you had to present the bill in person, of course, and flatter him a bit. And woe betide you if you accidentally charged a penny or two extra.

'For instance,' Wetherall continued, clearly watching the scorcher as he wheeled with a screech of tyres and brakes at the end of the street and came back again, 'I'm thinking of setting up a cycling club.'

Eppie's ears pricked up. 'There's already a club in town. The Wheelers.' To which he had the honour to belong.

'A *Conservative* Cycling Club,' said Wetherall in the tone of a missionary. 'Composed of good strong young men ardent for the good of their country. Eager to better themselves physically and mentally and store up strength to do great things.'

Eppie wasn't sure where to start with *that* proposal. Probably best to say nothing at all. Hairdressers weren't paid to have opinions, or at least not opinions contrary to their customers. But whatever next? A Liberal Cycling Club? A Catholic Cycling Club? A Grocers' Cycling Club? Cycling was cycling, and entirely above such trivialities as politics. Ah yes, he knew what would annoy a man like Wetherall and with any luck convince him to abandon the idea entirely – given that people like Wetherall hate anything smacking of controversy.

'I take it, Mr Wetherall, that there'd be a ladies' club attached?'

Wetherall started in horror and nearly lost the other ear. Eppie didn't allow him to get a word out. 'After all, it would be wise to make sure that the fairer sex too are fitted, mentally and physically, for *their* duty to society …'

Wetherall seemed on the verge of panic. Maybe he was afraid Eppie was going to mention that dreadful three-letter word beginning with S. What was the Wetherall household like, Eppie wondered. There was a wife and daughter, wasn't there?

'Absolutely, absolutely! As mothers of the next generation, they must certainly be strong and resolute. But of course, they cannot be allowed to strain themselves too much.'

Why ever had Eppie started this? He was only going to get more and more annoyed at Wetherall's posturing. A customer was a customer and all Eppie had to worry about was giving him a good haircut and getting paid.

The scorcher came back yet again, still nose down, arse up. The bicycle was slightly too large for him; he was having to stretch his legs to their fullest extent to reach the pedals. That was going to cause him muscle problems before too long. How old was he? Sixteen? Fancied himself, obviously. Why was he racing up and down the street, being barked at by excited dogs and grumbled at by pedestrians trying to cross the road? Ah yes, he was showing off for that young lady strolling with her mama, outside the baker's. Quite a good looking young lady – very young as a matter of fact. And her mama was stylish too. Wetherall was giving *her* the eye. A ladies' man, Mr Charles Albert Frederick Wetherall. Well, Eppie wasn't adverse to a nice-looking woman, either, not adverse to *looking*. When it came to considering doing more than looking, it never occurred to him. No one was as beautiful as Alma.

He glanced at the clock. He was at severe risk of being late. Charles Albert Frederick Wetherall was still in meditative state. Still gazing at the stylish mama and her daughter.

'Yes,' he said again. 'Still lots of things to do before I – er – leave.' What an odd mood he was in! He focused on Eppie's reflected image in the glass. 'The Easter Monday sports … You *will* be taking part, of course.'

Alarm bells pinged gently in the back of Eppie's mind. 'Yes,' he agreed cautiously.

'The five-mile race?'

'All the races.'

'Don't overtax yourself,' Wetherall said firmly. 'When one has a goal in mind, it is best to concentrate on that to the exclusion of all lesser objectives.'

'The five-mile race?'

'Precisely.'

Which meant, of course, that Wetherall had a bet on Eppie to win. That probably meant he was bound to lose. And Wetherall was known to bet very substantial sums. A hundred pounds on last year's Derby, apparently. Unless that was one of those rumours it was wiser to ignore. Eppie was inclined to believe it.

'And cycling can be a dangerous sport if one is distracted.'

'Which is why,' Eppie said, 'I never allow myself to be distracted while riding.'

But Wetherall's mind had drifted again. 'Yes,' he said with an air of grim determination. 'A very great deal to do.'

Almost as if he felt he was doomed! Well, if he didn't get a move on with whatever was on today's list to achieve, he was. He stood a serious risk of meeting his fate at Eppie's hands. Today. Now!

Wetherall was on his way out of the shop but another man was on his way in. A dapper man neat in police uniform, with a rather too splendid moustache. Inspector Crellin, with that beaming smile that didn't quite manage to hide the anxiety that seemed to plague the man. Eppie glanced at the clock. He *couldn't* fit someone else in! But Crellin was shaking his head.

'Now, now, Mr Epford, don't worry. I know you always close on Wednesday and Saturday afternoons during the season. I just wanted to tell you I'm sending a little business your way.'

Well, there was no disobliging the police but in Eppie's experience they never did favours. Crellin must want something.

'Oh yes?' he said cautiously. 'What kind of business?'

'Edict of the powers that be.' Inspector Crellin chortled in a menacing sort of way and pointed towards the ceiling as if to imply that not only the chief constable but the heavenly hosts had had a hand in it. 'All police officers are to be clean shaven.'

Eppie stared at him. 'No whiskers?'

That was going to cause a stir. Most police officers of his acquaintance thought that a good set of whiskers added to their air of authority.

'Nasty couple of cases in London. Policemen grabbed by their whiskers by malefactors eager to make their escape.' Crellin beamed. Did he really think Eppie didn't realize there was something else behind this visit? 'All whiskers have to go in the next month. I've told my men they're to come here to you. They'll be on your doorstep in the morning.'

It was the most ridiculous thing he'd ever heard. But then policemen were prone to daft ideas. Inspector Crellin smoothed down his uniform coat and leant his impeccably creamed head close. He smelled so strongly of tobacco he nearly set Eppie coughing. Was that splendid moustache doomed for the scissors too, or would Crellin conveniently assume the edict applied only to the lower ranks?

'Doing the five miles at the Easter Sports, are you?'

Eppie sighed. 'I'm planning to take part in all the races.'

The inspector tapped his nose. 'And we all know who is going to win, don't we? I've got a little money on you.'

Oh Lord, was everyone betting on him? Very flattering. But the inspector had been stung last August Bank Holiday when Eppie had had a puncture in the back straight on the final lap and trailed in dead last in the half-mile spurt. He really didn't want to be responsible for sending the inspector to the very edge of bankruptcy yet again.

'Obviously I can't *guarantee* winning …'

'Beat them out of sight, you will.' And the inspector sidled out of the shop, turning back at the last minute to wink.

Eppie shut the door behind the inspector rather more firmly than he'd intended, with a push that set the bell jangling. He was going to be late. He locked the door, glanced around the shop. Nothing much to check. His apprentice, Harry, was never in on Wednesdays, so Eppie was able to keep things straight as he went along – Harry had a lot to learn. He was young, admittedly, but sixteen was amply old enough to know what to do. At Harry's age … Eppie caught himself up. He was in danger of thinking himself into old age – he was only twenty-six himself, but the early death of a father tends to make one grow older more quickly.

He went into the back room, made sure the kettle was off the heat. As usual it was a bit too warm in there because of the range which kept the water hot. He took off his apron, tidied his hair in the small mirror that hung above the sink, and slid on his jacket. Checked he looked presentable. Alma didn't particularly care about the way a man looked, or said she didn't, but he wouldn't want her to be ashamed to be seen with him. He took the keys off the hook, unlocked the back door, took one last glance around. Good God, *Cycling* – he mustn't forget that!

Outside in the street, with the magazine safely under his arm, he was nearly mown down by the scorcher. That's what happens when your attention is more on the ladies than on your riding. But there was no time to give the lad what for – he was going to be late. He hurried off down the hill, noticing that the lad was only riding on the flat bit at the top of the hill. Ridiculous.

He'd gone about three steps when he heard a great scraping of metal and furious barking. He glanced back. The lad and the bike were in a tangle on the ground, and a large Labrador was running away, tail between its legs. Well, Eppie could have told him that would happen. If there was one thing dogs loved, it was scaring cyclists.

The tea-room was a small building nestling between an ironmonger's and a dressmaker's. A little too *nice* for Eppie's tastes – all chintz and frills and furbelows. On the good side, however, it catered for the sparrow-sized appetites of the ladies, which was fine as far as Eppie was concerned, because the last thing he could afford to do was eat excessively. He was in training after all. Going hungry was part of the deal – you couldn't win races without it.

A pair of ladies came out as he got to the door. Naturally, he stood back – they separated with a fond peck on the cheek. One of them was exceedingly good-looking, though not in the first flush of youth – Eppie watched her off along the street.

And who was it who was meeting her, just outside the baker's? Mr Charles Albert Frederick Wetherall. He surely could not be meeting a lady friend in public! Outrageously blatant. Of course, Eppie was just about to meet a young lady in public too, but at least he was not married to someone else.

He glanced around the tea-room as he went in. Half a dozen ladies in there all glanced up as the bell chimed his entrance. Oh, and one rather harassed looking gentleman at the back, just looking at his watch as Eppie entered.

And Alma.

She sat at the table she preferred, in the corner, next to the little window that gave onto the courtyard at the back of the building. The sunlight caught sparks of fire from her red hair, piled up on her head in the demurest of schoolmistress styles. How Eppie would love to get his hands on that hair. And not in a professional capacity.

She smiled at him, her whole face lighting up, the skin about her eyes crinkling. Eppie walked across the tea-room as if floating.

'Mr Epford,' Alma said primly.

'Miss Gains.'

'I trust you are well?'

'Very well, thank you. I trust you had a good ride over from Carlisle?'

'I enjoyed it very much, yes. It was good exercise and I needed to make sure my new tyres were serviceable.'

Thirty miles and Alma talked about it as if it was a mere potter down local streets.

He sat smiling at her. Why did his wits always seem to desert him at moments like this? Extraordinary how hard it could be talking to someone you wanted to talk to so badly. He pulled the magazine from under his arm. 'I have just collected the latest edition of *Cycling*.'

'Oh indeed? I assume it is as interesting as always.'

'Indeed. The *Asked and Answered* section is most illuminating. It has some exceedingly interesting items on cycling for ladies.'

'I would be most interested to hear about that.' She gestured to the empty seat opposite her. 'Would you care to join me, Mr Epford? I have not yet ordered.'

He sat down with as much alacrity as if a hundred men were competing for the chair. He could never work out why a hundred men were *not* competing for the chair. Could no one else not see how wonderful she was?

The waitress sauntered across with the primmest of airs. She couldn't be fooled, of course. Customers came and went but the staff were here every day and she must have seen the same little charade acted out every Wednesday for the last two months at least. They ordered tea and cakes, and she went away again with the tiniest of smirks.

Eppie checked that no one was listening and relaxed. He laid the magazine on the table.

'Page sixteen.'

Alma opened it. The advice by 'a lady' was accompanied by a sketch of an energetic young woman on a bicycle in blouse, skirt and boater. Alma gave a little sigh.

'How on earth is one supposed to race in such a costume? Ankle length skirts! Guaranteed to catch in the gears!'

The waitress brought the tea and a selection of little cakes. Alma took the smallest, and most chocolatey; Eppie helped himself to a small portion of lemon drizzle cake. Alma poured the tea.

'Easter's only three weeks away.'

Eppie nodded. 'Thank goodness. Sometimes the start of the season seems an age off.'

'The training's going well?'

He sighed. 'I had a cold at the weekend – all the rain on Friday, I think. It set me back a day or two, but otherwise there's been no real problem.' He lowered his voice, glanced around to make sure no one could hear. Goodness, was that Wetherall again, hesitating outside the window? Looking furtive. Actually, Eppie was probably looking furtive too. And for the same reason. 'And *your* training?'

She regarded him impishly. '*Very* well. I'm indebted to you for your advice about posture on the bicycle – I'm riding the mile much faster than ever before.'

They fell into a comfortable chat about training. Keeping their voices low of course. It was one thing for a hairdresser to race his bicycle but for a lady to be interested in competition was totally different. And a schoolteacher too!

'I'd love to go out in the morning to train,' Alma said ruefully 'But Mama would want to know what I was doing and—' She broke off. 'Eppie – I beg your pardon, *Mr Epford*. Is something wrong?'

He started. 'I'm so sorry – it's just Councillor Wetherall. He's parading up and down the street as if on guard duty.'

Alma twisted in her seat and stared. Wetherall sauntered past the window again, his head craned towards the other side of the street. Alma glanced back at Eppie, rolled her eyes. 'Mrs Cartwright.'

'I'm sorry?'

'The wife of the highways engineer.'

'Not the fellow who's forbidden racing on the road?'

'Well.' Alma was obviously trying to be fair. 'That edict *has* come down from the Cycling Union. And the government. He's only trying to enforce the ban.'

'It's still stupid,' Eppie said tartly, but left the subject alone because he knew Alma and he were of one accord in that matter. 'I've never met the wife – only ever seen her at a distance.'

'Very handsome. I've heard her husband keeps a *very* close eye on her.' Alma grinned suddenly. 'Though possibly not closely enough!'

Wetherall stopped suddenly, thrust his hands behind his back, stood legs akimbo. His back was rigid. The scorcher suddenly shot past again. Eppie sighed. 'I had hoped his machine had been wrecked.'

'Horribly bad technique,' Alma said disapprovingly. 'Ah, there's Mrs Cartwright.'

The lady was inclining her head. Only Wetherall's back could be seen but it was obvious he was preening.

'Isn't it amazing,' Alma said, 'what lengths people will go to to hide a truth that's absolutely obvious to everyone else?'

And she looked at Eppie, and smiled.

'Oh dear,' he said. 'I hope not. I mean, I hope it's not obvious – I mean—'

She stiffened. 'Are you ashamed to be seen with me, Mr Epford?'

'I wouldn't be here in that case,' he retorted. 'I'm merely concerned for your reputation. I know your headmaster is very strict.'

Alma, a little pinker than before around the cheeks, ate the remainder of her chocolate cake.

'I beg your pardon. I wasn't thinking clearly.' She dusted the cake crumbs from her fingers. 'Did you know there is a new young man cycling in Carlisle? A Mr Howie. He's extremely good.'

And they were off again immediately, chatting so comfortably that the tea cooled and the clock over the fireplace ticked on. Outside, the wife of the highways engineer smiled on the rapidly-unbending Charles Albert Frederick Wetherall, and the scorcher went past one last time, still nose to the handlebars and arse to the sky. Eppie wondered why one crash wasn't enough to teach him a lesson. He'd come a big cropper soon.

As would Charles Albert Frederick Wetherall. The highways engineer was a big strong man with huge whiskers and bigger muscles. And a helping of jealousy big enough to fuel a volcano.

One cyclist, one councillor, and a married lady all dicing with danger. Eppie looked at the earnest face and glorious red hair of the love of his life, and wondered if he was treading the same route …

2

THE REST OF the afternoon was very dull. No doubt accounts have to be done, but when you're thinking of a young lady with red hair, the attractions of income and expenditure are non-existent. The house was none too warm either. March is a chilly month. Eppie put out his books on the kitchen table, where the fire in the range was contentedly crackling away, heating the hot water in the boiler, and pondered pages that didn't quite balance. In the end, he decided a cup of tea might clear his mind.

The kettle took a gratifyingly long time to boil and he stood by the range waiting for it, feeling a great sense of contentment. The house was small and some, he knew, would have called it stuffy, even confining – it was only a terraced house after all, with a room or two downstairs and another two upstairs – but every room had its memories and that made a difference. Even now, he could sometimes turn around and expect to see his mother sitting at the kitchen table. Or to hear his father clattering down the stairs, calling out that he was off to the shop.

If only he could bring Alma here. But he could only do that if she had a ring on her finger, and he had his doubts that she would marry him. There was the job for one thing. If she married, she'd have to give that up – no married woman was allowed to teach. And Alma seemed to enjoy her job, despite the headmaster's oddities. She was a very independent woman, which was why he liked her.

Even more unfortunately, he had a feeling she rather enjoyed the little bit of cloak and dagger the present situation called for. He'd seen a glint in her eye when she sat up primly and called him *Mr Epford* as if they were mere social acquaintances. A glint of amusement, if he wasn't much mistaken.

He drank the tea, finished the accounts, glanced at the clock. Dusk was gathering in the street outside – it wouldn't be long before it was dark. He must check lighting-up time. There were plenty of constables in the town who enjoyed bringing unwary cyclists up in court for having no lights. He went upstairs and changed into his road cycling kit, Norfolk jacket and knickerbockers, with thickish stockings, given that it was still early in the year. Once he got pedalling, he'd warm up. Back in the kitchen, he wrapped some cake and some bread and cheese in little packets and stuffed as much as he could into the pockets of his jacket. Then, having checked everything in the house was safe and secure, he went out into the back yard.

His three bicycles stood side by side. The Ordinary was leant against the yard wall – he could not resist giving it a pat as he passed. How out-of-date and old-fashioned it looked now, with its huge front wheel and its tiny back wheel. And the pedals attached directly to the front wheel which so severely limited the speed you could travel at. And he'd thought it the height of modernity when he bought it!

The Safety bicycles now – they were a different matter. His Rudge path racer, feather light, tyres thin as paper, dropped handlebars – goodness, but it was a good machine. Sleek as the wind. And then his road racer, which he used every day, propped against the wall of the outside convenience. A nice machine, a very nice machine indeed. The one that was nearest to his heart – 24lbs only in weight, 4½ inch tread on the tyres. Beautiful. Perfect for racing on the roads.

If only that was still legal.

He didn't have time to admire the machines or he'd be late. He wheeled the road racer to the yard gate and out into the cobbled back lane. He lit the heavy lamp on the front, swung his leg over the bar and pushed himself back in the saddle. His feet found the pedals easily and he was off, out into the quiet streets.

Hardly anyone around. A touch of frost in the air. Not enough to make the roads slippery. Past a brewery dray with big placid Shire horses. Cyclists were supposed to frighten horses? Absolute nonsense! Cart and carriage drivers didn't know how to drive properly, that's what it was. A policeman on the corner of the road … Eppie slowed slightly. The policeman gave him a long hard look. But he must have seen the lamp on the front of the cycle. Eppie rode past, out onto the main street, past his own shop, down the long hill that led towards the harbour. The road racer was light on a patch of cobbles, smooth as silk over the road.

The corner at the bottom was sharp. He slowed almost to a halt. A carriage was coming towards him, the horses trotting briskly, right down the middle of the road, and the coachman apparently not even noticing him. Eppie had to move sharply to attract his attention. The horses jibbed and the coachman swore at him. The carriage swung past. And inside …

Ridiculous. The man was haunting him today. Charles Albert Frederick Wetherall staring out of the window. He looked as if he didn't know where he was. Eppie stared back at him. Wetherall's face was a mask of bleakness. Whatever was wrong with him? He looked like a man who'd lost everything.

Well, it was none of Eppie's business. He rode on, heading for the road north. If the highways engineer hadn't had his mind so much on the doings of his wife, he might have made sure something was done about this part of the road. Just as it left town, between the plush houses of the wealthier citizens, it degenerated at the edges into gravel and crumbling metal. Which was absolutely fine – Eppie kept to the crown on the road – until another cart blundered towards him and nearly mowed him down. Eppie swung off to the side, waited in the shelter of a hedge until the thing had passed. It had a huge load of logs – heaven only knows where that was going.

He thought when he set off again that he had a problem. Something felt not quite right about the machine. He dismounted. The wealthy apparently didn't like street lights very much either, so he could see very little in the darkness. A single light was burning a little way up the street, at the entrance to a small alley, and he wheeled the bicycle into its light. His first suspicion was that he had a puncture – under the light of the gas lamp he checked the back wheel.

Nothing but a couple of largish stones caught in the tread from the gravel at the side of the road. He prised them out, checked to make sure they hadn't pierced the tyre. It looked fine. He only hoped he wouldn't find he had a slow puncture – if he had, it probably wouldn't manifest itself until he was miles out in the countryside with not much option but to walk all the way home again.

A glimpse of movement.

He glanced up the alley. It ran between two houses; in the wall of the house on the left-hand side was a small lighted window. Even as he looked, the curtain fell back down across the glass.

Someone had been watching him.

Suspicious lot, the wealthy. Probably suspected every passer-by of wanting to rob them.

After all that, he had to ride hard to make his rendezvous in time. Thankful for the fact that it was a fine night and moonlit – not a full moon, but not far off. He was only going to be a little late.

He turned off the main road to Carlisle about ten miles out of town, just beyond the railway bridge into a small rural road. Only a hundred yards or so further on was the ruin of what had been a toll cottage. The building itself was roofless, but the walls were secure, and the outline of a very small garden could just be seen between the cottage and road.

With a white patch of paper stuck in the hedge by the broken-down gate.

Eppie climbed off his machine and leant down for the paper. The *Carlisle Journal*, of today's date. The morning edition, of course, as Alma would have picked it up before she left. He hesitated for a moment, as he always did. It was risky meeting like this – risky to Alma's reputation – and Eppie would hate to be the cause of any hurt to her. But really, what harm were they doing? And who would see them?

Round the corner, there was a gap in the hedge. He squeezed through, making sure the branches did not scratch the bicycle. Then trundled the machine across what had been a lawn, and round the back of the 'house'.

'Mr Epford,' Alma's voice said. 'What a surprise to see you here.'

She giggled.

She came out of the shadows of the ruin, the moon glinting on her hair. She had changed her clothes. Instead of the neat schoolmistress garb she had worn in the tea-room, she'd donned a Norfolk jacket and …

No, he really shouldn't look. He told himself she had been eminently sensible. No long skirts, just loose knickerbockers – almost the same outfit he was wearing in fact. The knickerbockers covered her legs from top to knee, with stockings over very shapely calves …

An eminently sensible choice. He must keep telling himself that.

He gave her a decorous peck on the cheek. 'Ready, Miss Gains?'

'Indeed.'

She disappeared into the ruin again while Eppie busied himself taking the lamp off his machine. When she came back, she had her own bicycle, similarly devoid of anything that might weigh her down. He took the lamp and his bag into the ruin, left them in a little pile with Alma's belongings behind fallen roof slates. Coming out into the moonlight again, he found Alma examining her machine to make sure the wheels were running smoothly.

'If we're stopped by a constable for not having lights, I'll pay your fine.'

'You will not!' she said indignantly. 'I've a good job and I'll pay my own way.' She gave him a sideways look. 'But if we *do* get stopped, you can cover my escape. And then I'll pay *your* fine as a reward for helping me to evade the law.'

He laughed.

They wheeled the machines back to the main road and mounted just under the railway bridge. From there, the road headed north, at first in a straight line and then in increasingly tortuous twists and turns.

'Five miles?' Eppie said, knowing that Alma knew the roads as well as he did.

'I'll see you there!' she yelled, threw herself onto her machine and was off.

He pedalled off after her, deliberately – at first – allowing her to stay ahead, by a yard or two. The roads were deserted, of course. Few people travelled after dark, unless they absolutely had to. So they raced along empty metal, swung round corners on the wrong side of the road or in the middle, cut off curves in the route. On the straighter bits of road, Eppie found it easy enough to catch Alma up but she was nimbler at the turns – he found himself watching her, trying to see how she did it. She was extraordinarily good at anticipating obstacles like potholes and loose stones, reacted more quickly than he did. And she was smaller and lighter than he was, so that she flew up the inclines and hills. He was certain he could catch her any time he wanted, but she was swift and agile – she would certainly beat a good few of the fellows in the Easter Monday races. If they would only allow her to compete.

She pushed him hard. They flew up the roads. Eppie's breath came fast and shallow; his heart beat ramped up bit by bit. Picking out the twists and turns of the road wasn't easy in the moonlight, some of the shadows were almost black, and more than once he misjudged and almost overshot a corner despite knowing the road well. But nothing could beat this! Riding on the path, on that cinder track around the cricket pitch, was so tame and dull – just round and round endlessly. The entire race on the path depended almost exclusively on speed; here on the road, there was so much more, so many factors to take into account – a man had to be quick-witted, quick to react, resolute and courageous. Why on earth should anyone want to ban this, just because a few drivers couldn't control their horses?

Alma was still ahead although on a couple of occasions Eppie feinted to overtake her before dropping back again. They were coming up to the signpost that marked five miles from their departure point when Eppie trod hard on the pedals and launched himself into his sprint. Alma at once cut across the road, took his ground. He was forced to swerve violently, and in the extra second that manoeuvre cost him, she was across the junction and coming to a halt by the sign-post.

'I won!'

She had, and fairly too. More or less.

They pottered back along the roads again, more cautiously this time, warming down, keeping their legs supple.

'Look at the roads,' Eppie said. 'We haven't met a single carriage or cart. The last traffic I saw was in Maryport. Just a cart and – oh yes, I saw Mr Wetherall, heading away from his house. In a hurry, I think. And looking very sombre.'

Alma laughed. 'Perhaps Mrs Cartwright is becoming too demanding.'

'I really think you shouldn't talk about Mrs Cartwright,' Eppie said with mock severity. 'Or at least, not about certain aspects of her behaviour.'

'Just because I'm a single woman doesn't mean I'm ignorant,' Alma retorted. 'Nor does it mean I'm not a good bicyclist.' She paused for a moment, said casually, 'I haven't heard yet about my entry for the races on Easter Monday. But I saw the vicar and he looked on me very disapprovingly and said something about ladies being fragile creatures. I think he'll insist the committee reject my application.'

'The man's an idiot,' Eppie said.

There was a moment's silence. Then Alma said, 'Eppie, you are the *dearest* man.'

He couldn't say anything. Nothing at all. And when they got back to the cottage and took out the food they had brought, he found it extraordinarily difficult to eat. Just sitting next to Alma was astonishingly affecting and when she touched him on the arm, just once, just accidentally as they both reached for a wedge of cheese, he had a most unfortunate reaction …

He shifted away from her slightly and murmured apologies.

'Eppie,' Alma said, as they packed up the remains of the food and hung the lamps back on the machines. 'You know I'm not in the least a fast woman.'

'Except on the bicycle, of course,' he murmured.

'Exactly.' And she leant towards him, and planted a kiss swiftly on his lips. Then she swung herself astride her machine and disappeared down the main road towards Carlisle and home.

Eppie floated back into town. And met only one carriage as he pedalled dreamily back into town. Councillor Wetherall, still at the window, still stared bleakly and unseeingly at the passing houses.

3

Eppie rolled out of bed early next morning, as he'd had faith he would, despite his late night. Do something often enough and it becomes an ineradicable habit. It was still dark. He washed quickly, put on his cycling gear. Not the Norfolk jacket and knickerbockers this time – proper cycling shorts and vest. He snatched a cup of tea and a sandwich. Then he was out of the house, shivering in the cold morning, and cycling on the sleek path racer towards the cricket ground through streets that were full of miners plodding home from the last shift, grim and grimy faced. The path racer was much too light for comfortable travelling on the roads and he took the corners carefully. In high winds, he'd sometimes been blown across the road.

On the edge of the town, the cricket ground was deserted. He let himself in by the small gate in the high wall rather than go all the way round the other side of the ground to the main gate, and wheeled his bicycle down the steep grassy incline. The track was merely a mown oval in one corner of the cricket ground, barely a quarter of a mile round – five laps to a mile – and it was about time all the talk of replacing it with a cinder track came to fruition.

It still wasn't fully light, though there was enough light to see the path by. Eppie left his food bag and his emergency set of tools on the steps of the cricket pavilion, mounted his machine again and got down to work.

Training was almost his favourite part of racing. He didn't go very fast to start with, just a nice roll round a few times to make sure he was warmed up and his muscles supple. Then he slowly increased the pace, got down over his handlebars and dedicated himself to putting in some hard yards. Riding round and round at a regular pace, not too fast, but not slow either. At the end of every mile, he put the pedals down hard and sprinted for the line, getting his heartbeat up and his blood racing, then settled down again. More miles. Round and round.

Someone was watching him from the grassy bank. The slope had been levelled in places, into rudimentary terraces, and a single figure was hunched about halfway up. A male figure. Eppie couldn't distinguish who. After the events of the previous day, his thoughts went immediately to Charles Albert Frederick Wetherall, but a gentleman would never have sat like that.

Round and round, and the man sat on. Eppie tried to concentrate on what he was doing but his back prickled. A sense of unease grew. He knew better than to give in to it. He'd decided to do a certain number of miles and he intended to do them. He brought his attention back, managed to discipline himself not to look towards the grassy slope every time he came to that end of the track. The rhythm came back into his legs, his breath evened out. Only one mile left to do. Another five times round the path and he sprinted for the last time, putting every last ounce of his energy into it, burst across the faint painted line in the grass and stopped pedalling, allowed the machine to roll to a halt.

'You'll never win the five miles that way,' said a harsh voice behind him.

The man had come down off the slope. Eppie twisted round. Dick Sibson, still grimy-faced from his shift at the pit. Looking at the dirt ground into the lines of his face, you'd have thought him fifty, not twenty-five. But under the grime, he was annoyingly handsome, in a devil-may-care sort of way. He never had any trouble attracting the ladies – as Eppie's mother would have said, he scrubbed up well. In his Sunday best, on a stroll in the park, he could have his choice, and not just of his own class either. Eppie didn't know whether to envy him, or hate him for it.

'I won it last year,' Eppie said mildly. There was never any point in taking Dick on – he never changed his mind, never conceded any ground. He rode that way too.

'Riding round and round,' Dick said contemptuously. 'What good does that do?'

'Builds up stamina.'

'It's speed you need.'

Eppie was reminded of the scorcher, pedalling furiously up and down the high street. 'Yes,' he agreed, readily. 'That too.'

'Soft,' Dick said.

Oh Lord, not that old chestnut again. In Dick's book, only men who did hard physical labour were real men. And there was nothing harder than hewing the coal out of the underground seams, in the near-dark, knowing that the gas could come creeping up on you and kill you before you knew it was there. Hairdressing? Some men had it easy. And to make it worse, Eppie earned more money than Dick did. He had a house he owned, not rented rooms. Every time Dick came round to Eppie's house, he cast a cynical glance round and muttered something about inherited wealth. Wealth! Eppie's father had worked hard for what he'd got, and so did Eppie.

For one thing, Dick never had to put up with customers like Charles Albert Frederick Wetherall.

'I'm going to win this year,' Dick said. Not in the manner of a boast, but in the way of a man stating a fixed intention and an inevitable outcome.

'We'll see.'

'No,' Dick corrected. 'I'm telling you for sure, Eppie Epford. I'm winning. Because when the stakes are high, *I* don't chicken out.'

Meaning he thought Eppie would. No doubt because he was a *soft hairdresser*.

Dick prodded him in the chest. 'So don't set your heart on those new tyres you want to spend the prize money on. Or were you going to wine and dine that lady friend of yours?'

Eppie stared, his heart squeezed in alarm. Surely Dick couldn't know about

Alma? He knew better than to temporize with the man, though. Denial always looks like a guilty conscience.

'You aren't by any chance referring to Miss Gains? The schoolteacher from Carlisle who wishes to compete in the Easter races?'

Dick sneered. 'You didn't think you could sit all afternoon in the tea-rooms with her without someone noticing, did you?'

Eppie managed a smile. 'If people gossiped every time a man met a chance acquaintance in a tea-room, the world would be awash in rumours.' He laughed. 'Actually, it is, isn't it?'

He nodded cheerfully at Dick and wished him good day then wheeled his machine off up the slope towards the gate, maintaining his light-hearted expression. While all the time longing to take the man's throat between his hands and squeeze tight. If the fellow intended to slander Alma's good name ... Heaven forbid he find out about their late-night races – he would draw entirely the wrong conclusions!

Of course, it would be wiser to stop the said late-night races. Except it was the only time they could talk without reserve, the only time they could race each other. The only time he could race on the road ...

Why the devil was life so complicated?

His apprentice, Harry, was already in the shop and came out into the yard as Eppie wheeled his road racer in through the back gate an hour or so later. Washed, dressed in his workday clothes, invigorated by his exercise, conscious of a good hour or more of training put in, Eppie was ready for anything. And there was a nice bit of early spring sunshine about too.

'There are three policemen at the door,' Harry said, sounding young and bewildered and just a touch frightened.

Eppie was startled. 'Did they say why?'

'They're just standing outside.'

Eppie propped the machine against the outside convenience and went through the back room into the shop. On the other side of the front door, lounging about self-consciously, were three very large, very burly uniformed constables. All with fine examples of bushy beards and side whiskers.

'Don't worry, Harry,' Eppie said. 'It's just business. Go and put the kettle on.'

He had five constables in that morning, all wistfully regarding their luxuriant whiskers in the shop's mirrors one last time before Eppie shaved them off.

'All this business about being clean-shaven,' one said scornfully as Eppie chopped off one side of his drooping moustache. 'If you ask me, it's because the Chief Constable *can't* get his beard to grow.'

'No doubt,' Eppie murmured, overlooking the obvious slur on the Chief Constable's virility.

'And as for it being dangerous! I've had my whiskers grabbed hold of any number of times by the most villainous of men and never once have they got the better of me!'

'*I* wouldn't take on a fine fellow like you,' Eppie said admiringly.

It was twelve before Harry could brew that cup of tea for him. He'd never had so many policemen in the shop before. Still, any business was good business. In a brief lull without customers, he sat in the back room leafing idly through the paper and sipping his pint of tea. Alma had brought a tin of biscuits for him and he nibbled on one while he read. She was a fine cook. There wasn't much in the paper, though the highways engineer came up in the minutes of the council meeting – evidently strong things had been said about the state of the roads. Not enough repairs after the winter's frosts, in some people's opinions, too many potholes still. Wetherall had had his say about housing for the poor and so had his Liberal opponents. Someone had seen a field full of poppies in full bloom somewhere in the south – a likely story: in March? A fish caught with a gold ring in its belly: he must take up the sport if that sort of thing was going to happen.

'Mr Epford?' Harry said nervously. 'There's another policeman here …'

He sighed and went out into the shop again.

It was Constable Banks, a pleasant enough fellow – most of the time – who usually patrolled the streets in the middle of town. He had whiskers that made his head look almost twice as wide as it was in actual fact. Eppie whisked the towel around him and set about sharpening the razor.

'And how are you, Mr Banks?'

'Enjoying life, Mr Epford. Enjoying life. Still riding that bicycle of yours?'

'I am indeed.'

'On Easter Monday? At the sports?'

Eppie hesitated. 'Yes …'

'In the five miles? I've put ten shillings on you.'

Eppie groaned inwardly. If he failed and the constable lost as much as ten shillings – *ten* shillings! – he'd probably have to promise him free haircuts for the rest of his life or see the unpleasant side of the man. They said he harboured grudges. Why couldn't people just enjoy the race for its own sake? Wasn't winning the main thing in itself? He lathered the constable up and tested the razor.

He had the right side of the constable's face clean-shaven when they heard the whistle. The shop door was shut and Eppie only half-imagined he'd heard something but the constable's head came up at once and Eppie felt him stiffen.

Then another blast, closer now, and the constable leapt up, tore the towel from his neck. He was out of the shop in seconds.

Eppie hesitated then went after him.

Outside, in the thin sunshine, shoppers were looking around in vague puzzlement. An elegantly dressed woman had her hand to her bosom as if frightened. Another blast on the whistle. Constable Banks shot off across the road as if fired from a cannon. Eppie scuttled in his wake, dodging that damned scorcher. He heard the lad shout and then a screech of metal. Serve the idiot right if he'd crashed again. He should know how to handle his machine.

Across the pavement, into an alley. At the far end, silhouetted against the light, was the unmistakable figure of another constable. He yelled at them in alarm. Constable Banks came to a sudden halt and Eppie cannoned into the back of him.

They stared down at the ground at their feet. A body. A plainly dead body. A man all huddled, curled up as if he'd been trying to protect himself. Tangled in an expensive overcoat, his hat tumbled to one side. And even in this poor light, Eppie could see that his head was lying in a pool of blood.

'Gawd,' said Constable Banks. 'That's nasty. Who is he?'

'Charles Albert Frederick Wetherall,' Eppie said, then corrected himself. 'I beg your pardon, the *late* Charles Albert Frederick Wetherall.'

4

EPPIE STOOD STOCK still, looking down at Wetherall's hunched body. If ever there was a case of hubris, this was surely it. All those plans Wetherall had talked about yesterday, all the things he was going to do before he *passed from this vale of tears*. All nothing now. Positively frightening, in fact. What if it had been Eppie? You never knew …

Constable Banks was having problems with his colleague. 'How did you find him? Well, come on, man, tell me!'

The other constable was just staring. Well, that wasn't entirely surprising – it's not often you see a police officer clean-shaven on the right side of his face and fully bearded and moustachioed on the left side. Perhaps now was not a good time to remind Constable Banks of the situation. Eppie took a step back, suddenly realized he was about to step in dog mess and hopped about on one foot until he was certain he could put the other foot down cleanly.

'Well, it's obvious what happened, isn't it?' Banks said, starting to point left and right, ludicrously like a man directing traffic. 'Bloody accident.' He pointed out to the street. 'He's walking down the street.' A flick of the elbow towards the far end of the alley where the gates of a cart yard loomed. 'He's heading towards the cart yard. Something needs doing to his carriage, no doubt. He comes in here, it's a bit dark, he doesn't see the dog mess.' A dramatic gesture suggesting the turbulence of great winds. 'He slips, goes arse upwards, lands on his back and hits his head on the cobbles.' He looked down, must have realized that the alley was metalled – presumably because it led to the cart yard – and amended, 'On a stone. Or the wall.'

Eppie looked down. The dog mess had indeed been smeared across the hard surface of the alley, obviously by an unwary foot. He bent down and peered at the crown of Wetherall's head. In the small bald patch – well, quite a large bald patch, actually – there was a jagged cut and the skull around the cut looked depressed and hollow. He winced. Not nice.

Wetherall's dead expression was interesting: perfectly calm, composed, as if he'd had no idea of what was going to happen. He lay on his right side, that arm bent underneath him, and his left arm relaxed against his side, with the fingers slightly bent as if he had been about to take hold of the open edge of his coat and rearrange it over his gold watch. The body was in the middle of the alley, about two feet from the nearest wall, and there were no large, or even small, stones about.

'An accident,' Banks said. 'Stupid bloody accident. Sent someone for the inspector, have you?'

'It wasn't an accident,' Eppie said.

They looked at him. A whole crowd of people were gathering behind the second constable, peering in and trying to see what was going on; he said hurriedly, 'I'll just go and clear this lot away.' Eppie was left facing Constable Banks.

'It wasn't an accident,' he said firmly. 'I won't deny the dog mess has been stepped in but there's none on the Councillor's shoes.'

'Now, Mr Epford,' Constable Banks said. The shaven side of his face was bright red. 'Thank you for your assistance. I think you should get back to your shop.'

'He can't have hit his head on the wall because he's lying too far from it. And if he *had* slipped on the dog mess and fallen on his back, he wouldn't have been anywhere near the wall. Anyway, he's not lying on his back. And there's no stone he could have hit his head against. And if you look, you can see the wound is on the top of his head, not on the back, which is where it would have been if he'd fallen. And it's been done by something with a sharp edge, but roughly round. Sort of. Could have been a hammer, I suppose. A big one.' He took a deep breath. 'He's been hit over the head.' He was extraordinarily reluctant to draw the obvious conclusion but it had to be said. 'He's been murdered.'

'Now, now, Mr Epford,' the constable said soothingly. 'You go back to work and have a nice cup of tea. Everything will be all right. You just leave this to me.'

'And it wasn't for the sake of robbery,' Eppie said. 'His gold watch is still …'

'Goodbye, Mr Epford!' Constable Banks said menacingly.

Eppie gave up.

Harry was waiting just outside the shop, straining to see across the road and obviously desperate to know what was going on. Eppie ushered him back into the shop.

'Nothing to get worried about, Harry.' Or was it? It wasn't nice to think there was a murderer about. In Maryport! Nothing like that ever happened here. Well, nothing exciting ever did. Apart from the bicycle racing.

'They're saying someone's dead, Mr E.'

'Councillor Wetherall.' Eppie shut the shop door. 'Is that kettle on?'

'Yes, Mr E. I'll make a pot, shall I?' Harry scampered into the back room. 'It's only the councillor, is it? And I thought it must be something interesting. Heart, was it?'

'The police are saying it must have been an accident.'

Harry was even more disappointed. 'Just knocked down, was he? Not that scorcher? Just a traffic accident. Nothing much after all.'

'Unless you're Councillor Wetherall. Unless you *were* Councillor Wetherall.'

Inspector Crellin arrived just as Eppie was closing up the shop for the day. Harry was sweeping hair from beneath the chairs. Eppie took one look at the inspector and knew it was not a social call. Not a business call either, if by that you meant Eppie's business.

'Eppie,' the inspector said reproachfully. 'You've been setting Constable Banks' back up.'

Eppie would have preferred to have been called *Mr Epford* – that would have been polite. Crellin's manner suggested the crowd yelling at the sports, and they weren't at the sports. There was a certain respect due. He said formally, 'Good afternoon, Inspector. I'm sorry Constable Banks didn't get his full shave. If he comes back here first thing tomorrow, I'll sort it out. Things, as it were, got in the way.'

The inspector chuckled. 'It's a bit late for sorting it out, Eppie – the lads have all seen him and they're never going to let him forget it. But that's not the problem, lad. You've been letting your imagination run away with you.'

And the inspector was letting his familiarity run away with *him*. No doubt a man in his fifties does look on a man of twenty-six as a young whippersnapper but it's not polite to let that affect your behaviour towards him in front of his apprentice.

'Harry,' Eppie said. 'Go and sort out in the back room.'

'I haven't finished here …'

'The back room, Harry.'

Harry went into the back room. If the inspector had wanted a bet, he could have bet on Harry listening at the door, but he wouldn't have got very good odds.

'Inspector,' Eppie said with a distinct trace of hauteur in his voice, 'if this is about Councillor Wetherall's death, then I'd rather you came straight out and said so.'

'A tragedy.' The inspector shook his head sadly but there was a shrewd sharp look in his eyes. 'A tragic accident.'

Oh well, in for a penny, in for a pound. 'It didn't look like an accident to me.'

'Trust me, lad. We've had the experts in. The doctors have had a look at him and they say he slipped in the dog – ah – mess. And, of course, there's the family. The wife and daughter.'

'And Mrs Cartwright?'

The inspector looked puzzled – it seemed genuine to Eppie. 'The daughter, you mean? No, no, she's not married. Though there's a young man in the offing, I'm told. Mr Epford …' He put a hand on Eppie's arm. 'Leave this to us, eh?' And this time there was no mistaking the pleading in his voice. Good Lord, the man was – well, was *scared* too strong a word to use?

Well, what could he do? The body would have been taken away by now, the alley would have been cleared up and Constable Banks would have told his story. And Eppie would look like a gawping sensation-seeker.

'When's the inquest?'

'Nothing's fixed yet.' The inspector was still watching him closely. 'The coroner is away for the day and won't be back till tomorrow. But there's no need for you to worry, Mr Epford – you won't be needed as a witness.'

It was a *fait accompli* then. They'd decided what they wanted the coroner to hear and it wasn't what Eppie was likely to say. Well, they did have the family to think of – they'd obviously be upset and it couldn't be nice to think someone had bashed your husband or father over the head with a blunt instrument. Even if it was what had happened. But surely the family would want to know the truth? Wouldn't they be egging the inspector on to find the murderer?

Maybe Eppie had been wrong. If only he'd stayed a bit longer in the alley, looked at things again …

Crellin was smiling encouragingly. Eppie sighed. 'Very well, Inspector. And you'll send the constable back for the rest of his shave?'

'I'll even pay for it myself,' the inspector said with a chuckle. And he went off, leaving Eppie with a very nasty taste in his mouth. The inspector would certainly pay a great deal of money for that shave, with a wink and a whispered 'For your trouble, Eppie.' For his trouble in not going to the inquest. For his trouble in not making a fuss.

He'd just been offered a bribe.

5

EPPIE HAD NO intention of going to the inquest which was scheduled for the early afternoon, in the Town Hall – in the Council Chamber to be precise, which seemed appropriate, given the profession of the deceased. Well, by profession he'd been a gentleman, of course, but as a councillor it seemed allowable he should have a little pomp and ceremony about his departure. Eppie was definitely not going to go. He had work to do, in the shop. Of course he could leave Harry in charge – he was a competent lad and would know what he was not capable of. Mostly. But he'd certainly lose money …

On the other hand, perhaps Harry ought to be given a chance to show what he could do.

Of course, the local press would be there and Eppie would read what happened in the paper soon enough. But that wasn't like seeing and hearing for yourself, was it?

The inspector wouldn't like seeing him there.

It was open to the public. Any inquest was. His turning up wouldn't mean a thing. In fact, it would probably be odder if he didn't turn up. Everyone else would be there.

No, he wouldn't go.

The council chamber was crowded. The entire town must be there, from shopkeepers and labourers to the gentry – as Eppie heard a lady say just as he got to the doorway, 'There's nothing more interesting than a good death, is there?' The coroner, standing chatting to his clerk, was Mr Senhouse, a burly middle-aged lawyer who looked like a building labourer, only more expensively dressed – he had a penchant for the latest fashions and the money to indulge his tastes. The elegant and rather staid figures of Industry, Arts and Science looked down from stained-glass windows, from swirls of flowers and frozen birds in flight; the roof timbers overhead somehow suggested a church. Voices echoed, or were lost in multiple whispers in the high corners of the roof.

Eppie hesitated at the door, heard one of those whispers speak his name. He scanned the crowd of eager onlookers, and spotted Amos Danson, tall and spindly, with impeccably coiffed hair brushed to suggest he'd carelessly run his fingers through it and tossed it back. He was waving at Eppie to attract his attention, and pointed energetically at an empty place on the bench beside him. Eppie squeezed through the crowd.

Amos shifted to allow him room. Just as Eppie got there, he thought he heard someone else say his name. He glanced round, saw Dick Sibson standing at the back, in his best clothes, looking remarkably spruce and clean, with other cycling cronies and a couple of women sidling close. The sort of women who are no better than they should be, and who like a strong man. Dick was giving them measuring looks as if trying to decide which one he preferred.

He did not want to have to listen to Dick condemning his training methods twice in one day – he nodded at Dick and slipped into the seat beside Amos.

'Welcome to the show, my boy. All the attractions of the fair, the idiosyncrasies of the deceased laid bare, all his misdoings. Do you know he was adamantly against the latest proposals for the harbour?'

'No,' Eppie said, 'and it doesn't interest me in the least.'

Amos nodded. 'It wouldn't interest the paper's readers either. So I'm hoping for some scandalous revelations.' He brandished a notebook in which he'd already scribbled some mysterious squiggles. 'Though I don't hold out much hope. Trust a politician to slip on a dog turd.'

Eppie said nothing. When you chatted to Amos, there was always the danger you'd see your comments in the next edition of the local rag.

The coroner called everyone to order, in a commanding tone that made everyone jump. 'Constable Fawcett!'

Fawcett, a young, red-faced, pimply man, turned out to be the constable who'd found the body. He had obviously been warned to say as little as possible. He had apparently literally tripped over the body on his beat and had blown his whistle at once. He gave the strong impression that he was only too glad the more experienced Constable Banks had happened on the scene. His most frequent and fervent utterance was 'I couldn't say, m'Lord'. The coroner, clearly increasingly irritated, dismissed him and said sonorously, 'Constable Banks!'

There was a great stir and Constable Banks trod heavily to the front of the room. He'd enlisted someone to shave off the remaining half of his beard and moustache. So much for Inspector Crellin's suspicious offer of riches. Banks looked unfamiliar and surprisingly young in his clean-shaven state.

'Me Lud.'

The coroner did not bother to correct the form of address; in fact he looked as if he rather liked it.

'You discovered the body, I believe, Constable.'

Constable Banks launched into an energetic account of what had happened, gesticulating widely at the coroner and the jury. He'd been in the barber's when he heard a whistle and dashed out to find out what was going on. He described the dog mess in loving detail, and explained his theory of the accident, waxing lyrical about unexpected tragedies in the midst of happiness and success. Eppie almost expected him to burst into biblical references about *in the middle of life we are in death* or whatever the correct words were. He did manage a reference to Wetherall being *cut down in his prime*. The coroner looked dubious.

'And you saw no one about the scene except Constable Fawcett?'

'No, me Lud. Well, apart from Mr Epford.'

Everyone, absolutely everybody, turned to look at Eppie. Why, oh why had he come? Amos whispered, 'You been hiding something from me, Eppie?'

The coroner looked down his nose at Eppie. 'And why was Mr Epford there?'

'I think he was sight-seeing, me Lud.'

Eppie sighed. That was probably true. Not that he'd thought of it that way – he'd just dashed off out of curiosity. But everyone else had too.

Constable Banks was allowed to go and was succeeded by the diminutive, red-eyed Doctor Graham, who seemed to want to vie with the coroner for the loudest, most echoing voice in the chamber.

'The deceased,' he pronounced, 'died from a blow to the head, which fractured his skull. He would have died at once, absolutely straight away.'

The coroner nodded. 'And is it your opinion that he hit his head against the wall, or against the ground when he fell?'

'Neither,' said the doctor robustly. 'Totally the wrong idea. Someone hit him over the head.'

So much, Eppie thought, for the inspector's plan to keep suspicion at bay.

Amos crowed with laughter, half the women in the room gasped in horror, and the coroner's clerk started hushing everyone with pompous indignation. The coroner frowned.

'Whatever makes you think that?'

'Bloody obvious. The wound was on the top of the head, not the back. Anyway, if he's slipped on dog shit, ten to one he would have fallen flat on his face, not on his back. That way he would have broken his nose, not his head.'

The coroner pursed his lips. 'Could something have fallen on his head from above?'

'Not unless it was dropped by a bloody passing seagull. Besides, there was nothing on the ground. Unless that idiotic constable picked it up in a fit of absent-mindedness.'

Amos scribbled away furiously. 'Banks *is* an idiot, you know,' he said out of the corner of his mouth.

'If you ask me,' the doctor said. 'It was a bloody hammer. And it *would* have been bloody afterwards. Very bloody. There was a pool of the stuff under the deceased's head. Well, obviously. You can't go around hitting someone over the head without getting splashed.'

More gasping from the women. The jurymen looked horrified. Someone caused a rumpus by fainting at the back of the room.

'Umm,' said the coroner considering. 'Did you measure the deceased? How tall was he?'

'Six feet exactly.'

'So if someone hit him over the head, that person would have had to be taller than six feet?'

The doctor shifted, started flexing his right hand, mimed a blow or two. Women shuddered audibly.

'Not necessarily,' he decided eventually. 'But at least the same height. If you had a hammer in your hand, you'd gain an inch or two in reach which would help. Say roughly the same. And before you ask, a man. No woman would have anything like the strength required.'

'And is there any way you can calculate roughly what time the attack took place?'

'Oh come on, man!' the doctor exploded. 'The councillor was still bloody warm!'

'Thank you very much, Doctor,' the coroner said. 'If I may say so, admirable evidence well presented.'

Eppie and Amos looked at each other. 'It's all right,' Amos whispered. 'Doctor

Graham never recognizes irony.'

The doctor strode out of the court.

'Miss Wetherall,' intoned the coroner.

More gasps from the ladies, then a rather envious murmur. Behind Eppie, a middle-aged woman said sourly, 'More money than sense.'

The young lady who hesitated at the back of the court was no more than eighteen years old, hair angelically blonde, pale skin rosy about the cheeks. She was wearing a black gown of course, but with frills and furbelows, discreetly done. A bonnet shaded her face, a lace handkerchief was clutched in her left hand.

Amos leant sideways again. 'I always distrust handkerchiefs.'

The young lady was propelled forward by a gentle push from a tall elegant gentleman of about thirty years of age. Amos muttered, 'The fiancé.'

Eppie said, 'That looks a fashionable gown to me.'

'Oh, it's the latest thing,' Amos agreed. 'My Belle wangled one just like it out of me the other day. Only in mauve. Who would want to wear mauve? I ask you, my dear fellow, mauve!'

The young lady gave her name as Miss Violet Daisy Rose Wetherall. (Amos rolled his eyes.) She explained that her mother was prostrated and unable to attend the court but she herself had been determined to come, 'for dear Papa's sake'. (The ladies murmured in sympathy and the jurymen nodded approvingly.) Miss Wetherall, Eppie thought, was taking note of her effect on the gentlemen in the court, and making sure it was favourable. She even cast a glance towards the onlookers at the back of the room and Eppie could have sworn that her gaze lingered briefly on Dick before the handkerchief came into play again. She explained that she had last seen 'dear Papa' at breakfast on the day of his *passing* and had spent the day with an old school friend, only hearing the news when she returned home in the evening.

'And how did your papa seem at breakfast, my dear?' said the coroner. 'Was he in good spirits?'

'Oh very!' Miss Wetherall took a deep breath that shuddered slightly. 'He had so many plans. He was very concerned about the poor and had lots of schemes to help them. And he was looking forward to my wedding next year.'

'He had no concerns, no worries? No one had in any way threatened him, or caused him any alarms?'

Miss Wetherall hesitated. A lock of her blonde hair fell across her shoulder, across the black fabric of her fashionable mourning gown. 'He said nothing but …'

'But?' prompted the coroner.

Miss Wetherall cast him a doubtful luminous look. 'It's just – well, I may be wrong but – well, you see things, don't you, and—'

Amos scowled, mumbled, 'Don't you just hate young women who've been taught to have no opinions of their own?'

The coroner encouraged Miss Wetherall to go on. She took another of those shuddering breaths. 'It was Wednesday night,' she said. 'The night before last. The last night of his …' Her voice failed her; a woman murmured loudly, 'There, there, love.'

'On Wednesday evening,' Miss Wetherall said more firmly. 'I was in the parlour, embroidering. My trousseau.' She cast a tremulous smile in the direction of her fiancé; he nodded supportively. 'The parlour is on the corner of the house, with a window out into the alley that runs between our house and the next.'

An alley? Eppie shifted uncomfortably. Wednesday night? He'd stopped to remove those stones from his tyres somewhere in those streets. There'd been an alley, hadn't there, and a curtain twitching too. Oh Lord …

'It was very quiet.' Miss Wetherall was warming to her task, but she cast little glances at the coroner as if to make sure of his approval. 'I heard footsteps outside – well, that's not unusual, even at that time of night. I mean, the coachman goes that way, and the gardener too. Then I heard my father's voice. He sounded …'

'Yes?' said the coroner, encouragingly.

'Angry.' She seemed to take courage, plunged on. 'I couldn't hear exactly what he was saying – it was all muffled – but he was certainly annoyed with someone. And there was another man there too – I could hear him saying something. And then my father raised his voice and I distinctly heard him say "How dare you threaten me!"'

Sensation in court, as Amos would no doubt write. Like Miss Wetherall, Eppie could not hear exactly what was being said, as everyone was saying whatever it was at the same time as everyone else in court. Amos was muttering too, more to himself than Eppie. Eppie stared at Miss Wetherall. How sweet and young and inoffensive she looked. How demure. How could anyone actually be like that? She must have been protected all her life. Was that actually good for her? Oh dear, he must stop moralizing.

'I went to the window,' she said, 'because I was, well, a little alarmed. I thought perhaps I ought to send for one of the servants, to help Papa. I thought it must be a pedlar or a beggar trying to get money from Papa.'

'And what did you see, my dear?'

'It was so dark outside. But I could see Papa, just on the other side of the alley, as if he had been stopped suddenly – he looked as if he was about to walk away.

The other man had his back to me so I could not see his face.'

Murmurs of disappointment. The coroner was not a man to be discouraged, however.

'Was he tall or short?'

Miss Wetherall considered. 'Of medium height, I think. With dark hair well-cut and slicked back. A slight man.'

Amos flicked a glance at Eppie as if to check what he looked like. Yes, Eppie thought, with a lowering of spirits, he did fit the description.

'And then Papa said, "I'll give you no money, sir. Out of my way." And the man said, "You'll regret this." Papa said again, "I'll give you no money." And he strode off towards the back of the house.'

Amos was frowning. He leant towards Eppie, whispered, 'Maybe he knew about some dark secret of Wetherall's and was trying to get money out of him.'

'Blackmail?' Eppie was startled.

'Some woman involved, I bet you.'

'But everyone knows about Wetherall's affairs. Well, apart from his wife. Possibly.'

The coroner was frowning at the court – Eppie and Amos weren't the only ones whispering. Eppie shook his head. Why was Miss Wetherall telling this story? Didn't she realize it could cast her father in a very bad light? Amos wouldn't be the only one wondering what secrets Wetherall had had.

'And this man,' the coroner asked. 'What did he do then?'

Miss Wetherall cast a look around the chamber. Her gaze oddly seemed to linger on Eppie. 'He turned and went off towards the road.'

'And did you see his face then?'

'No ...' she said reluctantly. Another flicker of a glance at Eppie, and a quick glance away. 'At least, not clearly. Only from the back.'

Amos glanced at Eppie.

'And then ...' Miss Wetherall hurried on. 'And then he rode off.'

'He had a horse? That doesn't sound like a pedlar or a beggar.'

'No,' she said. 'He rode off on a *bicycle*. Very quickly. I think he was what they call ...' She hesitated, pronounced the word carefully, as if it wasn't quite polite. 'A *scorcher*.'

And Eppie suddenly found that *everyone* was looking at him.

6

'And when he rode off on his *bicycle* – did you see him then? Do you see him in this court, for instance?'

She looked directly at Eppie. He was not mistaken. She *did*. And why did the coroner say the word *bicycle* in such a contemptuous tone?

'No, no,' she said hurriedly. 'I didn't see him clearly, I told you I didn't see him clearly.' She started to cry.

For a few minutes everything was kindly chaos. A middle-aged woman near Miss Wetherall got up, put her arm round her and said, 'There, there, love, don't cry.' The coroner called for a glass of water. 'Or, better still, lemonade!' The jurymen looked concerned. Amos leant in close to Eppie's ear. 'You didn't know the fellow, did you?'

'I cut his hair,' Eppie said through gritted teeth.

This was ridiculous. Why was everyone looking at him? Lots of people rode bicycles. Admittedly, his picture had been in the paper last August when he won the five-mile handicap. He rather wished he hadn't let Amos write that piece about him, even if he had cut it out and stuck it in his scrapbook.

'Mr Edward Epford,' the coroner intoned.

So much for his evidence not being needed. Eppie looked round and met the inspector's eye. Crellin frowned furiously at him – Eppie took that to mean he wasn't supposed to mention what he'd seen in the alley. But surely that couldn't hurt now, given the doctor's evidence? He got up just as Amos gave him an encouraging pat on the arm.

He wasn't used to being in front of so many people. And hairdressers were good at listening, not at talking. Everyone seemed to be hanging on his every word. Worse, the coroner was looking at him as if he was an interesting specimen of some disgusting beetle and he couldn't see a single customer on the jury. And it would be really nice if Dick would stop smirking at him, and start paying more attention to the blonde hanging on his arm.

'Did you know the deceased?'

Well, the obvious thing to do was to tell the truth. 'Yes.' Why was his voice squeaking? He hadn't squeaked like that since he was eleven. He cleared his throat. Murmuring in the back rows of the chamber.

'Well, explain!' said the coroner irritably.

'He's a customer. He *was* a customer. I cut his hair.'

'Do you know him well?'

'Only as a customer,' Eppie repeated. 'I occasionally see – *saw* – him in the street but never to talk to.'

'And when did you last see him?'

Oh Lord. Eppie took a deep breath. 'Wednesday.'

Miss Wetherall cast her eyes down to her hands clasped in her lap. Why on earth should she think it was him she'd seen? More sensation amongst the crowds in court. Even the stained-glass elegantly-robed female figures of Industry, Arts and Science seemed eager to hear what Eppie was about to say.

'I cut his hair,' he repeated. Good Lord, he was beginning to sound like an idiot. 'He was my last customer before I closed at midday.'

'And did he seem at ease?'

'Perfectly at ease. He was talking about various council matters.'

'And anything else?'

'He was thinking of setting up a cycling club,' Eppie said, not without reluctance. A sea of faces all staring at him. He deliberately looked across to where Amos was, in the hope of seeing a friendly expression, but Amos had his head down and was scribbling away. Dick Sibson was directly behind him.

'A cycling club? Of what kind?'

'A Conservative Cycling Club.' There were twitters of laughter from the audience. The coroner frowned them down. 'And did you agree with this?'

'He wasn't asking for my agreement,' Eppie said. 'He was just telling me his plans.'

The coroner looked at him from under his brows. 'He was confiding his plans to his hairdresser?'

Eppie was stung by his tone of incredulity. 'Some people do.'

'*I* don't,' the coroner said repressively.

More titters.

'Mr Epford,' the coroner said. 'Where were you on Wednesday evening?'

Eppie opened his mouth and shut it again.

'Well?'

'I was out training.'

'*Training*?'

Eppie would have been a lot happier if the coroner hadn't had such an expert line in contemptuous disbelief.

'It's only three weeks until the Easter Sports and I hope to win some of the races there.'

'On your bicycle?'

'Yes.'

'And you *train* for that?' The coroner looked astonished. 'I would have thought no special preparation would be necessary.'

'Well, it is,' Eppie said.

'Indeed? And what does this *training* consist of?'

'Getting the hard yards in. Riding as many miles as possible in order to build up your stamina and endurance.'

Trust Dick to grin so contemptuously at this point. They'd see. When it came to the sports. Dick would learn that Eppie's methods worked.

'And where did you do this training on Wednesday?'

'On the road north.'

'On the road.' The coroner's eyebrows shot up. 'Is that not illegal?'

Drat it. 'No,' Eppie said. '*Racing* on the road is illegal. Simply riding the bicycle is not.'

'Scorching along, I dare say.'

'No. I am not a scorcher. I train for endurance, not speed.'

'Doesn't sound a good idea to me.' The coroner smirked. 'It's no good having all the endurance in the world if you don't have the speed to beat the other fellows. Eh?'

Eppie said nothing. It was apparent that the coroner was not a cyclist himself. Probably had a stable full of horses.

'Of course,' the coroner said. 'The house of Mr Wetherall lies on the road north, does it not?'

'Does it?' Eppie stared at Dick. The fellow was still grinning. There was a streak of malicious enjoyment in that grin – Eppie would have words with him later. And what on earth was Amos still finding to write down?

'You did not happen to see Mr Wetherall by any chance?'

'As a matter of fact, I did.' Eppie said loudly. 'Twice, to be precise.'

He was getting very tired of all this noise in court. Why on earth was the coroner not shutting them all up? And why was that stout man on the jury scowling?

'At the bottom of the main street, I was nearly run down by a carriage taking the corner too widely. I waited for it to pass and I saw Mr Wetherall in the window of the carriage. Then, much later, on my way back, I saw him and the carriage, again, going in the other direction.'

'And what did he say to you?'

'Nothing. The carriage didn't stop. I don't think he even saw me, either time.'

The coroner pursed his lips. Behind him, in the stained-glass window, Industry seemed to be doing the same thing, with an extra, sceptical, twist to her mouth.

'And you did not stop at his house?'

'I don't know where he lives.'

'Oh yes, you do,' the coroner said with unmistakable glee. 'I just told you. On the road north. Were you alone, Mr Epford?'

Alarm bells started clanging, as loudly as if the verger was ringing them in the church tower just down the hill. How could he possibly tell them about meeting Alma? They'd all make the same assumption. Her reputation would be in tatters. She'd lose her job.

'Totally alone,' he said firmly. 'I always train alone. No two riders go, or want to go, at the same pace.'

'No one else with you at any time in the evening?'

'No.'

'And you didn't stop anywhere?'

'No.'

'Not at all?'

'Not at all.'

He had just lied. In court. Oh Lord, it must be so obvious ...

Silence in the chamber. Eppie lifted his head and stared back at the coroner.

'Very well,' said the coroner. 'You may go.'

Eppie felt as if he was escaping. But he walked sedately back down into the body of the chamber and took his place beside Amos. Who looked at him with a judicious pursing of his mouth.

There was little else. A variety of gentlemen were called, business associates of Wetherall, who all testified that he was a man of principle who didn't have an enemy in the world. To a man, they thought he must have been murdered by some ruffian who went round doing that sort of thing all the time. After a great deal of this, there was some rather more interesting information from Wetherall's solicitor, who revealed the terms of the will. Everything was left to Wetherall's daughter, providing she did not marry against the wishes of her trustees, but with a life interest in the property to her mother. Small bequests to the servants and mourning rings for a variety of friends. No reference to any other family members – Wetherall had apparently been an only child. Since the coroner pointed out that the doctor had been adamant that the blow could not have been inflicted by a woman, the will eliminated the question of inheritance as a motive for an attack on Wetherall.

The jury's verdict was inevitable: murder by person, or persons, unknown. Eppie was only relieved that the foreman of the jury didn't look at him when he pronounced the decision.

Amos took Eppie by the arm as they turned to edge out of court with the rest of the crowd who were eagerly debating the appalling events so noisily that Amos had to raise his voice.

'Public house, my dear fellow. Or have you sworn off beer in the interests of training?'

'I could be persuaded to break my rule,' Eppie said, feeling almost weak with relief.

Amos knew every hostelry in the town – he had probably been in them all in search of information at one time or another. Eppie found himself in one of those less than salubrious snugs with sawdust on the floor and tables sticky with spilt beer. Three or four dogs roamed sinuously through the table legs and stared beseechingly up at drinkers. Amos tipped a little puddle of beer onto the floor, and a mongrel lapped it up eagerly.

'You know the best places.' Eppie sniffed at his beer and took a cautious sip. It managed to be both weak and acrid at the same time. Not worth breaking his training for.

Amos was taking huge gulps of his pint. 'You're in there, Eppie. That young lady really took a shine to you.'

Eppie stared at him. You never knew with Amos – sometimes he was being sarcastic, and sometimes he was being perfectly serious. 'Miss Wetherall?'

'She was staring at you the whole time. You're a good-looking fellow, you know.' And he shook his own mane of hair back as if waiting for a similar compliment.

Eppie had no intention of indulging him. Besides, he was astonished that Amos had apparently not picked up the undercurrent of suspicion in the coroner's questioning. He couldn't have imagined it, surely?

'What do *you* suppose happened?' he asked curiously. Amos had an explanation for everything and Eppie usually found the explanations convincing.

'Robbery, obviously.'

'No, no. He still had his gold watch.'

Amos raised an eyebrow. 'Nothing said about that in court. Are you sure, my boy?'

'I saw it.'

'A *thwarted* robbery, then. The constable – the first one with the whistle – disturbed the robber before he could get his loot.'

'I suppose he might have. Though no one's said anything about seeing someone running off – and those are busy streets. Someone would surely have seen a fugitive. And why has no one explained that trip Wetherall made on Wednesday night? Why haven't they questioned his coachman?'

'Because,' Amos pointed out, 'no one knew anything about the trip until you mentioned it in your evidence.'

'The *coachman* did.'

'Why should they have talked to him? That was Wednesday night. It's what happened just before his murder on Thursday that they're interested in.'

'They were interested in Miss Wetherall's story of an argument on Wednesday evening.'

'That suggests a motive for the murder. The coach trip does not. My dear fellow, ten to one he was just off to see one of his mistresses. Are you going to drink that beer?'

'No, it's not worth the money.'

'My money.' Amos drained his own glass and started on Eppie's. The mongrel was staring up pleadingly again – Amos poured it more beer.

'Doesn't it strike you as odd that the murder took place in broad daylight?'

'Told you – attempted robbery. The thief saw Wetherall and took his chance.'

'Why was Wetherall in that alley?'

'He was going to the cart yard.'

'Why?'

'To buy a cart?'

'Why?'

'Eppie! You're as bad as a five-year-old.'

He nearly said *You're not the one against whom insinuations are being made.* But maybe he was wrong. Maybe he'd misinterpreted the coroner's questions. After all, he wasn't the only cyclist in town, even if superficially he fitted Miss Wetherall's description of the man with whom her father had had an argument.

'Anyway,' he said. 'Miss Wetherall's account of the unknown man's argument with her father doesn't make sense. Or at least the conclusions drawn from that meeting don't make sense. If that man was threatening Wetherall, that gives Wetherall a motive for killing him, not the other way round.'

Amos nodded. 'True. And Miss W ought to think carefully about what she says. If said unknown was demanding money, then he presumably knows something to Wetherall's discredit. Does Miss W seriously want to damage her father's memory?'

'She presumably wants to find his murderer.'

'Don't you believe it, my boy. Most women simply want to brush nasty things under the carpet. You'd be amazed how my Belle clams up and refuses to talk when unpleasant topics are in the offing.'

Eppie tried to imagine Alma refusing to discuss serious matters, and failed.

'I think,' Amos said slowly, emerging from the pint with foam on his lips. 'We are missing the obvious here. Wetherall was chairman of the Conservative Association. There must be a political motive.'

'Just about every Liberal in town probably hated him,' Eppie said, depressed. 'And there are an awful lot of Liberals.'

'Indeed there are!' Amos winked. 'And I know them all.' He drank the remainder of the beer in one draught. 'Time to question a few of them, I think.' He squeezed out of his corner and slapped Eppie on the back. 'Keep up the training, lad – I've ten bob on you to win the five miles on Easter Monday!'

And he strode out, leaving Eppie to the beseeching gaze of the mongrel.

At home, Eppie hunted in a drawer and found an old postcard of the harbour. He addressed it to Alma in Carlisle.

Dear Miss Gains, I regret that I find myself unable to honour our appointment this Saturday. I will contact you again when I am able to confirm another date. Yr humble servt &c. Edward Epford.

In other words: *Do not come to Maryport this weekend.*

There was no way he was going to let suspicion come anywhere near her.

7

HE WHEELED THE road racer out into the back lane and shut the gate. Mounting, he pedalled out into the street and the faint light of dawn. Nice and slowly. Don't do anything too strenuous until you're properly warmed up. By the time he reached the cricket ground, his muscles would be nice and supple, ready for a good few laps.

'Oi!'

He rolled to a halt. Even in that one shouted syllable he recognized Inspector Crellin's dulcet tones. He put a foot to the ground, twisted in the saddle. The inspector was sprinting across the road from the front of the house. Surprisingly nimble – Eppie would never have expected it of him.

'Oi!'

'Can I help you, Inspector?' He was afraid he already knew the answer to that – there was only one reason the inspector should come to his home.

'Where're you off to?'

That wasn't a good start. No *Mr Epford*. No polite greetings or inanities. Just *Oi – where're you off to?*

'Training. At the cricket ground.'

'I want to ask you some questions.'

Well, there was no point in pretending ignorance. 'About seeing Mr Wetherall on Wednesday evening?'

'Too right,' the inspector said. His face was red from running – Eppie could almost feel the heat radiating off it. The inspector was spry but not fit. Too much beer, probably. 'I want you down the station now.'

Some things have to be nipped in the bud. Eppie took his hands off the handlebars and leant back in the saddle. 'I'm perfectly prepared to be cooperative, Inspector, but I don't like the tone of voice you're taking. Politeness doesn't cost anything.'

The inspector opened his mouth and shut it again. Eppie dropped forward onto his handlebars. 'I'll see you at the station.' And he put the pedals down hard and sprinted off along the street.

He arrived at the station a full five minutes before the inspector's cab rolled up. The station was a rather dull building, with flat-faced windows and a brown door. Crellin didn't so much as look at it when he hopped out of the cab.

'Right, *Mr* Epford, inside if you please. Oi!'

Eppie stared at him. 'What *now*?'

'You can't take that bike inside. Prop it against that wall.'

'I can't leave it outside!' Eppie was appalled. 'It'll be stolen.'

The inspector gave it a critical look. 'It's just about the ugliest bike I ever saw. Flimsy too. Surprised it takes your weight. Who would want that?'

'It's a Rudge road racer! It was horribly expensive. And the tyres alone …'

The inspector sniffed. 'Lot of money to spend on a hobby.'

A hobby. Eppie suddenly saw himself as the inspector must see him: a young man with more money than sense, who went out in all weathers and got himself hot and sweaty, and sometimes sodden wet if it was raining, riding round and round and round and round the cricket pitch. *Waste of time*, he'd say.

'And in case you hadn't noticed, there's a police officer outside that door. No one's going to steal your bicycle with him standing there.'

The police officer looked bored and half-asleep. Resigned, Eppie carefully leant the bike against the wall, taking care not to scratch the machine.

He followed the inspector into the building. Inside, it wasn't any different from any other building in the town, except possibly that it smelt rather stuffy, and oddly – he sniffed – very lemony. Something used in the cleaning, maybe. Everyone was looking at him. Three or four uniformed constables, and two elderly ladies, very respectably dressed, who turned their heads away from him ostentatiously. He was suddenly very aware he was dressed in his skimpy cycling gear. At least the building was well-heated. Over-heated, in fact. No doubt that was why it was so stuffy.

The inspector's office was small and cramped, with several desks nudging each other at the corners. The inspector squeezed through to a chair with its back to a small window and gestured Eppie to another on the other side of the desk. The chair was bare and wooden, and the seat felt cold against Eppie's bare legs.

'Now,' Crellin said, staring hard at him. 'About this little expedition of yours on Wednesday night. Why didn't you tell me about it?'

'You didn't ask.'

The inspector looked as if he was thinking of taking that reply as a piece of impertinence. 'A man is murdered and you didn't think about telling the police a bit of evidence?'

'You told me to stay out of it.' Eppie pointed out. 'You said it was an accident. And if it *was* an accident, then it didn't matter where Wetherall was going the previous night, did it?'

'It *wasn't* an accident …'

'I know. *I* told you that.'

'I knew all along,' Crellin said airily. 'I thought it was suspicious from the first. My comments about it being an accident were meant to lull the fears of the guilty party. And I don't think you should play around with me.'

'I'm not.' And he wasn't deceived by Crellin's protestations that he'd known it was murder all along. 'What do you want to know about Wednesday?'

The inspector looked as if he felt he was losing control of this situation. 'Where were you going?'

'Training.'

'I didn't ask you *what* you were doing. I asked *where* you were going.'

Eppie described his route, missing out only the ruined toll cottage and his meeting with Alma.

'How fast were you going?'

Eppie eyed Crellin. That was a trick question, if ever he heard one. If he said he was going fast, then Crellin would have him up for dangerous riding, or racing on the roads even though he'd been – allegedly – on his own.

'I don't go fast. I'm training for endurance. Which simply means riding as many miles as possible at a steady pace. Besides—' Eppie decided to take the fight to the inspector, 'there's a law against riding too fast on the road, isn't there?'

'There's a rule against racing,' the inspector said tartly, 'and if I find out that you were meeting some of your pals for clandestine races …'

'No,' Eppie said, 'I was not.' Really, lying was a surprisingly easy habit to acquire.

His firmness seemed to disconcert Crellin. He pursed his lips. 'This time you saw Mr Wetherall, then. On the Wednesday night.'

'I saw him twice. Once on my way out to train and once on the way back.' Eppie described the encounters as best he could, though there was little to tell. He thought the inspector was not particularly impressed by his description of Wetherall as looking *bleak*. And, truth to tell, he was beginning to wonder himself. Maybe Wetherall had just been weighed down by affairs of state: that contentious housing for the poor, for instance.

'And you didn't stop.'

'No.' Eppie suddenly remembered the problem with his brakes. 'Except …'

The inspector leant forward like a cat about to pounce. 'There was a stop, wasn't there? There *was* a stop!'

'I had some stones caught in the rear tyre,' Eppie explained. 'I had to stop to get them out. But it was just a quick stop.' He was horrified to realize he sounded defensive. 'I just paused at the side of the road. I didn't see anyone or—' That twitch of the curtain – someone had been watching him. Well, he hadn't *actually* seen anyone. 'I didn't see anyone, or speak to them.'

'So it was just a coincidence that you stopped outside the councillor's house.'

Eppie set his jaw. 'Did I?'

'His daughter saw you! She heard you talking with her father! You saw him, didn't you? You spoke to him, and threatened him and then you saw him drive off in his carriage. That's what you did, isn't it? You didn't just stop outside his house by accident – you deliberately stopped there to talk to him. Didn't you?'

'No.'

'What did you talk to him about when he came to your shop on Wednesday morning? Why did he come to see you?'

'He came for a haircut.' Eppie lost patience. 'Oh, this is ridiculous! Why on earth should I want to threaten Wetherall?'

'You wanted money out of him,' the inspector said with relish. 'He told you some secret while you were cutting his hair one day. Men are always more relaxed in the hairdressers and let out all sorts of secrets.'

Eppie started racking his brains for anything Crellin might have told him. Nothing, unfortunately, came to mind. 'If you let me get some decent training in, I could get money from winning races!'

The inspector breathed in noisily. Three times.

'Anyway,' Eppie said, giving in to a rash impulse. 'Mr Wetherall was killed in that alley in broad daylight. And I was in my shop all the time.'

'Really?' The inspector's head came up. 'And I suppose you have witnesses to that?'

Eppie beamed. It really was impossible not to be triumphalist sometimes. 'I was shaving some customers. Taking their whiskers off.' He could see from the inspector's face that he already knew what Eppie was going to say. 'Constable Gill, Constable Armstrong, Constable Tinnion and Constable Banks. Only I only got halfway through Constable Banks when the whistle sounded.'

He thought Crellin might explode. His face went bright red with the effort of not saying what he thought. Which would probably have been very rude.

'You could have nipped out between customers!'

'My apprentice Harry was there all the time. He would have known I'd gone.'

'You could have paid him to keep quiet!'

Now it was Eppie desperately trying not to tell Crellin what he thought. And he would *definitely* have been very rude.

'How would I have known Wetherall was going to be in that alley?'

'He always went that way to the Town Hall. He was on his way to a meeting. You could have made an arrangement to meet him there.'

'Why?'

'To threaten him for money like you did on Wednesday night.'

'It wasn't me threatening him on Wednesday night! And what would be the point in killing someone you're trying to get money out of? Dead men can't do their accounts.'

Crellin leant forward across the desk with a nasty leer. 'You lost your temper and killed him when he said no.'

'He was six feet tall,' Eppie said. 'I'm five foot six.'

Crellin's mouth opened. Next he was going to say Eppie took a stool with him, to stand on, so he could reach high enough to hit Wetherall over the head. He was breathing heavily.

'Right,' he said, finally. 'You can go.'

Eppie smiled on him. 'Mr Epford,' he prompted

The inspector ground his teeth. 'You can go, *Mr Epford*!' He managed to make it sound like a threat.

Eppie pottered out to the front of the building, weak-kneed with relief. This was ridiculous. How could anyone suspect him? How could he stop them suspecting him?

As he got to the street door, two women came in and he automatically stood back for them. Both were dressed in mourning. A tall, severe, middle-aged woman who never so much as looked at him, and a young woman who cast him a demure *thank you* as she went past.

Violet Daisy Rose Wetherall. The other lady was presumably her mother. A model of rectitude, obviously. Women like that, in Eppie's experience, were so down on everyone who appeared to be enjoying themselves because they were too afraid to join in. But how odd that Miss Wetherall didn't seem to recognize him. She'd looked at him so directly at the inquest.

But then Miss Violet Daisy Rose had a number of things to explain. Her dress for instance. Just like the one at the inquest. Clearly made by an expert seamstress, and its elaborate frills and furbelows – its very *fashionable* frills and furbelows – suggested it must have taken quite a while to put together.

How very interesting.

8

AMOS DASHED INTO the shop at the very last minute, just as Eppie was closing.

'We're closing,' Eppie said. 'It's Saturday.'

'You and your half days! Wednesdays *and* Saturdays! How much money do you lose by closing twice a week?'

'Not half as much as I win in races if I use the half-days wisely for training.'

Amos grinned. 'You mean, of course, that you win the most wonderful elegant gentlemen's dressing cases and silver salvers.'

'Silver-plated.'

'Which of course are stacked on your shelves at home …'

Amos knew very well he sold them. As Amos, and everyone else, sold whatever they won.

He couldn't wait to get out on the bike. He'd had enough of this particular Saturday. At one point he'd had six customers sitting in the shop, refusing to be dealt with by Harry and insisting on having their hair cut only by Eppie. Since they were all obviously agog to know whether he had indeed murdered Charles Wetherall, and to ask as many questions as they could (the same questions every time), he was surprised they were willing to let him get anywhere near them with sharp scissors. And after being interrogated by each and every one of them, he wanted to get away from human beings altogether, and find some nice quiet road where he could ride along with no more noise than a few eager birds and the gentle whirring of bicycle wheels.

'Anyway, I don't want a haircut!' Amos swept back his flowing locks with an impatient hand. 'I want to talk.' He melodramatically cast a glance around but Eppie had already let Harry go home and there was no one else in the shop. 'About m-u-r-d-e-r.'

'I can spell, thank you. And that's exactly what I *don't* want to talk about. I've spent all morning being interrogated about *m-u-r-d-e-r* and no one seems to listen to what I say. At the time of the said *m-u-r-d-e-r*,' he added, speaking very clearly, 'I was disposing of the overgrown and not entirely hygienic whiskers of no fewer than four constables.'

Amos stared. 'What? No, never mind. Come to the King's Arms, my boy, and I'll tell you what I've found out about our distinguished deceased's political doings. And they weren't particularly hygienic either.'

'I'm in training and I had a beer last night.'

'No, you didn't. I drank it. And I'll drink yours again today if you want. Come on!'

Fifteen minutes later, in the King's Arms, Amos was still grumbling about the length of time it took Eppie to close up the shop.

'I've got valuable equipment in there,' Eppie said, settling himself in the corner by the fire. 'A thief could get a good price for that lot. It would be silly simply to forget to lock the doors. Right – what have you found out?'

'Well.' Amos took a great gulp of the first pint. 'There's a lot of the sort of stuff you'd expect. Political bickerings, claims of deals struck and principles betrayed. You know the kind of things you hear around all politicians – they have no principles and are simply doing it because they crave power. Which, as we all know, is exactly true. However, I'm damned if I can find anything which might prompt someone to murder the fellow. I mean, you don't kill someone because *you* think the money should be spent on housing for the poor and *he* thinks it should be spent on a new statue for the town square.'

'Whose statue did he want?'

'Whose d'you think? His own. No, everyone says one of two things about our deceased councillor: either he was the best thing that ever happened to this town – he was a man of strong principles and righteous morals – or he was an irritating bastard with no thought of anyone's good except his own. No one, however, seems to have felt particularly strongly either way.'

Eppie shifted away from the fire which was beginning to roast one side of him. 'No sensible murderer would make his dislike of his victim public, surely.'

'Except,' Amos said, ignoring him, 'one man who has been loud in his dislike of our esteemed deceased councillor. One Algernon George Maitland.'

'Maitland?' Eppie frowned. 'Is that the Liberal fellow?'

Amos finished the first pint. The landlord appeared at his shoulder and put a plate down on the table in front of him. A huge meat pie with potatoes and gravy. Amos grabbed his cutlery. 'I didn't order one for you, my dear fellow. I thought with you being in training and so on, you wouldn't want to eat.'

'I certainly wouldn't want to eat that.' Eppie could feel the weight of that meal in his stomach just by looking at it. 'If you eat meals like that every night you'll grow as portly as the *esteemed deceased*.'

Amos scoffed. 'This is merely something to whet my appetite. Belle will have another meal for me when I get back home. And, for your information, *portly* is a description no one will ever be able to apply to me. Good healthy food, Eppie. That's what you need. Build you up, give you strength. You're far too thin.'

'Maitland,' Eppie said, determinedly bringing the conversation back to the point.

'Well.' Amos ploughed on with his pie, speaking through it and spitting fragments of food out as he did so. Eppie moved back, out of firing range. 'Algernon Maitland is about thirty years old, son of whatshisname Maitland. Fellow who rebuilt that big house between Keswick and Penrith. Family have been there for ever. And Liberal for ever too. The old man was an acquired taste, they say – you either loathed him or loved him. The son is the same, very suave, very up with things, determined to change the entire world as long as it does what he tells it. Not got the best reputation as far as the ladies are concerned. Has been known to frequent the less than savoury females – bar maids and the like, fisher girls, that sort – and none too gentle with them, either. Apparently.'

'You mean, he's known to be violent?'

'Not hit anyone over the head, if that's what you're thinking. Well, not as far as I know. And being a bit rough with a barmaid isn't exactly the same as hitting a man over the head with a blunt instrument.'

'No,' Eppie agreed. 'It's much worse. At least a grown man has the strength to fight back.'

Amos made a face. 'Don't get overheated, my dear fellow. The point is – he's engaged to Wetherall's daughter, or wants to be, at least. The flower girl.'

'Violet Daisy Rose.'

'That's the one. Now, the rumours are that Maitland may have a nice house and grounds and plenty of huntin' and fishin' and shootin', but he doesn't have any ready cash to go with it. Rumours say he's been cutting back on the number of servants in his town house here in Maryport. And some of his shipping interests have been less than spectacular. A couple of ships he had interests in sank last year. Wetherall on the other hand does have a lot of cash. *Did*. And Violet Daisy thingy is his sole heiress.'

'Sounds like a good idea all round then. The marriage, I mean. Maitland will get the dowry when he marries and the expectations of his wife's inheritance in years to come will placate any creditors.'

'Ideal,' Amos agreed. 'Except for the political angle.' He speared a large piece of meat on the end of his knife and sucked it off the point. 'His only daughter marry a Liberal? Heaven forbid. Well, *Wetherall* forbid – forbade the match, that is. He actually said the words: *Over my dead body*. Tempting fate, clearly.'

'Who told you this?'

Amos tapped his nose. 'Ask me no questions, get no lies. No writer ever tells, you know that. But it was someone I trust. Someone who's been reliable before.'

Eppie contemplated the fire. The smell of Amos's pie was making his stomach growl. 'What are you suggesting? That Maitland murdered Wetherall to remove his objection to the marriage? Or that Violet Daisy Rose did it? It hardly seems worth it. Once she's of age, she can marry whoever she likes.'

'But that's three years off. My friend tells me Maitland can't wait that long.'

'Then the easiest way is to carry the daughter off to Gretna Green. Once they were married over the anvil, Wetherall would have had to accept the marriage or ruin his daughter's reputation. He would have brought them back, pretended the daughter had been off to visit some aunt or other, then had them married again in pomp and ceremony as if for the first time.'

'Maybe that never occurred to them.'

Silence while Amos worked his way through the pie and potatoes and beer. Eppie wondered how long he would be able to hold out against the enticing smell. He had to get home where he could make himself something more suitable to eat.

'It all seems very thin to me. I can see Maitland might have had reason to dispose of Wetherall, but there's nothing to suggest he actually did so. And what was the murder weapon?'

'Hammer,' Amos said with his mouth full. 'That's what the doctor said.'

'But in that case the murderer must have taken it with him – I mean, you don't just find hammers lying around in alleys, do you? So that means the murderer went along *intending* to kill Wetherall. It wasn't just a spur of the moment thing.'

'Maybe it was a cobble then.'

'It wasn't a cobbled alley. And there wasn't anything lying on the ground. If it was a cobble, then the murderer had to have made off with it – and what do you do with a cobble? Put it in your pocket? It'd be a bit obvious, wouldn't it?' Though the same thing applied to the hammer, of course.

'Bloody public place to kill someone.' Amos swigged beer. 'I mean, it's one thing to lose your temper and lash out, but to actually *choose* it as a murder site – that's plain silly.'

'Though it was safe enough,' Eppie pointed out. 'No one actually saw the murderer. It's not a well-used alley. Although according to Crellin, Wetherall apparently always went that way to council meetings.'

'There you are, then!' Amos said triumphantly. 'Not everyone would know that, but Maitland would.'

'You can't be sure of that.'

'Prospective son-in-law, fellow council member – of course he'd know.'

Eppie sighed. 'I'd say the highways engineer had just as strong a motive. And he might have known which way Wetherall went, too.'

Amos sat up straight. 'The highways engineer? What about the highways engineer?'

Eppie sighed. For a man who prided himself on knowing everything, Amos knew remarkably little sometimes. He explained about Mrs Cartwright and the rendezvous he'd witnessed on Thursday morning.

'I bet you never told the police about that,' Amos said.

That was true; he hadn't.

'I forgot,' he said, knowing how lame that sounded.

'Never mind.' Amos waggled his knife at him. 'I'll check that out too. Leave it all to me, Eppie, my lad. You just concentrate on riding that machine of yours as fast as you can. I cannot tell you how alarmed I was to hear you were training for endurance. Endurance! Speed, my lad, that's what you need!'

'I know what I'm doing, Amos.'

Amos crowed. 'You better had. Remember that ten bob I've got riding on you in that five miles on Easter Monday.'

Eppie sighed.

*

Even with the public house far behind, the smell seemed to linger on his clothes. Eppie felt almost faint with hunger as he wheeled his machine into the back yard of his house in the early afternoon. Which was ridiculous as he would not normally have eaten before this time anyway …

He stopped dead. In the corner, beside the huge bulk of the Ordinary and the sleek lines of the path racer, was a third bicycle. A lady's bicycle. He turned.

Alma was sitting on the back doorstep.

9

SHE LEAPT UP when she saw him. 'Eppie! Are you all right? The police let you go?!'

He was appalled. 'You shouldn't be sitting out here in the cold!'

'I'm fine, Eppie.'

'And it's starting to rain. You could have gone inside – there's a spare key …' And he found himself showing her whether it was hidden. Then he realized what it must look like. A single man showing a single lady where his spare key was kept! Whatever must she think? She was blushing! 'I don't mean, I mean, I wasn't …'

She was calmer than he was. 'Don't you think we'd better go in? In case your neighbours are looking out?'

He glanced up at the windows of the neighbouring houses. Mrs James on one side was deaf as a post, but Mrs McCormack on the other side was an avid window-haunter. Hurriedly, he unlocked the back door and let Alma in. She stood just inside the door, breathing in the aroma of the house while he went back, locked the gate and made sure his bicycle was propped safely against the yard wall. He would come out and clean it later.

What on earth was he going to say to Alma when he went back in? But she had come here of her own accord; he'd never so much as hinted that she might visit him. So in a way, she'd taken the initiative—

He went back into the house. Alma already had the kettle on the range in the kitchen and was looking for some potatoes in the pantry. She'd also found his mother's apron and was wearing it. He decided not to make a big thing of it. (He was *very* pleased.)

'I sent you a postcard. Yesterday. Telling you not to come to Maryport.'

She looked up. 'Yes, I got it last night. But honestly, Eppie, writing something like that just drives me mad with curiosity. And then this morning Dick Sibson sent me a telegram. He said the police had arrested you and wanted to charge you with killing Councillor Wetherall.'

When it was said as baldly as that, it sounded incredibly bad.

'He had no right to worry you,' Eppie said.

That was so like Dick – always had to know what was going on, always had to stick his nose in.

'But he was right? You are a suspect?'

'I wasn't arrested but Inspector Crellin did want to question me.' He sighed. 'I think, in all honesty, he had to.'

Alma was regarding him with clear blue eyes and a steady look. He knew that look – she was defying him to lie to her, or to hide the truth to protect her. She was a member of the fairer sex but she was not soft by any manner of means.

He brought plates and cups out of the cupboard and laid them neatly on the kitchen table. He virtually lived in this room. He couldn't remember the last time the front parlour had been used – in his mother's time probably.

'The councillor was an important man and now the inquest jury have decided he was murdered, the inspector has to investigate every possibility. And the man the daughter saw outside the house on Wednesday night fitted my description – or rather, I fitted his description.' He added gloomily, 'Actually, I think it might indeed have been me she saw. I passed the house on my way to meet you.'

'The headmaster told me Mr Wetherall had died,' Alma said, smoothing the apron. 'You know how he always finds things out. But he didn't know many details. Tell me all about it – right from the beginning.'

He told her everything he could remember while she peeled potatoes. He had a couple of chops on the slate slab in the pantry; he brought them out and put them in the frying pan. Nice lean chops with plenty of meat on them. He left them to fry in their own juices while he chopped up carrots and turnips. Thinking back to Amos's pie in the public houses, just the memory of all that grease and heavy pastry turned his stomach. And if he had eaten there, he'd have missed *this*.

'So,' Alma said, watching for the water to boil around the potatoes. 'You were down by Mr Wetherall's house that evening, even though you didn't know it. Miss Wetherall may have seen you when you stopped to sort out the bicycle. That's all very well, but why should she say she saw you have a conversation with her father when it isn't true?'

Eppie stared at the carrot in his hand. 'There's something very odd about that girl. Why should she tell that story?'

'Eppie! You're not listening. That's what I just asked!'

'No, you asked why she said I was the man arguing with her father. I'm wondering why she told the story at all. Look—' He waved the sharp knife at her. 'She said she thought it was a beggar trying to get some money out of her father. But Amos straight away saw there was another explanation. Suppose the man had some knowledge about Wetherall? Suppose he was threatening to reveal that knowledge unless Wetherall paid up? By telling that story, Miss Wetherall has planted the suspicion her father might have had something to hide. Would you tell a story like that? A story that might discredit someone close to you?'

'She could hardly have pretended it didn't happen.' The potatoes boiled, Alma moved them slightly off the hot plate.

'Why not? No one else knew about it.'

'But she wants her father's murderer found.'

Eppie squinted at the carrot, chopped it in pieces and dropped it into the pan with its fellows.

'I suppose. And there's another thing: the dress she was wearing to the inquest and another one this morning in the police station.'

'Her mourning dresses?'

'Very stylish and elaborate. Bang up-to-date.' He described them as best he could. 'I meant to check if she had any other relatives who died recently.'

'No.' Alma shook her head. 'The headmaster knows all about the family – met them a dozen times at Education Committee meetings, apparently. And he knows family members in Carlisle – distant cousins of some sort. Both Wetherall and his wife are only children and both sets of their parents died years ago. They did have about five children but Violet Rose Daisy was the only one to survive. No recent deaths in the family. Maybe they just have a very good dressmaker who turned out the dresses quickly.'

'Violet Daisy Rose. They looked London-made to me. I wish you could see them – you'd know better than me. Did the headmaster tell you anything more?'

Alma nodded. 'We had a full hour over tea this morning. But there was nothing much of real interest. Except there's a young man in prospect of whom Wetherall did not approve.' She added darkly, 'A Liberal. *Persona non grata*.' She grinned. 'The headmaster, after stressing that he *never* gossips, implied that Miss Violet Daisy whatshername and this Algernon Maitland were somewhat closer acquainted than they should be.'

Eppie pursed his lips. 'Amos thought there was a rush about the marriage because Maitland is short of money. But if they had – er – *anticipated* the marriage, there could have been another reason for hurry.'

Alma nodded. 'They could even have done it deliberately, to force her father's hand. No man would sacrifice the reputation of his daughter, however unpleasant he found his prospective son-in-law's politics.'

'But it doesn't give Maitland a reason to kill Wetherall,' Eppie pointed out. 'Quite the opposite. Now Wetherall's dead, no marriage can take place until the mourning year is over and by that time any child would have been born. If she is with child, they need to marry now.'

Alma poked him in the arm. 'There's one certain way of knowing if she is or isn't. If she is, she'll take herself off to the country, or the wilds of Scotland, or even the south of France – *to get over Papa's death*, of course. And she won't be back for months and months …'

There was a knock on the street door and suddenly the cosy atmosphere disappeared entirely. Eppie thought, *we're not married and she's in my house and we're cooking dinner together and it looks like we've done it dozens of times before and no one will believe me when I say we haven't …*

Alma looked round wildly. 'Don't answer it!'

Another knock. What if it was Crellin?

The plates had been put on the top of the range to warm. Eppie took one of them and put it back in the cupboard, together with one of the cups and saucers Alma had put out for the tea. He took one set of cutlery off the table and put it back in the drawer. The knock came again.

'You can't go upstairs because you'd have to pass the front window. Hide in the pantry.'

Alma gave him an exasperated look but obeyed. Eppie went through into the hall, calling out as he went, 'I'm coming.' His heart was beating as fast as if he'd just won a sprint. He pulled open the front door.

It was not the police. It was Violet Daisy Rose Wetherall, looking at him as wildly as Alma had. 'Let me in, please!'

'I can't do that!' His voice had risen, was rather shrill. He cleared his throat. 'Miss Wetherall – you are a single lady and I am a single man. We cannot, I mean, you cannot, it would not be proper …' *And besides, there's another lady hidden in the pantry …* He had to find a way of persuading her this was *totally* unwise. 'But what would your mother say?'

She stiffened. 'My mother knows that she can trust me.'

Eppie wouldn't have trusted her. He *didn't* trust her. 'But—'

'I can't stand on the doorstep!' And while he was blinking at her unexpectedly sharp tone, she pushed past him into the house.

He closed the door. She stood looking about her with what was unmistakably shock. 'You live *here?*' She seemed to shake herself. 'I'm sorry, I didn't mean to be rude, it's just when one is used to something a little more spacious …'

Eppie took pity on her. Besides, he didn't want to argue with her – she'd come here for some specific reason and he badly wanted to know what it was. 'Can I offer you some tea?'

He regretted the offer immediately. The pantry was only just off the kitchen – if Alma accidentally made a noise, Miss Wetherall might hear. On the other hand, Alma would be able to hear what Miss Wetherall was saying. Which meant that she would have no doubts there was nothing untoward between himself and the young lady. He didn't want her to think he was in the habit of inviting young ladies into his home.

Miss Wetherall followed him into the kitchen and he saw her casting sly little glances about the range and the cupboards. Her gaze slid across the door to the pantry – the door was slightly ajar but she didn't appear to see anything suspicious. She sat down at the table when he invited her to do so but said in obvious puzzlement, 'Do you have no separate dining room?'

Eppie diplomatically refrained from pointing out the difference between the Wetheralls' income and his own, got the second cup and saucer out again and poured the milk in first then the tea. It had brewed nicely and was strong, just the way it should be. Miss Wetherall sipped cautiously as if she was a trifle wary of it. He thought he saw her wince.

'What lovely china,' she said brightly.

'It belonged to my mother. Her pride and joy. Miss Wetherall …'

'I know,' she said and suddenly she was a demure young lady again, dropping her gaze so he could see only her nearly-closed eyelids. 'You're wondering why I'm here.' She took a deep breath, and put the cup and saucer down on the table. 'I wanted to apologize.'

Well, if she could be direct, so could he. 'For insinuating at the inquest that I was the one arguing with your father the night before his death?'

'*Someone* argued with him,' she said a little sharply. 'But – I, I – I never meant to imply it was you. I never said it was. It was just – you do look a little like him. And he had an accent like yours.'

'Most people hereabouts do.'

'I know it caused trouble for you,' she burst out passionately. 'Mama told me Inspector Crellin questioned you today. But he can't seriously think you did it. If he says you did, then I'll tell him I made a mistake, that it wasn't you.'

For a moment, he couldn't think what to say to that. At least she was trying to put things right.

'Thank you but I don't think I'll need help. I can prove I was elsewhere when your father was killed.'

She looked disconcerted. 'You can? I, I didn't know.'

'But I'm very grateful to you for coming here to try and help.' She seemed a little agitated; he had a suspicion that she wanted to say something else. 'If you're worried about finding out who did murder your father, I'm sure Inspector Crellin is very capable …' He rather wished he could have sounded more convincing on that point. Well, he couldn't be blamed for asking a question or two of his own. 'You said you thought the man you heard arguing with him was asking for money.'

'A beggar, probably,' she said.

'Or could it have been someone he knew? I was just wondering … well, if he had offended anyone? Or annoyed them. I know he was a man of firm opinions and if someone had disagreed with him, or felt he had been disadvantaged in some way by him …' Oh Lord, how could you ask a woman if her father had had a guilty secret?

'I know nothing about Papa's affairs,' she said, back to her demure self. 'Ladies do not meddle in that sort of thing.'

Eppie could almost imagine he heard Alma's snort from the depths of the pantry. He plunged on – he'd probably never have another opportunity to speak to Miss Wetherall in private so it was wise to make the most of it.

'You look very charming, Miss Wetherall. That dress is delightful.'

She blushed prettily. 'Thank you! I had it made by one of the best dressmakers in London.'

'Delightful,' he said again. Pleased with himself. 'This must be a distressing time – I mean, you were probably looking forward to your wedding …'

She put up a hand to her eyes – from somewhere a whiter-than-white lace handkerchief had appeared. 'Of course, we can't possibly think of anything of the sort until we have mourned Papa properly.'

'Of course not. I'm sure Mr Maitland would not ask it of you.'

'He's the kindest of men,' she said. Odd how she was hiding her face with that handkerchief. Or was he being overly suspicious? She hesitated, then lowered the handkerchief, revealing a tear-stained face. 'Oh, I have heard people saying such unkind things about you, Mr Epford – I wouldn't blame you if you simply decided to shake the dust of this place off your feet for ever and it's all *my* fault!' She started to cry. 'I mean, every time I hear someone say something, I try to put things straight, but, oh … I have made such a mess of things.'

Ah, now he had it. He'd met young ladies like her before. Their *modus operandi* was to blame themselves for something they thought they'd done wrong, before someone else blamed them. That way, everyone rushed to tell them it wasn't their fault, even if it was. He hated that. He said blandly, 'Never mind.'

She looked at him uncertainly but if she had anything else to say, she evidently decided not to say it. He saw her to the door, where she hesitated. 'I wonder if you …'

'Yes?'

'… if you could check that there is no one outside.'

He would have liked to hear something humble in her tone, but instead it was something quite different. It was the tone she must use with servants. An order disguised as a polite request. She was very good at it too – he found himself already reaching for the door before he could catch himself up. But after all, she was right – it was best to make sure she was unobserved.

He opened the door and looked out – into the face of Mrs McCormack.

She was wrapped up in shawls and bonnets, with her arms folded across her ample chest, and looked round at him with eager anticipation. Obviously just passing on the way to her own house but eager enough to stop. He cursed silently.

'Oh,' he said. 'I thought it was raining.'

He thought he sounded idiotic but Mrs McCormack apparently did not. She launched into a violent condemnation of the recent weather, assured herself he must hate it as much as she did.

'Out on that machine,' she said scornfully. 'You'll catch your death of cold. You ought to wrap yourself up more. Here …' She snapped her fingers. 'I've got a scarf that belonged to my old man – he was wearing it when he died, you know. Dropped dead in Senhouse Street …'

Eppie had heard the story of Mr McCormack's death many a time and had no desire to hear it again. But he said brightly, 'That's very kind of you. I'd love that scarf. Do you have it now? I'm going training later this afternoon.'

She stared at him in astonishment then bustled into action. 'I'll get it. You just wait a minute …'

He did. He waited until she'd bustled herself through the front door of her house and then hurriedly told Miss Wetherall to go. The girl almost ran off down the street. There were a few anxious moments before she completely disappeared, but she'd gone before Mrs McCormack came back and said, puzzled, that she thought she'd heard someone running down the street.

'I didn't hear anyone,' Eppie said with as much innocence as he could muster. And gently shut the door against her.

The scarf was horrible – a bright mauve. And it smelt of cabbage.

10

'Well,' Eppie said, seeing Alma's face as he let her out of the pantry. 'At least she apologized.'

'She wanted something.' Alma headed for the tea pot, felt the outside, obviously found it cold, reached to put the kettle on again. 'That sort always does. And the thing she wants is her own way.'

'She knows how to get it too. I've a feeling that if her father had survived, she'd have twisted him round her little finger and got his approval of her marriage to Maitland.'

'She's been spoilt,' Alma said tartly. 'Coming here on her own like that! *My* mother would never have allowed me to do anything like that.'

'Presumably Mrs Wetherall doesn't know.'

'She *ought* to know. '

'You're here without your aunt knowing,' Eppie pointed out, realizing the unwisdom of that comment straight away. Too late, Alma's head went up; for a moment, he thought she was going to say something sharp. But then she said impishly, 'So I am,' and straightened the apron. 'At least we know now the girl's not with child.' The kettle began to sing.

'We do?'

'Certainly. No woman with child would ever have regarded the prospect of waiting for marriage with such equanimity. Now.' She lifted the kettle and poured water into the teapot to warm it, swilled the pot out. 'Clearly this is up to us. Inspector Crellin obviously has no idea who killed Councillor Wetherall and I doubt very much anyone else does either. So *we're* going to have to sort it out and clear your name.'

Remarkable how soothing the sound of a boiling kettle could be. And the voice of a determined woman, particularly when it was one particular woman.

'What we need to do,' Alma said, making more tea, 'is to work out who might have wanted to kill Councillor Wetherall. Then we can eliminate them one at a time until we are left with the guilty man. Or woman.' She lifted the pan lid to check on the progress of the potatoes. 'But we'll do it over dinner.'

She served up the food and they sat down at the kitchen table, opposite each other, like his mother and father had used to do. If only he could see a way to persuade Alma to marry him. But she'd never leave her job. Still, he wasn't going to give up – only five years ago he'd never have envisaged himself carrying off all the prizes at the Easter Sports and he'd come up only one prize short last year. This year he'd get the lot – he was absolutely determined on it.

In the meantime, he was beginning to be very interested in the matter of who had killed Charles Albert Frederick Wetherall. There was of course the need to prove his own innocence. He might have been able to prove he was in his shop when the man died but it wouldn't take a lot to change Inspector Crellin's mind – what if the doctor had been wrong and Wetherall had died earlier, for instance? And there was the puzzle itself, which increasingly intrigued him.

Alma cut up her chop neatly. 'The headmaster says that almost every murder is carried out by a member of the murdered person's family.'

'There are only two: Wetherall's wife and daughter.'

'What do we know about his wife?'

'Her name is Maud Margaret.' Alma rolled her eyes. Eppie added, 'And she was an only child.'

Alma considered, chewing on the meat. 'And the daughter?'

'Violet Daisy Rose. Also an only child – or at least the only one to survive. Likes her own way. Is engaged to a Liberal against her father's wishes but is not with child. And she likes to get her dresses made in London. Including her mourning dress.'

'But she's barely five feet four.' Alma smiled sweetly. 'I was peeking through the pantry door, trying to see that dress. Which is *very* fashionable, incidentally, and has far more frills than one person could possibly need. Her father was over six feet tall. How could she have hit him over the head? If he'd been sitting in a chair at home, she could have done it, but in an alley in the middle of town, he'd have been standing up.'

'Unless he bent down of course. Maybe she dropped that handkerchief?'

'A totally useless article,' Alma said, almost crossly. 'Lace! Probably cost more than my entire wardrobe.'

'On the other hand, aren't female murderers supposed to use poison?'

'I wouldn't know,' Alma said. 'I've never met one. At least, not as far as I know.'

Eppie chewed his way through a few carrots and potatoes. He was eating almost as much as Amos but the difference was that he was going to work it off again in the morning with a long ride with Alma. A good few miles under their belts, along the coast road maybe, with a few sprints thrown in. Which reminded him …

'Have you heard about your entry for the Easter Sports yet?'

'Not yet. What about the servants?'

'Ah – I found out about them at the inquest. Two maids, a cook, and a manservant who acts as a butler, a valet and anything else that needs to be done. A gardener comes in twice a week.'

'Any of them with a grudge against Wetherall?'

'It would have to be a strong grudge to want to kill your employer. Suppose the widow decides to retrench and fires you?'

'A discharged servant with a grudge then?'

'Could be.' His heart sank. How was he supposed to find out about that? Inspector Crellin could just go off and talk to anyone and expect to get answers, but no one had to answer Eppie and it would look suspicious if he even asked. 'Inspector Crellin must have thought about the servants. I suspect they must all have been in the house.'

Alma got up and started clearing up the plates; Eppie said, 'There's some apples in the pantry and some cheese.'

'Good,' she said. 'You get them while I clear up.'

The cheese was in its covered bowl on the slate slab and the apples in a basket. Alma put sharp knives on the table. 'Tell me exactly what was said in this argument Violet thingy overheard.'

'She said she couldn't hear much. Just her father saying "How dare you threaten me!" And then a little later "I'll give you no money."'

'He could have been a beggar, I suppose …'

'No, he couldn't,' Eppie retorted. 'She said his hair was well cut, which was one of the things that made people suspect me. And he rode off on a bicycle. What beggar could afford either stylish haircuts or a bicycle?'

'He could have stolen the bicycle,' Alma pointed out.

'Then he would have sold it straight away, not ridden around on it. Supposing the true owner had spotted him? And a beggar would be in greater need of money than of transport.'

Alma cut her apple into slices. 'It *must* be the fiancé. Algernon Maitland. A man wouldn't hesitate to hit another one over the head.'

Eppie blinked. This seemed rather too great a generalization.

'How tall is he?'

'Maitland? From what I saw of him at the inquest – about six feet tall.'

'If he's in dire need of money and Wetherall was blocking the match …'

'Miss Wetherall can't be the only unmarried heiress in the county,' Eppie protested. 'Maitland could simply have gone elsewhere. And as I said before, Wetherall's death delays any marriage.'

Alma set her knife neatly on her empty plate. 'We must have missed someone. How about the police constable?'

Eppie was disconcerted. 'Constable Banks?'

'No, the one who discovered the body. Who'd look twice if they saw a constable talking to a man in an alley?'

'I would.' Alma gave him an exasperated look. 'Well, I would! I'd wonder if the man had done something wrong and I'd want to see if I could find out what.'

An hour or so later, when they'd thoroughly exhausted the possibilities of the malice of the population at large, and Councillor Wetherall's circle of friends and family in particular, Alma reluctantly got up to leave, and to go to her aunt's a few streets away where she usually stayed overnight on occasions like this. In the yard, Eppie glanced up at the cloudy sky and fancied he felt a spot or two of rain.

'I'll come with you.'

Alma shook her head. 'You know my aunt's neighbours are as bad as Mrs McCormack. They mustn't see you – the news would be halfway round the town by morning. I'll simply imply I spent all day training on the roads between here and Carlisle.'

'I don't like the thought of you going even a street or two on your own. It's getting dark.'

She laughed softly. 'Eppie Epford – you know the streets are well-lit all the way! I'll be fine. See you tomorrow.' And she leant over to peck him decorously on the cheek.

He saw her out of the yard all the same and watched her to the end of the street. He'd done no training whatsoever all afternoon what with spending time with Amos and then with Alma. And he didn't care one jot. He finished the accounts, read the paper thoroughly and had an early night.

And then he spent Sunday like he spent all Sundays these days. A happy Sunday with Alma. He met her as usual on the Silloth road just before noon and stopped as if surprised to see her.

'Miss Gains!'

'Mr Epford.' An elderly gentleman nodded at Alma; she inclined her head in return. 'Mr Epford – how nice to meet you here. I was just going for a long ride. Training, you know. On the coast road.'

'How delightful. Would you object to me accompanying you?'

'No, no, not at all.'

And they rode off along the road with Alma in front, nodding to her acquaintances and even stopping once to talk to an old school friend. Eppie dawdled on ahead and let her catch him up. Then they were out of the streets and onto the exposed sea road, fighting a strong headwind that had a tendency occasionally to swirl into a crosswind, as if it wanted to keep them guessing. Heads down, scorching along, but with a great deal more science and technique than the lad who used the High Street to impress the ladies. Breath coming hard and gasping, heart thudding, exhilarated.

They ate at an isolated little café they often patronized, where the owner was a cycling aficionado and knew all the local racers. She saw them all go past her door and was shrewd enough to give Eppie and Alma a few hints as to who was in form and who was not. And since she was not married to the local farmer who delivered her supplies daily but might as well have been, she wasn't inclined to remark on the significance, or otherwise, of an unrelated lady and gentleman riding out together.

At the door of the café, they parted. Alma turned north for Carlisle, sighing at the thought of having to make a meal for her mother and four younger siblings.

'And I can't even come over on Wednesday as usual. The headmaster and I have to go through the children's textbooks – it's a long time since we had new ones and there are several that really need replacing. Mr Thurnam the bookseller is coming in to advise us.'

A whole week until he'd see her again. Eppie's heart sank.

He reached home before dark and occupied his mind by taking the road racer to pieces, cleaning and oiling everything that needed to be cleaned and oiled, and putting it together again. He slept soundly, and in the morning went to the track for an hour before work as usual. He was the only one there, though he did fancy at the beginning that he saw Dick Sibson at the back of the cricket pavilion. Dick didn't wheel his machine out, however, which he always did when there was the slightest chance of a race, particularly one he thought he might win, so Eppie must have been mistaken. A pity, he had a bone to pick with Dick about that telegram he'd sent to Alma.

He went home, washed, changed and went to the shop.

And opened the back door onto a scene of devastation.

11

HE STOOD IN the doorway, staring. It was only a small room behind the shop, with space for two or three chairs and a tiny table at which Harry ate the pies and cakes his mother baked for him and at which Eppie wrote his bills. The smallest of ranges in the corner where they boiled a kettle and which they stoked up in winter to keep the shop warm and the water hot. Shelves where Eppie kept his records and letter books, and the bills and receipts from customers and suppliers.

The chairs had been overturned and smashed, the table lurched on three legs. Ledgers in a heap on the floor, torn-out pages scattered around them. The kettle on its side, with the side caved in. Cups were smashed and one handle lay on the floor at his feet like a question mark.

Carefully, Eppie shut the back door. He did not need to look to see if any money had been stolen because he kept none here. He picked his way through the debris into the shop. Oddly, it looked untouched. Everything in its place, everything as neat as ever.

Except for one mirror – a small one he kept on the counter so he could show the customers the backs of their own heads. It had been cracked diagonally – only one or two shards of glass had fallen from it, but when he looked at his own reflection, his face seemed split into two, disjointed, askew. Unrecognizable.

A knock on the door. It must be Harry, forgotten his key again. Only a sliver of clothing was visible through the front window of the shop. He went to the door, peered through the blind. Not Harry – Dick Sibson.

Sighing, he unlocked the door. 'We're not open yet.'

Dick shook his head, waved a piece of paper at him. He looked sour. He'd probably come straight from the pit – he'd washed but not particularly well. 'What does this mean?'

Eppie stood back and let him in, locked the door again. He took the paper and recognized Alma's neat handwriting. Amongst the smudges caused by the coal dust on Dick's fingers.

'It's an entry form for the Easter Sports. From Miss Gains. How did you get hold of it?'

'The secretary of the Sports says you're supporting her entry.'

Eppie nodded. 'I told him I didn't see why women shouldn't compete.'

'You,' Dick said, 'are a complete idiot!'

Eppie had to pause a moment to get the better of his temper. 'Thank you for that compliment. Look, Dick, if Miss Gains isn't able to keep up with the male competitors, she'll simply go out the back of the race, and probably drop out when she gets distanced. If she *is* good enough …' Dick snorted. 'Then she'll keep up and we men will simply have to do something to beat her, won't we? Either way, there's no problem.'

Dick's face had gone red – the black lines of coal dust stood out on it vividly.

He might like the ladies but he had a clear idea of where they should and shouldn't be and a cycle race clearly wasn't one of those places. He grabbed back the paper.

'She'll probably fall off herself at the first corner and bring the rest of us down. Or expect us to make way for her politely when it comes to cornering!'

'Don't be ridiculous!'

'And if this stupid woman is allowed in, there'll be dozens of females who want to ride the races.'

'Good,' Eppie said. 'Well, if that's all, Dick, you'll have to excuse me – I have work to do. And if you don't mind, I don't think any lady should be referred to in the sort of terms you have just used.'

He went back to the door and opened it to let Dick out. Dick didn't move. He stooped to pick up the broken mirror.

'Well, well, it looks like you need to tread carefully, Eppie – a broken mirror means seven years' bad luck.' He grinned maliciously. 'That five-mile race might prove more difficult than you think!'

'I'm not superstitious.' He realized he was crossing his fingers and uncrossed them.

'Get angry, did you? Throw something at it?' Dick waved the paper at him again. 'Worried she'll beat you?'

'Goodbye, Dick.'

But Dick was turning on his heels. 'No, no, wait a while. There's something on the floor. Bits of glass. More than you'd expect from a mirror that size.' He was taking the opportunity to give the shop a good look over. And Eppie, of course, had left the door into the back room open. Chuckling, Dick strolled through.

'Good Lord, you really did get annoyed, didn't you?'

Eppie sighed. 'I didn't do it. It was like this when I came in a few minutes ago.'

Dick stood in the doorway, looking first at the inner room then out at the shop. 'Bit odd they smashed up the inner room but didn't bother with the shop. Well, apart from the mirror.'

'They'd have been visible from the street, wouldn't they – if they were in the shop. In the back, no one would have seen them.'

'Anything stolen?' Dick seemed in a good humour now. Maybe it was the pleasure of seeing someone else's problems.

'Not that I can see.'

'You sure?'

'I'm sure!'

Dick frowned. 'That reporter fellow – the idiot who thinks he can ride a bicycle – Amos someone or other. He told me you'd been trying to find out who killed Wetherall.'

'Not exactly. Or at least …' He remembered the speculation he and Alma had indulged in on Saturday night. 'The police seemed at one point to think I'd done it. I thought that if I could prove someone else had been the culprit, they might leave me alone.'

'Maybe you've been ruffling feathers,' Dick mused. With some glee, it has to be said. 'Someone thinks you should stop poking your nose in.'

'I *haven't* been …'

'That Amos fellow said he'd been looking at the councillor's political friends on your behalf. *At your request*, he said.'

Dear God, suppose Dick was right. Suppose this mess had been the murderer's way of telling him to mind his own business. The fellow might try and get back at Amos too!

'I've got to go.'

'Wait, wait!' Dick rolled his eyes. 'You need those chairs and table mended.'

'I need new ones! If you don't mind …'

'I'll do it for you. A favour to a friend.'

Eppie hesitated. Dick was a good carpenter, in his spare time away from the pit. He'd made chairs and other stuff for many a clumsy-fingered man. He could be an infuriating fellow but he did help out his friends. In return for a little *consideration*.

'How much do you want for the job?'

Now Dick was screwing up his face in a parody of thinking.

'Just tell me! I've got to dash off.'

'I'll take your Ordinary as payment.'

'The *Ordinary*? Why? You can't ride it.'

Dick, as usual, took him the wrong way. 'I can ride any bike. I cut my eye teeth riding Ordinaries with much bigger wheels than that puny machine you keep in your back yard, and in all winds and weathers!'

'I mean,' Eppie said, through gritted teeth, 'there are no longer any races for Ordinaries, and if you plan to ride it about the streets, half the small boys in town will throw stones at you. Well, even more stones than they usually throw at cyclists.'

'I can enter it for the novelty bicycle competitions.'

There was an edge of savageness in Dick's voice that made it hard to tell if he was serious or viciously joking. Still, Eppie needed the chairs mending and he'd been trying to sell the Ordinary for years.

'It's a deal.'

Another knock at the door. This time it *was* Harry, looking about him with horror, and staring at the broken mirror with particular alarm. It was at times like these that Eppie felt inclined to join in those idiotic comments bandied about concerning 'the youth of today'.

'Harry – I have to go off and sort things out. Keep the shop closed, this morning at least, and do what you can to tidy up.'

'What do I do about the mirror?' Harry asked nervously.

'Wrap it up in newspaper and put it in the bin.'

'I'll help you,' Dick said, with such relish that Eppie suspected he was probably going to regale Harry with tales of horrid bad luck caused by broken mirrors. He'd probably come back to find that Harry wanted to hand in his notice.

'I'll take the chairs away too. I'll go and get my hand-cart.' And he insisted on accompanying Eppie down the street, when all Eppie wanted was to get away and make sure Amos was all right. He was probably making an entire mountain range out of a wormcast, but he wouldn't be happy until he knew that for certain.

Amos lived in a neat town house on the western edge of the town, not far from the harbour. He liked to say he had a sea view, but if he did, it must have been from the attic, standing on tiptoe. In truth, the house was terraced like Eppie's, but with a little more style, which meant it had cost more. Or would have, if Eppie had not inherited his house from his parents. The other difference was the quiet. In Eppie's street, there was always someone coming and going, or looking out; in Amos's it was as if everyone had suddenly decided to go off and live somewhere else and leave the place deserted.

For a while he thought Amos must have joined the throng. He had to knock for a good five minutes before getting even a hint of a response. Then it was only an upstairs window being drawn up slightly and Amos's voice issuing from behind net curtains. 'Who the devil is it? If it's a bill, push it through the box.'

'Amos! I've got to talk to you!'

Amos's head abruptly shoved itself through the window, looking ridiculously disembodied. 'Eppie? I want to have a word with you, my man!'

Then there was an equally long gap before the thud of running footsteps sounded. Amos was apparently dashing down the stairs. The door was jerked open, but all Eppie had was a view of Amos's disappearing back.

'Come in, come in!'

He shut the door and followed the disappearing back into the kitchen at the rear of the house. The room was stiflingly hot and Amos already had the kettle on the range, making the place even more stuffy. Eppie almost had to gasp for breath. Amos was buttoning up his shirt. He ostentatiously produced a wide yawn.

'Late night, Eppie, my dear fellow. Covering one of those terrible charity balls. Didn't get to bed until the small hours. But don't apologize for disturbing my beauty sleep. What time is it?'

'Morning,' Eppie said. He'd had experience of Amos's 'charity balls'. Once or twice he'd taken the trouble to look them up and had found them to be entirely fictitious. He'd carefully avoided wondering what Amos was really doing instead. 'I need to talk to you about Wetherall.'

Amos took a brandy bottle out of a cupboard and poured himself a glassful. He put the bottle back in the cupboard. There was something slightly odd about his demeanour, something – *edgy*.

'You won't want one, will you, being in training? It's good you want to talk to me about Wetherall, I want to talk to you about Maitland.'

'You've found out more about him?'

'I've found out he's been asking about you.'

This was so unexpected Eppie was thrown off-balance, mentally rather than physically. 'About me?'

'About your cycling activities, to be precise. He asked the vicar, who as you know is a member of the Cricket Club committee and who graciously presents the prizes at our little race meetings.'

Eppie hurriedly decided to steer the conversation in a different direction. The vicar's rather tactless remarks on presenting Amos with second prize in last year's half mile handicap had gone down in legend, and were a sore point, particularly as quite a few riders thought it the height of hilarity to repeat them, usually when drunk.

'What did he want to know?'

Amos was never above picking at sores. 'The vicar, who as you know believes himself an expert on cycling matters when he knows nothing at all, said he believed he was indeed *au fait* with your personal details.'

'What *are* you rabbiting on about?' Eppie exploded, then was brought up short by a delicately-expressed female yawn from the doorway of the kitchen. Mrs Danson shuffled past him, lustrous dark hair half up, half down, clutching a robe about her. Bare toes beneath the robe, the hint of a bare ankle. Eppie stared wildly out of the kitchen window at the house opposite. He hadn't needed any proof of why Amos was lying in bed late, and he very much wished it hadn't presented itself.

Mrs Danson warmed the teapot, naturally letting go of the robe to do so. Eppie closed his eyes. When he opened them again, she was smiling at him. It wouldn't have been so bad if she'd been ugly or even squint-eyed, but Belle Danson was a storming beauty with wide liquid brown eyes and a smile to rival Helen of Troy's. Well, obviously, Amos would never have married anyone but a beauty.

'Tea, Mr Epford?'

'Thank you.'

'Did Amos tell you about the vicar?'

'Many times.'

'I hadn't finished.' Amos pushed his brandy glass behind a potted plant out of his wife's eyeline.

She said, 'Don't worry, I've already seen it. The vicar told the whole story to his wife, of course, and she told me at the meeting of the Ladies' Guild. Apparently, Mr Maitland has been recommended to put some money on you at the Easter Sports.'

Eppie sagged. 'Is that all?' All? No, on second thoughts, he really didn't like all this pressure to win. He wanted to win simply because, well, he wanted to win.

'It's all right,' Amos said, still uncharacteristically sharp. 'The vicar told him not to.'

Belle Danson handed Eppie a china cup and saucer of a Chinese pattern. There was barely a quarter of a cupful of tea in it, with a solitary tea-leaf floating on top.

'The vicar told him he shouldn't bother, because at the August Sports you'd been a poor second at least ten yards behind the winner, and you only got that because the man challenging you crashed on the last bend. You evidently can hardly keep the machine upright.'

Eppie winced and tried not to look at Amos. The vicar's recall of events was obviously a great deal better than his memory for names.

'The point is,' Amos said loudly, 'the whole thing was a ruse ...'

'Because,' Belle said, 'the vicar's wife told me that the vicar told her that the carriage maker told him that Maitland hasn't paid his bills for two years and he – the carriage maker, that is – has been obliged to refuse to do any more work for him. And apparently Mr Maitland has been desperately trying to persuade the railway companies to buy land from him for a new line. Only the railway companies don't want it, because the line wouldn't go anywhere and wouldn't link up with any other line.'

'Algernon Maitland,' Amos said, 'as I told you before, is flat broke.'

Eppie sighed. 'So why do you want to tell me again?'

'If Maitland has no money,' Belle Danson said, 'He can't afford to bet on you, can he? So his query to the vicar was just to find out more about you. He told the vicar, according to the vicar's wife, that you'd been pointed out to him at the inquest.'

'He wants to know more about you,' Amos agreed.

He looked at them, at Amos, who was wearing short sleeves and, even beneath that odd edginess, the smug look he always had after a good night's 'sleep'. At Belle, who had let the robe slip open again, to reveal slightly more than she intended, or at least slightly more than Eppie hoped she intended.

'And did the vicar tell him I was a hairdresser? Did he by any chance even tell him the address of my shop?'

'Not exactly,' Belle said. 'He told Maitland you were a journalist with the *Courant* and lived somewhere around the harbour.'

'Eppie,' Amos said pleadingly. 'You don't think Maitland *did* murder Wetherall, do you? I mean, he wouldn't do anything violent, would he?'

12

RIDICULOUSLY EPPIE FOUND himself spending the next half hour reassuring Amos. 'It doesn't matter that the vicar mistook you for me. Maitland will simply take one look at you and realize the mistake. He's seen me at the inquest, he knows my name. He can't be deceived.'

'Of course he might want to question you about Eppie,' Belle said limpidly. 'But I'm sure he wouldn't do anything rash.'

Amos scowled at this piece of provocation. Eppie didn't blame him. A wife ought to be supportive, not mischievous. Though Belle Danson probably had a few crosses to bear where Amos was concerned.

'You could go and see him.' Amos seized Eppie's arm. 'Make sure he knows the vicar's confused.'

'Me!' He was in danger of getting shrill again. He said, 'No. Why should I? Amos, everything will be fine …'

He made his escape at last, having managed to reassure Amos that he was safe. He trudged down the street wearily. And he'd forgotten to tell Amos what had happened in the shop! Could the burglar have been Maitland? More likely someone doing it on his orders. But why? Because he didn't want Eppie interfering in the business about Wetherall's death? That suggested he had something to hide. Maybe he'd done it?

He forced himself to walk more briskly, began to feel more hopeful. It was barely ten in the morning and no real harm had been done. There'd been no attempt to hurt him or – he winced – *kill* him. The shop had been a warning to mind his own business and that was all. If he chose, he could heed that warning, carry on training for the sports and let the inspector deal with the death of Charles Albert Frederick Wetherall.

He wasn't going to, though. On principle. How dare Maitland think he could intimidate Eppie and get away with it, probably just because he was a hairdresser and a tradesman, and Maitland was a gentleman. And if it wasn't Maitland behind the burglary but someone else, the same principle still applied. No giving in! You don't carry off the victory that way!

He marched into the shop and cannoned straight into Inspector Crellin. The man beamed at him.

'Nice mess in here.' He actually sounded as if he liked the look of it.

Despite all the time Eppie had been away, Harry was only just starting to clear up the debris. The chairs and the table had disappeared but the floor of the back room was still covered in papers and broken crockery.

'Inspector Crellin came to see you,' Harry said, leaning on his brush, 'and he saw all the mess and wanted to know what had happened. I told him we've had a burglary.'

The inspector *did* look as if he was enjoying himself. 'You should have reported it.'

'Nothing was taken.'

'The thieves must have been disturbed.'

'Maybe they thought I kept money here. Maybe they smashed everything when they realized I didn't and they weren't going to get anything for their trouble.'

'No trophies nicked? No cycling cups, or gold medals, or silver-plated cufflinks?'

Eppie took a deep breath. Crellin knew well enough that all the cyclists sold their prizes for cash. It still wasn't wise to admit it, though – Crellin was quite capable of going to the National Cycling Union and telling them. And then Eppie would lose his amateur status and wouldn't be able to compete.

'They're all at home.'

'Must come round and see them sometimes,' Crellin said. Eppie didn't issue an invitation – as a result there was a bit of a silence. Crellin broke it. 'As a matter of fact, as young Harry says, I was coming to see you anyway.'

And he couldn't even boil a kettle and make a cup of tea to fortify himself. 'More questions about Wetherall?'

'*Mr* Wetherall. I've been told you know his daughter.'

'I saw her at the inquest.'

'I meant socially.' Crellin beamed. 'Someone saw you in the main street with her.'

'No, they didn't,' Eppie retorted. Rather relieved, as a matter of fact. For a moment, he'd suspected Mrs McCormack might have seen Violet Daisy Rose behind Eppie's front door on Saturday night.

'And in the tea-rooms just down the road.'

'That was …' Eppie stopped. Someone had seen him with Alma and had mistaken her for Miss Wetherall. But it was ridiculous – Alma and Miss Wetherall looked nothing like each other. Alma was tall and slim and red-headed; Miss Wetherall was shorter, blonde and already – even if it was a bit cruel to say so – tending to be a little plump. Maybe it was puppy fat. Yes, that was more charitable. But if Eppie said he'd been with Alma in the tea-rooms, that risked Crellin investigating her, and maybe he'd find out she came to see Eppie, and that they raced on the road, alone, with no chaperone, and then Alma's reputation would be at risk. On the other hand, maybe Crellin would find out the truth anyway. Surely he'd go and question the staff at the tea-rooms …

'Yes?' Crellin said encouragingly. Harry was pretending to sweep up but Eppie could almost see his ears flapping.

'If they're referring to last Wednesday afternoon,' Eppie said, as coolly as if he was diving for the narrowest of gaps in the last spurt for the finish line, 'then I was *not* with Miss Wetherall. When I went into the tea-rooms, I came by chance upon a young lady from Carlisle – well, she's from this town, actually, but she now works in Carlisle. We've met once or twice at the sports and we fell into conversation.'

'About cycling?'

'About the respective advantages of pneumatic, cushion and solid tyres, as a matter of fact.'

Crellin looked blank but recovered himself quickly. 'And the young lady's name?'

He really did not want to have to tell him. 'Miss Alma Gains.'

'Oh, I know her,' Harry said. 'She's the young lady that wants to ride in the Easter Sports, isn't she? Mr Sibson was telling me about her. He doesn't think it ought to be allowed.'

Eppie couldn't help himself. He said, 'Perhaps he thinks she'll beat him.'

That tickled Crellin's fancy; he chortled. 'Dick Sibson thinks a lot of himself. Not a bad wheeler, mind. You're going to have to watch him in the five miles.'

'I will,' Eppie said, suddenly desperate for a bit of solitude and quiet. 'I'll take care not to trip over him when I come round and lap him.'

Crellin roared with laughter. 'You're a one, Mr Epford! That's the way to deal with him. And may I compliment you on your good sense? Because I've already had a little word with the ladies serving in the tea-rooms and they tell me the lady you were talking to was tall and red-headed, not short and blonde.'

'Then why did you ask me?'

'To see how truthful you were, of course!' And Crellin sauntered out of the shop, grinning.

Eppie sagged, not knowing whether to be relieved or annoyed.

'I didn't know you were consulting lawyers, Mr E,' Harry said.

Eppie glanced round. Harry was picking up the ledgers and apparently trying to sort out which pages had come from which book. But in the middle of the snowfall of loose papers there was a big brown envelope from which papers had obviously dropped out when Harry picked it up. A heavy sheaf of legal-looking papers. Eppie flicked the corners of the bundle, caught the name *Wetherall*. What on earth...?

'Just something I was looking after for a friend, Harry.' He slid the papers back into the envelope. Feeling his heart beat almost as fast as it did when he was about to start a race. Not from nerves, from excitement. Not a warning, not a burglary. Quite the opposite in fact. The intruder had not *taken* something, he had *left* something.

It was a long afternoon. He shaved another three constables, cut hair and chatted to customers without hearing a single word he himself said. He was a bit annoyed Inspector Crellin had shown not the slightest interest in investigating the burglary. He was a policeman, wasn't he? Didn't policemen have to do something about crimes? Still, it was probably better he hadn't done anything. He might have found the papers and then how would Eppie have explained it all?

Who'd left the papers? And why? Why did they want him to read them? Was there something there they wanted him to know? Why? Why should anyone want him to know anything? If the break-in had been a warning to him to mind his own business, that at least would have made sense. Nice simple motivation, nice simple message. A murderer *would* want to discourage him taking an interest.

But to give him information which would probably only make him even more curious was very odd. As if the intruder – whoever it had been – had wanted him to know more, had wanted to encourage his investigation of the murder. But if the papers held significant information, why not take them to the police? The only answer Eppie could think of to that was that the person who'd left the papers had something to hide. Maybe not murder, but something that made them want to avoid the police.

But what? And why?

Amos was right; he was beginning to sound like a five-year-old. *Why, why, why?*

Which was odd, really, come to think of it. Why not *who, who, who?*

Having supper on his own was getting increasingly tedious. He almost didn't feel like having anything at all, but knew he'd regret it tomorrow when he tried to put in a good training session. He'd brought the big brown envelope home with him and put it on the table, out of his reach to make sure he didn't splash it with gravy or grease. It lay there in the gaslight like an anarchist's unexploded bomb. He wasn't sure he *wanted* to look at its contents.

Actually, he wanted very badly to look at the contents. He just wasn't sure it was a good idea.

He washed and wiped up, slowly and deliberately, trying to gain himself a little time. He made himself a cup of tea and was pleased to find the biscuit tin empty – he had a sweet tooth but it didn't do to indulge it. Then he sat down at the table again and looked at the big brown envelope.

Oh, well. In for a penny, in for a pound.

The bundle of papers had been folded together for a long time and were springy and impossible to flatten – he used plates to hold them down so he could read them. First was a pedigree across which linked names sprawled. Almost every one a Wetherall, with spouses added, of course. The family went all the way back to 1525, apparently, to minor nobility, but then every pedigree he'd seen seemed to go back to some medieval baron or other. It seemed obligatory to prove that even if you weren't noble yourself, you had noble blood. All Eppie's ancestors had been hairdressers. Probably one of them had shaved the beard of Peregrin Anthonie Richarde Weatherawl in 1520-something.

Following the pedigree down to the present day, it appeared that Violet Daisy Rose had been the youngest child of Maud Margaret and Charles A. F. Wetherall, and that her four elder siblings, all boys, had all died in infancy. Maud Margaret herself had been born in London and was an only child; Charles Albert

Frederick had no siblings either but had had one great-great-uncle, from whom some extremely distant cousins had descended.

The next paper was the will – a copy presumably – of Wetherall's father, Albert George Wetherall, made in 1840 and proved after his death at the age of thirty-five some five years later. Fifty years ago. Nothing very complicated: a few bequests to servants and old friends, and the estate left to be divided equally between *my son, Charles and any other legitimate heirs of my body.* Then a letter from a lawyer informing the family he was putting a notice in *the relevant papers* to ask any debtors and creditors of the late Albert George to come forward, with the relevant cutting pinned to the letter. Next, a letter from a vicar in Carlisle saying that the attached copies of extracts from his church registers were indeed accurate copies of the originals. The attached copies were for Albert George's marriage with Catherine Sarah Johnson of Carlisle in April 1836, and Charles Albert Frederick's birth, thirteen months later, in May 1837.

Which was all very interesting but Eppie didn't have the least idea why anyone would want him to know all this.

He gave up and went to bed.

13

Eppie slept badly and was annoyed with himself. Sleep was important – he never trained well when he was tired. He was tempted to forgo his early morning trip to the cricket ground but that way lay failure. Going out to train when he felt like it was easy – it was going out when he *didn't* feel like it that made the difference.

It was raining. Not heavily, just a steady nasty drizzle that soaked his woollen shorts and jersey. By the time he reached the cricket ground he was convinced of two things: one, no one else was going to be there, and two, everyone else was sensible and he was a complete idiot.

The narrow gate from the road was unlocked as always. He wheeled his machine through and carried it down the grassy slope to the track at the bottom. Riding over to the pavilion, he dismounted, put down his bag of food, which also contained his house keys, on the topmost step, in the corner where the overhanging roof of the veranda created a dry patch. The pavilion door was supposed to be locked but the padlock had been hung so it looked closed but wasn't. He indulged his curiosity and tugged at the door. It came open after a little resistance and let out a warm stale smell of old sweat and boiled cabbage. He changed his mind about sheltering inside, didn't bother to look inside after all and shut the door again, rearranging the padlock to make it look secure.

He fished out a small wedge of cheese and munched on it as he thought out his programme for the day. He needed to practise his sprinting – Dick could put on a good spurt at the end of a race. Eppie usually dealt with Dick's spurting speed by riding away from him on the last lap – if he wasn't there, he couldn't dash past to take the win – but he couldn't count on that happening …

'Mr Epford.'

He jumped, startled out of his wits. He'd convinced himself he was totally alone. And a woman too.

He turned on his heels, looked up at the woman who'd come out of the pavilion. Obviously not as fastidious as he was as regards smells. For a moment, he failed to recognize her but as she came down the steps she put back the veil of her large black hat. Mrs Maud Margaret Wetherall.

She was what his mother would have described as 'a stately woman'. She walked as if she had a steel rod down the back of her elegant mourning dress. There were no signs of tears on her hard face.

'I understand you are acquainted with my daughter, Mr Epford?' He involuntarily sighed and she added sharply, 'I'm glad to see you take this so seriously.'

He *hated* sarcasm and from the mouth of a woman it seemed even worse than from a man. Particularly from an elegant rich woman who was obviously intent upon impressing him with her higher social standing. He'd endured the sort of look she was giving him any number of times: contempt.

'I've already spoken to Inspector Crellin about this. It's a mistake. Your daughter was mistaken for another lady.'

She raised one finely chiselled eyebrow. 'Your wife, perhaps?'

That was said particularly nastily, clearly suggesting she suspected him of immorality. 'A lady I met by chance in the tea-rooms. A cycling acquaintance.'

'Then you have *not* been talking to my daughter?'

He would have loved to have been able to answer *no* to that but he felt he'd been lying rather too often recently.

'I can't see why you should think I would. What would either of us have to say to the other?'

'I rather thought,' she said, giving him the tiniest of sneering smiles, 'you might be trying to persuade her she did not see you outside our house on Wednesday night last week.'

'On the contrary,' Eppie said, 'I think she might indeed have seen me.' That clearly disconcerted her; he added, 'I had a problem with my bicycle and stopped to rectify the matter. Inspector Crellin and I have discussed that too.'

She seemed about to speak again but he plunged on. The only way to deal with women of her sort was to stop them in their tracks.

'Did you know that the chief constable has decreed that no police officers should have whiskers?'

She made an angry gesture. 'Don't fool with me, *Mr* Epford. You'll regret it.'

He straightened. 'Is that a threat?'

'It's what you choose to make of it.' She swept round, clearly about to make off.

He stepped in front of her. 'Mrs Wetherall. Thanks to the Chief Constable's decree, I had four police constables in my shop at the time of your husband's death. You may have heard that I was in the middle of shaving Constable Banks when the whistle sounded. If you suspect that, for some strange unfathomable reason, I killed your husband, you can put the idea out of your head. I did not.'

She lifted her head and stared him directly in the eyes. 'Do not cross me, Mr Epford. I am not one of those mothers who allows her daughter to run wild. I know *exactly* what she is doing, and what's more, I know that she thinks exactly as I do.'

Did she really believe that? Looking into her eyes, Eppie rather thought she did. And that *he* believed that Mrs Maud Margaret Wetherall was a woman of her words, not to be trifled with.

'If I find out at any time that you are attempting to put pressure on my daughter to change her story, be assured I *will* take action. And you will very much regret living in this town.' She flicked the veil down over her eyes. 'I have a great deal of influence, Mr Epford.' She made off across the wet grass and up the steep slope towards the gate.

He watched her, sighing. Obviously someone who always wanted the last word. Ridiculous. Unfortunately, she also showed all the signs of being a woman who badly wanted someone to blame for her husband's death but didn't much mind who. The first fellow to hand would do. Which didn't bode well for Eppie.

Slow ironic applause from behind him. He swung round to see Dick lounging against the side of the pavilion.

'That's the way to woo the ladies, *Mr* Epford!'

'How much did you hear?'

'Almost all of it.' Dick jerked his head towards the back of the pavilion. 'I came in from the main road. First thing I hear is you talking with a lady – I thought I'd interrupted a little tryst with your little friend from Carlisle.'

'I've told you …'

'So I trod carefully, *silently* even, to see what was going on. I thought I was going to have sure and certain evidence of your dalliance!' He gave Eppie a sneer. 'Not even the most gullible will believe you were having an assignation with a woman of *that* age. Remind me to give you a little advice on how to deal with the ladies. Later, after I've beaten you in the Easter Sports.'

'No, thank you,' Eppie said politely. 'I know you're the expert, Dick, but I'm happy to go on in my own way.'

'I can tell you how to get on the right side of a woman like that. Women like that want a strong man, Eppie – one that stands no nonsense. And I tell you – her daughter's the same.'

This was coming dangerously close to the sort of thing Eppie thought unpleasant. 'I always treat women with respect.'

Dick nodded. 'That's always been your trouble. They don't like it, Eppie.'

'Nonsense!' He could imagine what Alma would say if he tried to lay down the law to her and 'stand no nonsense', as Dick put it. She'd probably walk out on him. And quite right too.

'I'm right,' Dick said. 'Just you try it and see. Now, does this woman seriously believe you murdered her husband?'

'I'm not sure she's thinking at all,' Eppie retorted. 'Now, if you don't mind, I have a training session to do.'

'Good,' Dick said. 'So do I.'

Inwardly, Eppie groaned. Even more so when he got a good look at the bicycle Dick wheeled out from the shelter of the pavilion.

'You've bought a new machine.'

Dick smirked. 'It's the latest model from Elswick. New light frame. Look …'

Eppie let the details wash over him. He didn't need them. He could see that the machine was probably the fastest thing on two wheels. Depressing. Except for the fact, of course, that even the fastest machine in the world needed a rider, and this particular rider had his weaknesses. One of them being to think that natural ability was all you needed to win races.

He was right about Dick's idea of a training session: never mind practising the things you weren't much good at, or building up your strength – just race all out. But under the present conditions that wasn't a good idea. Even walking across the wet grass to get on the track was dangerously slippery and the close-cut grass track was like an ice-rink on the bends. Dick patently didn't care – he was off, hurtling along the back straight, and on to the slight banking at the far end while

Eppie was still climbing onto his machine. Eppie sighed, got his pedals sorted and started off carefully.

And promptly skidded and fell off.

The impact on the ground was hard against his backside but he knew he hadn't done himself any damage. He sat on the sodden grass, rain splattering on him from above and soaking through his woollen cycling shorts from below, and watched Dick disappear round the banking and into the curve of the track as it worked its way round the bottom of the cricket pitch. Into the front straight. Well, he didn't mind looking a fool in Dick's eyes. All the better, in fact. When Dick thought his opponent was a fool, he got complacent and did rash things. It was in Eppie's interests to appear incompetent, or at the very least out of form. If he was going to play on Dick's weaknesses, best to get the campaign going here and now.

He sat on the grass until Dick came round towards him – when he was certain Dick could see him, he got up, putting a hand to his right shoulder as if it hurt.

Dick was grinning as he hurtled up towards Eppie, he yelled, 'Collar bone?'

Eppie rubbed, wincing. 'Nothing broken. Just bruised.'

Dick braked to a halt. His front wheel skidded but he brought it under control easily. Eppie begrudgingly had to admit that Dick was a good bicycle handler.

'Are we going to have this race or not?'

'I came to train.'

'You need to *race*.' Dick leant on his handlebar. 'Come on, and don't fall off again!'

He didn't fall off, but he did deliberately get a slow start so that Dick was able to ride away from him. He then put on some speed in the back straight and nearly caught Dick before letting him get away on the banking again. He knew he couldn't overplay his hand – Dick would never believe that – so he kept it close, and ended the lap only a yard or two behind Dick.

'Now,' Dick said. 'I'm going to give you some advice, Eppie. Make a better rider of you.'

'Oh yes? What precisely?'

Dick bared his teeth. 'Enter the novices' race!'

Eppie watched him wheel away and head back across the wet pitch to the gate onto the main road. Maybe his ruse had been rather more transparent than he'd thought …

Harry said, 'Mr Danson called in, Mr E. Just a couple of minutes ago. Said he had to go to the Annual Meeting of the Florists' Society. He left a note.'

A customer was already waiting and Eppie jerked his head at Harry to get him settled while he went into the back room to sort himself out. The lack of furniture reminded him of his 'burglary' and the papers he had locked up in his bureau at home. And of Dick. Drat the man – he'd probably botch the repair of that furniture deliberately as a way of getting back at Eppie for trying to fool him this morning. Eppie would end up with wobbly chairs and a lopsided table.

He unfolded the note from Amos.

It said: *You do know that Councillor Wetherall's funeral is this afternoon, don't you? 2 o'clock. Parish Church. See you there.*

Eppie sighed. This was clearly going to be one of those days.

14

HE UNLUCKILY HAD a pernickety customer who was impervious to hints so he was already running late when Dick came into the shop. He nodded to Harry to clear up the fallen hair and reached for his jacket.

'I can't stop, Dick. I'm off to Wetherall's funeral.'

Dick grinned. 'Amongst all the nobs. Wear your best clothes, Eppie! I won't keep you long.'

'You won't keep me at all,' Eppie retorted. 'Harry, mind you put the notice on the door to say we'll be open again later.'

Dick stepped in front of him as he headed for the door. 'It's about the table and chairs. It's going to cost more than I thought to repair them.'

Eppie stopped. So that was it – Dick was trying to get more money out of him. 'Are you saying the Ordinary won't cover the costs?'

'I've been thinking about that. I was going to do it up and sell it on, but I might not be able to get rid of it quickly.'

Eppie could have told him *that*. He had been trying to get rid of the thing for years. 'That's not my problem. We had an agreement.'

'If you check *Cycling* magazine, they're only going for a couple of pounds at most and that's not going to cover the cost of repairing the furniture, let alone my time.'

'Two pounds?' He could have gone out and bought new furniture for that! 'Look, can we talk about this later. I'm going to be late …'

'It depends how soon you want your chairs back, doesn't it?'

This really wasn't worth the fight. Dick wouldn't give in. He never did. That was his prime virtue as a racer. He might get his tactics hopelessly wrong, and didn't have a clue about training, but he never gave up. Eppie had seen him come back from ridiculous situations.

'I'll give you an extra pound.'

Dick squinted at him. 'One pound ten.'

'One pound ten shillings! Not a chance. Throw the stuff on the scrapheap and I'll buy new.'

'A guinea then.'

Always let the other man think he's won – until you sprint past him on the line. 'Oh, all right then! But make me up a bill so I've got it for my accounts.'

And after all that, of course, he was late. By the time he got home to change into his most sombre clothes, then dashed back into the centre of town to the church, the street outside the church was filled with bystanders, some just beginning to drift away, others doggedly deciding to stand in the thickening rain. Directly outside the church was the hearse, with its four black beplumed horses and its elaborate crepe drapings; there must have been flowers but they'd probably been taken inside the church with the coffin.

The church was packed – for a moment Eppie thought he'd come too late for a seat. All the people at the back were the shopkeepers and tradesmen of the town – the great and the good presumably were at the front of the church. The lower orders were not particularly concerned with maintaining strict silence; most of them seemed to be speculating on the identity of the murderer and there were a few interested looks cast at Eppie. And goodness, there was Dick in an ill-fitting coat so out of fashion he must have had it ten years at least. Why hadn't he said he was coming?

Someone was whispering, a hoarse hiss that was more penetrating than all the mutterings at the back. No, it was a hiss. Amos was waving vigorously to him from a back pew. Beside him, Belle was splendid in a slightly out-of-date black gown, and a new hat with a delightful and totally undevout veil. More people were looking at her than at the vicar at the front of the church. Odd she should have felt the need to come, but then some women actually like funerals.

Amos made room for Eppie. 'You're late. The flowers were white lilies. The widow's wearing a most attractive set of black pearls, plus a sorrowful stoop and at least three startlingly white handkerchiefs. With lace. The daughter sobs a lot.'

As if on cue, Eppie heard a sob from the front of the church. By straining slightly, he could see the coffin, on trestles in the nave, with a sheaf of white lilies on top of it. An array of black hats clearly denoted ladies in the front pew. A fair few bare-headed gentlemen behind them, mostly silver-haired. And the vicar, standing prayer book in hand, giving the muttering tradesmen at the back a stern look.

'Dearly beloved …'

He hadn't got the wrong place in the service book, had he? Eppie wouldn't have put it past him. Hard to imagine that that benign gentleman in black cassock and white surplice was a demon fast bowler. Well, he had been in his youth, and he was still capable of bowling out an unwary batsman. Only much more slowly.

No, he had the right place. He uttered a few words of sombre greeting then launched into the usual sentences and prayers, and admonitions to live a good life before you were snatched away unexpectedly in the vigour of your youth. Eppie had heard him intoning similar sentences to batsmen trudging back to the pavilion. But surely describing Wetherall as being snatched away in the vigour of his youth was a bit much – he'd been fifty-eight if he was a day.

Eppie allowed his mind to drift. Most of his neighbours were obviously doing the same. Belle dropped her handkerchief as she sat up after a prayer – it was retrieved by the smiling gentleman on the other side of her. She whispered her thanks; Amos, who'd been scribbling away, vigorously dug her in the ribs and she gasped. Eppie peeked over Amos's arm.

'What are you writing?'

Amos showed him a list of names. 'You always have to have a full list of attendees for the paper.'

'You can't identify all those – you can only see the backs of their heads!'

Amos nodded. 'True. But every one of these *will* be here – they need to be seen to be here. Look, the gentlemen of the Conservative Association—'

A man in front turned and hushed him. Amos waited until the man had turned away again, then made a face at the back of his head.

'And if they *aren't* here,' he whispered, lowering his voice only by the merest fraction, 'they'll want people to think they were.'

'In other words,' Eppie whispered, 'you're making it up.'

'You have summed journalism up in a single sentence! Well done!'

The vicar intoned on, then there was a lull. Some music would have been nice. There was nothing wrong in having music at a funeral. A hymn or two perhaps so Eppie could get up and stretch his legs after all this kneeling and sitting. It wasn't good for him to keep still so long – he needed to keep supple. He yawned. Amos looked up from his scribbling.

'Is there *no* respect for the deceased?'

Looking round at the gossiping tradesmen and the shopkeepers glancing impatiently at their watches, Eppie said, 'I don't think so. I'm surprised you're here, given what the vicar thinks and that he told Maitland you were me.'

Amos beamed. 'All sorted, my dear fellow. I met Maitland at the church door and he addressed me by name. By my *correct* name. I told him the vicar gets confused and that he really meant you. When I described you to him, he remarked that he'd seen you at the inquest and had known the vicar was wrong all along. A false alarm, my boy.'

Eppie rolled his eyes. Trust Amos to get in a fuss about nothing. Oh Lord, and here came a eulogy. If he hadn't caught Inspector Crellin's eye at that moment, Eppie would have eased his way out of the church with a hand on his stomach to imply great need. But Crellin was looking at him with an odd calculation, so Eppie sat tight.

The man who climbed the steps to the pulpit was young, black-haired, impeccably and expensively and fashionably dressed. The very man they had been talking about – Algernon Maitland. He must have been asked by the widow to say a few words. He certainly knew how to hold an audience – before uttering a word, he let his gaze sweep over the congregation, seeming to settle unnervingly on Eppie for a moment before moving on.

Amos leant to whisper in Eppie's ear. 'Know what he's doing? He's fixing his gaze on a point on the back wall of the church, just above the heads of the congregation. Then everyone in the church gets the impression that he's looking directly at them. Clever but not exactly original.'

'As a future member of the Wetherall family,' the young man began. How old was he? Thirty? 'This sad duty falls to my lot ...'

Amos sighed audibly.

'I had hoped,' the young man said, and paused for a moment to smile down at the ladies in the front pew – a sad poignant sympathetic smile, 'to be able to call Charles Wetherall my father-in-law before too long ...'

'Not a penny to his name,' Amos muttered. 'All that glisters is not gold.'

It was unusually perceptive of Amos to realize that Eppie had been on the verge of being impressed by Maitland. Eppie took a grip on himself and tried to look at the man through Amos's eyes. *Clever but not original* had been Amos's verdict on Maitland's approach – was that what he would say of the man himself? It was tempting to agree. As Eppie listened to the rolling phrases and heard just how wonderful a man Charles Albert Frederick Wetherall had been, how devoted a father and loving a husband, and such a keen advocate of so many good causes, he heard nothing new, nothing he wouldn't have expected to hear. But then what else was Maitland to say? He was hardly likely to stand up and say 'I disliked the man intensely – he was a fool and an idiot and was unfaithful to his wife.'

That would have been more entertaining, though.

All things come to an end and the vicar finally nodded at the undertaker's men who sidled out of pews to heave the coffin onto their shoulders. The vicar warned the congregation that only the family would be welcome at the graveside. Heads were bowed as the coffin came on its slow stately way back up the nave. The pall-bearers' faces were set in solemn lines, the widow and daughter came behind, dabbing at wet eyes under their concealing veils. Maitland gently held out his arm for the widow to take and she glanced up at him. Actually, she looked rather too glad to be obliged – that was a warm smile she gave Maitland. Eppie wondered how grieving a widow she really was – although, admittedly, he wouldn't much have liked being married to Charles Albert Frederick Wetherall either.

Maitland looked directly at Eppie.

He did. He absolutely did. There was no doubt of it. There was even a tiny smirk on his lips, and a fractional nod of his head. Then the procession was past, and with a loud comfortable clearing of throats, and shuffling of feet, and clattering of dropped bags and books, the congregation got up, as if released from the worst of ordeals. Belle, behind Eppie, said loudly, 'Oh, you *are* kind. I'm not usually this clumsy, dropping things all the time …'

Amos said menacingly, 'Come on, *dear*,' and shouldered past Eppie, his hand firmly on Belle's elbow, guiding her towards the church door. Belle gave Eppie a mischievous smile.

'Fine woman,' said a man nearby.

Out in the street the rain had eased, there were a mere few spots in the air. The cortege was disappearing round the side of the church. There must be a family vault, otherwise they would have been off to the cemetery. Charles Albert Frederick Wetherall would lie here, under the weight of the church, a few streets away from the town hall where he'd strutted and posed and espoused unpopular causes, probably *because* they were unpopular, a few streets away from the home where he'd been threatened only the night before his death. Would they put up a statue to him as he'd hoped? That, Eppie thought, probably depended on the reason for his murder. If he'd been killed for his political views, then yes; if he'd been killed by a jealous husband, then probably no.

Which, of course, brought Eppie to the matter of the highways engineer, who, conveniently, was a mere three yards in front of him.

'Mr Cartwright!'

The man looked round. Heavy lines of tiredness about his eyes, a weary droop of his shoulders. He was one of those grey men: grey hair, grey eyes, grey skin, enormous grey whiskers – he was accustomed to usually wearing a kind of tweed that was somehow more grey than brown. A big man but looking diminished today.

'Mr Epford. If this is about bicycle racing on the roads, I'm afraid I cannot discuss this now. Perhaps another time …'

Did he seriously think Eppie would accost him about such matters on an occasion like this? He shook his head.

'I merely wanted to express my condolences to the family and since I can't, for obvious reasons, come close to them at the moment, I wondered if you'd pass them on, on an appropriate occasion in the near future.'

Cartwright startled him by laughing, harshly. 'Me? Pass on your condolences? No, Mr Epford. I'm rather afraid I can't do that.' He seemed to think he'd been a trifle too sharp, softened his voice. 'I'm afraid I have little contact with the Wetherall family apart from official business. I suggest you write a note of condolence – I'm sure the family would be grateful to receive it.' And with a tight little smile that was apparently meant to be friendly, he turned for the street.

Amos said in Eppie's ear, 'Now there's a man who's under a great deal of stress. Looks like the rumours about his wife are true.'

'You can't say that!' Eppie protested. 'You've no evidence – it's just guesswork. The man might be ill …'

Amos snorted. 'I'm off to write up my report. Do you want to be listed as amongst the mourners?'

'You can say I was present,' Eppie retorted. 'I'm not hypocritical enough to say I mourn a man I hardly knew!'

Thanks to Maitland's verbosity – the eulogy had lasted the best part of an hour – it hardly seemed worthwhile to reopen the shop. But business was business and Eppie wanted a new pair of pneumatic tyres. Though given the fact he was going to have to pay for the repairs to the shop after the 'burglary', he probably wouldn't be able to afford them, no matter how hard he worked.

He stayed open for two or three hours and was so busy he started to wonder whether the tyres weren't within reach before the Sports after all. Quite a few people wandered in and out of the dispersing funeral crowds to have a haircut or a shave, and a good gossip. At times the shop was so full of customers, the noise was almost deafening, with wild ideas about the murder being thrown backwards and forwards.

Everyone had a theory apparently, from the fairly obvious ('It was a thief, wasn't it? I heard they'd torn the clothes off his back to sell'), to the distinctly outré ('I heard that he got on the wrong side of some Chinese villains when he was in London last year, and I saw a Chinaman down by the harbour just two days before he died').

Dick was in the shop when this last theory was put forward and withered it in the bud with a laconic, 'I heard it was a woman.'

Three or four men looked at each other in thoughtful silence.

'I had heard he liked the ladies,' one man said finally, but he sounded distinctly disappointed.

At last the shop was empty. Harry got the brush out to sweep up the last of the hair from the floor; Eppie started to rearrange his tools and to reckon up the money he'd taken. The door swung open with a jangle. He looked up, ready to say 'We're closed,' but never got the words out.

It was Inspector Crellin. Looking grim. 'Good evening, *Mr* Epford.'

'We're just—'

'I was wondering why you were late for Mr Wetherall's funeral this afternoon.'

'Why?' Eppie asked. 'Is it a crime?' No, no, that really was not a clever thing to have said!

'That,' Crellin said, 'depends on *why* you were late.'

15

EPPIE TOOK THE inspector through into the back and regretted that too. The inspector squinted around the room. 'Not got the table and chairs mended yet?'

'We're negotiating the price,' Eppie said darkly. 'Inspector, what's all this about the funeral?'

Crellin straightened and wriggled himself into a sterner position, the one he must put on to question suspects. Which worried Eppie no end.

'Can I ask why you were late for the funeral, Mr Epford?'

'You can,' Eppie said. There was a little silence.

'And your reply would be?' added the inspector, obviously annoyed. Heat 1 to Eppie.

'Why do you want to know? Why does it matter when I turned up? Don't they say "better late than never"? I might not have gone at all.'

'Just give me the reason, sir,' the inspector said. Extraordinary – the more polite he became, the ruder he sounded. Out in the shop, Harry could be heard clattering around.

Eppie gave in. What was the point in being awkward for the sake of it?

'I was late closing the shop because of a last-minute customer. Then I had to get home to put on suitable clothes and then come back to the church. It took me longer than I'd expected.'

'That's all?'

'That's all.' He was dying to ask if there should have been more, but he was beginning to think it was unwise to ask for trouble. Anyway, it was apparently heading his way of its own accord – no sense in encouraging it.

'You didn't happen to take the long way round to the church? Via Mr Wetherall's home?'

'No.' Eppie was astonished. 'Why should I?'

'Well, sir, you might want to remove some incriminating evidence. Some papers, for instance. And take a little money at the same time if you're lucky, pick up a few loose coins that have been left lying around. Break a window, climb in – nothing could be simpler.'

Alarm bells starting ringing. Eppie could hear them so clearly he almost looked round for them.

'Papers? Incriminating evidence?' He gathered his wits. 'Evidence can only be incriminating if you've done something, and I haven't.' He glared at Crellin, which seemed to amuse the inspector.

'Are you sure, sir?'

'Of course I'm sure!'

'It's just that one of the neighbours saw someone who looked pretty much like you. First Miss Wetherall thinks she saw you, then a neighbour. Mrs Wetherall and Mr Maitland are looking long and hard at you, Mr Epford, I don't mind saying so.'

Eppie opened his mouth, shut it again. Crellin was lying. He had to be. If he'd had good strong evidence from one of the neighbours, then he'd just have come along and arrested Eppie straight away. And what Mrs Wetherall and Mr Maitland thought of him was neither here nor there as far as Eppie was concerned.

'Let me get this straight,' he said. 'Has there been a burglary at the Wetheralls' house?'

'What do you think?'

'I think there has been,' Eppie said cordially. 'I think the entire household, including the servants, got behind the hearse and went off to the church and someone nipped in behind their backs and burgled the house. What an unkind thing to do.'

Crellin was going an interesting shade of brick red. 'This is no laughing matter, sir!'

'I'm not laughing,' Eppie protested. 'I know how upsetting a burglary can be.' He looked round pointedly. 'Very well, if you want a precise answer, I was nowhere near Wetherall's house. But I doubt I can prove it. Even if you talk to my neighbours – and I can assure you they *will* have seen me coming and going, and *will* have noticed I was wearing my mourning clothes – they won't be able to tell you that I didn't go via the Wetherall's house. I was riding my bicycle – I suppose I might have had time to go round that way.'

That was a risky thing to say but it had the effect he'd suspected it might – Crellin backed off at once. 'I'm just investigating all the evidence, Mr Epford. When a neighbour says they thought they saw someone, I can't ignore it.'

'I don't know any of the neighbours, so how would they know me?'

They could have seen him at the inquest, he thought belatedly, but this did not seem to occur to Crellin. 'You mistake me, Mr Epford. I said they saw someone whose description fitted yours.'

To do him justice, he had, but the intention had clearly been to imply the neighbour had definitively identified Eppie. He decided to be magnanimous. 'I see your point though – if papers were taken as well as money, then it suggests it wasn't just an opportunistic burglar. Do you know *what* papers are missing?'

Crellin puckered up at once. 'Excuse me, Mr Epford, but that's confidential information. We can't go around telling everyone exactly what clues we have, can we?'

Though they could apparently go around accusing innocent people on nothing but a whim. 'Of course not. I beg your pardon. Is that all, Inspector?'

Crellin smiled. 'Not quite, Mr Epford. You haven't yet convinced me you had a good reason for not reporting your burglary.'

Good heavens! Eppie had thought that had been dealt with – that he'd passed it off quite nicely. And now Crellin was saying he hadn't forgotten about it and wasn't going to forget about it.

'Inspector,' he said, spreading his hands appealingly, 'I've lost half a day's trading with the inquest, and half a day more with the funeral and I can't afford any more time off, even to report a burglary. Especially when nothing was taken.' He put the merest suggestion of a whine in his voice. 'You know it's hard to make a living nowadays and …'

'All right, all right!' Crellin straightened up into his policeman stance again and waggled a finger – actually waggled a finger! – at Eppie. 'You'd do better in the business if you didn't keep taking half days off to train.' Which was not a reasonable thing to say when you had a bet on a man to win a race – did no one think he had to work at it? They seemed to think he could just turn up and carry all before him. 'Now,' Crellin went on, 'I'm going to tell you straight, Mr Epford. I know people don't always think it worthwhile reporting every little thing to the police, but you've got to see it from my point of view. There's a burglary at the house of my murder victim, following close on to a burglary at the house of my principal suspect – that can't be a coincidence.'

Eppie almost reeled. *Principal suspect*!

'How am I to solve crimes, if people don't tell me everything?'

'I'm sorry,' Eppie said humbly, when really he felt like hitting the inspector. Principal suspect, indeed! 'I'll make sure that if anything else happens, you'll be the first to know.'

'Good,' Crellin said and made a quick exit. So quick an exit, in fact, that Eppie rather thought the inspector knew he was skating on thin ice. Or at least that he was making an exit while he was still on top of the argument.

He'd just promised to tell the inspector everything and he hadn't mentioned a word about those papers sitting in his desk at home. Wetherall family papers. Which had been stolen from the Wetherall house while the family and servants were at the funeral. No, hang on a minute. They couldn't have been. He'd had them in his possession since Monday morning. Which meant they had been purloined from the Wetheralls over the weekend. Well, they'd been preoccupied of course, maybe they hadn't looked for the papers until this evening. After the funeral maybe – when the lawyer wanted to make sure he had all the deceased's bills and so on, to administer the estate. Or would that have been done earlier?

So had there been a burglary at the Wetheralls' or not? Had someone just gone to the desk and found the papers missing and *assumed* they'd been stolen? Hadn't Crellin said a window had been broken? And that neighbour Crellin had quoted? Maybe there'd been a burglary with some money stolen and they'd assumed the papers had gone in the robbery too. Or maybe none of it had really happened – maybe Crellin had just been trying to force Eppie to say something inadvisable.

What a mess.

At home, finally, with some relief, he got out the papers again while his supper was cooking, flicked through them once more. He'd missed nothing: a will, newspaper advertisements, certificates of marriage and birth. The obvious conclusion to draw was that there'd been some doubt of Charles Wetherall's legitimacy. But – he read the copy certificates several times – the dates were fine: Wetherall had been born thirteen months after his parents' marriage. Of course they *were* just copies, but why should any vicar lie as to their authenticity? Unfortunately, given the date on the letter accompanying the copies, this vicar must be long dead, so there was no chance of asking him. Eppie could check the original registers of course but what excuse could he give for doing that?

He couldn't see anything else in the papers that looked significant. Unless the will was a forgery? But if it *was*, and therefore invalid, it wouldn't matter in the least. Apart from the small bequests to friends and servants, everything had been left to the son – Charles Albert Frederick. Exactly as it would have been if the father had died intestate.

No, none of it made sense. But one thing was clear: he really didn't want to be caught with these papers. He'd take them with him when he next went to see Alma, and ask her to find a hiding place for them. In the meantime, he hid them with his spare hoard of emergency cash, under the floorboard beneath the bedroom carpet, ate his dinner and went to bed.

He was definitely going to have to sort this out.

16

EPPIE LIVED ON a knife-edge for three days. He seemed to be forever seeing Crellin in the street and every time they passed the inspector looked at him oddly. Or just looked at him. At any moment, Eppie expected to feel a hand on his shoulder and to hear Crellin intoning whatever words it is that policemen intone when they arrest someone. Eppie didn't know exactly what those words were and he didn't want to find out. Chief suspect!

He'd never thought he'd be pleased that Alma couldn't visit. He didn't want her mixed up in this. Though he did feel rather lonely. Amos seemed to be tied up with endless 'charity balls', and he didn't even see Dick at his early morning training sessions at the track. Anyway, there was no one he could talk to as well as Alma.

At least the rumour-mongers in town now seemed to be convinced that Wetherall had been murdered by a robber. Everyone, it seemed, had their own tales of being accosted in the street by someone highly suspicious, usually – inevitably – someone Irish or a railway navvy, or both. Though Eppie did catch one or two people looking suspiciously at him. Or was that his imagination? And were there fewer customers than usual?

Oh, this was ridiculous! He was going to ignore it all and concentrate on his training.

Early Saturday afternoon, he put on his Norfolk jacket and knickerbockers, and packed his usual bag for expeditions. A warm sweater in case the weather turned colder. Various tools in case he had a puncture or other mechanical failure. Some of Alma's specially-made cakes which staved off hunger better than anything else he knew. No water, of course, better not to drink too much while riding – he'd stop at a café somewhere for a cup of tea.

And the papers. He thought twice before taking them out of their hiding place. The last thing he wanted to do was to implicate Alma in anything potentially, or actually, criminal, but he found himself particularly wanting her opinion on them. On his situation generally. (*Chief suspect*!) He didn't want to worry her, of course, but he rather thought she wasn't the type of woman who *did* get worried. No matter the situation, she always had a suggestion of something they could do. Besides, he wasn't idiotic enough to suppose the police wouldn't find the papers if they chose to search his house. Crellin and his men must have seen every hiding place ever thought of.

He pushed the brown envelope to the bottom of his bag and piled the food on top of it.

Out in the yard, he checked the Safety over, as usual, before taking it out. The Ordinary behind it seemed oddly reproachful. How long was it since he'd taken it out? Three years at least. The first time he'd ridden it he'd been so proud, sitting up there, perched above the front wheel, bowling along, high above the road and the pavements. Very proud. Until the little boys started throwing stones at him to try and knock him off. They'd roared with laughter at every wobble.

Why on earth had Dick thought he could sell it? *Cycling* was full of hopefuls with 54-inch wheelers languishing in their back yards.

Out onto the road, not breathing easily until he was beyond the houses and onto the Silloth road. His first race ever had been on this road – a three-mile handicap to the toll-house and back. He'd come second and won a silver cruet. Got fifteen shillings for it from the man who haunted the corners of every race meet, hiding behind bushes even though everyone knew he was there and the organizers turned a blind eye to him.

Onto a straight mile or so of road, he felt the need to stretch his legs, put his head down, chin to the handlebar, and started to build up speed. A few pedestrians trudging solidly along with baskets or boxes; a man with two dogs that jumped up and barked furiously as Eppie pedalled furiously past. One dogcart with a young girl in charge of the horse – she didn't even seem to notice Eppie, nor did her horse. See, it *was* possible for cyclists and horses to co-exist on the roads!

He hit a pothole. The machine bucked under him and he fought it back upright. Nasty. Well, potentially nasty. Potholes were the big downside of road racing.

He worked his way north. At Thursby, he stopped at a café for a pot of tea and a piece of lemon cake. Two other cyclists in the café were talking about the church bicycle parade which was due to take place in a few weeks' time. Silly idea. He'd gone once, with the Wheelers, and the vicar had droned on, as vicars do, while everyone else anxiously stared out of the windows and watched the rain clouds gather. Inevitably, the moment he released them and they stepped outside, the heavens opened and they all got sodden.

On the machine again. He should easily be in Carlisle by tea-time. There'd not be much daylight left, not at this time of year, but he'd get an hour or so in at the track and, with any luck, a race against Alma and anyone else who happened to be there. He wasn't dressed properly for the track, of course, but that wouldn't matter for once.

North of Thursby, he got on the road to Dalston. A nasty little narrow road – you always had to be careful not to go too fast because there might be a farm wagon round the corner, or a couple of countrywomen off to market. Farm dogs were liable to suddenly leap out of field gateways at you. Windy country too – sudden gusts could knock you off the bike. On one run with the Wheelers, a crosswind had come howling across the open field just as they rode past the windmill, and the next minute a neat line of cyclists two by two were scattered in little clumps along the road as the weaker riders let the gaps go.

Someone was coming up behind him. A single horse by the sound of it. Just as he got to the narrowest part of the road between the windmill and the town. He hesitated, then pulled into the gateway to a field, under a darkish clump of trees that were just hinting at green leaves. At first he thought he'd misjudged the situation, that the horse was further off than he'd estimated, but then it appeared, a handsome bay, trot-trotting down the centre of the road. Ridden by a gentleman in a thick riding coat, with a muffler around his throat and a hat pulled down over his face. Between them, the muffler and the hat obscured nearly all the man's face …

Somehow Eppie had the feeling that under the muffler, pulled up around the lower part of his face, the man was smiling.

The horse came to a halt, sidled. Eppie leant back against the field gate, as nonchalant as he could be, given that he didn't feel nonchalant at all.

'Good afternoon,' he said cordially. 'Nice day.'

The man laughed. Eppie knew at once who he was. Then the whip came up in his hand.

Eppie had nowhere to go. The gate blocked his way behind and the horse blocked his way back onto the road. The whip lashed down. He threw up his left arm to protect himself and took the blow just above his wrist. Pain seared all the way to his shoulder. He thought the man would hit again, twisted to try and move away, lost his balance. Toppled backwards, caught himself in the bicycle. They went down in a tangle of man and metal. The top tube cracked down hard on Eppie's right leg, he banged his head against the field gate.

By the time he'd disentangled himself, the horseman was halfway down the road to Dalston. The echo of a laugh drifted back.

The gate to Colonel Binning's field in Carlisle was always closed, but every cyclist in Cumberland knew how to trip the lock. Eppie swung himself down off his machine, winced as his right leg complained. There'd be an enormous bruise there in the morning. He wheeled his bike into the field, shut the gate behind him.

The cinder track took up a considerable part of the large field. Larger than the one in Maryport, a good quarter of a mile round. A solitary cyclist was riding hard at the far end of the track, just broaching the banking at the far corner and starting up the back straight. Eppie stood and watched her for a while, admiring her style and speed. If only she'd been born a man, she'd be beating them all on the path, including Eppie, particularly over the short distances.

Though he was glad she hadn't – been born a man, that is.

As Alma worked her way up the back straight, he stood waiting for her, absent-mindedly rubbing his arm where the whip had hit. Was there anyone else there? Maybe he could hear voices from the pavilion on the other side of the field? Yes, a couple of men came out to gesticulate and point. Committee members obviously, probably planning the Easter sports, working out the places for the marquees and the judges' stand and so on. There'd been significant organizational problems last year that needed to be rectified.

Alma was grinning hugely as she sprinted up to him. 'Good news! They've accepted me! They've accepted my entry to the Maryport Sports on Easter Monday!'

'Good gracious!' He was startled, but pleased. 'They've had a brainstorm! They've actually seen sense. I'd never have believed it of them!'

'Well,' she said, laughing. 'We are almost in the twentieth century, aren't we?'

'Yes, but they could have come into the nineteenth a bit quicker!'

'Eppie,' she said. 'What's wrong?' He started to protest but she interrupted him. 'Eppie Epford, don't even *think* of lying to me. You'd never get away with it, I know you too well. You've come off your machine, haven't you? You crashed on the way here. You're not hurt?'

'I didn't crash.'

She gave him a rueful look. 'Don't look at me as if I've insulted you horribly. Everyone falls off now and again.'

'I didn't crash,' he repeated. 'And just now, all I'd like to do is put in a couple of hours' training.'

She studied him for a moment. 'You're sure you're not hurt?'

'The odd bruise, that's all. Let's warm up with a few leisurely laps. Two laps then a sprint, then another two.'

She nodded, took him at his word without any more protesting and rode back onto the track. He went after her, but his bruised leg ached even more now. It had pained him badly when he got back onto the bike near Dalston but had eased as he had ridden – stopping, however, seemed to have started it complaining again. He got back into the rhythm of riding eventually but Alma beat him easily, twice.

After the third sprint, she eased off, dropped back beside him, pedalling lazily as the back bend came up.

'Eppie, this is silly. You're obviously not right. You're not pedalling with your usual fluency. If you're injured and you keep riding, you'll only make things worse.'

She was right. He cruised to a halt.

'All right. Let's go and have some supper and I'll tell you what happened.'

'Good,' she said. 'I don't think I could have borne not knowing any longer!'

Ensconced in their usual little tea-rooms in English Street, at the table reserved for them every other Saturday evening, they let the little waitress come and go, and chatted about the Easter Sports until they were confident no one could overhear. Then, as Alma tucked into her beef – she wasn't one of those *ladylike* eaters, thank goodness, all small portions and two peas on a fork – Eppie explained about his encounter on the Dalston road. It was a short recital and he played it down as best he could, but even so Alma stopped chewing and, after a moment, laid her cutlery on the plate.

He'd intended to say more, to reassure her that it'd been nothing, just an idiotic horseman taking things to preposterous lengths, but one look at her face stopped the implied lies in his mouth. He stumbled to a halt, added, 'It *is* only a bruise or two. Nothing broken. I was lucky, really.'

She looked down at her plate, pursing her lips. Then she looked up at him from under her eyelashes. 'You recognized him, didn't you? Who was it?'

He glanced round. There were few people in the room and they were all engaged in pleasant conversation over their meals. He nodded.

'Algernon Maitland.'

17

EPPIE HAD GONE off his food – he pushed his plate away.

'Somehow the family have got it into their heads that I killed Wetherall and they're out to get me. You didn't hear Maitland's laugh as he rode away – pure malice.'

And hadn't Amos told him there were unsavoury rumours about Maitland mistreating his mistresses? After his encounter on the road today, Eppie could well believe it.

'But why should they be so convinced it's you? I know the girl implied you were the man arguing with her father but she retracted that later.'

'Mrs Wetherall clearly thinks I put pressure on her to do so.' He explained his encounter with the widow at the track.

Alma was thinking things through with a delightful little crease between her eyes. 'Surely Mr Sibson will say he accidentally delayed you in the shop?'

'Who knows what Dick might do? He doesn't like to get involved in things. And even if he does, I might still have had time to do it. Suppose I'd taken my clothes for the funeral to the shop and changed there, instead of spending time going home. Then I could have gone to Wetherall's house, and still had time to get back to the funeral.'

Alma nodded. 'But the inspector's clearly lying about the neighbours. They can't have seen you because you weren't there.'

Eppie sighed. 'Some people are sensation seekers and Crellin can be credulous, especially when he *wants* to believe something. All the neighbours would have to do is say they saw a shadow roughly my size and shape, and he'd jump on them.'

'We have to go right back to the beginning.' Alma poured herself another cup of tea. '*Why* are the family so determined to blame you?' She tilted her head. 'Would you call me a suspicious person?'

'Not at all,' he said promptly. 'I think you're a very good judge of character.'

She nodded, accepting the compliment in that matter-of-fact way he loved. 'Well, I wouldn't swear Maitland must be the murderer, because I don't know where he was when his prospective father-in-law died, but he plainly has a motive – given his money problems and Wetherall's opposition to the match with Violet Daisy Rose. So I'm wondering if he thinks you know something to his detriment. If he thinks Mr Wetherall told you something under the seal of the confessional, so to speak.'

'I wish people would stop thinking my customers confide all their secrets in me! They do talk a lot, but it's mostly gossip about other people.'

Alma took a delicate sip of tea. 'Or perhaps you saw something at the scene of the crime.'

'I can't imagine what.'

'The police of course didn't see it.'

'Well,' he admitted. 'Sometimes I think Inspector Crellin wouldn't recognize a clue if it hit him, but then he turns round and is surprisingly shrewd. But the doctor isn't stupid. *He* examined the scene very thoroughly – surely he would have spotted something untoward?'

'Unless it had been removed before he got there.'

Eppie frowned and felt hungry again. If they were to do a long training ride tomorrow, as usual, he needed to have a good meal. He tucked into his steak and kidney again.

'But I was the only one on the scene apart from the police until the doctor arrived and I didn't remove anything.'

'Then the police did. How much do you trust Constable Banks?'

He chewed on a nice piece of kidney. 'I've never had cause to trust or distrust him. The only contact I've ever had with him is over his head. Literally.'

Alma nodded and stared absently at the elderly couple at the next table. 'I still think the suggestion I made last week is a good one. About Miss Wetherall.' She tucked into her food again. 'Suppose she accosted her father in the alley – she must surely know he usually went that way.'

'We talked about that before – we agreed the height difference was a problem.'

'Not with that handkerchief,' Alma said darkly. She seemed to be taken by that scrap of lace, and not in a good way. 'They're talking. She's pretending to be upset, dabbing at her eyes. *Oh Papa.*' Her imitation of the young lady was wickedly accurate. '*How could you think of forbidding my marriage? You are ruining my life for ever!* She drops the handkerchief. *Oh! My handkerchief! Would you be so obliging as to pick it up, Papa*? Papa bends down – she hits him over the head and runs off, forgetting the handkerchief.'

'What did she hit him with?'

'Her parasol.'

'A parasol would hardly have given him a headache!'

She looked annoyed. 'Then she had something heavy in her bag.'

He nodded to say that he allowed her that, even though he couldn't imagine Miss Wetherall with a hammer. But as he picked apart a particularly succulent potato boiled with mint, he said, 'There was no handkerchief there when I arrived.'

'Then it was something else she dropped. Something that rolled away into a corner, perhaps. You didn't have time to spot it before Constable Banks sent you away but Maitland thinks you may have. He's attacking you in order to protect his fiancée.'

'I don't like this,' Eppie said, not meaning the potato, which he liked a great deal. 'Are you saying he intends to kill me?'

'No, no, it's just a warning. *Stay out of my business.*'

He sighed. 'There's so much going on that I can't make head or tail of. Take the burglary at the shop, for instance—'

Alma put her cutlery down with a clatter. 'What burglary?' Her voice rose. 'Eppie! What haven't you told me?!'

He'd forgotten he hadn't seen her all week. Well, he hadn't forgotten the fact – he'd missed her bitterly – but he'd forgotten it meant he hadn't told her about the burglary at the shop. She listened calmly enough, but a kind of mulish determination started to form on her face. Hurriedly, he reached down into his bag, on the floor at his feet.

'Nothing was taken. On the contrary – whoever broke in *left* something. These.'

He handed her the papers and there was silence as she read through them. He called to the waitress for another pot of tea. Alma had her schoolmistress air on, as she always did when she started to read – he adored that slightly severe look, that air of concentration. The new pot of tea arrived; Eppie ordered two portions of bread and butter pudding, and stirred the pot thoroughly.

Alma put the papers down and was silent for a moment. 'I can't see any reason why anyone should want you to see those papers. There's nothing untoward about them at all.'

'The only thing I can think of is that the register entries are faked. Or that the vicar of the time copied them incorrectly.'

Alma consulted the papers again. 'They're from the registers of St Cuthbert's.

We could go along and ask the present vicar if we could see the registers. I know him well – he's one of the governors of the school. We could tell him we're in search of one of your uncles or aunts or some such story.'

'That would be a lie.' He shifted uneasily – he had been stretching the truth rather too much recently.

'Eppie,' she said. 'Do you want to know what's going on or not?'

He considered this, together with the bread and butter pudding which conveniently arrived on the table at that precise moment.

'Actually,' he said, when the waitress had gone. 'Yes. Very badly.'

'Good.' Alma reached for her spoon. 'We'll go and see the vicar straight after supper – he'll be writing his sermon for tomorrow and will be only too glad to be interrupted.'

She was right. The vicar, Mr Jones, wore a slightly harried air when he answered the door of the vicarage to them himself but his face cleared when he saw Alma.

'My dear Miss Gains!' His voice carried the merest hint of a Welsh accent. 'How delightful of you to pay me a visit! I was just writing my sermon but never mind, never mind. Come on in. And this is?'

'Mr Epford from Maryport.' Alma smiled sweetly. 'He's a neighbour of my aunt's and has a query he wishes to put to you.'

They followed the vicar into a dark and gloomy den. A small fire flickered in the grate and one lamp burned on a table strewn with papers. But the vicar turned up the gas lights and suddenly the room was cosy and welcoming, with deep armchairs by the fire and a delicate, more feminine sofa plainly intended for lady visitors. They waited politely for Alma to seat herself on this; the vicar waved Eppie to an armchair and sank into the oldest, sloppiest chair himself. He looked at them expectantly, a burly man who patently liked his food and drink.

'A query, Mr Epford? Would it by any chance be …' He leant forward with a conspiratorial air. '… a personal matter?' He smiled at Alma.

Eppie said hurriedly, 'No, no, I mean …' He wished it was.

'It's about a long lost great-uncle,' Alma said. 'Well, half-great-uncle. You see, Mr Epford's grandfather married twice and the two halves of the family lost touch – I won't go into reasons, you understand?'

The vicar nodded. 'Rifts in the family. You would be amazed how often it happens. Sad, very sad.'

'But now there's the matter of an inheritance. Nothing large, but Mr Epford would like to make sure that it goes to the right people, should there be any living descendants.'

The vicar complimented Eppie on his probity and family feeling. Eppie said nothing. He was still staring at Alma in amazement at this farrago of nonsense. Lost in admiration at her inventiveness and her *sangfroid* in relating this invented story without a scintilla of embarrassment or self-consciousness. If he could have proposed there and then, he would have.

'So,' Alma said. 'We were wondering if we could look at your parish registers to verify one or two matters.'

'Indeed, indeed. What in particular?'

Eppie was moved by a spirit of emulation. Somehow he wanted to prove he was worthy of all this effort on his behalf. If only he could think of something to add. But Alma needed no help.

'We'd like to check one or two family events, to make sure we're not heading off on a wild goose chase. Mr Epford's grandfather married in your church, and his eldest son was baptized here, so we'd like to check to make sure those events did indeed take place.'

'Well, that should be easy enough. The marriage registers and the baptismal registers. I shall go and get them straight away. What dates were you wanting?' Mr Jones patted his pockets and brought out a set of keys. 'If you would be so kind as to wait here … Oh! I should have offered you something to drink. Of course I should …'

'We've just had supper,' Alma said.

He looked relieved. 'Oh good. My daily help, you know, has gone home and …'

He smiled and pottered out of the room.

The registers were surprisingly thin books, printed with the relevant forms and filled out in a variety of handwritings good and bad. The vicar, fortunately, had no interest in helping them search, but merely checked that he'd brought them the correct volumes before pottering out of the room again.

They began with the marriage volume and quickly found the marriage of Wetherall's parents. The details had indeed been noted correctly in the copies. The baptism was rather more difficult to find. The parish was a large one, and baptisms legion. Alma eventually turned up the page for May 1837 and found nothing. She went back to the beginning of the year and started searching methodically.

The vicar came back with an enormous pot of tea covered by a cosy in the shape of a country cottage complete with hollyhocks embroidered by the front door. The most fragile and ugly of tea cups and saucers rattled on a tray. Eppie shifted the marriage registers to allow him to place the tray on the desk. There was a plate of rather sad-looking biscuits too. The vicar stood up, easing his back slightly.

'My dear late wife's favourite tea service.'

'Oh,' Eppie said. 'They're delightful.'

They made their escape close on two hours later, having listened to most of the vicar's tales of marriages and funerals that had gone wrong – and there had been a lot of them. Walking back onto English Street, where all the shops were shut but the taverns open, havens of light and warmth in the night, Alma said, 'He's lonely.'

Eppie nodded.

'And we've found out nothing that we didn't already know. Except that the vicar of the time wrote *appallingly* and Charles Wetherall was born in July, not May. Which means he was actually born fifteen months after his parents' marriage and is – or was – perfectly legitimate.'

'We've eliminated one possibility, I suppose,' Eppie said gloomily.

'And how many other possibilities are we left with?'

Eppie contemplated the nearest tavern and thought that it was about time he and his bicycle went to his hotel. 'None.'

'Exactly,' Alma said.

They stood under a street lamp and looked about them at the passers-by, the shop windows, anything and anyone but each other.

'Well, good night …' Eppie hesitated and added cautiously, '*dear.*'

Alma beamed. 'Good night, Eppie. Same time as always tomorrow?'

'Indeed.'

And he floated off towards his hotel on a wave of exultation. She had allowed him to call her *dear*. She had not objected. Ridiculous to be so – so happy. But he was. There was still a fair bit to worry about – Maitland, Inspector Crellin, *chief suspect* – but just for tonight, he was going to forget all about that.

Dear!

18

Eppie refused to let the situation spoil his Sunday with Alma. He woke up feeling distinctly stiff in leg and arm, and knew he wouldn't be at his best, but all training was valuable unless you pushed yourself when you were really sick. By the time he'd cycled from his hotel to the castle, which was their usual meeting point, his aches and pains had eased and they put in a good ride, heading north into Scotland, keeping up a steady pace, occasionally spurting for milestones or bridges or the outer edges of villages. Alma won almost all of these sprints which just showed how much Eppie was under par because of that leg.

They parted at the castle again in mid-afternoon to allow Eppie time to get home to Maryport in the light. Alma hesitated as she was about to ride off.

'I wondered last night if we'd missed something about those papers.'

'We must have.'

'No, no, I thought of something specific. We know that the parents married in St Cuthbert's when they said they did, but I wondered if there was a legal impediment – something that rendered the marriage not valid.'

Eppie stared at her. 'Like a previous marriage, you mean? There's nothing in the papers to suggest that.' He sighed. 'Come to that, there's nothing in the papers to suggest they're connected with Wetherall's murder, except they must be. Why else should anyone have sent me them?'

'Actually,' Alma said with a slight edge of apology in her voice. She sat back on her saddle, steadying herself on the machine with one foot on the ground. 'I had a thought about that too. What if they were simply meant to incriminate you? Someone put them in your shop, arranged what looked like a burglary at Wetherall's house while the funeral was going on then sent Inspector Crellin after you. He was supposed to find the documents in your shop and charge you with the burglary.'

'Why me?!' Eppie protested, horrified. 'What have *I* done?'

Alma put up a hand as if to stop him. 'Calm down, Eppie – it didn't work, did it? You were too quick for them. We *will* sort this out, I promise you. All we have to do is take it one step at a time.'

'They can't have been meant for Crellin to find. They were left a good two or three days before the burglary – I was bound to find them before Crellin turned up. They *must* be significant.'

'I suppose so,' she conceded, albeit a trifle reluctantly. 'Very well, I'll check out the wife's side of the family – Wetherall's mother, that is – since they were a Carlisle family. You must check out Wetherall's father. His family's details will be in the Maryport registers. I wonder how they met.'

'Probably at some ball,' Eppie said, gloomily. 'Or on a hunt.'

Alma laughed. 'I'm certain it wouldn't be while doing an honest day's toil! Eppie, dear, you must go or you'll be out in the dark and you haven't got your lamp on your bicycle. I don't want to see your name in the police court records!'

And she leant across and pecked his cheek before riding off at top speed down Castle Street.

Eppie almost floated home.

He paid the price for his enthusiasm. By the time he cycled into the outskirts of Maryport, his leg was aching furiously. He'd overdone it. He'd be hobbling for days and Dick was bound to see him and enjoy a gloat or two. He eased down and took the streets into the centre of town more slowly.

'Eppie!'

He braked to a halt, glanced around. Across the street, almost outside Eppie's shop, Amos was waving vigorously at him. Eppie cycled across.

'I've been looking for you, my boy! I went to your house first then came here in case you were tidying up the effects of your burglary. God, but you look exhausted.'

'Went too far,' Eppie said. 'What did you want to see me about?'

He jerked his head towards a low wall that jutted out from a shop a couple of yards down the street, dismounted and wheeled the bike towards it. Amos almost shrieked. 'You're limping! You will be fit for the sports, won't you? You're not going to pull out!'

'It's just a bruise,' Eppie said irritably, propping the bicycle against a wall. 'I'll be fine. And if you hadn't put money on me, you wouldn't need to worry.'

'But I did put money on you,' Amos retorted, sitting down beside him on the low wall. 'And let me tell you, it's a serious situation. If you don't come up with the win, Eppie my lad, yours truly will be deep in trouble. Rent wise, if you follow my meaning.'

Eppie stared. 'What about your salary from the paper? That's not exactly small.'

'Alas, it disappears so quickly. Belle gets her due and then the rest …' He made a *phutt* noise. 'All gone.'

'On what?'

Amos grinned. 'Betting mostly. Eppie, my boy, stop trying to get me on the straight and narrow. I won't have it.'

'You're an idiot,' Eppie said tartly. 'Betting to win money to cover your betting – what kind of logic is that?'

'None at all,' Amos agreed cheerfully, 'But it *is* a great deal of fun. Are you going to listen to me or are you planning to preach me any more sermons?'

'Go on.'

'I have been, as you know, checking out the political connections of our late, sadly deceased Chairman of the Conservative Association, with a view to deciding if any of them had any motive to dispose of him.'

'And?'

'Seven.'

'What?'

'Seven of them had issued threats against him in the last three months.'

'I'm glad I'm not that unpopular. How could he live knowing that seven people wanted to kill him?'

'Well, to be fair, not all of them threatened to *kill* him. Two or three threatened to find the rottenest tomatoes they could and pelt him with them, that sort of thing, but they all admit to hating the man. And there are at least another ten who were less outspoken but probably just as annoyed. And not all Liberals either. A fair few were of his own political persuasion.'

Eppie groaned and eased his aching leg. The street lights were beginning to glow faintly pink as dusk gathered.

'How are we going to check all of them out? It'll take an age!'

'Ah.' Amos waggled a finger. 'That's the good news I have for you. We don't have to check any of them out.'

'But …'

'Because, like you, they can all prove where they were. Did you never stop to wonder, my boy, where Charles Albert Frederick Wetherall was going when he was murdered?'

'Crellin said he was going to the Town Hall. For a meeting.' Goodness, he was tired. He wanted to get home, eat, sleep …

Amos beamed. 'Exactly! A council meeting for which he was late. Every single one of the men who might have had cause, motive or desire to kill him were sitting in the Town Hall at the time, debating whether to ratify the minutes of the previous meeting. They are all, I repeat, *all* in the clear.'

Eppie stared at him. 'You think that's good news?'

'Saves us a huge amount of work, my boy.'

'I was thinking more of who it left as the *chief suspect*.' A sudden thought struck him. 'Does *all* include Algernon Maitland?'

'It does.'

'He couldn't have murdered Wetherall?'

'Not unless he possesses the ability to be in two places at once.'

'And the highways engineer – Mr Cartwright?'

'Reporting on plans to repair the bridge by the park.'

Eppie groaned.

Amos was grinning. 'Don't despair. There'll be some nice juicy scandal somewhere – it's just a matter of ferreting it out. And you know how good I am at ferreting. Now my boy, it's off home with you. Get yourself a decent night's sleep, rest that leg and be ready to put in a good stint of training tomorrow morning.'

'Thank you, Amos, I don't need your advice.'

'I'm just protecting my investment.' Amos got up and hitched Eppie's machine off the wall. 'Come on. Get on and get off – home!'

Eppie didn't have the energy to do anything else. He got on the bicycle and pedalled off. Behind him, he heard Amos shout.

Which was a *really* good thing. Because when he turned round to try and see if Amos had forgotten to tell him something, he spotted the unmistakable figure of Constable Banks lumbering out of a side street, with his whistle halfway to his mouth.

It was past lighting up time!

He shot off down the nearest side street, put his head down and scorched dangerously round a corner, barely avoiding clipping the curb. Behind him, Banks' whistle sounded. He veered down a cobbled alley, past the broken down doors of house yards. Out the other end and straight across the street into another alley. From there it was only another two turns to the long run downhill to his house.

He was breathing heavily and his heart was pounding with both exertion and alarm. He took the cobbles too fast, skidded on a slippery patch at the far end of the alley and nearly came down. Another whistle, further away this time. Surely Constable Banks *must* have recognized him – the light hadn't been *that* bad. But of course he'd been on foot and couldn't match Eppie's speed …

He heard a third whistle, rather distant, as he turned onto the hill, and coasted down towards his street with a sigh of relief. Even so, he nearly misjudged the right-angled bend into the back alley in his tiredness and had to slow almost to a stop. In his back yard, he hooked his lamp onto the bicycle and turned it on. By the time he'd sorted out his bag and clothes in the house, the lamp would be warm.

He'd just turned it off, ten minutes or so later, when he heard a peremptory rap on the front door. He limped back from the yard and through the house just in time to yank the door open on the second bang. Constable Banks stood outside, his hand still, or again, raised to knock. He was completely clean-shaven, in a manner of speaking. The whiskers had gone but he was plainly growing a new covering of stubble.

'I'm having you,' he said. 'Riding without lights!'

Eppie summoned up the memory of Alma lying to the vicar. That was the spirit he needed right now. 'I never ride without lights.'

'I saw you!'

'Perhaps you did. I've not long come in. But there *is* a lamp on my machine.'

'Where is it? I want to see it.'

Eppie let the constable see he was indignant and led the way through the house to the back yard. The constable sneered when he saw the bike decked out with the light.

'You've just put that on!'

'Well, if I have, it'll be cold, won't it? If I've been using it, it'll be warm. You feel it.'

Constable Banks looked as if he suspected a trick, which was, of course, astute of him. But he lumbered over to the machine and put his hand on the lamp.

'Barely warm,' he sneered. He rubbed his hand against his thick overcoat. 'Let me tell you, Epford, you step out of line just once more and I'll have you!' And he headed for the back gate beyond the machines, stopping only to wave at the Ordinary. 'Murderous machines! I saw a dog killed by one of those. Ride that in the street and I'll have you for causing danger to life and limb – and don't think I won't do it!'

He slammed the gate behind him. But not before Eppie saw him blowing on the fingers with which he'd tested the lamp.

19

It rained. All night. A heavy rain that battered against the windows of Eppie's bedroom and rattled the casements. He slept fitfully, woken every so often by the sound of the storm, drifting off again uneasily. When he finally awoke, and knew for a certainty he wouldn't doze off again, it was still dark; he checked his watch and realized it was almost time to get up for his training.

It was still raining but the worst violence of the downpour had eased and he pedalled along the road in a depressing drizzle. His leg, as he expected, had stiffened up and he had pain from his arm when he gripped hard on the handlebar. He almost turned back home for an indulgent breakfast but gritted his teeth and carried on. A few heavily laden carts passed him, a cluster of miners heading home from the pit, but it was generally quiet. Because it was still only twilight, he'd left the lamp on the bicycle and it was an extra weight that irritated him – the machine didn't quite feel its usual self. But he didn't feel like another run in with Constable Banks. At least not for another day or so – until Banks remembered he had a bet on Eppie and needed to be protecting his investment, not clapping it in prison.

The gate to the cricket ground swung open onto the grassy bank with its improvised seating. The grass was sodden and almost lethal; twice Eppie slid helplessly a few yards. Breathing heavily, he reached the path – he was lucky not to have broken an ankle.

He prodded the grass track with a toe. It must have been cut the previous night because it was almost as clean-shaven as Constable Banks. Unfortunately, it had been cut almost *too* short – the heavy rain had soaked into the ground and produced a surface that was half-grass, half-mud. It looked unrideable.

Gloomily, Eppie trudged across the width of the track, towards the pavilion. The back straight was often in better condition than the front – it might be possible to do a few sprints up and down. He was loathe to waste all his effort in actually getting up and out of the house.

The back straight looked tolerable. Wet but not muddy. Eppie took the lamp off the bicycle and put it on the top step of the pavilion, together with his packet of food, bent to check the machine over …

A lady said, 'If I may have a word, Mr Epford …'

He spun round, thinking: *Not again!* Was he never to get a full session of training? Just like Maud Margaret Wetherall the other day, she'd come out of the shelter of the pavilion. A tall woman dressed in dull lilac, as if in half-mourning, a dress with an elegant fringe – expensive but not in the latest fashion. A heavy veil obscured her face but, to judge by her voice, she was slightly younger than Mrs Wetherall – mid-forties perhaps.

He bowed. 'Ma'am. You have the advantage of me, I think.'

She nodded, hesitated, then lifted her veil to reveal a tear-stained face, clear blue eyes, the neatest of noses and a surprisingly weak mouth. Blonde hair, just starting to grey, framed the face.

'Mrs Cartwright …'

She hushed him in what sounded very like panic. 'Mr Epford – I am risking my reputation coming here to see you. If we were seen together, it would be interpreted as an assignation.'

That was all he needed – to be accused of an illicit affair with a married woman. 'Why come here then?'

She let the veil fall again. Behind its thin protection, he saw her bite her lip. 'I need to speak to you. About – about Charles Wetherall.'

He didn't feel inclined to help her out and said nothing. She added irritably, 'Mr Epford, there seems to be nothing secret in small towns like these. You must be aware of my – connection to Mr Wetherall!' She sagged a little. 'Everyone else seems to know.'

'Except your husband?'

She laughed bitterly. 'Oh, he knows too. It pays him to keep quiet. Or it did. Charles smoothed his way to his present appointment. As a kind of present to me.'

Eppie winced. He would not have been happy to be the absent Mr Cartwright. No wonder he hadn't wanted to talk at the funeral.

He wasn't much enjoying this situation and was as aware as Mrs Cartwright of the dangers of it, but it did seem an unparalleled, and probably unrepeatable, opportunity to question the lady.

'Is that appointment in any danger now Mr Wetherall is dead?'

'It is not!' She sounded so indignant he half expected her to flounce off. 'William is excellent at what he does. He is highly thought of in all quarters.'

In which case, Eppie thought, a man might not think it necessary to keep on the good side of his original benefactor. Which was different, of course, from planning to murder him. And Cartwright would have had to enlist help and get someone else to do the killing for him, given that he was sitting in a council chamber at the time of Wetherall's death.

'And you know of no one who had reason to kill Mr Wetherall?'

'It was probably that wife of his,' she said darkly. 'She is the most impossible, intransigent, obstinate, offensive woman I ever met! Absolutely determined to get her own way!'

Like mother, like daughter then. But no doubt Maud Margaret would say something similar of her husband's mistress.

'Did she know of your affair?'

She turned into a hissing termagant. 'Mr Epford! I thank you not to speak of things about which you know nothing! My – *connection* with Charles was one of deeply-felt emotion. We were in love. But his wife would not allow him a divorce nor would my husband hear of it. We were forced to meet in secret, to snatch stolen moments here and there. Fate, Mr Epford, has always been against us. We were supposed to marry when we were young, but his father sent him off to London where he met *that woman* and was forced into marrying her. Money! That was his father's watchword. Money, above everything else, even his son's happiness!'

She ground to a halt, breathing heavily. A pretty story: Eppie suspected she believed it herself. It might even have been true. But that didn't make it any the less sordid. From the little he'd seen of Charles Albert Frederick Wetherall over the bald spot on the crown of his head, Wetherall had not been a sentimental man – Eppie found it hard to imagine him ever in love. And if Alma was married to someone else, Eppie would certainly not have endangered her happiness and her reputation, by instituting an illicit relationship with her. As for considering divorce – scandalous!

'But I want to make it clear,' Mrs Cartwright said, her voice unsteady. 'That the – *attachment* was over. Charles said he could not bear to see me suffering in such a way, that it was better we should part. That's how noble he was, Mr Epford! Always a man of principle!'

Eppie wondered how this fitted in with the other affairs Wetherall was rumoured to have had. He had a sneaking feeling that the 'cannot bear see you suffering' speech might have been trotted out on more than one occasion.

'Mrs Cartwright,' he said. 'Why did you want to talk to me?'

For a moment, she seemed to have forgotten it was she who had instigated this conversation. She was making an audible effort to calm herself down, to control her ragged breathing. Eventually, she said, 'There was a man he was afraid of. Someone who kept coming to see him. He wouldn't tell me who. At first I thought it was you – I mean, after his death, when people kept saying you were somehow involved. But then I realized it couldn't be. The day before he died, I met him in the High Street, just outside your shop. He told me you were the best barber in town. He would never have spoken of you in that way if you'd been the man threatening him.'

Well, it was something to know he could have called upon Wetherall for a business testimonial, if only he was not dead.

'Did he say why he was afraid of this man?'

'He knew something. Something Charles wanted kept quiet. I think it was a family matter. I must admit he never told me very much but I got the impression it was about his daughter.'

Perhaps it had been Miss Wetherall's relationship with Algernon Maitland. But that was common knowledge – or at least common rumour – surely?

'You never saw this man?'

'Only once. And not clearly, even then. I was in my carriage and I saw Charles outside the ironmonger's. He came across to exchange a word or two, but then stopped suddenly and said he had to go. I saw him staring across the street and looked in that direction. There was a man but he was just going into a shop and I saw only his back view.'

'Which shop did he go into?'

'It was yours.' She hurried on as Eppie sighed. 'But it wasn't you. I could see you, through the window, cutting someone's hair.'

Well, that was reassuring. But it was less than comforting to think that not only had the victim been a customer, but so was the probable murderer.

'Can you describe this man? His clothes? His hair?'

'He didn't look particularly well-off, but not poor. A dark coat, a hat.' She shook her head. 'I think his hair was dark too. I'm sorry. If I could help more, I would. I want to find who killed Charles!'

There was real passion in her voice. He said, 'You need to tell the police this.'

She laughed bitterly. Again. 'Do you think Inspector Crellin is capable of finding a cake in the tea-rooms?'

'I'm not sure he's *that* bad. But …'

She nodded. 'Mr Epford. Let us be frank. Of all the people in this town, apart from myself, *you* have the most pressing reason to want to find Charles's killer. Because we both know that Inspector Crellin has his eye on you. He told my husband that he's perfectly aware you were in your shop at the time of Charles's death, but that he thinks the doctor might have been mistaken about the time of death and it was earlier, when you would have had an opportunity to carry out the crime.'

The very thing he'd feared! Though Eppie would back the doctor's judgement against Crellin's any day. This was Crellin trying to make the facts fit the theory, instead of the other way round.

'But why? Why should I want to kill a customer? And if I did, why should I then insist it was a murder when everyone else thought it an accident?'

She straightened – she'd plainly had enough of this conversation. 'Mr Epford. I don't particularly care who killed Charles. I just want that person to be caught. But I want the *right* person to be caught. And so, presumably, do you.'

She nodded politely and walked off towards the gate behind the pavilion.

He stood on the pavilion veranda, gloomily watching the drizzle pearl the grass with tiny beads. Well, he'd learnt something, both about Charles Wetherall and about his murderer. But it was all so vague as to be worthless. The murderer was probably a man wearing a dark suit and hat, possibly not very well-off, and he might have had dark hair. He was probably one of Eppie's customers. Eppie could think of dozens of his customers who fitted that description.

He'd lost heart for training but he went and did it anyway. He was after all, a racer.

The shop door was shut. He fished the keys out of his pocket; the bell jingled as he pushed the door open. Where was Harry? He should have been here half an hour ago, making sure everything was ready for business. He went through into the bare back room. No sign of Harry here either. No kettle on the hob, no cups put out ready for tea of the morning. No morning paper on the shelf for Eppie to browse through. This was unlike Harry – he was an ardent devotee of improving himself, always wanted to do everything thoroughly and efficiently. He'd actually said once he *liked* working for Eppie. Eppie had begun to think he had a good touch with hair, that he'd make a good partner one day a few years in the future.

Maybe he was ill. Eppie put the kettle on, took off his coat and hat, and hung them on the hook by the back door. He went round the shop, inspecting everything – Harry had done a good job of cleaning before he left the previous evening. He put out the tools of his trade, turned the notice on the door to *Open* and went back to make himself a cup of tea. It was fully fifteen minutes later when he realized he hadn't yet had a single customer.

He stood behind the window with its backwards lettering and stared out at the street. It was certainly a slow morning in town, not many people around, no doubt because of the rain. But even on days like this he should have customers by now.

He had a dreadful feeling he knew exactly why no one was coming in.

20

HALF AN HOUR after he'd opened, the door cracked ajar for the first time. A wary face poked through the gap. Harry. He scuttled in, with a scared glance back as if he thought someone might be watching him. They probably were, Eppie thought gloomily. During his time at the window he'd seen at least three groups of men hesitate outside the ironmonger's opposite, for a chat, and a point or a jerk of the head in the direction of Eppie's shop. If only he'd never gone out with Constable Banks to look at the body. If only he'd kept his mouth shut about it being murder.

'You're late, Harry,' he said severely.

Harry shook his head. He looked as if he was about to burst into tears – sometimes Eppie forgot he was only sixteen years old.

'I'm sorry, Mr E but I can't come any more. My mother says I'm to hand in my notice.'

He stood staring at Eppie, clearly holding his breath. Leaning back a little as if he dared not come too close. Eppie had heard stories about Harry's home. Harry's dad was a miner and, like most miners, liked his drink. He'd been known to use his hand and his belt. But then a lot of fathers did. *Spare the rod and spoil the child.*

'Harry,' Eppie said in a friendly tone. 'You're sixteen years old. You're a man now. Are you going to let your mother tell you what you can and cannot do?'

'She says I'm not to associate with you any longer. She says …' He faltered to a halt, flushing bright red.

Eppie nodded. 'You can be honest with me, Harry. I won't be angry. Tell me what she said.'

'She says you're a murderer!'

This time Harry flinched, although Eppie had not moved. Eppie said calmly, 'Harry. Your mother's wrong. However, I'm sure she's only concerned for your welfare. So, shall we agree that you can go home now and think about this for a couple of days, so you can decide what *you* think and what *you* want to do? Come back – let's say Thursday morning and tell me what you've decided. If you still want to give in your notice on Thursday, then I'll accept it. But I warn you, you'll have to work out your month.'

Now Harry looked really scared. 'I can't! My mam would hit me! And my da …?'

'Think about it, Harry,' Eppie said soothingly. 'And thank you for coming to tell me in person. I very much appreciate that. It was the act of an honourable, honest man.'

Harry flushed again. But he was standing a little taller when he made his hurried exit, accompanied by the jangle of the bell.

Eppie went on standing at the window. Well, at least it wouldn't matter too much if he was short-staffed, not if there were no customers.

Fifteen minutes later, he was rearranging his scissors for the twentieth time or so, when the door jangled open. A customer? Alas, no. He turned to see a man shouldering his way backwards through the door. Filthy shoulders, as a matter of fact – Dick might have washed after his shift at the pit, but he hadn't bothered to change his clothes. And he still managed to look debonair! Well, if you liked *debonair* a bit rough around the edges.

He was coming in backwards because he was pulling his handcart with the table tied upside down on it and the two chairs precariously perched on top. The wheels of the handcart were oily and made dark tracks across Eppie's floor. He started towards Dick, horrified.

'Don't bring that in here!'

Dick smirked at him. 'Don't you want them back?'

'Yes, but you could bring them in the back gate, into the yard!'

Too late. Dick was shutting the door, leaving a big grimy handprint on the white paint. 'What's the point? You need them in the back room, don't you?'

He parked the handcart in the middle of the shop and heaved one of the chairs off the back, pushed it into Eppie's hands and bent to untie the rope that had kept the rest of the load secure.

'Busy morning, eh?'

'There's no need to gloat,' Eppie said with dignity and took the chair into the back room. He half expected it to wobble on uneven legs when he set it down, but to do Dick justice he'd made a good job of it – the chair was steady and looked good. Apart from the grimy handprints on the back. Dick was a conscientious workman.

He went back into the shop and watched Dick tug at a recalcitrant knot.

'You must have heard a few rumours. Today or yesterday, maybe. About me.'

Dick looked up. He'd washed his face but some grime was never going to shift until the day he died. His black hair was wayward as ever, as if he never combed it. His shirt beneath the grimy jacket was surprisingly clean. He looked for a moment as if he was debating with himself whether to say anything or not, then he nodded.

'The inspector's been going round asking a lot of questions about you.'

'*You've* talked to him? What did he ask you?'

Dick considered. 'I'm parched. Make me a cup of tea and I'll tell you.'

Eppie sighed and went to make the tea.

By the time he had it brewed and stood – Dick liked his tea strong enough to walk out of the pot – Dick had brought the other chair and the table in, and stood them in the middle of the back room. When Eppie poured the tea, Dick sat down on one of the chairs, leaving an immediate smudge across its back. Well, Eppie didn't have anything better to do today – cleaning up after Dick would help fill his time.

'What did Crellin ask?' he repeated.

Dick gulped down the tea. 'He asked how long I'd known you, where we'd met and so on. If I had you cut my hair – that sort of thing. He wanted to know all about the Wheelers.'

'Why?'

'He seemed to think you're a demon racer who flies into a rage every time someone beats you, or even gets in front of you on the path.'

'Ridiculous! And what did you say to that?'

'I told him to come to watch you training. If he could see anything enraged about your endless endless *endless* pottering round the path at a speed scarcely faster than a tortoise, then I yielded to his wisdom.'

Sometimes he thought he hated Dick.

'You'll sing another tune when I beat you at the Easter Monday sports,' he said lightly. 'Anything else?'

'He wanted to know if you're short of money. Someone's told him you sold all your prizes last year for cash and he now suspects you're a betting man and have lost everything.' Dick was smirking – actually, Eppie didn't think he'd stopped smirking since he came into the shop. 'I made it clear of course that you're strictly an amateur like the rest of us and wouldn't dream of competing for cash.'

'Did you specifically tell him I don't sell my prizes?'

Dick drained his cup. 'Why should I say that? It wouldn't be true, would it? Any more tea?'

Eppie filled the cup with the last of the tea in the pot.

'That's better,' Dick said, sipping it. 'A decent strong cup at last.' He obviously liked it stewed. 'Eppie, everyone knows there's a little man at every sports, hiding behind the bushes down by the telegraph, busily handing out cash for unwanted gentlemen's dressing cases, cruets and toast stands. I know it, you know it and Inspector Crellin knows it. If you think it's any surprise to anyone to learn that we *amateurs* convert our prizes into ready cash, you're a bigger fool than I thought.'

'If Crellin reports the fact to the NUC, they'll prevent me competing.'

Dick grinned. 'That's the risk we all take.' He drank the rest of his tea, got up and stretched. 'Eppie, take some advice from a friend. You're in big trouble.'

Eppie remained seated. 'That's not advice. That's information.'

'Consider it an early Christmas present.'

'In March? Thank you.'

Dick did not hear the sarcasm, or perhaps chose not to hear it. 'I'll come round tonight to pick up the Ordinary.'

Eppie stared at him. 'I thought you wanted cash now.'

'I've changed my mind. I've got a buyer for the machine.'

Eppie sighed. 'Whatever you like.'

'Then I'll be round tonight. Early. Just in case the inspector has paid you another visit, and you – er – have to accompany him elsewhere.' Still smirking, he sauntered out into the shop. A moment later, Eppie heard the bell jangle and the shop door close. But only after the slightest of pauses.

He went out to see what that pause had been about.

Dick had turned the *Open* sign to *Closed*.

*

He rolled up his sleeves, fetched a bucket of hot water and some cloths, and got down to cleaning up the shop and his newly-repaired furniture. The oil from the wheels of Dick's handcart was particularly difficult to shift and he scrubbed and rubbed and tossed hot water across the floor and scrubbed again, and managed eventually to get rid not only of the oil but also a lot of his own frustration. He got more hot water and had a go at the grimy handprints on the inside and outside of the shop door. A man who happened to be passing along the pavement as Eppie opened the door decided to take a wide berth round him.

If there was one thing Eppie was clear on, it was that this had to stop. Now. He had to do something about this. He couldn't just sit here, or stand here, or scrub here, and wait for Crellin to come and arrest him, or for more disasters to fall on his head. He had to do something to rescue himself. His own self and his own resources, after all, were all a man had to rely on. He'd run this shop from an early age and he intended to run it into his old age, and to have a thriving business for his sons to inherit, and enough money for decent dowries for his daughters, and an annuity to take care of Alma should he predecease her. And he wasn't going to be deflected from those plans because of some ridiculous idea an idiotic policeman had got into his head!

So how was he going to deal with this? Well, he could itemize everything he knew and work out how it all fitted together. He put a bit of elbow power into the most stubborn mark on the outside of the door. He already knew that it was almost impossible that Wetherall had been murdered by one of his political opponents, given that they'd all been in a council meeting, and Crellin must surely have accounted for all the servants. (He really must check that, drop it casually into a conversation with Crellin somehow.) Which meant it *must* be a family matter. Maitland had been in the council chamber at the time of the murder too, so, whatever the problems with their respective heights, that left just Wetherall's wife and daughter. Where had they been?

Actually, there were other questions that needed to be asked as well. Was it a spur of the moment killing or had it been planned? If it had been planned, then someone had to know where Wetherall would be that morning. Who knew he had been off to the council meeting? Wife and daughter, obviously.

But if the murderer *had* been his wife or daughter, it would have been a lot easier to kill him at home. A little bit of rat poison in his stew or arsenic in his brandy, something like that. That would be far safer than hitting him over the head in public, or what might as well have been public. Maitland too could have murdered him in private – he could have met him in his study, hit him over the head, arranged it to look as if it had been an accident, as if Wetherall had tripped over a carpet and hit his head on the corner of a piece of furniture, perhaps. Much less risky. So the murderer was someone who had no choice but to kill Wetherall in the street, because that was the only place he *could* kill him, the only place they ever met.

That is, not a member of the family, after all!

He was left with the man Violet Daisy Rose had seen arguing with her father, who Mrs Cartwright had seen walking into Eppie's shop. The man whose description could fit half the population …

Now, now, take a deep breath and start again. This mysterious man clearly knew something about Wetherall, something discreditable and—

'Morning,' said Inspector Crellin. Eppie turned, soapy rag in hand. The inspector was standing on the pavement, beaming at him. 'You and I need to have a little talk, Mr Epford. You're not busy, are you?'

Eppie ground his teeth.

21

CRELLIN SHUT THE door with what Eppie thought was unnecessary force. The shop suddenly seemed very small and quiet, almost claustrophobic. Crellin was standing too close, but if Eppie took a step back it would look suspiciously as if he was trying to get away. He bent to rinse his cloth out in the bucket of cooling water, which was a mistake because when he straightened up again, Crellin was so close Eppie was *forced* to step back.

'Haircut, Inspector? I'm not sure I can fit you in.'

Crellin didn't seem to hear him. 'Nasty bruise that, Mr Epford.'

'What?'

'That bruise. On your left arm.'

Eppie glanced down. On his bare forearm, below the rolled-up material of his shirt, the flesh was a glorious mess of red, yellow and black.

'Oh, that bruise.' He cursed inwardly. How feeble that sounded!

Crellin said nothing. Eppie rinsed his cloth out again. Crellin was waiting for him to make an excuse but if he wanted one, or an explanation, he was going to have to ask for it. Only guilty men rushed to explain things away.

'And how did it happen?' Goodness, Crellin sounded annoyed! Quite an ugly sneer on his face.

Eppie peered at the vanishing mark more closely. 'Fell off my bike.' He hadn't appreciated before quite how useful that explanation might be.

'On the track, was this?'

Something in Crellin's voice warned him of a trap ahead. If he'd fallen off on the track, which was grass, he was unlikely to have sustained quite so bad a bruise …

'On the road.'

'Racing, were you?'

Eppie turned an innocent face to him. 'That's illegal, Inspector. I was on my way to Carlisle, as a matter of fact, to see some friends. If you don't want a haircut, what can I do for you?'

'You know full well what I've come about!'

Eppie shook his head. 'You'll have to lay it all out before me, Inspector, in short words and sentences.'

Crellin started forward as if he intended to grab hold of Eppie, but pulled back before he did anything rash. Which was just as well, as Eppie had the wall at his back and nowhere to go.

'Mr Epford. I'm very well aware that at the time Mr Wetherall died, you were in this shop giving haircuts to five of my constables. That is, if the gentleman died when the doctor says he did …'

A little pause. Eppie said, 'But?'

'Look,' Crellin said in a rush. 'You come clean about all this, tell me exactly what happened and why you did it, and …' He hesitated. 'I'll see what I can do.'

'Oh come on, Inspector!' Eppie said impatiently. 'If I turn out to be a murderer, then there's nothing you *can* do. It's the courts and the Assizes and the hangman's noose! And plainly, if you're asking me to explain all those things, you have not the slightest idea about this death and you're simply going round threatening people and hoping they're so scared, they confess without further ado!'

He stopped to draw breath, surprised at himself. Crellin looked surprised too, and – goodness, was that a touch of fear there too?

'Inspector,' Eppie said, as moderately as he could under the circumstances. 'I'm willing to bet you have the Chief Constable and goodness knows who else on your back, wanting an arrest within the next five minutes. Well, I have my reasons for wanting to find the man too. I don't want to find myself in prison or the condemned cell.' He gestured round the shop. 'And you can see what all this suspicion is doing to my business. But arresting me isn't going to help you. I'm not going to tell you all the things you don't know, because I don't know them either. And without evidence you're not going to convince a jury that I did it.'

Crellin was breathing heavily, snorting through his nose. His face had gone a nasty dull brick-red. Eppie waited. Holding his breath.

'Well,' Crellin said. 'There's one way you can prove your good faith, isn't there?'

'Is there?'

The Inspector looked as if he had to force the words out. 'You can help me solve this case.'

'If I could, I would. But …'

'Mr Epford!' Crellin took a deep breath and suddenly became human. 'Mr Epford, I'm at my wits' end! *You* saw that the affair was murder, right from the start. You told Constable Banks exactly why. You *see* things.' His ugly sneer was quite gone and in its place was a surprisingly pleading look. 'Mr Epford, I need help. I have to see Mrs Wetherall this evening to report the progress of the case and I have to have *something* to tell her.' He paused. 'Help me, Mr Epford. *Please* help me.'

The inspector cradled his cup of tea between his hands as if he was cold. He'd been a good listener and a good questioner as Eppie expounded his views on the public nature of the crime – Eppie had revised his opinion of him as a policeman. Slightly.

'So the wife and daughter and Maitland didn't do it, because if they had, they'd have done it at home. And the political cronies are out too because of the council meeting. And you've found out that all the servants were at home, having a nice cup of tea in the kitchen.' (Eppie was relieved to hear he had guessed correctly.) 'So we're left with this fellow who was trying to blackmail Wetherall. And he could be anyone in town.'

'Any *man* in town, yes.'

'Could have been a woman in disguise.'

Eppie shook his head. 'Miss Wetherall definitely heard a *man* arguing with her father.'

Crellin helped himself to another of Alma's biscuits which Eppie had put out only with the greatest reluctance because he wanted to encourage the inspector's sudden rush of cooperation.

'So Wetherall had a secret and we don't know what.'

Eppie thought of telling him about the family papers and decided against it, because he'd have had to explain why he'd kept the papers' existence a secret so far. He'd also omitted to mention Maitland's attack on him at Dalston, because Maitland, as they had just agreed, hadn't carried out Wetherall's murder. Unless he'd had an accomplice of course ...

Crellin chomped at the biscuit. 'Very nice, these. Home-made?'

'Yes.'

'*Very* nice. Well, in my experience, people don't just usually have a secret, they have three or four. A mistress, for instance, money troubles, a crime or two in their past – usually something small and silly they did when they were a boy but not the sort of thing a respectable Conservative Councillor would admit to now.'

'Wetherall's mistress is no secret. Everyone knows about Mrs Cartwright.'

Crellin stared. 'Mrs Cartwright? That was over a month or two ago. There's someone else now. Only I can't find out who.'

Actually Mrs Cartwright had admitted that to him this morning at the track, hadn't she? Eppie had completely forgotten. He made a mental note to ask Amos if he knew anything about Wetherall's latest interest.

'Do you know where Wetherall was going the night before his death?'

'It certainly wasn't an assignation with Mrs C,' Crellin said gloomily. 'She and her husband were at a dinner party with friends. Fourteen of them, "conversing" into the small hours.' He gave Eppie a helpless look. 'It's just – well, the murders I usually deal with are drunken brawls between miners, or a husband getting carried away when his wife doesn't have his supper on the table when he wants it.' He said vehemently, 'I hate it when crimes involve the gentry. More than my life's worth.' He munched on Alma's biscuit. 'Though I have to say the ladies are being most helpful – and Maitland. Never rude, always graciously accessible for questioning. No question of him being obstructive or leaving town. Totally cooperative – can't suspect any of them.'

It hadn't apparently occurred to him that a murderer would be totally stupid *not* to be cooperative.

'What does the coachman say?' Eppie said, trying to cheer the inspector up, or at least get his thoughts onto a more constructive path. 'Where did he say he took Wetherall?'

'To the Town Hall,' Crellin said gloomily. 'Then he was told to drive round for an hour and come back to pick his master up in the same place. Which he did. He says Wetherall was distracted when they set out and angry when they came back.'

'Maybe he wasn't meeting a woman. Maybe he'd had an altercation with a man.'

'And then he went back home and had an argument with another man who threatened to blackmail him? Not his evening, was it?'

'It was the same man – he followed Wetherall home.'

'Or one of them was a jealous husband.'

Eppie had another of Alma's biscuits himself. 'I haven't seen any sign that Wetherall was worried about people knowing about his affairs with the ladies. Mr Cartwright knows all about Mrs Cartwright's little fling. Obviously you don't *flaunt* that sort of thing but as long as you're discreet, nobody stirs the pot.'

'Jealous husbands don't always keep to the rules,' Crellin said. 'There's always someone who minds.'

'Well, it's unlikely to be Cartwright if the affair's over.' He thought back to his encounter with the man at the funeral. A big man but oddly not the sort he thought would ever take action over something he disliked. The sort of man who tends to give in just in case things get worse if he does anything.

'The husband of the new interest, then.' Crellin straightened. 'Yes, that's obviously the way to go. Wetherall has a new lady friend. This blackmailer fellow, whoever it is, finds out about it and threatens to reveal it to all and sundry. Wetherall tells him to go hang himself. Wetherall seems to have been a selfish so and so – he'd probably just have denied the thing point blank and let the lady take her chances. So the blackmailer gets annoyed and …' His voice trailed off.

'Kills Wetherall?' Eppie shook his head. 'Why should he do that? You can't get money out of a dead man.'

Crellin helped himself to another biscuit. 'Maybe Wetherall attacked *him* and the blackmailer was just trying to defend himself.'

'No – Wetherall was hit from behind, remember. He was walking away from his murderer.'

'Blast!' Crellin said in exasperation.

He was brooding on something. Eppie had seen the signs dozens of times before in normally garrulous customers who were unwontedly distracted or preoccupied. It usually came down to marital problems. Was Crellin married?

'Look,' Crellin said awkwardly. 'I don't want to – I mean, well, there are rumours …'

The man was obviously horribly embarrassed. Well, if he was paying attention to rumours, Eppie wasn't going to help him out. 'Oh yes?'

Crellin took the plunge. 'I hear that you're paying for the repairs to your furniture with one of your bicycles.'

'And?'

He could have sworn he heard Crellin's teeth grinding together. 'Which suggests you're having money troubles, Mr Epford! I still haven't seen those trophies of yours. I'm willing to bet they're nowhere to be seen …'

'So you don't want my help any longer?' Eppie said.

Crellin stopped, breathing heavily. After a long moment, he said, 'Just a rumour.'

And Eppie knew exactly who Crellin had heard the 'rumour' from – just wait till he saw Dick next!

'Did you know,' he said conversationally, 'there's a thriving market in Ordinaries? Just look at the advertisement columns in *Cycling*.'

'Really?' Crellin actually looked faintly interested.

'There are some high prices demanded for machines like that.' And never paid. 'Dick Sibson is getting a good bargain taking the Ordinary for payment.'

'I had no idea,' Crellin said. 'I thought no one rode the things nowadays.'

No one did. Which was why the advertisements kept appearing week after week. The same advertisements.

'Well, I apologize,' Crellin said with a handsomeness that made Eppie feel guilty. 'Obviously a misunderstanding on my part. I shall forget about it. Let's get back to business. The way to go is plainly to find out Wetherall's secret. And that's connected with where he was going that Wednesday evening.'

Eppie nodded and encouraged Crellin to steer the conversation away from unpalatable areas. He even went so far as to offer the inspector the last of Alma's biscuits. (Crellin fortunately waved it away.)

'If the carriage dropped him at the Town Hall and he thought he could conclude his business in an hour, then wherever he was going was close by. Unless he caught a cab of course. But even then he couldn't have travelled far. Not to get there and back in an hour.'

'A cab!' Crellin sat bolt upright. 'That's it. He must have caught a cab. There's half a dozen usually idle round the Town Hall. That should be easy to find out!' He gulped down the rest of the tea. 'Right, Mr Epford. I'm off to check that out.' He pushed back his chair and headed for the door. 'Leave it to me.'

And while Eppie was gaping open-mouthed at him, he disappeared into the shop. Eppie heard his footsteps echoing.

The footsteps hesitated and then came back. Crellin popped his head round the door. 'Thanks for the biscuits, sir. Very nice.'

And then he *was* off.

Leaving Eppie weak with relief.

22

EPPIE FINISHED IN the shop and moved into the back room to clean up his newly returned furniture. He ate the last biscuit, standing up, savouring every crumb of it. Wondering how far he could trust the inspector. It was odd when the only person an investigator felt he could turn to for help was his *chief suspect* but it would *not* be odd if Crellin turned against Eppie again later if no better candidate for murderer came into view. What chance would there be of finding a cabbie who remembered taking Wetherall somewhere that night? Well, there weren't that many cabbies in town and they'd all be gossiping about the murder so maybe they would know something. Assuming Wetherall *had* taken a cab that night.

An hour was not a long time. If Wetherall had had to get into a cab and drive across town, then see whoever he was meeting, then get the same or another cab back all in an hour, either he couldn't have gone far or the meeting must have been short. And if he'd not gone far, why take a cab at all? Why not walk? Unless Wetherall had been against walking on principle. The gentry often are.

On impulse, Eppie tidied himself up, put on his coat and hat and went out into the street. A passer-by took an unexpectedly wide berth around him. Eppie didn't recognize the man, maybe he was just imagining he'd been taking evasive action. He could always hope. He turned the sign on the shop door to *Closed* and locked it. Then he headed for the Town Hall.

The Town Hall was a neat and tidy building rather than a stylish one. Eppie walked right around it. The streets in this part of town weren't wide – not many streets in town were. Plenty of alleys going off in all directions, none of them terribly well lit. The odd dead end of a yard. Amazing how little he knew about streets which were almost on his doorstep. This close into the centre of town, almost all the buildings were shops or industrial premises, though people must live above them of course. Wetherall might have been going to see his latest love interest but surely she would have lived somewhere a bit nicer?

Maybe he needed to widen his circle of search. From the Town Hall, Wetherall could have walked quite a reasonable distance in a relatively short time, had his meeting, and then walked back in ample time to meet his carriage again. But how on earth could he guess which direction Wetherall might have headed in?

He went to the front of the Town Hall where Wetherall's coachman would certainly have dropped him. There were a few steps up to the main door into the Town Hall but that would have been locked at that time of night. Wetherall must have told his coachman he was going in the side door, which was on the right of the building. Eppie walked round that way, paused on the corner, looking back.

If he'd been the coachman, where would he have driven? Not down the road to the harbour – much too rough an area, particularly at night. Not out into the country either, not on unlit roads where thieves might be about. He'd probably have done a roundabout route: down the hill to the bottom, round the edge of the town centre, back out towards the nice residential areas where Wetherall lived, back in again. He'd have driven around in circles a few times, just keeping the horses moving at a gentle trot.

Wetherall would have known that. Since he obviously wouldn't have wanted the coachman to see what he was doing, he'd have gone off in the opposite direction. Eppie set off towards the side door, came to an abrupt halt. Maybe Wetherall had just waited until the coachman had disappeared, and then headed in the same direction …

In short, there was no way of knowing where Wetherall had gone. Blast!

The side door was under an arcade. A rough-looking man was leaning over peering at the ground by the door. He obviously heard Eppie's step and glanced up.

'Spare some change, mate?'

Eppie was about to shake his head but the tramp said, 'Nah – of course not,' without waiting for him to reply. 'Lousy town, this. Folks don't even leave cigars lying around any more.'

'Cigars?' Eppie said lightly. 'Did they ever?'

'Did last week.'

'A whole cigar?'

'Three. In this doorway.' The tramp pointed. 'But I've come back every day since and nary a one.'

'Someone must have dropped them.'

'Was only two the week previous. And one the week before that. None this week.'

Now Eppie was really taking notice. 'Always on a Monday?'

'Nah, Wednesday.'

'It's Monday today …'

'Well, the gent could have changed his habits, couldn't he?'

'I don't suppose,' Eppie said cautiously, 'you've ever seen the man who left the cigars?'

The tramp looked triumphant. 'I might have. Who's to say?'

Eppie sighed and dug in his pockets, produced a sixpence. The tramp inspected it. 'Nah, didn't see anyone.'

A shilling got the same result. When Eppie produced a half crown, the tramp grinned. 'Reckon it could be worth more than that to you.'

'No. It isn't.'

The tramp grabbed at the half crown. 'Tall gent, well-dressed, expensive-like. Getting on a bit. Had a bit of weight on him. Stopped here every Wednesday night, smoked a cigar, dropped one on the ground. Next week it was two. Then last time it was three. And do you know what happened to that gent?'

Eppie nodded. 'He was murdered. And if you know that, you must know there'd be no more cigars. You've been hanging round here ever since, waiting for someone to come past who'd know the significance of what you saw and reward you for it.'

The tramp grinned. 'A man's got to make a living, hasn't he?'

'Did you see anyone with him?'

'That's worth another half crown.'

'It's worth sixpence.'

'Shilling.'

'Deal.'

The tramp grabbed that coin too. 'A working man, dark coat, hat pulled down over his ears. Only he wasn't actually with the gent. The gent smoked his cigar, ground it out, walked off. Then a few minutes later the other fellow turned up, looked at the cigars and walked off again.'

'He didn't pick up the cigars?'

'Maybe he was kindly leaving them for a hard-working man like me,' the tramp sneered.

'Did they go off in the same direction?'

'Yes, but …'

'Three shillings and sixpence,' Eppie said in his best no-nonsense voice, 'is ample payment. You're making a tidy sum already. Answer my questions!'

The tramp pointed across the street to an alley. 'The gent went that way. The working man followed him. I heard voices. They were arguing in there.'

'What did they say?'

'Didn't hear.'

Eppie started to protest but the tramp cut in. 'I wanted the cigars, didn't I? What did I care what they were saying?'

'Maybe the first time,' Eppie said, 'but the second and third times? You had no curiosity at all?'

'Curiosity don't pay.'

'Any information you overheard might.'

The tramp pursed up his lips, seemed to be struggling with himself. 'I might have heard something,' he said finally, but there was not the slightest conviction in his voice. 'All right,' he said, evidently judging Eppie's reaction by his expression. 'I didn't hear anything, right? They were talking too low, right down the other end of the alley. I just caught something about money. I did go round the streets to try and get closer to them at the other end – the second time that was – but by the time I got there, they'd gone.'

'Where?'

'The gent was just heading back for the Town Hall. I didn't see where the other fellow went.'

'And what did the gent do when he got back to the Town Hall?'

The tramp made a dismissive gesture. 'Why should I care? I had work to do, didn't I?'

'Looking for more cigars? Or coins in the gutter?'

The tramp leant closer. Decaying breath washed over Eppie; he tried not to flinch.

'You'd be surprised how good a living you can make from picking up coins and cigars. Or maybe you wouldn't.' And he winked and limped away.

Eppie stared at the ground by the door for a moment. Wetherall had been keeping a regular assignation, with a man who might have been his murderer. He'd come here, lit a cigar, dropped it on the ground as a signal. (Why the different numbers of cigars each week?) Then he walked off into the alley. The other man turned up a minute later, saw the cigar which presumably indicated that Wetherall was waiting for him and went to keep the assignation. They were lucky the tramp hadn't got in first and run off with the cigars.

He walked over to the alley the tramp had indicated. It was much like all the other alleys in town, long, thin and dirty, though it took a sharp turn which prevented him from seeing the far end. The ground was cobbled at this end but looked as if it was metalled further down. He looked round first to check there was no one nearby – he didn't want to get himself robbed – then started down the alley.

Halfway down, just as the alley took that sharp turn to the right, he realized where he was. Another alley came in from the left: a dead end leading to a carriage yard. He was at a T-junction. And the far end of the alley, the one he hadn't been able to see from the Town Hall, was where Wetherall had been killed.

He stood by a darker patch of metalled ground at the far end of the alley, wondering if it was Wetherall's dried blood he was looking at. So now he knew what Wetherall had been doing that night, even if he didn't know who the man was, or what business Wetherall had had with him.

But …

He walked back to the shop. Could this working man be the man Miss Wetherall had overheard her father arguing with? That would mean they'd met in the alley near the Town Hall, talked, and then the man had followed Wetherall back home to continue the argument there. Did that sound likely? And was it the man Mrs Cartwright had seen going into Eppie's shop?

He put the key in the shop door, turned the notice on the door to *Open* and went into the back room to take off his coat and hat, stared at the last grubby chair. Why should a blackmailer want to kill his victim? As he'd said to Crellin, it didn't make sense. It had to be someone else. But who?

There was a knock on the door. He went back out into the shop. A police constable, resplendent in uniform, was peering through the glass door. Sighing, Eppie opened the door. The constable was very young and very anxious.

'Are you closed?'

Eppie resisted the temptation to point at the *Open* sign.

'I've just got back. Did you want to talk to me?' What now? Had he infringed some regulation simply by walking around town?

The constable peered uncertainly at him.

'I want to … er …' He indicated his very be-whiskered face. 'I mean, the inspector sent me along to get rid of them.' He looked like he wanted to cry at the very thought.

Eppie ushered him in and sat him down in the chair in front of the mirror. He was the first of four that pottered reluctantly along that afternoon and their presence encouraged two or three other men to come in off the street, though whether *they* wanted a haircut or were hoping to see an arrest wasn't clear. Eppie got to work. Wondering whether the presence of the constables was a peace offering from the inspector.

Or a bribe. *Help me and I'll help you …*

23

CIGARS. LOATHSOME SMELLY things. Didn't do your breathing on the bicycle any good either. That was something Amos forgot. He liked a good smoke sometimes.

Always said he could take it or leave it but recently it had been more take than leave. Silly thing for a serious cyclist to do.

This was ridiculous! He was rambling. Eppie turned onto his back and stared at the ceiling. Or at least at the darkness where the ceiling was. The curtains were good and thick so the bedroom was nicely dark. Eppie hated light when it came to sleeping – he never slept so well when the room wasn't completely dark. And was that rain?

He groaned and turned over. He might as well get up and make himself a cup of tea – he was never going to sleep with all this going round in his mind. He struggled out from under the clinging blankets, urinated in the chamber pot and trudged downstairs. Put the lights on and filled the kettle. Nice sound, a kettle boiling. Soothing. He found the teapot, put in three spoonful of tea as usual then remembered he hadn't warmed the pot. Too late now.

He lifted one corner of the curtain and looked out into the yard, faintly lit by a street lamp at the far end of the lane. A few spots of rain against the panes, nothing much. Dick hadn't come by for the Ordinary; it still stood against the wall of the privy with the two Safety machines beside it. Maybe he'd had to work a different shift at the pit. A pity; Eppie had been looking forward to picking a bone with Dick about giving Crellin the impression Eppie was hard up for money. He'd been looking forward to saying his piece about that. He was annoyed he couldn't get it off his chest.

A dark man. He couldn't get Mrs Cartwright's description of the murderer out of his mind. (*Was* he the murderer? There was no proof of that, of course.) Probably something like a clerk. Not well off but not poor either, if he could afford a decent haircut. How many hundreds of men like that were there in Maryport? And there was no reason he should be from the town itself. He could be from one of the local villages, or one of the towns further down the coast – Workington or Whitehaven. He needed more than a description of the man's hair and clothes!

Why hadn't the man picked up the cigars and taken them with him? Good cigars were expensive, and if the man was unscrupulous enough to commit murder, picking up cigars from the street would hardly have bothered him. Wouldn't be particularly clean, of course.

Maybe he didn't smoke.

Well, that narrowed the suspects down a bit – there must be a few men who didn't smoke. Somewhere. Apart from himself.

'Ridiculous,' he said out loud. He made the tea, let it brew and drank a cup standing up. Then he went back upstairs, got into bed and fell asleep instantly.

Waking to a sudden noise.

He was lying on his left side and found himself staring at a slightly lighter patch of darkness where the curtains closed across the window. He tilted his head to listen. Nothing. He must have imagined it. Or maybe it was a cart passing outside in the street. What time was it? He patted the bedside table for his watch and managed to make out it was around three in the morning.

Not the milkman then.

He held his breath. Nothing. Definitely his imagination. He closed his eyes, pulled the blankets up around his ears. Definitely nothing. No point in getting up again.

He got up, found his slippers, pulled on his dressing robe and padded out onto the landing. He could see an odd stripe downstairs in the darkness. He peered at it. A very dim light, coming through the gap between the open kitchen door and the doorjamb.

He'd closed the door. He always closed the door. The kitchen window didn't fit properly and there was a fearsome draught when it was windy.

He went back into the bedroom, to the corner by the window, and stooped for the poker he kept there. Not much use in a bedroom without a fire. Unless you wanted to protect yourself. His father had always kept it there and he'd unthinkingly carried on the tradition, was glad of it now. He hefted the poker in his hand, went silently back onto the landing.

Down the stairs one by one. They didn't usually creak but he knew the places that were prone to it and kept close to the wall to avoid them. The door to the kitchen was definitely open and he could feel a cold draught on his bare ankles. It was strong enough to stir the thin fabric of his nightshirt. The back door must be open.

Burglars.

Odd that he'd never been burgled before but that it should happen now, twice, just when he'd got himself mixed up in a murder. He held his breath as he slid down the last few steps. The hall was small, barely three steps wide. He girded himself up mentally, lifted the poker high and took the three steps in a rush. Pushed the kitchen door open—

Something in the corner of his eye. He was turning as the blow came down. He instinctively swung up the poker. The hollow thud of wood on metal. He ducked away, got hold of the door handle. Swung round, bringing the door back with him, let go. The door swung on, into the face of his assailant.

A blur in the darkness as the man moved. Out of the way of the door. Eppie felt for the edge of the kitchen table, got his fingers round it and heaved. The table went over, with a crash of the crockery he'd put out for the morning.

Movement. A grunt. Not where he'd expected the man to be. To his right, somewhere by the cupboards.

How the devil can you fight when the only light is the dimmest orange glow through curtains? Discretion was obviously called for. Eppie stumbled back across the kitchen, fallen crockery crunching underfoot, heading for where he knew the door into the hall was. The only alternative was to head for the yard and he'd no wish to find himself locked out of his own home in his nightshirt. He banged his nose on the door, panicked a moment, found the open gap, dashed into the hall.

He needed to get into the front parlour. If he could get behind the door in there, pull the man's own trick on him …

The back door slammed.

He waited two, maybe three minutes, surrounded by blessed darkness. Not a sound. Had the intruder gone? What if he'd just slammed the back door and was still inside, hiding behind the kitchen door again?

He felt an hysterical urge to laugh. He was standing in the darkness of the parlour, the intruder was probably standing in the darkness of the kitchen, both of them trying to wait the other person out … How long was he going to stand here like a statue, poker raised? How long was the intruder prepared to linger? Darkness prickled at his eyes.

Oh, this was preposterous! He strode back into the hall, and blinked at a blur of light. The intruder had turned on the lights in the kitchen, very low but surprisingly dazzling after the darkness of the rest of the house. Surely he wouldn't do that if he was still there. Cautiously, Eppie tiptoed into the kitchen, poker raised, grabbed the door handle and swung the door wide. Poker raised for an attack …

No one behind the door this time.

The back door was shut. There was no one in the kitchen.

He went back out into the hall again. Could the intruder have come back into the house while he was in the parlour, gone upstairs maybe, still be lurking, waiting for him?

He searched the house, turning up all the lights as he went, until the house was ablaze. Even then, he didn't feel safe. He checked the locks on the front door five times, every window at least twice.

Finally he came to the back door again. He took a deep breath, made sure he had the key in the pocket of his dressing robe, and stepped out into the yard, poker gripped tightly in his hand.

The light from that street lamp was good enough to show him the yard clearly enough, though there were dark patches of shadow. The back gate was unlatched, not quite closed. The yard was empty. Unless the man was hiding in the privy … Eppie whipped the door open and was faced only with the wooden seat and the usual acrid whiff.

He pushed the door closed again. A spot or two of rain splattered on his right hand. He went to the back gate. The lock had been forced in a white glare of fresh wood visible even in this poor light. Out into the cobbled back lane. No one about. He'd been unlucky surely: there was no way the burglar could have known which house belonged to which person – from the lane, the back yards and gates all looked the same.

He closed the gate on the latch and wedged a few old bricks behind it. If anyone tried to get in that way again, the bricks would screech against the ground and alert him.

Now all he had to do was go back to bed and try to sleep.

He knew an impossibility when he faced one. He stood in the middle of the yard breathing deeply to calm himself, as if it was the beginning of a race. It was far better he got down to some tidying up. The kitchen was a bit of a mess and maybe the intruder had stolen something. It would also be a good idea to decide whether to let Inspector Crellin know what had happened. If it was just a burglary, there was hardly any point – he hadn't got even a *bad* look at the intruder. Just a blur, a shadow in the darkness. But was it just an innocent burglary, if there could be such a thing? Surely this *had* to be connected with Wetherall's death …

He stared at the wheels of his racer. The pneumatic tyres were flat. He bent to examine them. They'd been slashed. Cut to ribbons. All the wheels on all three machines, the Ordinary included. Dick was not going to be pleased about that! Come to that, he was pretty mad about it himself. But it settled one thing. His idea that this might have been an opportunist thief was well wide of the mark. An ordinary thief wouldn't have slashed the tyres – he'd simply have stolen the machines. They were by far the most valuable things Eppie owned.

And moreover, the tyres must have been slashed when the burglar first arrived – he surely couldn't have had time or inclination to do it after Eppie had disturbed him. And if the slashing of the tyres had been the first thing he'd done, then it had been the most important thing. Which meant the object of the visit was not to steal anything but to intimidate Eppie.

This 'burglary' was *definitely* connected with Wetherall's murder.

A fact which was confirmed when he found the note on the floor beneath the upturned kitchen table. The intruder must have trodden on it in the chaos of the table coming down, because there was a dirty footprint across the nice clean expensive paper. On it was written, in beautifully copperplate letters: *You would probably find it more congenial to live somewhere else in the country. I advise you to move quickly.*

24

RUN AWAY? NEVER! Eppie went to the shop as usual next morning, not entirely sure, admittedly, that he'd be able to carry on a coherent conversation given he was so tired. He'd got back to bed eventually and dozed fitfully and then, annoyingly, slept through his morning training session. He hated missing it. And now he was walking around in a daze. Though it hardly mattered since he'd have no customers.

He wasn't quite right. A couple of his regulars came in and told him they didn't believe a word of what was being said about him. He was grateful for their support but rather wished they hadn't been so detailed about the rumours doing the rounds. Or that the elderly builder hadn't chortled over a joke about Sweeney Todd.

The postman delivered some bills and Eppie went into the back room to brew tea. He still hadn't managed to get all Dick's grimy handprints off the chairs. He was staring gloomily at one particularly prominent mark when the bell jangled. He peered back into the shop.

'Talk of the devil.'

Dick scowled. He had on his working clothes. Bare-headed too, his black hair windswept.

'If you don't want to talk to me …'

'It was only a manner of speaking – I was just contemplating your handprint on one of my chairs. Tea?' He called back over his shoulder. 'What are you doing here? Shouldn't you be on a shift at the pit?'

Dick came through to the back with him. 'I've changed shifts so I can get some proper sleep and training in before the Easter Sports. Which is why I didn't come round to collect the Ordinary last night. Besides, I heard rumours you'd left town.'

'I have not!' Eppie said forcibly. 'And I don't intend to either.'

Dick shook his head. 'They say the inspector's hot on your heels.'

What was he supposed to say to that? *No, as a matter of fact he's asked me to help him out?* Crellin wouldn't thank him for that: it would be all round town that the inspector didn't have a clue what he was doing. He used the pouring of tea to cover his indecision.

'And whose fault is that? Why did you tell him I'd insisted on paying with the Ordinary? He thinks I'm on the verge of bankruptcy!'

Dick was obviously amused. 'He asked how much I charged for the repairs.'

'Why?'

'I don't know. The fellow's an idiot. Who knows how he thinks.'

'You didn't have to say anything about the Ordinary.'

'I couldn't say *nothing* or he'd have thought I was hiding something!'

Instead of which, Crellin thought *Eppie* was hiding something. He handed Dick the cup of tea with a bad grace. Dick had a point, which made it difficult to carp at him. But he'd been looking forward to telling Dick off and it had all been a bit of a damp squib. Not satisfying at all. Maybe he was too tired to deal with this sort of thing today.

'It's odd you should talk about me leaving town. Someone else thinks I ought to.' He told Dick about his 'burglary' and found himself easier in his mind for relating the story.

Not that Dick was sympathetic. 'Good God, Eppie! How do you get yourself in these messes?'

'I can hardly be blamed for someone trying to burgle my house!' Eppie was so indignant he nearly threw Dick out there and then.

Dick flung himself down in one of the chairs. He could have chosen the one which was still dirty. 'Let's take this one thing at a time. Was anything stolen?'

'No,' Eppie admitted – reluctantly, because he could already see where this was going.

'Damaged?'

'Yes – he slashed my tyres. All of them. It'll cost me a fortune to repair them.'

'Don't tell me you don't have spares, Eppie!'

He sipped tea, said defensively, 'Well, yes, but not of that quality. Besides, that's not the point, is it?'

Dick looked at him thoughtfully. 'Did he slash the tyres of the Ordinary too?'

Eppie sighed. 'Yes.'

'I'm not taking it with damaged tyres.'

'It's not ...'

'You'll have to put new ones on.'

Eppie stared at him in horror. 'How am I going to get hold of a new front tyre for that thing? It'll be a nightmare. Do they even make them any more?'

'Must do. Some people still ride them.'

'It'll be horribly expensive.'

'Your problem, not mine.'

'I'll pay you in cash, like we agreed before.'

To his relief, Dick merely shrugged. 'If you insist. I'll draw up a bill and drop it in next time I'm this way. Any other damage?'

'No. Except what got trampled in our fight.'

'And he tried to attack you personally?'

Eppie contemplated this. 'I probably disturbed him. He no doubt heard me coming downstairs and grabbed something to defend himself. And he might have been going to steal something but didn't have the chance because of my intervention.'

'Or he could have been intending to attack you all along.'

'Thank you for that cheerful thought.'

'Have you considered the possibility he made that loud noise *deliberately*, to wake you up?'

'This isn't helping, you know.'

The sardonic face creased into a malicious grin. 'You never said you wanted *comfort*, Eppie. You never said you wanted me to tell lies so you could ignore the obvious. There's a distinct possibility this man broke into your house to frighten you. That note is the key – it warns you to leave town. Your so-called burglar was there to suggest what might happen if you don't.'

'Oh Lord.' Eppie sipped more tea in an effort to calm himself down. It wasn't working. 'You mean I've got to look forward to more of this?'

Dick contemplated him in silence, then got up, pushed his empty cup onto the table. 'Why don't you take a holiday?'

'What?'

'You're always talking about doing a cycle tour of the Isle of Man. Pack a few things and go. Just take a week away. It won't hurt the shop, if no one's coming in. And you'll be safe.'

'I can't go on a cycle tour now!' Eppie protested aghast. 'Not in the run up to the Easter Sports! Pottering round hilly roads in the Isle of Man won't be good training for races on the flat of the path.' Though the island did seem to produce some extraordinarily good cyclists.

'Eppie, your life could be at stake here. At the moment, they only want to frighten you but they could change their minds and opt for something worse.'

'They could try to kill me!?' How he hated his voice when it got shrill like that. He took a deep breath. 'Why should anyone want to kill me?'

'Now, now,' Dick said soothingly. 'Don't panic.'

'I'm not panicking! Anyway, *you'd* be panicking if someone wanted to kill you. This is ridiculous. First I'm accused of murder, now someone wants to do away with me. What have I done to bring this on myself?'

Dick shook his head. 'You rushed out to see Wetherall's body, Eppie. And you were loud in your insistence that it was murder. If you'd kept your mouth shut, the police would have said it was an accident and everything would be over and done with now.'

Eppie stared at him. Dick was a tall man – well, as far as Eppie was concerned anyway – and all that hewing of coal had given him muscles to spare. (Which of course isn't necessarily good on a bicycle. You don't need bulging muscles in your arms. Even steering the machine round corners is largely a matter of redistributing body weight.) And all of that weight and height and muscle was, as far as Eppie could see, advising him to run away. Which suggested exactly what Dick thought of him. Probably just because he was small and slight and a hairdresser.

'No,' he said firmly. 'Dick, as far as I can tell, Wetherall was not a nice man and maybe the people who disliked him had a point or two in their favour. But whoever killed Wetherall might make a habit of knocking people over the head and might have half the town council in his sights. Or you. Or perfectly innocent butchers and bakers. You can't ignore murder. And,' he added, with what he recognized uneasily as a touch of defiance, 'I'm not going to.'

Dick shook his head and went off without another word. And as if in reward for Eppie's good intentions, half a dozen people came in the afternoon and sat in his chair as if everything was normal and they weren't submitting themselves to the scissors and razors of a suspected murderer.

All in all, he thought later, sweeping up the stray hair from the floor in the calm after he'd turned the sign to *Closed*, all this business had deflected him from the matter of the cigars. Wetherall had had a long-standing arrangement with his murderer, to meet once a week. He got his coachman to run him to the Town Hall, then he stood in the doorway and smoked a cigar which would look perfectly normal to anyone who passed by. He then dropped the cigar as a signal to the other man and walked off to the pre-arranged rendezvous. The other man came along, saw the cigar and went off to keep the rendezvous.

Why the different number of cigars? It couldn't be just a simple signal saying *I'm here* because then the number wouldn't matter. And the tramp had said they met in the same place every time so it couldn't refer to a house number or a place to meet or anything like that.

Eppie gave up on that, swept the hair onto a piece of newspaper. What would Wetherall and this other fellow have talked about? Something secret, obviously. Maybe they were in a conspiracy together? To do what? It couldn't have anything to do with Wetherall's affairs of the heart, surely. If the other man was a wronged husband, they wouldn't have met on a regular basis. Anyway there was no evidence that Wetherall had his flings outside his own social class, except for some vague rumours. Though some rumours sometimes surely must be true.

A gentleman and a labouring man in secret meetings. One thing was for sure, those talks involved nothing legal.

He threw the cuttings into the bin and stopped dead outside the back door, casting his eyes to heaven. He was an idiot. The whole thing was ridiculously simple. Thanks to that conversation overheard by Miss Wetherall. The man was blackmailing Wetherall because of this secret – whatever it was – and the meetings were to hand over the money. The number of cigars referred to different amounts. Ten shillings, twenty shillings, thirty shillings – perhaps, outrageously, thirty *pounds*. Perhaps at the last meeting, the murderer had wanted more, Wetherall had refused and the man had followed him home to threaten him. But hang on, it was Wetherall dropping the cigars, not the murderer; if the murderer was demanding money, wouldn't he be dictating the amounts demanded?

Blast. And it had been such a good theory too. Not that it would explain Wetherall's murder. It always came back to the fact that no blackmailer would be stupid enough to kill his victim. That simply spelled the end of the money. And it had clearly been a planned murder, not something done on an angry impulse, because Wetherall had been hit from behind by someone who'd brought a heavy weapon with him.

Oh well, he'd progressed – a little – even if he hadn't got all of it right in his head yet. But what had Wetherall been blackmailed about? Not an affair, because Wetherall had been surprisingly open about them.

Which brought Eppie back to those papers that had been left in his shop. He'd forgotten all about them and he'd promised Alma to look up Wetherall's side of the family. He'd go round and see the vicar tonight. But it wouldn't be pleasant – not if he had to listen to the vicar's strong views on cycling.

25

He knew something was wrong the moment he pushed open the front door of his house. Something was *different*. Unless it was the lingering unease from the previous night ...

He was late, having had to stay behind to do all Harry's jobs. He'd been rushing too, wanting to see the vicar before it was too late in the evening, and when you're in a rush, things tend to have to be done twice. And now he'd come home to tidy himself up before going to the vicarage and something was wrong ...

The house should have been completely dark. Instead there was a blur of light under the kitchen door.

Not again!

He had no weapon on him and the poker was back in its place upstairs in his bedroom. The only thing he had was his keys. He cupped them in his right hand, so that one peeked out from between the fingers of his clenched fist. A deep breath. He shoulder-charged the kitchen door, yelled, 'I'm armed! Stand still!' and prayed the intruder would make a bolt for the back door.

Alma shrieked in shock.

Eppie stumbled to a halt inches away from her. The kitchen was dimly lit and cosy, the table was laid, the delicious smell of a stew wafted from the range ...

Alma flung herself into his arms. 'Eppie, thank goodness you're all right! I was so worried. Except I saw you in the shop and ...' Then she said, 'Oh!' and hurriedly took a step back. She was wearing his mother's apron again. 'I mean, I'm sorry – I shouldn't be – I didn't mean to be so forward. Eppie, *are* you all right?'

He wasn't. He'd hardly had time to get used to having her in his arms, before he had to get used to *not* having her in his arms. He didn't know that wasn't the worst thing about today.

'What are you doing here?'

'Dick Sibson sent me another telegram, saying you'd been hurt. Something about a burglary. And the headmaster said I should come straight away, so he gave me the last two hours off school and I cycled over. Luckily, I came past the shop, of course, and I saw it was open and you were inside so I knew Mr Sibson had exaggerated. So I let myself in using the spare key you showed me and I've made supper. I had to really push hard against the back gate to open it but I put the bricks back. Is that the way the burglar got in? Are you sure you're all right? I mean, not even a bruise?'

All this was so unexpected, Eppie didn't know where to begin. 'The headmaster? He knows about us? I mean ...' He picked his words carefully. 'He knows we're friends?'

She blushed. 'I told him you were a neighbour of my aunt's. And he's very interested in cycling.' She gave him an innocent look. 'Or rather, in certain aspects of it.'

He said with grim foreboding, 'He bets on races?'

'He has two pounds on you to win the five miles handicap on Easter Monday.'

'Two pounds!' If Eppie had two pounds to spare he wouldn't bet with it. He could think of hundreds of more useful things he could spend such a substantial sum on. And Dick was still sending Alma telegrams – after what Eppie had said the last time! Dick had probably envisaged Alma fainting in horror. Instead of which she'd leapt on her bicycle and come straight to his aid.

Actually, in one sense, Dick had done him a favour ...

With difficulty, he concentrated on the matter in hand.

'No, not even a bruise.' He added, with some pride, 'I saw him off. With a poker!'

Alma grinned in delight. 'Tell me all about it and I'll serve you up some supper.'

He couldn't think of anything more delightful. He took off his coat and hat, and even, at Alma's invitation, his jacket. In shirt sleeves, he washed his hands then sat down at the head of the table. Alma put a plate full of stew down in front of him, fetched her own and sat down to one side. Satisfyingly close. She fished in the pocket of her apron and laid something on the table. The sheet of paper with the beautiful handwriting and the dirty footprint.

'You left it on the table.'

Eppie sighed, and between mouthfuls of the stew, explained what had happened. Alma listened in silence, eating as heartily as he did, soft roundels of carrot, squares of swede, chewy chunks of good-quality stewing beef. All in a deliciously thick gravy. Alma really was an extraordinary cook and, of course, knew exactly what, or what not, to give a racing cyclist.

When he'd finished, there was silence for a moment. Alma eventually said, 'It wasn't a common or garden burglary, was it? It was meant to frighten you.'

He nodded. 'To make me run off.'

'Which would certainly make everyone think you guilty of the murder. Eppie,' She put down her knife and fork. 'Inspector Crellin is hardly a wonderfully intelligent detective but he does know he has to find someone for Wetherall's murder. The death of such a prominent man can't go unpunished. And no matter how much he wants you to help him now—' He had explained Crellin's visit to the shop as well – 'if he can't find anyone else he will settle for arresting you.'

'That's what I thought,' he said glumly. 'Perhaps I *should* go away. It would be better than being arrested. Dick suggested the Isle of Man.'

'Not in the cycling season,' Alma protested. 'In the autumn maybe. We could go there for our honeymoon.'

Eppie looked at her. She looked back.

'So we could,' he said. He took a deep breath. 'You'd have to give up your job. No married woman can teach.'

'We'll talk about that later. Now, have you checked out Wetherall's family background?'

'No, I got distracted.' And he launched into a description of the cigar business. She held up a hand to stop him. 'Wait.'

There was an apple crumble in the oven.

He tucked into tart strong apples and sweet crumble, and described his adventure with the tramp, and, as an afterthought, his conversation with Mrs Cartwright who thought the murderer could be one of his customers. That led to Crellin's theory that there was another woman in view, someone who was a woman of a lower social status.

'Not that I've heard that said anywhere else.'

'Mr Danson would know.' Alma waved a spoonful of crumble at him. 'Didn't you say he investigated all Wetherall's political connections and that many of them didn't like him much? If there were rumours about another woman they'd be glad to pass them on.'

'Amos didn't mention anything.'

'Perhaps he should go back and ask them.'

Eppie wolfed down the last of his crumble and got up to put the kettle on. 'He'd enjoy that. You think that there may be a jealous husband?'

'I think this mysterious man who was having meetings with Wetherall could have been a jealous husband, yes. And an unscrupulous one.' Alma clearly warmed to her theory. 'Instead of trying to stop the relationship, or fighting Wetherall because of it, he might have decided to blackmail Wetherall instead. If the woman is of low social status, money might be more important to her and her husband than honour. Perhaps they even trapped Wetherall into the relationship?'

Eppie warmed the pot and sat back down to consider this. 'I suppose it depends quite how low the family are socially. I mean, if the woman is no better than – than—'

'A prostitute,' Alma said encouragingly.

'A woman of low morals,' Eppie said, unable to use that word in front of Alma, 'then it really would damage Wetherall's reputation if the liaison was known. But if she is, say, the wife of a tradesman, then the liaison would be of more concern to the husband than to Wetherall. Alma, these gentry people aren't like you and me – they don't trouble themselves over things like this.' He thought of telling her about Maitland's goings on with half the barmaids in town then thought *better not*. 'Everyone knew about Mrs Cartwright, but nobody shunned either Wetherall or her. It's only if an affair's flaunted that people start condemning it.'

'Not everyone is so immoral,' she pointed out. 'Maybe Wetherall came across a husband who *did* trouble himself over it.'

'That's what Inspector Crellin said.' He sighed. 'It just doesn't seem right to me. Maybe it's something else entirely.' He got up again to make the tea from the boiling kettle. 'Every idea I have seems to end nowhere.'

Alma thanked him as he put a cup and saucer in front of her, picked up her spoon to stir in some milk – she was a devotee of *after* not *before*.

'Then we need to think things through again and come up with some better ideas.'

It sounded almost like an instruction but Eppie accepted it meekly. He knew that tone. Alma was a great one for not giving up.

He moved the bricks and let her out the back gate. As she was wheeling her bicycle into the cobbled lane, reality suddenly struck him. 'Alma – are we …?'

She looked at him encouragingly.

He hardly dared say it. 'Betrothed?'

She smiled fondly and leaned forward to peck his cheek. 'We are. Though I suspect it would be better not to tell anyone just yet.'

He nodded. 'I'd rather sort this Wetherall business out first. But – Alma—' He wanted to say something but didn't quite know what. In the end it came out, rather lamely, as 'Thank you.'

She shook her head. 'No, thank *you*, Eppie.'

He was startled. 'For what?'

'For being who you are.' She started. 'I nearly forgot to leave your spare key!' She pulled it out of her coat pocket and held it out to him.

He took it. It was still warm from her body. He shivered. 'I'll put it back in its usual place.'

She nodded, hesitated, then, with the neat economy of movement that characterized her, mounted her bicycle. He held it steady for her for a moment, with a hand on the back of the saddle; she nodded and he let go.

She wasn't going far, just to her aunt's house, where she'd stay overnight as she usually did, then ride to Carlisle at first light. He watched her to the end of the back lane, unwilling to let her go. Never mind, it wouldn't be for long. The end of the year at most, or the beginning of the next. He'd need to sort out this matter though, and quickly – they wouldn't be able to marry if the business was still suffering.

At the end of the lane, Alma slowed, glanced right, then left.

A man leapt out at her.

26

IN THE LIGHT of the distant street lamp, Eppie had a brief glimpse of the attacker. Burly, muffled up in coat and hat and scarf. His weight crashed against Alma's slight figure on the bicycle – she went over in a screech of metal. The attacker fell on top of her. A grunt, a scuffle. The man grabbed a handful of coat at Alma's throat.

But Eppie was already running. Yelling at the top of his voice. He stumbled on the cobbles, got his balance again, ran again. Alma was fighting back, lashing out with her right hand, kicking her attacker on the shins …

Eppie stooped for a loose cobble, hurled it. It fell short, bounced up and clipped the man on the thigh. He roared in pain, dropped Alma back into the tangle of bicycle, swung to face Eppie.

A glimpse of eyes in the thin strip between pulled-up scarf and pulled-down hat. Then he was away, sprinting across the road into the mouth of another back alley. This one curved away and he was out of sight in seconds.

Eppie didn't waste time going after him. Alma was struggling to get up, still with the machine on top of her. He lifted it off. She was gritting her teeth. And she put up her hand to her left shoulder in a gesture so common amongst cyclists that Eppie knew instantly what had happened.

She grimaced. 'I think I've broken my collar bone.'

He helped her up. She supported herself against the back wall of a yard. 'I think I can get to my aunt's. But you'll have to wheel my bicycle for me.'

'You're not going anywhere.' Eppie inspected her bicycle – it actually looked less damaged than she did. 'You're coming back with me.'

He steeled himself for her protests, but she said nothing. When he glanced at her, he saw, even in this light, how pale she was. She was screwing up her face as if she felt queasy. He leant the machine against the wall, and put his arm around her shoulder. 'Come on.'

He got her back into the kitchen, sat her down at the table, went back for the machine and put it in the yard beside his own. When he shut the back gate, he piled not only the bricks but the Ordinary against it too.

In the kitchen, Alma had put her head down on the table, resting it on her uninjured right arm. Her left arm hung by her side.

She heard him come back in and lifted her head. She was *very* pale.

'It's painful,' she said.

'I'm going to ask Mrs McCormack to send her girl for the doctor.'

'No!' She sat up suddenly, cried out in pain. 'Eppie, whatever will people say? If you tell Mrs McCormack you have an unmarried woman in the house, the news will be all over town in half an hour – and you can't afford any more damage to your reputation at this moment!'

'I'd rather that than leave you in pain,' Eppie said and went out. Ridiculous that she should worry over him and not think of her own reputation!

Mrs McCormack and the girl who did for her were sat over a companionable pot of tea in the mistress's kitchen. They were only too eager to help. Eppie spun them a tale about hearing a noise in the street and going out to see Miss Gains lying in the road having fallen off her bicycle. Mrs McCormack indulged in a fit of tutting.

'Say what you like, Mr Epford, but those machines are dangerous.'

He nodded meekly. 'They can be.'

The maid was sent off for the doctor. Mrs McCormack unfortunately, as Eppie had anticipated, could not bear to be left out of anything remotely interesting and insisted on going back to Eppie's house 'to bear Miss Gains company'. She simpered at Eppie, which was not becoming in a woman of her age. 'As a chaperone, you might say.'

'I'm grateful,' Eppie said and was ashamed – just a little – to hear the sarcasm in his own voice. Mrs McCormack did not. And he *was* grateful to her when they got back to his own house because Mrs McCormack had evidently assisted at more than one sickbed (and, he suspected, more than one deathbed) and knew exactly what to do. She had the kettle on for 'a nice cup of weak tea' straight away, put her hand on Alma's forehead, which was apparently soothing, tutted over her temperature and started clucking at her, saying, 'there, there' a great deal which Alma, surprisingly, did not seem to find annoying. By the time the maid came back with the doctor, Alma actually had some colour in her cheeks.

The doctor stood in the kitchen doorway looking at her. 'Fell off one of those damned machines, did you?'

Alma nodded then winced. 'A dog …'

'Far too many dogs in the world,' the doctor said and swung round on Eppie. 'Well, what are you doing here?'

Eppie stared. 'I live here.'

'No, no, man! You can't stay here while I examine a lady!'

'Wouldn't be proper,' said Mrs McCormack, tutting.

Eppie was forced to retreat to the parlour, where he paced in frustration, trying desperately to hear what was going on in the kitchen and miserably failing. Of course, the moment he stopped trying to listen, he distinctly heard Alma cry out in pain. And then he was startled when the parlour door was flung open and the doctor strode in.

'All done! Lady's fine. No serious damage.'

'Not a broken collar bone then?'

'Cracked,' the doctor said. 'But not broken. Not nice, of course, but maybe she'll learn her lesson.'

Eppie said cautiously, 'Which is?'

'Women,' said the doctor, 'should not ride infernal machines. They should confine themselves to being driven in carriages in a dignified manner.'

'I see,' Eppie said. 'Well, Doctor – thank you for coming and …'

'If young ladies persist in flouting the conventions, which are conventions for very good reasons, they will end up paying the bill. In a very literal sense in this case. And I don't come cheap.'

'If you would send the bill to me, Doctor …'

'Miss Gains has already dealt with that matter. She is insisting that no expense should come to you on her account – you have after all done all that is right and proper in rescuing her from the consequences of her own folly. She is, I must say, appropriately grateful.'

'Oh good,' Eppie said.

'I'll just see the young lady to Mrs McCormack's and then I'll be off.'

He turned for the door. Eppie dodged in front of him. 'To Mrs McCormack's?'

The doctor looked astonished. 'Well, where else could she go?'

Eppie cursed himself. Of course Alma couldn't stay here. 'Her aunt lives nearby.'

'We've been through that. Not near enough. And Mrs McCormack volunteered her spare room. She'll take care of Miss Gains. I have to say her ministrations would drive me mad but the ladies seem to like that sort of thing.'

Eppie had a mere glimpse of Alma being ushered out of the front door. She was a little hunched over, holding her right hand to her injured left shoulder and grimacing in pain so much that Eppie wondered if the doctor was right about the bone not being broken. Mrs McCormack was all for hustling her straight down the street immediately but at the last moment Alma turned and held out her uninjured hand to him.

'Mr Epford, I must thank you for your kind help …'

He had only a moment to shake her warm hand before Mrs McCormack chivvied her off next door. The doctor strode off to his carriage and Eppie was left alone on his own doorstep. Knowing there was an attacker in the neighbourhood and that the said attacker had attacked Alma to get back at Eppie. And if that was not a bitter enough pill to swallow, Alma was now unprotected, in a house populated only by an old woman and a young maid who looked as if she'd be scared of anything larger than a Jack Russell terrier.

Eppie would protect her. Even if he had to sit on her doorstep all night.

The nights were still cold at this time of year – he looked out a thick coat and scarf and muffled himself up. Then he went out the front door, locking it carefully behind him. He'd have preferred to go out of the back door but that would have meant leaving the back gate insecure. With any luck Mrs McCormack would still be ministering to Alma and not looking out of her windows. He walked calmly along the street, took a left turn and came to the corner where Alma had been attacked.

Attacked. Odd how quickly one became used to such things. Only a week or so ago, the most pressing matters he faced were whether his best scissors were still sharp, and how soon he could afford a new set of pneumatic tyres. Now his racing bike was sitting in the back yard with slashed tyres, he hadn't even thought of replacing them with the spares, let alone considered whether those spares were going to be good enough to win him the races on Easter Monday. And if he didn't win that race, he wouldn't have enough money to buy himself a new pair of top-notch tyres to enable him to win other races …

That, he supposed, was what was known as a vicious circle. What seemed a lot more vicious to him was that someone had decided to get back at him by hurting Alma. And that was *totally* unacceptable.

He scrutinized the ground at the corner. The street lamp didn't cast a particularly good light and he'd have preferred to leave the job till morning, but by then a few dozen miners would have tramped over this pavement on their way to or from the pit. What was he looking for? A cigar would be nice. Or a button. Or a convenient piece of paper with someone's name on it.

All he found were a few skid marks where Alma's machine had come to grief.

'Lost something?'

He must have jumped a good couple of inches in the air. Constable Banks enjoyed that. When Eppie landed again and got a good look at the constable's face, the man was grinning broadly. No, he wasn't – he was smirking. Why did people always have to smirk?

'A ten shilling note,' Eppie said. 'At least, I lost it on the way home. I thought it might be here.'

He eyed Banks. The constable had a thick overcoat on over the uniform, which Eppie rather thought was not regulation. And that overcoat had a big smear of something greasy at the bottom of the hem on the left hand side ...

'Going home?' Eppie asked. When he knew full well Constable Banks lived down by the harbour.

'Nah,' Banks said. 'I live down by the harbour.'

Eppie sighed.

'Something wrong, Mr E?'

'Mr Epford to you!' Eppie was sharper than he intended, but only Harry was allowed to call him that. And he was sick and tired of the police interfering in his life. Chief suspect, indeed!

'You're on duty then?'

Banks thrust his face into Eppie's. 'I am. And I don't like people who are suspiciously snooping around at this time of night.'

Eppie stood his ground. 'If I see anyone suspiciously snooping around, I'll tell them you said so.'

'Don't you be clever with me, Epford!'

'I wouldn't dream of it.' Banks probably wouldn't understand if he was.

'What are you doing out here?!'

'I told you, I dropped some money on the way home.' Actually, it probably wasn't a good idea to keep that story up – Banks would sooner or later find out all the gossip, and part of that gossip would be Mrs McCormack's choice tidbits about Alma's bicycle accident. 'Anyway, it was a good job I decided to come out to look for it, because there was a bicycle accident.'

Banks chortled again. 'Fell off, did you?'

'Not me. A lady. Because of a dog that dashed out into the road.'

Banks patently did not believe him. 'And where is this *lady* now?'

'The lady – who happens to be a very respectable schoolmistress – is at Mrs McCormack's. The doctor has already seen her and is of the opinion that she is not badly hurt.'

Banks was breathing heavily. 'Mrs McCormack's? I'll check that out, you know.'

'Be my guest.'

Banks looked at him once more then swung round and stomped off down the street and round the corner. He obviously didn't believe Eppie. Which was mutual, as a matter of fact. Because Eppie wasn't sure he believed Constable Banks.

Banks looked a bit bigger in build than the man Eppie had glimpsed attacking Alma, but it *had* been only a glimpse and Eppie had been more concerned with rescuing Alma than taking a detailed inventory of the man's appearance. The height was about right and that coat and scarf of Bell's would fit. He was wearing a helmet now of course but that's not to say he mightn't have swapped it briefly for a hat earlier. He'd hardly have attacked someone wearing such an obvious part of his uniform.

But why? Why should Banks have attacked Alma? Crellin would never have sanctioned it, that was for sure. If he was the attacker, Banks was acting on his own.

He could have murdered Wetherall. Admittedly, he'd been sitting in Eppie's chair when the body was discovered but he'd come straight in only a minute or two before, and he could have come down the alley on his way to Eppie's shop. Eppie even started to wonder if the constable hadn't been just a trifle out of breath when he arrived. Suppose he'd passed Wetherall in the alley – Wetherall wouldn't have taken the slightest notice of him. Once the two men had passed, Banks could have swung round and hit him over the head with his truncheon. Wielded by such a big man and one experienced in using it, there'd have been no problem at all in striking a fatal blow. And it solved the mystery of where the murder weapon had gone. Banks had walked off with it and no one would have thought anything of it. Policemen always wear truncheons.

Now all he had to do is work out why on earth Constable Banks should want to kill Wetherall.

27

'God, you look awful,' Amos said.

He had come round the path in his usual all-or-nothing manner, accelerating out of the last bend as if his back wheel was on fire and he was trying to get away from it. A couple of other riders were racing each other down the back straight – riders Eppie had never seen before. Whatever had happened to his nice quiet all-on-his-own early morning training session?

'Late night,' he said, dumping his bag on the steps of the pavilion and looking in some despair at the spare set of tyres now adorning the bicycle propped against the pavilion wall. There was a reason they were his spare set and it was a matter of quality.

'Late night?' Amos had a way of jumping off his machine as if it was a horse. Eppie half-expected to see him pat the handlebars affectionately. 'Eppie, that's not good. It's only two weeks till the Sports. You can't afford to let the training go!'

'Don't worry. Your bet is safe.' Nothing like sounding confident when he wasn't. 'Amos, someone was lurking around my house last night and attacked ...' He hesitated, then plunged on. If there was anyone he could certainly trust, it was Amos. 'A certain friend of mine when – er – she left my house.'

'She?' Amos smirked. 'Say no more, my boy, I know what you mean.'

'No, you don't,' Eppie retorted. 'The lady in question is totally respectable.'

'She just happened to pay you a visit.'

'We were talking.'

'Of course you were. Tell me all, Eppie!'

He explained what had happened. Amos, he noted, was rather more sombre than he'd expected. Serious, even. That didn't happen very often. They let the two riders scramble past – lots of enthusiasm there but no science. Pretty young. One at least looked as if he had potential. The other was just a scorcher.

'Did this attacker know you were there?'

Eppie considered. 'I think he must have. I mean, he must have been lurking around the corner and waiting for Alma – Miss Gains, I mean – to come past. Alma and I stood at my back gate for a moment or two talking, then she got on her machine and rode off. The attacker must have glanced down the lane to see if she was coming and if he did that, he must have seen me.'

'Well.' Amos pursed his lips. 'I can't see that he intended to kidnap her, or anything of that sort. He might have been a big man, but what was to prevent her screaming and attracting attention? He might have been trying to rob her, I suppose, but if he knew you were there and could rush to her rescue, that would have been a fool's errand too. So ...'

'He *wanted* me to see. It was a warning.'

Amos nodded. 'Looks like it, I'm afraid, my boy.'

Eppie filled him in on all of it: the burglary, the note suggesting he leave town, Dick's suggestion he take a trip to the Isle of Man. The two riders went round and round the path and, to Eppie's surprise, the scorcher began to get the better of the other lad.

Amos winced. 'Don't even think of leaving town, Eppie. Everyone will immediately say you killed Wetherall.'

'I'm not going to bring Alma into further danger!'

Amos patted him on the arm. 'Entirely proper of you to worry about her. But you can keep the lady out of danger simply by telling her to stay in Carlisle for a week or two. Out of sight, out of mind. They're using her to try to intimidate you. If she's not in the picture, they can't do that.'

Eppie sighed. 'I suppose not.' The scorcher was starting to draw away from his opponent. He certainly had stamina, and strength. 'I did wonder ...'

Amos nodded encouragingly. 'Go on, go on.'

'Whether it was Constable Banks.'

'My boy, let's sit in the pavilion out of the cold and discuss the matter.'

'It smells in there.'

Amos was already fingering the loose padlock but stopped. He shrugged. 'If you want to catch your death of cold, dear boy, don't let me stop you.' He plumped himself down on the pavilion steps. 'Explain everything!'

Eppie took Amos through his reasoning. Amos thought the constable might well have been able to carry out the murder on his way to dispose of his whiskers in Eppie's shop.

'But why? Why should a police constable, no matter how stupid, want to kill a man like Wetherall?'

The scorcher sprinted for the line and twisted in the saddle to gloat at his erstwhile rival.

'There's apparently a rumour that Wetherall was having an affair with a woman out of his usual social class. I don't know if Constable Banks is married ...'

'He is,' Amos said. 'But Mrs Banks not the sort of woman anyone has an affair with, let alone someone like Wetherall. For a start, she's a sensible woman. Belle knows her well, they shop at the same butcher's.'

'But the constable might have *thought* Wetherall was having an affair with her.'

Amos wrinkled up his nose. 'Bit tenuous, I'd say. You don't kill someone for having an affair with your wife without first making sure you're right.'

'*I* wouldn't,' Eppie said. 'But Constable Banks thought he could make murder go away just by telling me to go back to my shop and stop talking about it.'

'Actually,' Amos said thoughtfully. 'If he *was* guilty of Wetherall's murder, that would explain why he was so anxious to make out it was an accident.'

'See!' The two young riders were starting off on another race. 'I think I need to find out more about Constable Banks.'

Amos got up and stretched. 'Leave it to me.'

'No!' Eppie grabbed at his arm. 'Don't! If it *is* him, and you start asking questions, then you could be in danger too! Leave it alone, Amos. Let me deal with it – I can't be in any more danger than I am.'

Amos looked down at him, an odd expression on his face. 'You're serious about that?'

'I am.' Eppie got up and straightened his jersey. 'Now let me do some training.' He picked his machine off the wall. 'Or your ten shillings really will be at risk.'

Amos was rubbing his right thumb over the metal of his handlebar.

'Eppie,' he said softly, just as Eppie was about to ride off. 'You really can be a fool sometimes, you know.' He raised his voice as Eppie started to protest. 'My boy, if you think me the kind of man who deserts his friends in their hour of need, you have another think coming. It's about time I nailed my colours to some mast instead of just drifting through life. And, my boy, yours is the mast I'm nailing them to. Train well!' And he put his head down and scorched off towards the gate to the road.

It was starting to rain again by the time Eppie got home and of course he couldn't just wheel the machine into the back yard as usual because the obstacles behind the gate prevented it opening – he'd added more bricks to the pile to make sure of that, since Alma had managed to get in that way. So he had to go in the front door and carry the muddy machine through the hall and kitchen.

He'd hardly got back in the house from the yard before there was a knock on the front door. If it was Constable Banks, or even Inspector Crellin, he wasn't sure he had the patience to answer them civilly. He pulled open the door rather forcibly.

It was Alma. She made a face at him and dived into the house. 'Shut the door!'

He did so. 'Mrs McCormack?'

'Just as I got to the door to leave, the maid let the stew boil over in the kitchen and she had to dash back to tell the girl off. I don't think she saw which way I went but I don't want her to see me at your door.'

She looked pale, but a great deal better than when he'd last seen her the previous night. Her clothes had been beautifully pressed – it looked like Mrs

McCormack's girl was a lot better with clothes than with stews. But he didn't like the look of the sling that held her left arm still.

'You need to sit down.'

'No, I only want a word or two—'

'Into the kitchen,' he said firmly. 'I was just going to put the kettle on.'

She hung back. 'Don't be silly, Eppie. I know you normally just change into your work clothes and go straight off to the shop.'

'That doesn't mean I can't do things differently for once. Anyway, I don't have many customers just at the moment.' Or any.

He pulled a chair out from the table for her and waited resolutely until she sighed and sat down.

'I'm fine, Eppie. I promise you. I won't deny my shoulder's sore but the worst of the pain has gone. The doctor says I shouldn't use it very much but that's easier said than done!'

'What about the headmaster? Surely he'll be expecting you at school?'

'I sent him a telegram last night telling him I'd had an accident. Eppie, do you know who attacked me?'

He shook his head. 'Not exactly, no. I do have some suspicions.'

'Who?'

He hesitated, then pulled out the chair opposite her and sat down. 'You were attacked because someone wanted to frighten me.'

She nodded. 'I know that! They want you to leave town.'

'I'm not going anywhere.'

'I never thought you would.' She smiled, reached to pat his hand. 'You're not a man to run away.'

He felt a glow of gratification. 'But if you're here, they'll continue to try and use you to frighten me off.'

He knew by the sudden hardening of her mouth that he'd made a mistake somewhere though he couldn't quite fathom what it might be. He pressed on.

'You must go back to Carlisle, immediately, and stay there. Until this business is over, at least. Then you'll be safe. I'll look after your bicycle and you can take the train—'

She stood up very abruptly. 'While you stay here, in the line of fire?'

'Alma—'

'Edward Epford,' she said coldly. 'If you think I'm the kind of woman who abandons her betrothed the first moment trouble rears its head, you had better reconsider. And let me tell you, I am not flattered by your opinion of me!'

Belatedly, he leapt up, suddenly remembering his manners. 'I didn't mean …'

'I don't think you know what you mean,' she said with dignity, and turned for the front door. 'Meanwhile, if you want to talk to me, I will be at my aunt's. I'll send the headmaster another telegram to say I've had an unfortunate relapse and will be off school for several days.'

He stared, horrified. 'You're staying in Maryport …'

'No one,' she said, turning her back, 'absolutely *no one*, would drag me away from such a delightful place!'

28

No one was waiting when he arrived to open the shop. He was not surprised. Precisely three customers turned up all morning. He had to get this affair sorted soon or the business would go under and then he'd probably be waiting for ever to marry Alma.

And as if to taunt him, it was turning out a really nice day – sunny and bright. He'd seen bright blue and white crocuses in the park on his way to the shop, and the first daffodils. Spring was on its way. A great day for a bicycle ride. If he'd been on good terms with Alma.

A great day for a *long* ride. Halfway to Penrith, perhaps. He'd not slept well and somewhere in the small hours of the morning he'd wondered if he'd been neglecting a certain gentleman with money troubles. Of course, he might only have been suspicious of Maitland because the man had enjoyed a malicious trick at his expense, but there could be no denying that Maitland had a motive for killing Wetherall – to remove his opposition to the wedding with Violet Daisy Rose, and to acquire the man's money. Admittedly, Maitland would have to wait for the money until the mourning year was over, but creditors are usually more generous when they know their man has *expectations*.

So Eppie had decided to spend his half-day training riding out to Maitland's country house and having a look around. He didn't seriously think he'd find anything there but the idea made him feel better. It gave him the sense he was actually *doing* something, even if he really wasn't.

At which point he'd turned over in bed and groaned. He was not one for deceiving himself and he knew this trip was a fine example of futility. The only advantage it had was that he'd get some decent training in. Not that he particularly liked that road – he'd complained to Alma about its twists and turns and horrible surface more than once. And some of the hedges were so high you couldn't see what was coming the other way. Once he'd come face to face with a very startled and annoyed horse, and only just escaped a sharp bite.

And *cyclists* were supposed to be dangerous!

Halfway through the morning, as he was tidying up after one of the few customers of the day, a young boy came dashing in, already holding out his hand for money.

'Note for yer.'

'Who's it from?'

'Don't know.'

He was a grubby lad, looking very much as if he'd been down rolling in mud. Eppie pretended to consider. 'Don't want it.'

'Here, he said you'd give us a shilling!'

'Then whoever it is is an idiot – I never give more than thruppence. And I don't want to read notes from idiots.'

Now the lad was beginning to look disgruntled. 'Penny?'

Eppie gave him the penny and got the note in exchange. Amos's handwriting on the grubby sheet of paper. Which meant, given Amos's present financial state, that the lad probably *had* been told Eppie would pay him. The boy was halfway out the door when Eppie called him back.

'Let me give you a word of advice …'

'Aw, no,' the lad said. 'I 'ave enough of that from me da.'

'Never,' Eppie said, fishing in a pocket, 'settle for a penny. Always hold out for at least sixpence. After all, you have the advantage.' He waved the note. 'No one could possibly bear to let a letter addressed to them disappear out of the door. There'd always be a niggling suspicion it might have been a legacy. Hold out your hand.'

The lad looked uncertain but obeyed. Eppie took back the penny and gave him two thruppenny bits instead. The lad's face lit up. He clenched his fist at once and took a step backwards. Then he uttered the greatest compliment Eppie had had in days – 'You're a complete nutter, you!' – and ran for the street before Eppie could change his mind.

Eppie rather liked being thought mad. It made a change from being sensible, or dull, or just everyday.

Or suspicious.

Amos's note said:

Informants say Mrs B acting oddly recently. But then she is married to Const B.

And he has just insisted on buying a dog – one of those snappy terriers. No one corresponding to W's description seen around the lady. Besides, where would she have met him? Not looking good. Sorry. Will continue to ask around.
A
P.S. Yes, I am being very discreet.

Not very helpful. But the note only really confirmed something else that had occurred to Eppie during those long wakeful night hours. A tramp like the one who'd kindly informed him of the 'cigar meetings' would recognize every policeman in town. He'd probably been arrested by them all at one time or another. So, if Wetherall's co-conspirator had been Banks, why should the tramp not have said so? Unless he was planning to have a little chat with Banks himself at some point. Which, if the man was a murderer, would not be a good idea.

Eppie decided he'd had enough. He'd close the shop and go off to the tea-rooms for something to eat. A nice treat would help him feel better, though most treats, in his experience, tended to make him put on weight, and that wouldn't help him win on Easter Monday.

The tea-rooms were busy though the table in the corner he usually shared with Alma was conveniently free. The waitress came across with a harassed air.

'You won't want to order till the lady arrives, will you?'

He gritted his teeth. 'I'm on my own today.'

'Oh, I *am* sorry.' She was a young girl, with wispy blonde hair escaping in every direction from her cap. 'You haven't had an argument, have you?'

'Meat, pickle, potatoes and tea,' he said, coldly.

She drew herself up as if to say *well, be like that* and took herself off.

He'd brought the paper with him, in a vague hope that he might be able to concentrate on reading it. Failing that, it would make a useful screen to hide behind while he racked his brains and wondered what to do. Maybe a nice trip to the Isle of Man *would* be best …

'Mr Epford?'

He looked up, startled, and saw Violet Daisy Rose Wetherall, attired in a stylish black gown. He leapt out of his seat. She looked up at him from under the rim of her bonnet and limply held out her hand. He wasn't sure whether she expected him to do with it – he shook it, which seemed to amuse her.

'Do you mind if I join you?'

He could hardly say no. He pulled out a chair and she arranged herself on it. The waitress chose that moment to come back with a tray of tea, and Miss Wetherall looked limpidly up at her.

'Oh, is that for me? How delightful. Is it Earl Grey?'

The waitress put the tray down on the table and looked sideways at Eppie with a knowing look. She might as well have added 'Well, aren't you the one?' because that was what she was thinking.

'I'll fetch you some, love.'

Miss Wetherall pushed the teapot towards Eppie but kept the teacup for herself. 'I expect you're wondering why I want to talk to you.' She cast a glance around. The busyness of the rooms meant there was a great deal of noise which lessened the risk of anyone overhearing. She fidgeted with the spoon in her saucer. 'Mr Epford – I know I'm asking a great deal, but I desperately need advice and you're the only person I could think of. I'm so relieved – I thought you'd probably left town!'

Eppie consigned the Isle of Man to another year. If he was still at liberty. No one would ever be able to say Eppie Epford ran away from a contest.

Miss Wetherall was plainly disconcerted by his momentary lack of response; she batted her eyelids. 'You are so strong …'

Involuntarily he thought of what Dick had said, banished it from his mind. And she, he was tempted to reply, was so silly. She seemed not to care in the least what people thought of her behaviour, or going about the town on her own. Admittedly, Alma went about the town on her own too, and met him on her own, but she was a working woman and Miss Wetherall was at least five years younger than Alma and clearly not fit to be let out. Coming up to him in public like this! And when she had as good as accused him of being a murderer in court. And surely her mother must have warned her against him. He couldn't imagine why she shouldn't have.

The waitress brought the second tea tray and they were silent while she set the various pots and cups on the table.

'Something to eat?' she said to Miss Wetherall. The young lady shook her head and the waitress took herself off again.

Eppie commandeered a teacup and poured his tea.

'I would of course like to oblige you, if I could,' he said carefully, 'but surely it would be more appropriate to talk to your mother, or your fiancé?'

'I can't.' There was an edge to the young lady's voice, not hysteria, but certainly a hint of panic. She glanced around again – if she did much more of that, someone would start taking notice. Furtiveness was always more obvious than brazen behaviour. She pushed a slip of paper across the table. 'This was left for me this morning.'

This was a single sheet of paper folded in half, with the name *Miss Wetherall* on the outside. Inside were a few words in the same beautiful copperplate that had adorned the note left in Eppie's kitchen: *If you want to live a long and happy life, mourn your father and cease to wonder how he died.*

The waitress brought Eppie's cold meats and potatoes. He handed the note back to Miss Wetherall, and started to cut up his cold beef. It was hardly polite to eat while a lady did not, but she'd put herself into this situation.

Miss Wetherall looked puzzled by his reaction. 'That note is threatening me. It's saying that if I persist in trying to find out who killed Papa, they will—' Her voice failed her. 'Well, you understand. You *must* understand.'

He nodded, chewing.

'You can see why I don't want to worry Mama and Algernon with it.'

'No,' he said. 'Actually, I don't. I can't see that anyone is more qualified to protect you than your fiancé.'

'They'd never let me go out on my own again!' She leant forward, placed her hand on his arm. 'Mr Epford. Help me, *please*. Find out who killed Papa, then we can all sleep peacefully in our beds.'

Well, he might as well learn as much as he could while he had the chance. 'You said the note was "left" – by whom?'

'It was pushed under the front door during the night.'

She'd left the note lying on the table and he turned it over. 'Your maids do a good job.'

She frowned. 'I'm sorry?'

'Cleaning. The note's remarkably fresh for something that's been pushed along the floor.'

She foundered for a moment then said, 'I can't explain that.'

'And you don't think the maids looked inside the note to see what it said?'

She was outraged. 'Read my correspondence? They wouldn't dare!'

He was inclined to think that was her first genuine, uncalculated reaction since she'd arrived.

'Why do you think you're the one who has been threatened?' The tea was, unfortunately, stewed; he drank it anyway. 'After all, isn't it Inspector Crellin who's been investigating the matter?'

She took a deep breath. 'I was the one who persuaded him it wasn't an accident.'

'I know. I was at the inquest. You overheard your father arguing with someone in the lane behind your house. But having started the ball rolling, as it were, there's nothing you can do to stop it now.'

She sipped tea delicately, unable to resist showing him her good side as she did so. Her ear was a white perfect shape nestling amongst her artfully arranged hair. 'I think – I – I've found out something and I was going to tell the inspector about it.'

'I see.' He finished the beef and potatoes, and laid his knife and fork neatly across the plate. 'And you think this threat is intended to discourage you from passing this information on.'

She nodded.

'But that suggests someone knows you have this information. Who have you told?'

'No one!'

'That can't be true.' He looked at her over the top of his tea cup. Of course, she might believe everything she said. She could be being worked on as much as he was. She was a remarkably self-centred young lady and she probably never gave things much thought if they didn't impinge directly on her. Add to that her youthful age and her probable lack of experience of the world, and she'd be remarkably easy to fool. Particularly by someone who knew her well. Like a fiancé, for instance. 'And what is this information?'

She said in a subdued manner, 'The night Papa went out, the night before he – he died, I went out too.'

'To meet someone?'

She nodded. 'A – a young man.'

Eppie had a lowering feeling he really didn't want to know any more about this. 'Not your fiancé?'

She shook her head. 'Oh, it was silly. I can see that now. Algernon is everything a woman could want in a husband except …'

'You don't care for him?'

She glanced round surreptitiously. If only she wouldn't do that! 'He's so pompous. I mean, he's absolutely devoted to me, but …' She gave a little embarrassed laugh. 'He's not in the least handsome.'

'And someone else is?'

'I can't tell you his name!' Her mouth twisted. 'And besides, it doesn't matter, because I never saw him that night.' She looked down at her hands in her lap. 'I was a fool. He never came. I waited for him at the entrance to the park. And I waited, and waited, and then I realized he wasn't coming.' She gave him a watery glance. 'So I decided to go back home. Only I took a wrong turning and ended up behind the Town Hall. And I saw my father. With – with a woman. They were …'

She bit her lip and reached for her tea cup. Eppie waited. Wetherall and this woman could not have been doing anything particularly significant, not in such a public place. Kissing perhaps. But such a young lady would certainly have been shocked.

'I'm not fool enough to think it hadn't happened before,' she said. 'Papa was very attractive to certain kinds of women.'

Women, Eppie noted, not *ladies*.

'So I didn't tell Mama.' There was a trace of defiance in Miss Wetherall's tone. 'But I did realize one odd thing later – much later, only a day or so ago. She wasn't the sort of woman Papa would have normally associated with. She wasn't a woman of our class.'

Goodness, how did he ask her if the woman might have been a prostitute?

'She was very handsome,' Miss Wetherall said. 'Quite exotic in fact. And very respectably dressed. And I heard him talking to her …'

Now Eppie really was interested. 'You heard her name?'

She nodded. 'Belle,' she said. 'She was called Belle.'

29

'BELLE,' EPPIE SAID flatly, more to gain himself time than anything else. There must be lots of Belles in town surely. The door of the café jangled open again; the customers at the next table got up to leave.

'Her husband is a journalist.'

'How do you know that?'

'I've seen him at official dinners and charity balls. She accompanies him sometimes.' She added, 'They're both very *common*.'

'They're friends of mine,' Eppie said. Miss Wetherall merely looked puzzled. She was, admittedly, very young but Eppie was beginning to tire of using that excuse for her. 'As a matter of fact …'

'As a matter of fact,' said a steely voice just to his right, 'I believe this is *my* seat!'

Eppie shot to his feet. Alma stood like a vengeful, well, a vengeful something, a goddess, no, that was ridiculous, actually no, it wasn't. She could easily have posed for a statue of a goddess, tall, slender, gorgeously red-haired. The sling wouldn't quite have fitted though. She was definitely annoyed. Glaring down at Miss Wetherall, thank goodness – Eppie had no wish to endure that look.

Miss Wetherall was looking bewildered now, but the well-bred frostiness of her upbringing came to her rescue. 'I don't believe we've been introduced.'

'We don't need to be introduced,' Alma snapped. 'All you need to know is that I'm Mr Epford's fiancée.' And then the people at the next table were beginning to sit up and take notice. This morning Eppie had been merely the chief suspect in a murder; now he was going to get a reputation as a philanderer as well!

'Miss Wetherall was just leaving,' he said hurriedly.

Miss Wetherall was not flustered. On the contrary, she gathered her bag and gloves, then looked up at Eppie expectantly. He cursed inwardly and dashed round to pull her chair back.

'Thank you.' She gave Alma a limpid look. 'I wish I could say it has been a pleasure meeting you.'

'Well, *I* certainly shan't lie,' Alma said.

Miss Wetherall smiled faintly. 'Good day, Mr Epford. Thank you for your assistance.' And she made her delicate way through the tables to the door.

Alma glared at Eppie. He pulled the chair out further and assisted her to sit down. The waitress leapt in with obvious eagerness.

'D'you want some tea too?' She gathered up the various pots and cups that gave witness to Miss Wetherall's presence. 'The other young lady,' she smiled sweetly, 'had Earl Grey.'

'The other young lady,' Alma said tartly, 'is obviously more refined than I am.'

They waited until the waitress had tidied up and gone. Eppie sat down, and pushed away his empty plate, wondering if he should have another go at persuading Alma to go back to Carlisle. He would much rather she was safely out of the way but at the same time, he was rather pleased she wasn't.

Alma turned and stared coldly about the room. A number of people looked away quickly. She fixed Eppie with that stare.

'What did she want?'

Eppie took a deep breath. 'To give me some information about her father's death. Apparently she's too scared to go to the police with it. Or to her fiancé.'

The waitress set the tea things in front of Alma with something of a snap. Alma said coldly, 'Thank you.' The waitress *humfed* and went off. 'Are we supposed to believe that?'

'Apparently.' Eppie watched Alma trying to remove the tea pot lid and stir the tea one-handed. 'May I assist you?'

She gave him that look again then sighed. 'It's all right. I'm not going to bite your head off. Thank you. I'm finding it a trifle annoying to be so restricted. I can understand why such a poor little thing might be wary of the inspector but why should she not tell her fiancé or her mother at least?'

Eppie made sure they were not being listened to. 'Let's just say Miss Wetherall is not entirely committed to her present marriage plans, or at least – she admits the advantages of the match but has other – er – interests.'

'Does this other interest have a name?'

'No.' Keeping his voice low, he explained what Miss Wetherall had told him, up to the point where she'd admitted seeing her father with another woman.

'This doesn't make sense.' Alma shook her head. 'I thought Wetherall's expedition on that night was to meet his future murderer. Now we're being told it was apparently to meet a lady. If the man was blackmailing him over his dalliance, as we have speculated, why should Wetherall add fuel to the fire by meeting the lady only minutes after meeting the man?'

'Unless the meeting with the lady was fortuitous.'

'A respectable woman out on her own late at night in back alleyways? Nonsense.'

'Or the blackmail wasn't about a woman.'

'Then what *was* it about?'

'I give up!' Eppie said. 'I'm never going to get to the bottom of this. I think I'm going off to the Isle of Man after all. Permanently. They must need hairdressers there.'

'But they only have two race meetings a year.'

'Perhaps there's more to life than cycle racing.'

'No, there isn't,' Alma retorted. 'Eppie, what are you keeping from me?'

He sighed. 'Miss Wetherall knew who the woman was.'

He searched through his pockets for a scrap of paper and came up with a bill he'd paid a few days earlier and forgotten about. Alma handed him a stub of pencil.

'A schoolmistress always has writing implements about her.'

He scrawled *Belle Danson* on the back of the bill and pushed it across the table.

Alma's eyes widened. 'Surely not!'

'Apparently.'

'But I thought …' She hesitated. 'Some people are clearly unhappily married but others – well, I'd have been sure …'

He nodded. 'I'd have been sure I could trust Amos with my life.'

She lowered her voice. 'He may not know.'

'We were suggesting earlier that a jealous husband …'

'But he's too lazy!' Alma drank tea. Unlike Miss Wetherall, who had used the whole business of sipping and swallowing as a performance designed to attract, Alma plainly drank because she was thirsty. 'Well, there's one thing we can do. Ask the lady herself.'

Eppie said, 'You don't think *she* might have … I mean, if the whole thing was in danger of coming out, she might not have wanted that. And if they were in the habit of meeting in that alley, she might have sent a message to Wetherall suggesting he meet her there on the way to the council meeting. They met, argued, he refused to talk any more. Then she dropped something, he bent down to pick it up and she hit him over the head.'

'She must have gone intending to do it or she wouldn't have had the weapon.'

Eppie thought for a moment. 'There's no evidence to suggest that's what happened, is there?'

'No. But then there's no evidence.'

'Miss Wetherall's story is not entirely convincing either. A note pushed under the door but as clean as if the paper had just come from the factory. A note that wasn't sealed, so all the servants could have read it if they chose. And a threat that she should stop investigating her father's death when she's not doing so in the first place!'

'I'll tell you one thing for certain,' Alma said. 'I was wrong. She *is*.'

'She is what?'

Alma sighed. 'You know.'

'No.'

'You know!' She gestured meaningfully with her free hand.

'What?'

She mimed a rocking motion.

'Oh,' Eppie said. 'Really? Are you sure?'

'Absolutely. She didn't want anything to eat, did she?'

'No, is that a sign?'

'In the morning, it is.'

'But not in the afternoon?'

An elderly couple came to sit at the next table, with a great deal of fuss and confusion. Alma raised her voice a little. 'I would very much like to take a turn about the town, Mr Epford. Would you care to accompany me, or do you have to return to the shop?'

'I don't see why – I have no customers. I'd love to take a walk.'

He called the waitress over and paid, and they went out onto the street. Alma looked up and down the hill.

'Why don't we just visit Mrs Danson? Ask her whether the story is true?'

Eppie wasn't much inclined to agree. 'I've always wanted to ask the wife of one of my closest friends whether she's being unfaithful to her husband.'

Alma grinned. 'Eppie. We have to sort this matter out quickly, before the consequences get totally out of hand. If that means being a bit, well …'

'Rude?'

'A little *less than tactful*, well, so be it. Come on, where do they live?'

30

IT WAS NEVER quiet down by the harbour. Even on a damp day, when spots of rain in the air hint at the possibility of a shower, on one of those days when whatever you wear, you always wish you'd put on something thicker, when there are few people around and all of them are hurrying for the indoors, there's always something going on in the harbour. The shouts of men unloading a fishing boat, the squawk of seagulls wheeling overhead, the clatter and clash of machinery. The stink of the sea and of fish almost overwhelming.

On a sunny day like today, it looked almost pretty. Though still smelly. Alma regarded the houses on Amos's street.

'Elegant, stylish, quite large, I should imagine. But come down in the world.' She glanced at Eppie, rather cautiously – it wasn't a look he was used to seeing. 'The sort of place you live when you don't want to spend more money than you have to.'

'At least not on anything but betting.'

Alma looked at him sideways. 'Has he bet on you for the Easter Monday Sports?'

'Hasn't everyone?'

'I wonder … Eppie, do you suppose this affair could remotely be about the Sports? Perhaps someone has bet on one of your opponents and wants you to lose?'

'So much that they would kill someone to stop me competing?'

'Well, no.' She screwed up her face thoughtfully. 'But someone *is* trying to make you leave town.'

'Are you suggesting that whoever's trying to get me out of town isn't the person who killed Wetherall?'

'It might just be someone taking advantage of the situation for their own ends. And remember, your tyres were slashed by your intruder. That's not simply an attempt to intimidate you — it actually lessens your chances of winning.'

They'd come to Amos's front gate. Eppie stared glumly at the brown-painted front door. 'I'm confused enough as it is, without having two separate malefactors each with their own motives and objectives.'

Alma squeezed his arm. 'Just think of it as a road race. You against two other competitors. Will you let them beat you?'

Eppie stared at the door. It really was a horrible colour, and scratched in places too, particularly at the bottom, where it had obviously been kicked more than once.

'Of course not.'

'There you are then,' Alma said obscurely.

Eppie had to knock twice before he heard the distant sounds of movement within the house. A long moment before the door inched open. Belle's face, smudged with white, appeared in the crack. She looked from Eppie to Alma, a little anxiously, Eppie thought. Then she pulled the door open and disappeared back into the house, calling out, 'Shut the door behind you!'

She was baking. The smell of warm lemon cake drifted through the hall and made Eppie's stomach ache even after everything he'd just eaten. The kitchen was littered with cooking impedimenta: dirty bowls piled everywhere, every spoon and knife in the house on the kitchen table, a bag of flour that had split, chopping boards piled with dried fruit and candied peel and little piles of spices.

Belle wiped her hand across her forehead and left another smudge of white. She looked at the debris around her with something like helplessness. 'I always somehow get disorganized when I cook.'

'But it smells as if it's worth it,' Alma said.

Belle beamed. 'Thank you. Amos likes it.'

Eppie took his life in his hands with a deep breath. 'What about Charles Wetherall?'

Belle stilled. She was a remarkably fine-looking woman, even with her dark hair descending haphazardly onto her shoulders. She rubbed her hands together, scattering flour across the table.

'We never talked food.'

A little silence. Alma said, 'Will you tell us about it?'

Belle laughed, somewhat bitterly. 'Why should I?'

'Because I'm being suspected of murder,' Eppie said. 'And you know something about it. I won't tell Amos anything, if that's what worries you.'

She drew herself up. 'I'd make you both a cup of something but I don't think there's any space. Besides, I've still got an apple sponge to mix. Yes, I knew Wetherall. And don't expect me to be ashamed of it.'

Alma said – obviously trying to be gentle, 'You were having an affair with him.'

Belle roared with laughter. 'I was not! Mind you, that wasn't for want of trying on his part.' She straightened her apron which was stained with cocoa powder. 'We met at one of his charity balls and he made a play for me right at the start. All compliments and significant glances. Three days later I met him in the street and he made me a proposition – straight out – no arguing. "I could do you a lot of good," he says. "You could do me out of a good marriage and a fine husband," I say back. And he tells me straight he knows Amos is short of money and that means I am too, and he offers to buy me all sorts of jewels and such like.'

She jerked her head at a door in the corner of the kitchen – the pantry by the looks of it.

'They're in there.'

'Jewels?' Eppie echoed, startled.

'One necklace, pair of earrings, nice brooch. Bit old-fashioned, and the sort of respectable stuff you buy a wife. I wonder if she's missed them yet. He was a bit odd that way, you know, with money. Would cheat on his wife without a second thought, but take one penny more than you're entitled to and he'd be outraged. One night the woman behind the bar in the Red Lion gave him tuppence too much on the change and he gave her it back!' She laughed. 'Wouldn't catch me doing that! Said it was stealing and gentlemen don't steal. He was very keen on his responsibilities, you know. A gentleman does this, and a gentleman does that.' She sighed. 'Could get very wearing sometimes.'

She jerked her head at the pantry. 'The jewels are in the oatmeal. I was going to sell them, but when Wetherall met his comeuppance, I knew I'd have to leave it a good while. Which is annoying, as a matter of fact, because we could do with the money now.'

'That's why you encouraged him,' Alma said. 'So he'd give you presents.'

'That's the problem with men, love,' Belle said, in the manner of one delivering an essential lesson. 'They don't have any common sense.'

'Excuse me?' Eppie said.

'Fancy giving the jewels out before they get anything in return! Just asking for a sensible woman to walk off with the goods and deny them the payment.'

'Not all men …'

'And he was stupid enough to think he was in control,' Belle scoffed. 'I had him on a leash all the time. He was the one doing all the giving and I was the one who was doing all the getting.'

'Except for the night before he died,' Eppie said. 'He got something then, didn't he? Enough to shock one or two onlookers.'

Belle squinted at him. 'What are you on about, love? I never saw him the night before he died.'

'Behind the Town Hall.'

'What? In the street? Believe me, I made sure he always took me down the public house and bought me a drink or two – in a private room, out of sight of anyone who might talk to Amos.'

'I'm sorry,' Alma said. 'Let me see if I understand you properly. You encouraged Charles Wetherall because you needed the money …'

'It's Amos.' Belle sniffed the air. 'That cake smells ready. He's a lamb but he doesn't have a clue about money. They none of them do.'

'I do,' Eppie said.

'So we women have to step in and do something about it. And Amos would never hear of me getting a job, that would hurt his pride, poor thing. So I have to make do and mend. And since Charles Wetherall admired my beauty, I thought I had better make use of the opportunity.'

'Did he ever talk about his wife?'

'She didn't understand him,' Belle said. 'They never do. But by all accounts she led him a merry dance. Didn't mince her words and isn't above throwing the odd ornament around. Henpecked the poor fellow to within an inch of his life – though that was his story of course. I mean, he would say that, wouldn't he? Trying to get my sympathy.'

Alma nodded. 'That doesn't mean he wasn't telling the truth though. Did he ever say anything about being threatened, or being afraid of anyone?'

'He was too busy talking himself up. Men like to appear big and important, love …'

'Oh for heaven's sake!' Eppie exploded. 'I'm glad to have your opinion of me, Mrs Danson, but I don't have to stay to be insulted. Alma, I'll wait for you outside!'

She came out to him in the street in only a minute or two, as he stood in a patch of sunshine and moodily regarded the seagulls. She tucked her arm in his.

'Apparently Wetherall didn't object to Maitland because of his political principles. Or not *just* because of his political principles. Maitland was apparently altering IOUs.'

'Altering them? How?'

'Well – according to Wetherall – if Maitland was owed, say ten pounds by someone in gambling debts, he'd alter the IOU to read ten pounds and ten shillings. He did that a lot, apparently.'

'That's criminal!'

'Maybe that was Maitland's motive for killing Wetherall – because Wetherall knew about his cheating?'

'He doesn't need another motive. He's got dozens. He just didn't have the opportunity to do it.'

'The important thing,' Alma said, 'is that Mrs Danson didn't see Wetherall the night before he died. So either Miss Wetherall was mistaken or she lied.'

'Why should she lie?' Eppie stared along the street. The seagulls wheeled overhead; a cart laden with boxes of fish was trundling across the junction at the far end of the street. 'Maybe she's been lied to. By her fiancé. She's a very young and impressionable girl.'

Alma nodded. 'So now what?'

The answer was obvious. All this just increased his conviction that he needed to take a closer look at Maitland. Starting with his house. But he wasn't going to risk Alma by involving her in things like that.

'I'll have to go back to the shop. There might just be a customer or two.'

She nodded. 'I'll walk back there with you. And then I think I'd better go home to my aunt and reassure her that I haven't exhausted myself wandering round town.'

'You should go back to Carlisle.'

She looked sideways at him for a long moment.

'You *are* tired,' he pointed out.

'Yes, but …' She walked a few steps up the street with him. 'I must admit my shoulder is hurting me greatly.'

'And you don't want to try the headmaster's patience too much. If we're to save for our marriage …'

She straightened up, as if suddenly determined. 'Yes, you're right. But Eppie, I don't like to think of you alone …'

'I'll be fine. Trust me.'

She turned her eyes up to his and for a moment he thought she'd seen something in his face that made her suspicious. He did find it extraordinarily hard to lie to her.

'Very well,' she said. 'When's the next train?'

31

THE TRAIN WHISTLE sounded. As one, all the passengers waiting on the platform looked south, hunting for the tell-tale plume of smoke from the engine. Was that a wisp of it above the trees? Alma said, 'What are you going to do? This afternoon, I mean.'

'I thought I'd take a training ride. A long one. Get the cobwebs out of my legs.'

'And take your annoyance out on the roads?'

He nodded ruefully.

The plume of grey-black smoke was visible now, the slight breeze drifting it backwards, away from them. 'I've rather neglected training recently.'

She patted his arm. 'The odd day won't matter. Eppie …'

'Yes?'

'Don't do anything foolish, will you?'

'Believe me,' he said, 'I'm intent on keeping out of everybody's way. I'm hoping they'll forget about me.'

She gave him a mischievous look. 'That's harder than you think, you know.'

The train slowly made its way up the long straight stretch of track into the station. Other passengers were gathering up their possessions and pecking loved ones on the cheek. Eppie disentangled his arm from Alma's; they started down the platform towards the guard's van, Eppie wheeling Alma's bicycle.

'It's criminal you should have to pay for carriage of the bicycle.'

Alma laughed. 'Some things always annoy you!'

'It's luggage,' he said obstinately. 'Like someone else's Gladstone bag.'

'But bigger.' She was smiling now, as he'd hoped she would. She always laughed at him when he grumbled at the railway companies. The train ground to a halt, wheezing and groaning – a whole array of doors sprang open along its length. A child began coughing in the smoke of the engine.

He handed up the bicycle to the guard and for a moment was busy with the various arrangements, the checking of labels and tickets and all the rest of it. Walking Alma up to her carriage, he said, 'You're worried I might confront Amos.'

She nodded.

'Well, I won't. I don't believe for one moment Amos would have attacked Wetherall. He might have shouted at him or insulted him – but killed him? No, never.'

'How can you be sure?'

He hesitated, holding onto the carriage door so she could mount the step. Inside, three elderly ladies had already got their knitting out.

'It sounds dreadful, I know, but Amos is not a man who ...' He felt as if he was betraying Amos by telling the truth but it *was* the truth. 'He's not someone who achieves anything, good or bad. He's ineffectual.'

Alma hesitated, leant forward and pecked his cheek. 'It's good to be honest with oneself about one's friends. Too often, partiality blinds us.'

He desperately tried to lighten the mood. 'It doesn't deceive me as to *your* true worth. But I'll save my assessment of that until another occasion.'

'Eppie Epford,' she said chidingly. 'You are a rogue.' She put her foot on the step, then leant down towards him and whispered, '*Dear ...*'

He stepped back from the train as if he was floating, watched it grind its way out of the station and get up to speed on its way north.

'Very touching,' Crellin said, behind him. 'I thought for a moment you were off with the lady, Mr Epford. Glad to find I was wrong and you're not leaving town.'

Eppie glanced round. The inspector was looking tired and crumpled. One corner of his collar stuck up oddly as if he'd slept in it and awkwardly creased it. Perhaps he had. Eppie didn't have the least idea whether Crellin was married or not, but surely no wife would have let her husband out of the house looking like that – it would have reflected too badly on her housekeeping abilities.

Eppie turned for the station exit. 'As a matter of fact, I *am* leaving town.'

Crellin jerked to a halt. 'Oh yes?'

'For a training ride. A nice couple of hours on the road. Or possibly more. Ideal cycling weather.' Crellin was still regarding him with scepticism written large on his face. Eppie said, 'Do you want to win your bet on Easter Monday or not?'

The inspector looked disgruntled. Eppie suddenly realized one wonderful inescapable fact.

'You *can't* arrest me, can you? Whatever your opinion of my guilt or otherwise, if you arrest me, you'll lose the money you've bet on me at the Easter Sports!'

'I do my duty,' Crellin said, with dignity. 'And I do not allow my own personal interests to interfere with that.' A pity his tone of voice did not sound in the least convincing. He seemed to sag. 'Mr Epford, you've got to come up with something soon – you've no idea what pressure is being put on me!'

They came out into the street.

'Not as much pressure as there is on me,' Eppie pointed out. 'But, I assure you, I'm doing my best.'

A little reluctantly, he told Crellin about the incident with the cigars, feeling guilty because it had happened two days ago and he'd never so much as thought of telling the inspector. Crellin listened, and became increasingly bewildered.

'I can understand that Wetherall was arranging a meeting with this man but why the different numbers of cigars?'

'I wondered if they referred to differing amounts of money.'

'It might not be important,' Crellin said thoughtfully, but he sounded no more convincing than he had before. 'And this tramp …'

'I don't know who he was. Sorry – I should have got his name, shouldn't I?'

Crellin snorted. 'The chances of him telling you it truthfully are pretty small. All right, Mr Epford, leave the tramp to me. You go and have your training run. Which way are you going?'

This was plainly something Crellin was determined to know. Eppie gave way gracefully, for the sake of peace. 'Heading out towards Penrith.'

Crellin snorted again. 'Further than I'd like to go. You'll go out to Cockermouth, then Keswick, then over the hills eastwards?'

'Probably. It's only a vague intention.'

Crellin shook his head. 'Make it a firm intention, Mr Epford. Then I can rest easy.'

'Very well. Yes.'

Crellin nodded and went off. Eppie watched him go with some relief.

He pushed himself hard on the road towards Keswick and was glad of the effort. The machine was weighed down with his bag of food and clothes and with his lamp, essential given he'd be riding back in the dark. Pushing up the hills was correspondingly harder and slower, and he felt the strain in his legs and his heart beating more strongly than usual. On the hill out of Keswick, he realized he was pushing himself *too* hard and that anger was to blame. He slowed, concentrated on maintaining a steady regular pace and stopped at the first convenient place after the summit of the hill to dismount, and eat and drink.

The sun lent an extra charm to the magnificent scenery, so beloved of all touring cyclists. He stared at a sheep which was efficiently cropping the grass just over the fence against which he was leaning. In all this mess, he could be certain of only one thing: that Algernon Maitland had something to answer for. Why else should he have attacked Eppie on the way to Dalston? The business of the IOUs was significant, too, surely, and if he'd got wind of Miss Wetherall's wandering attentions, he might have wanted to move quickly to secure her. No, that wasn't right – Wetherall's death *delayed* the marriage even as it removed an obstacle to it.

Maitland could not have killed Wetherall personally – he'd been in the council meeting at the time. But he *could* have paid someone else to do it. The mysterious man who'd met Wetherall behind the Town Hall, who'd argued with him outside the Wetheralls' house. Who was trying to frame Eppie for the murder, by planting evidence in his shop, by trying to scare him off, and by trying to injure Alma?

Those notes were interesting. The one that had been left in Eppie's kitchen was in the hand of an educated man. The same hand had been on Miss Wetherall's note. But surely she would have recognized the handwriting if it had belonged to her fiancé?

The whole business was still hopelessly confused. He couldn't believe Alma's suggestion that there were two separate plots against him. But he was tired of sitting at home and waiting for yet another disaster to befall him. It was time he took the bull by the horns and did something. *Anything*. He could check whether the house was shut up, ask the locals about Maitland, whether he'd been behaving oddly, for instance. The innkeepers would know all sorts of gossip. Chances were he'd pick up nothing, but he had to try. If Maitland had been involved in the attack on Alma, even if he hadn't done it himself, he was not going to get away with it.

And he ought to be able to make his enquiries without Maitland knowing anything about it – he'd double-checked Maitland's whereabouts: he was attending a meeting of the council this afternoon.

All the same, as he laboured up and down the rolling roads, freewheeling into dips, standing on the pedals to get up the steeper inclines, battling a wind that seemed sometimes to want to be a headwind, sometimes a buffeting crosswind, he realized he was being followed.

At first, he thought he was just becoming obsessed with the idea of being persecuted. After all, these were picturesque roads full of holiday makers, and there'd be plenty of locals who cycled about their everyday business too. He'd heard that the blacksmith in Keswick had apparently built his own machine, though why he'd not simply gone for one of the most reputable and expert builders was a mystery. There was no reason at all why there should not be a hundred cyclists on this road. Even though it was, as he'd expected, pretty horrible – too many curves and twists to get up a decent speed, and potholes galore from the multitude of carriages that used it.

He couldn't say exactly why he knew he was being followed. There was certainly a cyclist behind him because he caught a glimpse of him on the many occasions the road took odd turns and doubled back on itself. He was riding into increasingly barren country and the dry stone walls were not high – if he glanced back he could see the cyclist, dark and lithe, climbing the same hills he had just come up.

He could be just a local. Well, there was one way to be sure.

At the inn at Threlkeld, he pulled off the road and concealed himself behind a large tree to one side of the inn yard where he could have a perfect view of the road. He waited.

Nobody came. Perhaps the cyclist had turned off – there'd been a few farms along the way. No, here he came, slowing as he crested the hill …

The cyclist put one foot on the ground, glanced round, frowning.

Eppie walked out of cover. 'Why are you following me, Dick?'

32

Dick regarded him in considerable exasperation. 'I could ask why *you're* hiding from me!'

'I asked first. Why are you following me?'

Dick pulled off the road and leant his machine against the tree alongside Eppie's. 'You'll shout me out.'

'Tell me the truth and we'll see.'

Dick was incapable of smiling, or grinning, in unalloyed pleasure like other people. The best he could manage, as now, was a sour, lopsided grimace.

'Crellin asked me to follow you.'

'The inspector!'

'Saw him at the railway station. I was on my way out for a training run anyway – he said you were off out, and he wanted an eye kept on you.'

'He still suspects me!'

'You're a suspicious character, Eppie.'

'I am not!'

'You were the first one to point out Wetherall was murdered—'

'Which should be a point in my favour.'

'And you had a motive—'

'Nonsense!'

'And you're clearly intent upon getting out of town.'

Eppie sighed. Even the most innocent move on his part, a mere afternoon out of town, and everyone immediately thought he was fleeing.

'Do the inspector a favour, Eppie.' Dick dug a package out of the bag on the back of his machine and started unwrapping a heavy-looking piece of cake. 'He doesn't seriously suspect you – if he did, he'd never have allowed you to leave town at all. He simply wants to know what you're doing.'

'Then why not ask one of his constables to follow me?'

'You'd recognize any one of them a mile off.'

'I recognize you too.'

'Yes, but I've a reason to be here and they wouldn't.'

'Oh good,' Eppie said. 'You mean the inspector thought that would make it easier for you to spy on me. And you agreed to do this? I don't exactly regard it as the act of a friend.'

Dick chewed his way through a portion of the cake, wrapped up the rest of it and stowed it back in his bag.

'You mean a friend isn't supposed to help you out? He isn't supposed to help cover up whatever nefarious mission you're off to carry out? No, don't interrupt. That lamp,' he pointed at the offending article on the front of Eppie's machine. 'You wouldn't be bringing that on a training run, or the bag of clothes. You've brought those because you're planning to be out after dark. The lamp is because you're a law-abiding citizen and don't want to get fined for not having lights after lighting-up time – the clothes are because it'll be cold in the evening. Now, why should you want to train after dark? Especially this far from home. Potholed roads like these can be treacherous even with a light. And if you do crash, just a fortnight before the Easter Sports – even if you don't do yourself much damage – just take a bit of skin off maybe – you'll lessen your chances of winning.'

He paused. Eppie was stunned by all this verbosity. It was usually as much as he could do to get two or three sentences out of Dick. Dick gave him that sour look again.

'You're not the only one who can *detect*, Eppie. And if you think I don't know that Algernon Maitland lives out this way, you're very much mistaken. You can't be paying him a friendly visit because he'll be at the council meeting. So what are you up to?'

'Training,' Eppie said obstinately.

'Because,' Dick said, 'I might just give you a hand.'

There was a convenient low wall only a short distance from the tree; they sat in sunshine, and Dick laughed.

'I never thought I'd end up confiding in you, Eppie. Rival number one on the track. I didn't think I'd ever give you any quarter.'

'What happens on the track and what happens off it are two different things.'

'Good old Eppie. Always stating the obvious.'

Eppie unwrapped one of Alma's biscuits, which looked a great deal more appetizing than Dick's heavy cake. 'What do you have against Maitland?'

Dick regarded an oak tree, with its bare crooked arms upheld against the sky. Sometimes getting him to talk seemed like trying to put air in a solid tyre.

'Came down the pit one day.'

'What, actually below ground?'

Dick laughed sourly. The sun caught his eyes and made them glint rather malevolently. And if that wasn't being over-fanciful Eppie didn't know what was.

'Not him – think he'd get himself dirty? He came to visit just as the shifts were changing. Wanted to look around to get some ideas on how to run a pit – thinking of buying one apparently. Or buying a share in one anyway. We'd just come up.' He turned those glinting eyes on Eppie. 'Ever been down the pit?'

'No, and I never intend to.'

'It's dark.'

'So I've always supposed.'

'And we came up into bright sunshine – lovely summer's day. Sunshine blinded me. I couldn't see a damn thing. Squinting and peering at shadows. I just headed for the gate with everyone else. You've been that way so often you know the path without thinking about it, your feet turn in the right direction of their own accord. Only this day there was a stupid idiot called Algernon Maitland in the way.'

'Ah,' Eppie said.

'And a patch of mud right behind him, because it had been raining overnight.'

'And the two of them made acquaintance?'

'If he hadn't been a stupid bastard in the wrong place, I'd never have barged into him and he'd never have fallen over.'

'He blamed you for the incident.'

'Wanted me fired. Came damn close to doing it too. Except the foreman had more sense. But I had to apologize, grovel to the man. And he was still demanding my dismissal even after that! So they said they'd fire me and got rid of him and then told me to lie low for a while. He was supposed to come back the next day and they told me not to come in for the next shift. So I didn't, and he didn't turn up and I lost the pay anyway.'

There was plainly a lot he was not saying, but for Dick this was already a great deal more than he usually said on personal matters.

'So,' he finished. 'If you're planning to do Maitland down, Eppie, I'll happily lend you a hand. More than happily. You think he murdered Wetherall.'

Eppie shook his head. Actually, having a helping hand would be nice, and with Alma not well and gone back home, and Amos being problematic at the moment, that didn't leave him with many people to call upon.

'Maitland couldn't have killed personally. He was in a council meeting. But he could have got someone else to do it. And he was certainly the one with the best reason for doing so.'

'Why?'

Eppie explained about Miss Wetherall and her father's reservations about the match. Dick laughed. 'Just because the fellow is a Liberal? God, there are worse things than having the wrong politics. Like not having enough money to eat or to pay the rent.'

'Don't forget the cheating on IOUs. The irony is that Miss Wetherall isn't too keen, either. Not handsome enough, apparently.'

'How do you know that?'

'She told me. The thing is, Maitland is apparently short of cash …'

Dick stared. 'Is he?'

'He's a betting man.'

Dick started to say something then stopped. Then started again. 'Then what was he doing talking about buying into a pit?'

'Bluffing? Or thinking about using his bride's wealth maybe. The point is that Miss Wetherall won't get the money until her father dies …' He stopped.

'What's wrong now?'

'I'm an idiot. I shouldn't be here. I should be in town. Because the person most at risk isn't me. It's *Mrs Wetherall*. Wetherall left his wife a life interest in the estate – the daughter won't get the money until the mother dies!'

Dick grabbed his arm as he leapt up. 'Wait, wait! *Think*, man! So the girl won't get the money until her mother dies – so what? Maitland can't have the woman killed here and now, even supposing you're right about him. One death is suspicious enough, but the moment two of them slip their moorings, even Crellin will get the message. There must be dozens of suspects to kill Wetherall, his political cronies, business partners, disgruntled employees. But the moment the woman dies too, that says *family* straight away. Maitland will be the first suspect in the firing line. No, he'll wait – marry the girl, invite the mother to live with them, arrange an accident in a year or two, or slip something into the woman's tea …'

Eppie shook his head. 'He can't wait that long. Everything I've heard suggests he needs the money *now*.'

'Then marrying the girl won't help. They can't go ahead with the ceremony until the year of mourning is out.'

'They might,' Eppie said. 'The girl may be with child.'

'Then Maitland didn't kill Wetherall,' Dick said. 'If there's a child on the way, Wetherall would have agreed to the marriage, to protect the family's reputation.'

Eppie couldn't sit still, couldn't stand still. He had to do something. Anything. He paced up and down the yard, to the tree and back, to the wall and back.

'Besides,' Dick said. 'What would you say to the woman? "Mrs Wetherall, your future son-in-law is plotting to kill you"? She'd ask you for evidence and you have none. Either that, or she'd just throw you out straight off.'

He had a point.

'And what are you planning to do at Maitland's country house? You're going to break in, aren't you? What good will that do you? He's hardly likely to have kept the murder weapon.'

'He didn't do it himself,' Eppie repeated. 'He was in a meeting. He had to have an accomplice.'

As usual, he was beginning to feel low, depressed even, in Dick's presence. Though the man was talking perfect sense. Perhaps that was it: Eppie persisted in hoping for something better than everyday common sense. Maybe that was why he raced, to get a little excitement into his life. Maybe that was why he was heading for Maitland's house now.

Though he didn't much like the excitement of being suspected of murder.

'Let's just do a ride round and go back to town,' Dick said. The edge of soothing in his voice was horribly annoying. Like a man trying to calm a fractious child. 'I haven't changed my shifts to go burgling. I want to get some training in and it's a damn good day for it. Mrs Wetherall's safe enough. Nothing's going to happen to her. And you're biased against Maitland because he's an arrogant bastard. Just sit at home and let the whole business die down. Everything will be nice and quiet by the time of the Easter Sports.'

Eppie paused in mid-step, turned from contemplation of the oak tree to stare at Dick. 'I'd have thought you'd want quite the opposite. If I'm in an agitated state at the Sports, I'll probably ride badly and you can get the better of me.'

Dick grinned, that nasty sour leer. 'I'm going to get the better of you anyway, Eppie.'

'Oh, that's better. I was beginning not to recognize you. All this concern for me. Not your usual style at all.'

Dick said, 'Crellin promised me a florin if I bring you back safe and sound.'

That took Eppie's breath away for a moment. Dick was taking money to keep an eye on him? Then he was genuinely amused.

'You know why, don't you? He admitted this morning he couldn't arrest me until after the Sports – he has ten shillings on me. No policeman could afford to lose that kind of money. Right!' He disentangled his machine from Dick's and swung his leg over the saddle. 'Come on then.'

There was no sign of movement from Dick. He eased the machine round in a circle, put a foot down again. Dick was still sitting on the wall, with such a look of anger on his face ...

'You don't like it, do you? You don't like the fact that Crellin's bet on me, not on you.'

Dick grabbed his bicycle. 'I'm going to beat the hell out of you on Easter Monday, Eppie. I'm going to be so far ahead of you, you'll be lucky to see my arse!'

'Don't count on it.' Eppie pedalled lazily to the road. 'Come on then, make your choice. Are you going back to town or are you coming to Maitland's house with me?'

Dick ran up beside him, pushing the machine. 'You're an idiot.'

How could he explain his total and utter conviction that this was what he had to do?

'No? See you later then.'

He trod down hard on the pedals and took the slope up out of the inn yard onto the road. As he crested the little summit, he twisted to glance back.

Dick was following him.

He grinned – and went gliding down the slope of the road with a mad feeling of exultation.

33

MAITLAND'S COUNTRY RESIDENCE was as different from his town residence as any place could be. The town house was stylish and modern, and on the few occasions Eppie had passed, had looked well-kept. The country house was little more than an uncomfortable amalgamation of a pele tower and a large farmhouse, with some added pretention from the days of King George. The tower, once an isolated stronghold against the invasions of the Scots, had been done up at some time with large windows, and had been allowed to be overgrown by a creeper of some sort – Eppie wasn't well up on plants. Then it presumably had the farmhouse attached, in the no-nonsense way of the border country, and *that* had then had windows added and a door with a rather clumsy porch which looked like it was an afterthought no one had quite had the nerve to admit didn't work.

Add in two false windows painted on the upper storey to produce a symmetrical frontage, a lot more creeper (ivy?) and an arch which presumably led to stables behind, and it all looked rather – well, indecisive. As if the occupants hadn't been able to agree on what kind of a house they wanted.

There were obvious signs of neglect too: a hayfield in front of the house which was probably supposed to be a lawn; roses which straggled everywhere and were clogged with weeds, a gravel carriage drive covered with grass.

'You're right,' Dick said. 'No money. Though he puts on a fine enough show in town.' He sounded bitter. 'Always has money enough for his women.'

'I wonder how much he owes.' Eppie looked around for a suitable place to leave his bicycle and settled on a corner behind the open lodge gates. The lodge itself looked deserted: no curtains at the windows, cobwebs drawing lines between the doorjamb and the door knob. 'I'm not sure there's anyone here.'

Dick pushed his machine even further back into bushes. 'Don't want it stolen. Anyone can see in through that gate.'

'You have a poor view of human nature.'

'A realistic one,' Dick retorted. 'Here, I forgot this.' He pulled a crumpled grimy piece of paper out of his pocket. 'The bill for your furniture. I was going to push it under your door.'

Eppie stuffed it in his own pocket. 'Come on then.' He set off along the carriage drive, only to be caught by the sleeve.

Dick glared at him. 'What are you doing?'

'I'm going to knock on the front door.'

'And ask if Maitland's in, I suppose?'

'Exactly.'

He ignored Dick's snort of derision and headed for that big clumsy porch with the door sheltering beneath it. There were curtains on the lower floors but none upstairs. No hint of movement inside. No dog. That was significant – landowners like Maitland always had dogs. One ought to have come bounding round from the stable yard by now, barking furiously.

The porch had cobwebs too, ornamenting the corners of the porch with heavy swags of grey. Eppie turned for the arch to the stable yard, trailed by Dick swearing softly beneath his breath. Under the arch, he stopped.

Dick walked into his back. 'What the devil are you playing at?'

Eppie pointed. In patches of hardened ground under the arch were the clear marks of horses' hooves.

'Ages old,' Dick scoffed.

'But they show someone still comes here.' And was that the hint of a wheel track too?

He went on, more cautiously, taking a step or two inside the yard to look around. Signs of neglect were obvious here too. Slates off the roof of the stable block on his right, a window broken in what was evidently the scullery. Grass growing verdantly between the cobbles of the yard.

He called, 'Hello? Anyone here?'

Behind him, Dick laughed out loud. 'My God, Eppie, you really are a fool, aren't you?'

'I don't know why you're here, if all you intend to do is insult me. I'm a hairdresser. Aren't we all soft fools, compared with you hardy miners?'

'That's right.'

Eppie went across to the stable block and just avoided stepping in horse droppings inside the door. The droppings were crusted over and looked a week or two old. The horse wasn't there now.

'It has to have been Maitland, surely. What other gentleman would want to come here?'

'You can't prove it was Maitland,' Dick said again with a wolfish grin. He was plainly enjoying baiting Eppie.

'Only a gentleman has a horse, or a professional man like a vicar.'

'Or a doctor.'

'Don't you read your *Cycling* magazine? Doctors nowadays are finding a tricycle much more convenient for their rounds. Apart from anything else, you don't have to feed it or call out someone to take care of it when it's sick.'

Eppie went back out into the yard, Dick trailing after him, still grinning. Across to the scullery door. He stood back. 'Notice anything?'

'No.'

'Exactly. No great swathes of cobwebs. Just the odd one or two.' He reached for the latch. The door resisted then gave way, opening onto darkness.

Dick took hold of his arm. 'Why should anyone leave the door open? This could be dangerous.'

'I'm not coming all this way and not having a look.' Eppie peered round the door. After a moment, his eyes adjusted to semi-darkness. He made out a Berlin sink, wooden draining board, the sad remains of a mangle with a broken leg. The whole place smelt musty and dank. 'Look. Footprints – heading straight through the scullery for the house. They've dusted over again slightly. All this suggests that someone was here relatively recently, maybe a week or two ago.'

Dick glanced around. 'Someone could have broken that window then opened the door from inside. Got in through the window, out through the door.'

Eppie peered at the window dubiously – it looked as if it might have been broken years ago.

'Why would Maitland need to break into his own house?'

'You don't *know* that it was Maitland who was here.'

Eppie sighed. 'So you keep reminding me.'

'All this *detection*,' Dick said contemptuously. 'It's guesswork.'

'I was right about Wetherall being murdered though, wasn't I?'

'That's your problem,' Dick said. 'You always think you're right.'

Eppie followed the trail of footsteps into the house. Beyond the scullery was a dusty passage, leading past an empty butler's pantry and steps down into, presumably, the cellar. Then a heavy door which took some pushing and they were out into the main part of the house. He looked round a hall heavily wood-panelled in an old-fashioned style. The windows on either side of the main door were filthy, dust-covered. Not much light.

The footsteps in the dust led across the hall to a door on the far side, but as they came to the bottom of a flight of stairs there was a confusion of prints and a fainter trail seemed to lead upwards. Eppie hesitated.

'If you think I'm going up there,' Dick said, 'you're very much mistaken. Those stairs look rotten.'

They did. Slightly reluctantly, Eppie headed for the door on the far side of the hall. It had been a dining room at some period, not too long ago – the dust was marked with round dimples where the legs of a long large table had stood. And the marks of at least six or seven chairs. He glanced at Dick, who put his hands on his hips in annoyance. 'If you're going to ask me if I notice anything again, I'll personally dispose of you and leave you here!'

'These are marks where a table and some chairs once stood. The dust in the room is thick, the product of months if not years. But the marks of the table legs have only a thin covering of dust. Therefore the furniture was removed recently. Note the pale patches on the walls too, where there used to be pictures. I haven't yet seen one stick of furniture in this house, apart from the broken mangle. He's been selling it all off.'

'You're right about him not having money then,' Dick said grimly. 'Where are you going now?!'

'Upstairs.'

'I told you, those steps are rotten.'

'I'll walk at the very edges.' He suited the action to the word, treading carefully up the sides of the bottom two or three steps. The owner of the footprints had done the same.

He stopped halfway up.

'Now what?'

'There are two sets of footprints, not one.' He stared down at Dick who was still hovering at the foot of the stairs. 'You can't see it on the bottom steps because the second man has stepped directly in the footsteps of the first. But it's clearer here.'

Dick came up behind him, looked silently at the evidence. 'So?'

Eppie went on up. It was remarkably lucky that all the carpets had been taken up – presumably they'd been valuable. That left bare floorboards where the footprints showed up clearly. They headed for a room just to the left of the landing, but when Eppie pushed the door open there was nothing, and no one, inside.

'The footsteps go on up to the attics,' Dick said. He'd not moved from the landing. Eppie nodded and sighed. Dick was plainly determined not to go up first – presumably he'd decided that if anyone was going to fall through the stairs it would be Eppie.

The stairs narrowed but were still remarkably fine – decent carving on the banisters. At the top Eppie started sneezing. 'The dust is even thicker up here.'

Dick pointed to the left. Eppie nodded and followed the scuff marks in the dust. All the way to the end room, where the owner, or owners, of the marks had evidently hesitated. There was a small window on the gable wall – Eppie peered out into the dilapidated stable yard.

'They must have paused here to look out.' He pushed open the door of the attic room. 'And then …'

Dick ploughed straight into the back of him. 'Go on in, for God's sake!'

'No,' Eppie said. 'I'd rather not. There's quite a lot of blood.'

34

THE ROOM STANK. A heavy tang of corruption that made Eppie want to retch. Odd – he hadn't felt that revulsion when he'd seen Wetherall's body. But then there'd only been a neat puddle of blood beneath the man's head. This was different – there were crawly things and buzzing things about the body and a green-grey tinge to what little skin he could see.

'God!' Dick said behind him. 'That's foul.'

Eppie inched forward. The man lay flat on his back, with his arms a little spread but not unnaturally so. A man who'd possibly been about forty, with luxuriant whiskers and the sort of clothes that are expensive but not particularly fashionable. The sort of clothes a professional man wears to inspire confidence in his solid worth.

There was no visible wound. Not from this distance, anyway, and Eppie had no difficulty in deciding against the idea of getting any closer. He glanced at Dick. Dick was standing in the doorway, looking oddly determined. As if he was forcing himself not to run off. Eppie knew exactly how that felt.

'That black stuff under the body looks like dried blood.'

Dick said nothing.

'So maybe he was stabbed? Or shot? Even if it wasn't immediately fatal, he'd have bled to death after his attacker ran off. Actually,' he amended conscientiously, 'he *must* have bled to death, because if the wound had killed him immediately, he wouldn't have bled at all.'

Dick rolled his eyes. 'Let's get out of here.'

'We have to report this to the local constable.'

'Report it!' Dick's voice rose a notch or two. 'Eppie, have you completely lost your wits? We're illegally in this house. We broke in.'

'No, we didn't – the door was open.'

'You think the police are going to believe that? The scullery window was broken – they'll say that's how we got in. They'll think you were burgling Maitland's house to get revenge on him for suggesting you murdered Wetherall. Add to that the fact you're already a murder suspect, and they'll clap you in prison!'

'But this man is a total stranger. Why should I have killed him?'

'You don't know who he is.' Dick gestured wildly at the body. He had control of his voice again but there was a distinct hint of panic in his tone. 'Suppose he turns out to be a diamond merchant from London who had a bag of stones worth millions? Which is now nowhere to be seen.'

'Oh, that's ridiculously far-fetched!'

'*You don't know!*' Dick insisted. 'You have not the slightest idea what you might be getting yourself into. But you do know …' He prodded Eppie in the chest. 'You *do* know you're the chief suspect for Wetherall's murder and you're deliberately getting yourself involved in another death. You're a complete idiot!'

'We can't just leave him lying here.'

'*I* can,' Dick said and suited the action to the word, striding out of the room.

Eppie looked at the body. The sound of Dick's footsteps, echoing in the uncurtained, uncarpeted house, faded down the stairs. Outside, a crow cawed, which was more than Eppie appreciated. Dick was right – and he didn't like that either. But it went against the grain to leave a man lying dead, uncoffined, unblessed and unburied. The man might have a wife and children wondering where he was. And he might, at the very least, be a clue to what exactly was going on …

Carefully, Eppie skirted the black fingers of dried blood and gingerly reached for the man's coat. Lifting the material carefully, trying not to disturb anything creeping or crawling or buzzing, he felt in the pockets for papers, or a notebook. Anything that might help identify the man. Nothing in the coat and he wasn't about to try turning the body over to get at any pockets at the man's back. There were a few coins in the trouser pockets. As far as he could tell that was the only money on the body. Had robbery been the motive then? Eppie peered at the man's hands. There were clear signs he'd once worn at least two rings – the paler bands of flesh around the fingers were unmistakable.

So was it as simple as the man had come to the house for some legitimate reason – to assess its worth at sale, for instance – and had been surprised by a tramp who was living here (having got in by the broken window) and killed for the valuables he had on him? That didn't sound unreasonable but it *would* mean that this second death wasn't connected to Wetherall's, that it was a mere coincidence.

Well, coincidences did happen.

At which point Eppie realized that if he was right and this man *had* been killed by a tramp, then said tramp might still be in residence in another room and might have no scruples about killing a second time …

He got up hurriedly – and spotted a corner of white beneath the man's right shoulder. Turning up his nose in distaste, he tugged at the corner. A business card, with writing in beautifully printed copperplate. It slid out at last, horribly blotched with blood. The blood obscured parts of the text but left enough for him to distinguish the essentials: *Philip Greenways* and a portion of an address in Lincoln's Inn, London. The man was – or had been – a lawyer.

He pushed the card back under the man's shoulder. Maybe he could tell the police anonymously and they could find the body and the card for themselves. He'd have to think about it. He headed for the stairs.

At the top of the flight, he thought he heard a noise downstairs.

'Dick?'

No answer. Probably Dick. Almost certainly Dick. No, he must be long gone. Probably cycling along the back lanes even now on his way back to Keswick. Then who'd made that noise? Damn it, he wished he hadn't thought of that tramp!

He ran down the stairs, reached the second storey. There was an entire mess of footprints on the landing – the original ones and their own. Dear God, their footprints would be in the dust of the room with the body too. He hesitated. Should he go back up and try and get rid of the footprints? He'd need a brush. Maybe there was one in the scullery.

He would never get involved in anything like this again, not ever. Maybe he should tell Crellin about the body after all. Could someone tell one set of footprints from another? Maybe, if there were identifying features. He stood on his left leg, holding onto the banister, and lifted his right foot to peer at the sole of his shoe. It didn't look anything out of the ordinary. No cuts or nicks. Nothing on the other shoe either.

This was ridiculous! He ran down the stairs and headed for the back of the house. If there was a brush in the scullery he'd use it, if not he'd just leave and hope for the best. If only he hadn't come here!

Through the heavy door into the servants' quarters. He stopped dead as the door clattered shut behind him.

'Dick?'

Someone was moving around here, definitely. In the cellar? At a run he headed for the scullery. Never mind who was here, never mind if he looked a fool. He just wanted to get out of this house. There was a dead man upstairs and the murderer might still be here. Eppie wasn't going to be the unlucky third victim. Absolutely definitely not.

He stumbled to a halt in the scullery. There was something wrong, something different.

The mangle. The mangle had been shifted.

He caught a glimpse of movement in the corner of the room, jolted into action. Sprinted for the back door to the yard. Something caught him a glancing blow on the back of his right shoulder. Pain stabbed through his arm. He kept running. Jerked the back door open. Out onto the uneven cobbles in the bright sunshine. He turned for the arch to the carriage drive, glanced back. A man stood in the doorway of the scullery, a hat pulled down, a muffler pulled up …

He didn't care who it was. He *particularly* didn't want to know who it was. He hurtled across the cobbles. The arch never seemed to get any closer! He stubbed a toe on an upraised cobble, flung out his arms to try and keep his balance, went down anyway, flat on his face. He gasped for air, winded, scrabbled to get up again. Running footsteps …

A woman shouted, 'Don't move! I'm armed!'

Alma?!

The footsteps got nearer. A tremendous bang. Eppie jumped, lay still. Now someone was shooting at him! Was this nightmare never going to end?

More running footsteps. Wait a minute – weren't they heading back for the house? He squirmed on the cobbles, peered back. Caught a glimpse of heels disappearing back into the scullery.

'Eppie!'

He got onto hands and knees. Alma was furiously beckoning to him from the arch. He scrambled up, sprinted over to her. She caught his arm as he dashed through the arch, hauled him to one side.

'Quick, on the bicycle!'

She had his machine there. He vaulted onto it in the best manner recommended by French doctors for athletic exercise. Alma was already on her machine, pedalling madly across the gravel carriage drive towards the lodge. He spurted after her, praying for no punctures.

The lodge gate loomed up ahead. Alma leaned her body weight over and took the bend to the right at top speed. She'd abandoned the sling, Eppie noticed.

He kept on her wheel, twisting and turning in the narrow lanes for at least two miles. Then he saw the urgency go out of her, her shoulders sagged, she slowed. She put out a hand to indicate she was pulling into the side of the road.

Eppie put a foot down. He was breathing heavily, but Alma was worse. She was pale; perspiration ran down her cheeks. Eppie put out a hand to steady her.

'Are you all right?'

She shook her head, put her hand up to her left shoulder. 'I think I may have made the injury worse.'

He glanced around. Beyond a field gate lay a small copse of trees with a heavy undergrowth of evergreen bushes. He pushed open the gate, ushered Alma through – she had hardly the strength to pedal. Once in the wood, he helped her off the machine, lowered her to a seat on a fallen tree trunk. He brought both machines deep into the wood and propped them behind some bushes. If they kept seated, they wouldn't be seen from the road.

Alma looked faint. Eppie broke open his bag, found the cup he had there, and went in search of a stream. When he came back with water, Alma was leaning against a silver birch and looking better. She sipped the water and, after a little hesitation, accepted his offer of one of her own cakes.

'What are you doing here? I saw you onto the train.'

'I got off at the next stop.' She regarded him with weak but fond amusement. 'Eppie, did you seriously think I was going to let you do anything so foolish as to search Maitland's house on your own?'

He sighed. 'You knew.'

'Of course I did! As soon as you said you were heading this way I knew you must be going to Maitland's house. You've always said you don't like this run so I knew you wouldn't be doing it for pleasure.'

He regarded her with admiration. 'Where did you get a gun?'

She managed a grin. 'I didn't. There was an old bucket by the arch and an ancient padlock on the outhouse door. The padlock was so rusty it came away in my hands. I dropped the padlock into the bucket and it made a lovely sound. It convinced *you*, didn't it?'

'As long as it convinced my attacker too. Alma, I found another dead body!'

He told her all that had happened and made her eat another piece of cake. She was looking much better but he couldn't imagine how she could have ridden all the way here, or how she was going to ride all the way back. Though they could just go to Keswick railway station and get the train back home from there …

'He was a lawyer?' she said at last. 'All the way from London. It must have been serious then.'

'I was wondering if he came up here to tell Maitland he was foreclosing on the estate. Maitland would have cause to kill him then – he wouldn't want anyone to know about that. All his local creditors would be on his back straight away.'

'But killing the lawyer wouldn't stop the foreclosure happening.'

'It would prevent the knowledge of it getting out.' He added, indignantly, 'I wasn't on my own anyway. Dick came with me. Didn't you see his bicycle next to mine?'

She shook her head. 'There was only yours, just inside the gate.'

So Dick had made off with great speed. There was a suspicious bit of Eppie that wondered if Dick had in fact realized rather earlier than Eppie that the murderer might still be around, and had decided that discretion, as the proverb insisted, was the better part of valour. Though warning your friends of possible danger wasn't apparently part of traditional advice.

'Do you think you can ride? I thought we'd go back to Keswick railway station and get the train from there.'

She bit her lip. 'I think so. If we go slowly. You don't think …'

'What?'

'That the man who attacked you might follow us?'

'No, no.' He shook his head. 'Not on the public highway. I know it's not particularly busy but it would be far too risky.'

All the same, he kept an eye open all the way back for anyone who might be following them – and he didn't tell Alma that he thought there was.

35

THE COST OF taking *two* bicycles on the train was exorbitant – so exorbitant Eppie resolved on the spot to write to *Cycling* about it. But it was worth it to hear Alma's relieved sigh as she sank into the seat in their compartment. She dozed off as they pulled out of Keswick heading for Cockermouth and by the time they'd gone two miles, her head was on his shoulder. He did not correct the elderly sentimental woman who murmured that 'his wife was tired out, poor thing.'

It was well past supper time, well past dark, when he left Alma at her aunt's to be cooed over and cosseted, and rode off back towards the town centre on his way home. He was desperately hungry and stopped to eat his last biscuit. It gave him a little extra energy to push down on the pedals. He went automatically, almost as if the machine knew its own way home, turning the corners without thinking much about it. His mind was on the scene in Maitland's house, the blood, the dead man staring up at the cracked ceiling. Someone's son, someone's husband, probably, someone's father.

He couldn't remember when he'd last been so angry.

He pulled up, putting his foot to the ground as an empty farm cart lumbered past, realized that he was almost opposite Wetherall's house. He wheeled across the road, peered between bushes. No lights at all. Not one. Surely even if the family was out, there'd be servants in the house. Presumably they'd be in the back, but even so lights would surely be kept burning at the front, if only to deter burglars.

He hesitated, looking down the lane that ran down the side of the house to the stables at the rear. It was almost completely dark. So dark he couldn't even see the window that had been lit the last time, the one from which Miss Wetherall said she'd looked out.

Something was nagging at him, something he couldn't put a name to. Something he thought he'd missed. Or that he hadn't seen that he should have. Something not quite right. He glanced around. No one in the street. Only the distant rear of the cart disappearing into the distance, heading out into the country.

He dismounted, turned his bicycle so it faced home and leant it against the hedge at the front of the Wetherall residence. Then he went, as softly as he could, down the cobbled lane.

The window in the wall on his left must be the one from which Miss Wetherall had looked out. It was a narrower window than he had imagined. Unlit. He cupped his hand against the glass and tried to peer in. Mere shadows inside. Not very helpful.

The rest of the wall was blank. At the back corner, the cobbled lane took a turn to the left into a smallish yard with a stable at the very rear. A horse snuffled inside the stable, its hooves clattering briefly on the floor. Eppie froze. Did horses whinny at the first whiff of an intruder like dogs did? Well, dogs barked, obviously, not whinnied, but …

This was ridiculous. He shouldn't be here. What on earth had he thought he might learn?

There was a small extension on the far side of the yard. Servants' quarters probably. A dim light behind closed curtains. A woman laughed. A rumble of lower voices. Eppie held his breath. He sidled across to one of the windows of the main house – there were only two on the ground floor. The curtains of the first one fortunately didn't quite meet; by shifting about he could see a banked-up fire, the embers glowing a cosy shade of red, lots of bookshelves, big leather armchairs, the corner of a desk. A very masculine room – Wetherall's den, apparently, though why a fire should have been lit there when he was dead was not obvious.

Eppie tiptoed to the next ground-floor window. The curtains here were undrawn. The faint light from the extension gleamed on a well-polished dining-room table with a silver centrepiece, rather vulgar from what Eppie could see of it – curling tendrils and extravagant flowers.

The woman laughed again inside the extension. The sound of a chair being scraped back.

Eppie bolted for the street.

He cycled up into town. Past the Town Hall, not being able to resist a detour to the side door to see if there were any more cigars. Of course not. No sign of the tramp either which was more to the point. He went on to the police station, propping his machine against a lamppost and praying no one would dare to steal it from such a place. Inside, the policeman at the desk was dozing, his head drooping against the wall. A black and white cat prowled through from the inner rooms, yawned at Eppie and strolled back again.

Eppie cautiously prodded the policeman. The man snorted, jumped, said sleepily, 'What?'

'I want to see Inspector Crellin.'

'Not here,' said the constable and let his head drop back against the wall.

Exasperated, Eppie went home. He'd have to see Crellin in the morning. How early did the inspector get in to work? If Eppie gave up his training session (again!) would he catch him first thing? Or should he go just before work and open the shop late? After all, the customers wouldn't be queuing up. But could he concentrate on training knowing that poor man was lying dead in Maitland's house?

He still had to take the bicycle in through the front of the house – he really must get that back gate fixed! He was fiddling with his front door keys when he heard a noise behind him. He swung, raising his fist …

Crellin jumped, face blanching. His hat fell off. 'Mr Epford!'

'I thought you were … someone else.' How lame that sounded! 'I thought someone was following me.'

'I haven't been following you! I've been waiting for you. For hours! I thought you weren't coming back. Let's go in, for God's sake.' He dipped to snatch up his hat, cast nervous glances around. 'All the neighbours will be watching. That McCormack woman. She knows everything that happens in town.'

Was it worth chatting to her and asking about Wetherall? Probably not.

'Well, everything that happens in this street, certainly,' Eppie admitted and pushed the door open. He gestured Crellin into the warm darkness but Crellin gave him a shove to go first. Did he suspect there was someone in here? Eppie wheeled the bicycle inside and set about turning up the lights and checking the rooms. Crellin shut the front door behind him with a bang, followed Eppie into the kitchen.

'I've got to talk to you.'

'I've just been to the police station to find you.' Eppie slipped off his coat, hung it over one of the kitchen chairs, headed for the kettle. 'I've found another body.'

Crellin had opened his mouth to say something. He shut it again. Stared. Opened his mouth again. 'Eh?'

'I went for a ride as I told you. I ended up at Maitland's country house, the other side of Keswick.'

'Just by chance, I dare say.'

Eppie decided not to rise to that sarcastic bait. 'The scullery window had been broken and the door was open. The whole place is deserted. Not a stick of furniture in the place, not a picture or carpet.'

'What, burglars?'

Eppie hadn't considered that. 'They'd hardly take the lot, would they?' He put the kettle on to boil. 'No, actually, judging by the dust, the furniture was long gone. And there was a body.'

'You *did* have a good look around, didn't you?'

There was an odd note in Crellin's voice, which made Eppie glance at him, puzzled. 'Don't tell me you haven't considered Maitland as a suspect for Wetherall's murder?'

'All the time,' Crellin said tartly. 'I don't break into his house to see what I can come up with, though.'

'I told you, I didn't break in. The door was open.' Eppie spread his hands. 'Would I be telling you this if I'd done anything wrong? I simply wanted to look around and see if I could find any clues.'

'Go on.'

Eppie got out cups and saucers.

'The dead man was in one of the attics.' He described the scene with no difficulty at all – he wasn't sure he would ever forget it. 'There was a business card lying under the body. He was a lawyer, from Lincoln's Inn, in London.'

The inspector pursed his lips. 'Looks like foreclosure, doesn't it? Knowing what we already know about Maitland's money troubles.'

'But why murder the solicitor? At most, you'd only buy yourself a little time. You can't stop foreclosure that way. Even more importantly, why kill someone in your own house? You'd be the first suspect. On the other hand, if you know someone else's house is empty, it would be an ideal place to do nefarious deeds.'

'Are you saying it could just be a coincidence? That some local who knows Maitland never stays in his house any more decided to use it as a convenient place to murder someone?'

'No,' Eppie said reluctantly, pouring water on the leaves in the teapot. 'That doesn't sound convincing, does it? And it gets even more complicated because someone attacked me as I was leaving the house. The murderer, I presume. But the victim had been dead a week or more, maybe two. So why had the murderer lingered there so long – or come back again?'

Crellin scowled at the teapot. 'I hate these cases. Give me a nice drunken brawl and a smashed head any time.'

'You got the smashed head,' Eppie pointed out. 'Though I don't think Wetherall's murderer was drunk.'

'So we have a dead councillor who was hit over the head in an alley and a dead lawyer who was either stabbed or shot in a stately home. Very nice.'

'I didn't see exactly how the lawyer died,' Eppie said conscientiously, 'but there was an awful lot of dried blood. We also have a mysterious man who may or may not have been conspiring with Wetherall. Or possibly threatening him.'

'Or just getting free cigars out of him.' Crellin brooded morosely. 'Well, you'd better give me this lawyer's name and address so I can write to his people in London and tell them he's dead. Maybe they'll know why he came up here.'

'There's more,' Eppie said, handing Crellin a cup and saucer. Crellin groaned. 'Don't worry, it's not another body.'

'Go on. I might as well have the worst of it all at once.' Crellin sipped the tea. 'I don't suppose you've got any of those nice biscuits left?'

'No, I haven't. I draw the line at feeding the constabulary.'

'I haven't had anything to eat all afternoon, thanks to having to wait for you.'

'I don't have any left.' Really, lying got easier every time you did it. 'On my way back here, I passed Wetherall's house and something nagged at me. I thought I'd go and have a look.'

'Oh yes?' Crellin said, in that nasty way policemen have. The way that tells you they anticipate you giving yourself away. Eppie thought carefully how to phrase what he was about to say.

'At the inquest Miss Wetherall said she was in the parlour doing some needlework when she heard her father outside arguing with someone. Someone in the alley at the side of the house.'

'That's right.'

'That's just the point. It *isn't* right. I had a good look at the house tonight. The only window on the side of the house next to the alley is a very narrow one. I couldn't see inside because there were no lights on, but from the position of the window it's obvious that it must give onto the hallway – it's just round the corner from the front door. Then you go down the alley and the house wall is completely blank. Round the back, the alley takes a turn to the left into a back yard. There's an extension which is obviously servants' quarters and there are also two ground-floor windows looking out onto the yard.'

Crellin nodded. 'That's where she was then.'

Eppie shook his head. 'One of the rooms was Wetherall's den or study, the other was a dining room.' He looked at Crellin. 'No parlour. Not on that side of the house. I'm willing to bet the parlour's at the front, on the other side of the front door. It would face south that way, which means it'll get a nice bit of sun in the afternoon. The back of the house faces north, which must make it dark and gloomy.'

'So,' Crellin said, sipping his tea as delicately as any young lady. 'You think Miss Wetherall was lying.'

'I know she was,' Eppie said boldly. 'Her story of overhearing her father arguing with someone was a complete fabrication. She did it deliberately, in order to create a suspect to blame for her father's death. I dare say she didn't mean to implicate anyone in particular, just to create a mysterious someone who couldn't be traced.'

'Why?' Crellin said.

'She's obviously in league with her fiancé. Maitland. Maybe she's afraid of him – he doesn't have a good reputation with regard to ladies, apparently. Or maybe she was happy to go along with it – she's a lot less innocent than she looks, you know. As a matter of fact, she's rather forward. I …'

He trailed off. Crellin had pursed his lips.

'What?'

'Ah,' Crellin said.

Eppie stared. 'What do you mean, *ah*?'

'I mean,' Crellin said, 'you're wrong.'

'Wrong about her lying or wrong about her conspiring with Maitland?'

'As far as the parlour thing is concerned, I'll have to go and have a look. I wouldn't be surprised, mind. She strikes me as a sly one. But you're definitely wrong about the conspiracy with Maitland. For one thing, he's not her fiancé anymore.'

'They've broken it off?' Eppie found himself stirring the tea in the pot energetically. It seemed to help him think. 'That's not to say they didn't plot together. Maybe that's what they argued about.'

'Not broken it off.' Crellin was enjoying himself. 'Not exactly.'

Eppie stared. 'They're married? Is that it? They got married while the girl is still in mourning?'

How obnoxious Crellin could be when he was triumphant. Eppie wished he *had* given him a piece of cake – perhaps it would have kept him sweet.

'No.' Crellin's grin was as wide as a mine pit. 'Maitland's got married, all right, but not to the girl. He's married the mother. The widow. Maud Margaret Wetherall. Twice as old as he is – and twice as rich.'

36

Eppie sat down in one of the kitchen chairs with a thump, got up again, stirred the pot one last time and poured himself a cup of tea. It was strong to the point of being stewed which did him a power of good.

'I know what happened.'

Crellin jumped and spilt tea over the front of his waistcoat. He slapped ineffectually at the wetness.

Eppie took Crellin's cup and topped it up again. 'They're all in it.'

'Who?' Crellin said, bewildered.

'Maitland, and Mrs and Miss Wetherall.'

Crellin said, 'Don't be daft.'

'I *knew* there was something wrong from the moment I saw that dress!' Eppie was exasperated with himself. 'But did I take any notice? No. I just thought: *that's odd* and went on ignoring it …'

'Mr Epford,' Crellin said very carefully. 'Crazy though it sounds, I have no choice but to listen to this idea of yours because otherwise I have absolutely no clue who did these murders. But if you want me to take it seriously, you're going to have to start at the beginning and explain things step by step!'

Eppie took a deep breath and pushed his tea cup to one side. 'Miss Wetherall's dress at the inquest.'

'She was wearing mourning.'

'Very fashionable mourning with lots of frills and flounces and bows and things. Newly-made mourning. *One day* after her father's death. Now I know dressmakers pride themselves on being able to turn out mourning clothes at the shortest of notice, but it wasn't the sort of ensemble you can get here in Maryport. It was London fashions, London-made. She admitted it to me. And given it was so up-to-date, it has to have been made *very* recently. Now I know transport is wonderfully quick these days but you can't send to London for clothes and get them back ready-made and properly fitting, without a fitting, if you see what I mean, in twenty-four hours!'

'Maybe she bought them for another relative who died recently.'

'The headmaster says not.'

'Who?'

'Sorry,' he said hurriedly. 'Someone a friend of mine knows. The only conclusion is that Miss Wetherall, *and* her mother, who has been wearing equally fashionable mourning, knew that Charles Albert Frederick was going to be deceased in the very near future. Add to that the fact that, as I've just proved, Miss Wetherall was lying when she said she heard and saw someone arguing with her father the night before he died, and there's obviously something very wrong.'

Crellin was shaking his head. 'You thought she was upset her father wouldn't allow her marriage to Maitland and therefore decided to get rid of him. But Maitland has gone and married her mother.'

'Miss Wetherall admitted to me only a day or so ago that she had another interest.'

Crellin sat up. 'Not the Smythe boy?'

'Oh really,' Eppie said crossly. 'Did you know all along and not tell me?'

'I didn't think it was relevant.'

'Well, it is. Obviously. Who is this Smythe boy?'

'Well, you didn't tell me about the dresses. He's the son of Mrs Smythe. The chandler's widow.'

Eppie made a face. 'The chandler? When I was a boy they were called Smith. Well, Wetherall certainly wouldn't have approved of that either – a tradesman's son with pretensions?'

'I thought they'd broken it off,' Crellin mused. 'Still … By getting rid of Wetherall, his daughter gets to marry her lowly suitor, and Maitland gets to marry Mrs Wetherall who'll get all the money – a life interest only, of course, but Maitland can spend that as well as any other money. He gets cash enough to pay off his creditors. And no doubt he gives his stepdaughter a nice little dowry as her share of the spoils. Of course, they have to put up with all the disapproval of marrying only a matter of weeks after Wetherall's death but it's not illegal.'

'Exactly.' Eppie was astonished at how pleased he felt. He'd actually come up with the answer! 'It also explains why Mrs Wetherall was a bit, well, shall we say, lax about her daughter's forward habits. Like visiting unmarried gentlemen like me.' He saw Crellin's frown, and hurried on. 'Never mind that. I'm willing to bet she knew all about the Smith boy – she would have been happy to let her daughter look where she liked, as long as she did it discreetly, because she wanted Maitland for herself! And all this business about me – well, they needed someone to be suspected of the murder, of course, to distract attention from themselves, and I was handy, because I'd shown such interest in Wetherall's death. Maybe there was an element of annoyance in it too, because if I hadn't taken a look at the murder scene, it might have passed off as an accident. So they decided to take revenge for that by casting suspicion on me. And by threatening me, to try and get me to leave town. That would immediately have made everyone think I did it.'

'Nice,' Crellin said admiringly.

Eppie felt a sense of foreboding. 'Go on, tell me you don't believe it.'

Crellin pondered. 'Well, it would have been a lot easier simply to work on Wetherall and get him to agree to the marriage between the girl and Maitland.'

'That wouldn't have helped Mrs Wetherall – she needed her husband to die so she could get her hands on the money.'

Crellin sighed. 'As a matter of fact, I *do* believe you. I daresay you haven't had to deal with those three as much as I have, and I can tell you I could believe anything of them. *Not nice* people masquerading as *really nice* principled upstanding citizens. There's only one problem. I can't go to court with only a couple of mourning dresses for evidence.'

'And the matter of the windows – proof Miss Wetherall made that story up.'

Crellin conceded this. 'But there's a whole load of stuff that doesn't fit in. What about these meetings Wetherall had with this mysterious man? I take it you're not suggesting the tramp made that up?'

'No,' Eppie admitted reluctantly.

'And the fact that the ladies were at home and Maitland at a council meeting when the murder took place, so none of them could have done it themselves.'

'They got the mysterious man to do it.'

'The one who was plotting something with Wetherall?'

'He might just have been *pretending* to plot with Wetherall, to gain his trust.'

'And the argument he had with him outside his home that night – that helped gain his trust too, did it?'

'That might never have happened. Remember, we've only Miss Wetherall's word for it and we've just proved she was lying.'

'Blast!' Crellin said feelingly. 'And where does the death of this lawyer come in? Maitland couldn't have done that – he's never left town once since Wetherall's death. Too busy comforting the ladies. Except for one visit to Carlisle to go to the hunt.'

Eppie knew all about *that* trip. He stared at the teapot. 'If the lawyer's been dead two weeks, his murder could have happened *before* Wetherall's death. Just.' He sighed. 'But we agreed Maitland wouldn't be stupid enough to leave a dead body in his own house.'

'Getting someone to do the dirty stuff could be dangerous,' Crellin mused. 'Hire someone like that and you give yourself into their hands. They could take it into their heads to blackmail you over it for the rest of your life. Maitland would find Wetherall's money slipping out of his hands faster than he expected.'

Eppie sat up. 'But that same person might be willing to spill the beans to us – well, to you. To the police. If he found it worth his while. Or if he got angry enough at Maitland.'

'No one is going to admit to murder and put the hangman's noose around his own neck,' Crellin said tartly. 'However angry he gets at the fellow who hired him.'

'Maybe he could be tricked into saying something …'

'If we knew who he was, of course.'

Eppie sighed.

Crellin got up. 'I'll go and sort that body out. And see if anyone knows who Miss Wetherall's new love interest is. I wonder if she *has* got back together with young Smythe …'

'You could try talking to Maitland too. If he thinks he's got away with murder, literally, he might be arrogant enough to let something slip.'

'Nice idea,' Crellin said dryly. 'If only he and his new lady wife hadn't gone off to London for their honeymoon. Out of reach of unpleasant gossip, I reckon. In London, no one need know they married inside the mourning period. Now, don't you start saying something rude, Mr Epford! How was I supposed to stop them? There's no evidence against them. Besides, they'd gone before I knew about it. What are *you* going to do?' He stared with sudden foreboding. 'If you're thinking of having a go at Maitland's town house, don't even consider it! It's full of servants still.'

Eppie threw the remains of the stewed tea down the sink. 'I'm going to have something to eat. Go to bed. Get up and train early tomorrow. And then I will finally get round to seeing the vicar.'

'Planning a wedding?' Crellin looked roguish.

'Not for a few years yet. It's something I ought to have done a while ago, but I kept getting distracted. I think I may know what those meetings between Wetherall and the unknown man were about.'

It rained. All night. For the first hour Eppie lay in bed, sighing heavily as the rain rattled against the window panes and gurgled down the drainpipes. After that, he decided he was going to sleep anyway and surprised himself by doing just that. Or so he found when he woke up next morning.

Some things had to take priority. Alma might be injured, someone might be out to attack him, someone had killed two men. But he was not going to miss training again. There were more important things in life than unpleasant people who were out to do mischief.

Mind you, he could have done without the nasty little surprise he had when he heard something crinkle in his coat pocket and realized it was the bill Dick had given him. Whatever had happened to the agreement they'd made on the price? Dick seemed to have forgotten it. He wasn't going to pay this much – it would definitely have been cheaper to buy new furniture!

The grass track was sodden wet, of course. Eppie decided there and then to put forward a proposal to the club to build a proper cinder track. How on earth was anyone supposed to train properly on sodden grass, let alone race on it? He was in no mood to be thwarted, however, he dumped his bag with his food on the cricket pavilion steps and set off, rather cautiously, admittedly, to do some hard laps.

Halfway through the session, it began to rain again. And Dick turned up and sat on the wet steps of the pavilion, watching Eppie rather sourly. Eppie was inclined to look back sourly. Quite apart from that bill, Dick had walked out on him last night and abandoning someone to a possibly dangerous fate was hardly the act of a friend. He sailed past Dick with his nose in the air. Dick grinned.

A little after nine in the morning, he was at the vicarage, knocking on the door. After a long wait, a neatly-dressed maid edged the door open. She said she'd see if the vicar was at home. Which was a polite way of saying she wasn't sure if the vicar would deign to see him.

He had to wait in a rather sterile looking parlour, which looked as if it was rarely used. None of the comfortable shabbiness of the Carlisle vicarage here. And here came the vicar himself, a thin man with silver hair, who looked as if he had never wielded anything heavier than a pen in his life, even though Eppie had seen him last year, dropping a devilish cricket ball half an inch in front of batsmen's noses. The last match he had broken two fingers, if Eppie remembered rightly, and neither was his own.

'Mr Temple? I was wondering if you could help me.'

The vicar looked on him more severely and folded his hands. 'If this is about the cycle track, I will not back down, Mr Epford. I stand by what I say. Unscrupulous cyclists are ruining the outfield – I fear we really must part company.'

Eppie was alarmed. The vicar was highly influential on the cricket club committee and if he said he wanted to get rid of the cycle track … Eppie resolutely focused on the matter in hand.

'No, actually this is a family matter. The question of a small legacy to a cousin. But I need to be certain the legacy is justified. I'd like to check various family events in your registers.'

The vicar looked down his nose. 'I usually only grant access to lawyers in matters such as these.'

'Indeed?' Eppie smiled. 'Then I'll go and get my lawyer, shall I? I think he said he'd be available on Wednesday afternoon.'

The vicar stiffened. 'Wednesday is impossible—' He broke off suddenly. 'Very well, tell me what you want and I will fetch it. Quickly, mind!'

Eppie had never before imagined it might be a good idea to know when the Cricket Club held its committee meetings.

37

He was astonished, as he turned the corner twenty minutes or so later, to see Harry outside the shop. The lad was walking backwards and forwards as if a whole swarm of gnats was after him, waving his hand about his face as if to ward them off. When he turned and saw Eppie walking towards him, a look of sheer panic crossed his face – he even backed off a step or two as if he was planning to bolt.

'M – M – Mr Ep – Epford …'

He couldn't have developed a stammer in two days, could he?

'Good morning, Harry,' Eppie said bracingly. 'Did you want to see me? Sorry I'm late – I had to see the vicar.'

Harry's face lit up. 'Are you and Miss Gains going to get married?'

Really, did the whole town know about them? They'd deceived themselves hugely, hadn't they, in thinking they had been so discreet.

'No,' Eppie said, then amended his tone as he saw Harry flinch. 'Not yet at any rate. Come on in, Harry.' He unlocked the door and ushered the boy inside. 'What can I do for you?'

'I want to come back,' Harry blurted out, looking as if he thought Eppie would throw him out straight away. 'My mother says I shouldn't, but I'm a grown man now and I say I shall. I know you're not a murderer, Mr E, and I don't care what anyone else says!'

Eppie rather wished that had been phrased slightly differently, but never mind.

'Harry,' he said. 'Put the kettle on!'

Harry fled into the back room with a cry of delight.

Eppie had hardly taken his coat off when the door opened with a jangle. He looked expectantly towards it, hoping it was a customer. It was Amos, hesitating in the open doorway.

It was the first time Eppie had seen him since he and Alma had spoken with Belle. Amos must know. Of course he must. Belle would have told him. And the last thing Eppie wanted was to lose Amos's friendship. He seized the initiative. Or tried to, at least.

'I'm sorry, Amos. For what happened the other day. Alma and I shouldn't have …'

Amos's face was set hard, his jaw clenched. His shoulders were up around his ears. He said stiffly, 'It's a sensitive matter.'

'Of course it is.'

Harry popped his head around the door from the back room. 'Tea, Mr D?'

'Make sure it stands a good time, Harry,' Eppie called. That was their private code for: *make yourself scarce for a while.*

'Course I will,' Harry said cheerfully. 'Just popping out to the bottom of the yard, Mr E. I – er – I'll be back in a while.'

Amos waited until they heard the back door of the shop shut. He ground out, 'She did it for me, Eppie. *Because* of me. Because we don't have any money, because I spend it all on stupid bets.'

'Yes, I know,' Eppie said, waiting.

'I'm not going to do it any more, Eppie. Never again. Betting, I mean.'

'Of course not, Amos.'

'I've learnt my lesson.'

'Of course you have.' Eppie quickly calculated. Was this the third time in twelve months Amos had 'learnt his lesson'? Maybe the fourth time. And totally sincere every time.

'That time you came round …'

'Amos,' Eppie said firmly. 'We were wrong to go and see Belle without your knowledge, and I apologize. I know you're in a difficult position, and I didn't for one minute mean to interfere in the relations between man and wife – I wasn't thinking properly. I was worried. About Alma, I mean, because …'

'For God's sake, shut up, Eppie!' Amos exploded. 'I want to tell you something for your own good and you're babbling on like a five-year-old! Wetherall told Belle something. Something important.'

Eppie frowned. 'You mean something that bears on his murder?'

'Exactly. The last time he saw her he said he'd written to a lawyer in London. He said there was something he had to put right. The man was coming to Maryport expressly to see him. The night before Wetherall was killed. Don't you see, that was where he was going in his carriage that night, when you saw him! If we can trace that lawyer, maybe we can find out what was going on.'

Eppie was staring open-mouthed at him. *Not* Maitland's lawyer? *Wetherall's* lawyer. Then what had he been doing at Maitland's house? And why hadn't Belle remembered this before? Though he had walked out on her in a little bit of, well, annoyance.

'We won't be able to trace him,' he said apologetically. 'Or rather, I already have.'

'Eppie ...' Amos said menacingly.

'He's dead.'

Amos looked incredulous so he explained.

'This lawyer must have known something significant,' Amos said. 'It can't be coincidence that he should turn up now and get himself killed. And probably at about the time of Wetherall's murder too, if you're right about how long he'd been dead—'

'Amos—'

'Don't interrupt me, Eppie, I'm thinking. His body was presumably left in the house with the idea that it wouldn't be found for weeks or months at which point it would have been unrecognizable – though leaving that card was a mistake. Ham-fisted.'

'Amos—'

'But if Wetherall wrote to this lawyer, then his office in London should have a copy of the letter which will explain what this is all about.'

'I don't need a letter.' He laughed. Remarkable how good it felt when all the elements of the puzzle started to come together. 'I know what this is all about. I know everything!'

'You can be absolutely infuriating!' Amos said. 'I've been wandering about town trying to trace this lawyer for you, and now you tell me you knew all about him?'

'Well, not till I discovered his body. And I don't know how he got to Maitland's house.'

'Give me some of that damned tea and I'll tell you exactly how.'

Harry had left the tea in the pot, and the cups ranged nicely on Dick's newly-repaired table. Amos sat down with a sigh of relief. 'I must have visited every inn in town yesterday afternoon to try and find that lawyer and my feet are still aching.'

Eppie poured milk and then tea into the cups. 'And?'

'He was staying at the Coach and Horses. Not the most expensive of hotels but pretty decent. They say he was supposed to stay a week but left after only one day. Took all his luggage with him. A coach came to get him – not a private coach but a plain one, probably hired. Trying to discover where that came from would be fun, I don't think!'

'Did they see the coachman, or was there anyone to meet the lawyer?'

'A servant, they said. So nondescript, they couldn't describe him. I got the impression they never really looked. People don't look much at servants, do they?'

'And they've no idea where he was going?'

'No. He said nothing, just paid his bill and went.'

'It has to have been Maitland's doing, surely?'

Amos sipped his tea and visibly relaxed. 'I checked at his town house – I happen to know one of the footmen there and he says Maitland's had no visitors for a month or more. To be honest, my boy, he hinted that Maitland can't afford to have visitors.'

'Well, it's obvious he was driven to Maitland's country estate where he was killed.'

'Why? Come on, Eppie, it's time you came clean. What do you mean? *You know everything*!'

Eppie beamed. Goodness, but it was a wonderful feeling to have all the answers!

'Wetherall had a conscience,' he said. 'Who would have thought it? He was going to tell everyone. Give it all back.'

Amos regarded him in exasperation. 'Give what all back?'

'His money.'

'You don't mean to tell me he stole it all!'

'Only in a manner of speaking.' Eppie leant against the wall and beamed. Harry made a remarkably good cup of tea. 'He wasn't entitled to it. Because …' No, really, he couldn't draw the moment out any longer. 'Because his parents weren't married.'

38

Amos stared open-mouthed. 'Not married! But my boy, wasn't a copy of his parents' marriage certificate left here when you were supposedly burgled? Wasn't it genuine?'

'Oh yes, absolutely. And Wetherall was born fifteen months later.' He leant forward and poked Amos in the chest, enjoying himself. 'Alma told me days ago to check out the Wetherall family in the registers here, and I kept forgetting. Besides, I thought the papers had only been left here to incriminate me and didn't really matter anyway.'

Amos groaned. 'Just get on with it, Eppie.'

'But I've checked the original now, in the local registers. Wetherall's father was married before. A mere two years before. What happened to that marriage, I don't know but he and his wife were plainly estranged – I don't suppose he'd have gone off courting in Carlisle if he'd actually been living with a wife here. Rather helpfully, the parish clerk of the time was one of those who put little notes in the margins: by the first marriage he put *An unequal marriage in age, the groom being twenty-three and the bride fifty-eight years of age.*'

'Money,' Amos said succinctly.

'Exactly – she was the widow of a London merchant. I found her death as well, two years later. This time the marginal note said *Died of grief.* The point is, Amos – the date of death was precisely *one day after* Wetherall's father's second marriage.'

'Not valid!' Amos crowed. 'The fellow was a bigamist.'

'Maybe it was a genuine mistake. Maybe he thought she'd already died. And if he took his new bride off on honeymoon somewhere, as Maitland has with Mrs Wetherall, then neither they nor anyone else here might have been aware of the problem. By the time they got back home, all the dates might easily have been muddled up.'

'But Wetherall somehow found out and was going to admit it to his London lawyer.' Amos leapt up and started pacing. 'Good God, that was brave of him. He'd have lost all the money – he wouldn't have been entitled to any of it.'

'Precisely. Though it doesn't sound much like him – I'd have bet he'd just keep quiet about it. According to the vicar, there are remote cousins in London who probably should have it all.'

'And Mrs and Miss Wetherall would have been paupers.'

'So they – and Maitland – wanted to get rid of Wetherall at top speed, straight away. And just in case he'd already told the London lawyer exactly what he was at, they had to kill him too.'

Amos nodded and prowled some more. 'There's still one major problem, Eppie.'

'Only one? I can think of three or four. Who did Maitland get to do the actual killings? What was this business of the cigars? How do I stop people trying to attack me and Alma? And – crucially – how do I get proof of all this?'

'That's …'

They heard the back door open. Harry called, 'Can I come back in now, Mr E?'

Amos paced in silence as Harry helped himself to tea and went out into the shop to lay out all the tools of Eppie's trade. Eppie felt an odd sense of gratitude – things seemed so *normal*. It was only an illusion, though. There were still plenty of things to do before *real* normality descended, and even when this matter was cleared up, he was likely to have lost some customers for good. Plenty of people believed in the proverb: *no smoke without fire.*

'Right,' Amos said. 'We need proof. What do we have so far?'

Eppie ticked the points off on his fingers. 'One: we have proof that Wetherall's parents weren't married. Two: it should be easy enough to get proof that he was going to do something about it if we can get hold of the letter he wrote to the London lawyer. Three: the mourning dresses suggest strongly that the Wetherall women knew in advance someone was going to die, and you can usually only know *that* if you're planning to do something about it yourself, or know someone who is. Four: there are some strongly suggestive things concerning Maitland. He attacks me; the London lawyer's found dead in his house; he's extraordinarily short of money; he marries Mrs W with astonishing speed in defiance of all the conventions. Five: Miss Wetherall lied about overhearing that conversation between her father and someone else. She invented the whole thing. Six: we know that Wetherall was having secret meetings with someone, complete with a large expenditure on cigars. Seven …' He paused to consider. 'It doesn't add up to a lot, does it?'

'It adds up to a lot of suspicion,' Amos agreed. 'Nothing that would convince a jury.'

'What would?' Eppie said glumly.

'A confession?'

'Oh, come on, Amos! Why should any of them confess? They're happily getting away with murder. And I dare say each and every one of them would point out that they had an alibi for the time of death.'

'Maitland hired a murderer, obviously.'

'And that's another thing! People don't just agree to murder someone just because they like doing that sort of thing! Maitland would have had to *pay* this man. And we know he has no money and is living on credit.'

'He could have promised him a cut of the inheritance.'

'You mean this man agreed to commit murder on credit? *I* wouldn't. I'd want to see the money up front.'

Amos gulped down the rest of his tea and poured the last, stewed, dribble of liquid out of the pot.

'Let's take this one thing at a time. This boy, Smith, Smythe, whatever he calls himself. The chandler's son Crellin thinks Miss Wetherall is walking out with. I know him, well, I've met him. Believe me, Eppie, he hasn't a solid bone in his body. All we'll have to do is ask nicely, and if he's involved in anything he'll tell us.'

'The inspector thought the affair had been broken off ages ago.'

'Well, he would, wouldn't he? If they were planning to do something then *apparently* breaking off the affair would be the obvious thing to do.' Amos swigged the dregs of tea and winced. 'Right, I'm off.'

'What? Where?'

'To talk to this lad Smith.'

Eppie pushed himself to his feet. 'I'm coming too.'

Amos looked bewildered. 'Don't you have a shop to run, my dear fellow?'

'Of course. And I've *so* many customers.'

He gave Harry strict instructions before he left, and told the lad he could do some basic shaving and cutting if any customers should deign to come in. Harry was whistling through his teeth as they left, not at all daunted by the prospect of being left to run the business on his own. There was something new about him, Eppie reflected. All of a sudden, in only a few days, he seemed to have grown up.

Well, a little, at least.

The harbour was almost deserted, apart from a whole squawking flock of seagulls that swooped so low Eppie kept instinctively ducking. No fishing boats – they must all be out at sea. That didn't stop the quayside from being an obstacle course, particularly for people in clean clothes: coils of tarred rope, abandoned and torn nets in huge piles, stacks of planks of wood, more than a few rotting carcasses of fish being ravaged by the raucous gulls.

The chandler's shop was halfway down the quayside and was occupied by half a dozen elderly men whose idea of an energetic day was plainly to smoke and drink and talk about how fishermen in their day had it really hard, unlike the easy times their sons and grandsons were complaining about. They were being watched by a young man in smart, almost too smart, clothes who looked as if he had nothing to do either and was pretty desperate about it.

Amos went straight up to him. 'Jimmy. Jimmy Smith!'

The boy hushed him, looking over his shoulder towards an inner room in obvious panic. 'Smythe, Smythe. It's *Smythe*.'

A woman was talking to someone in the back room: a pleasant enough sounding woman but Mrs Smith – Smythe – had been running this shop for ten or more years after the death of her husband and was making a success of it. That argued she was not a woman to be trifled with. How old was her son? Twenty or twenty-one? He looked almost younger than Harry.

Amos jerked his head towards the outside. 'Let's go for a pint.'

The boy looked tempted. 'I can't. I'm minding the shop.'

'We'll just stand outside then.'

For the first time, the boy showed signs of intelligence. 'Why?'

'I want to talk to you – about Miss Violet Daisy Rose Wetherall.'

'Her!' The boy's outburst was so violent, the old men looked round. The boy lowered his voice. 'She's a devil. My mother told me she was and I didn't take any notice. But she is.'

'Jilted you, did she?' Eppie said in his most sympathetic tone. 'That must have been horrible.'

'Yes, it was.' The boy seemed torn between sullenness and gratification that his torment had been acknowledged.

'Had someone else, did she?'

'I saw her with him. A rough fellow, though he obviously thought a lot of himself.'

Amos glanced at Eppie. 'You mean, not someone of her own class?'

'Oh, she never liked that. She preferred it.' The boy was bitter. 'She said she liked me because I wasn't one of those dressed-up soft idiots she met in her mother's drawing room. Then when she turned me over, she told me I wasn't hard enough for her liking. She said I'd do anything anyone told me. I didn't! I don't! But she wanted someone rough who'd knock her about. What kind of woman does that make her?'

Eppie thought of Maitland and his reputation. And his marriage. 'Like mother like daughter, I rather think. Do you know who this fellow was?'

The boy shook his head. 'I saw her with him but I don't know who he is.'

Eppie began to take alarm. 'Don't tell anyone you saw them together, for heaven's sake! Where was this?'

The boy looked bewildered. 'On the main street. Outside your shop. And then I saw her father with him. By the Town Hall.' He looked uncomfortable, admitted, 'I was following her. The night before her father died. I went to her house to see if I could see her. I wanted to make up with her. And I saw her go out. So I followed her. She walked up into town and met a man there – him.'

So Violet Daisy Rose's story had had a basis in fact. 'And then?'

'She hailed a cab and went off again. I couldn't follow her, so I followed the man instead. And he met her father in an alleyway.'

Amos patted him on the arm. 'Well done. Did you hear what they were saying?'

The boy shook his head. 'Well, not much. I couldn't get close to start with and when I did they were just finishing off their conversation. So I only heard one thing.'

'Which was?'

The boy looked from Amos to Eppie and back again. He looked acutely embarrassed. 'The man – the one I didn't know – he said "We'll wait then, until the Easter Sports. But I guarantee Eppie Epford won't be racing."'

There was a long moment of silence. Amos glanced at Eppie.

'I'm telling the truth,' the boy said ardently.

Eppie patted him on the arm. 'Yes, I know. Thank you, you've been very helpful.'

He jerked his head at Amos and they walked back out onto the quay where the seagulls had taken it into their heads to dive bomb a small white yappy dog. Or perhaps the dog had taken it into his head to leap up madly at the low-flying gulls.

'We've miscalculated,' Amos said. 'This *is* all about you, after all.'

39

'Drat,' Eppie said.

They walked along the Quayside, heading for the road up into town. Seagulls flapped about their feet, trying to get at the scraps of fish left on the cobbles.

'It all comes down to betting, doesn't it?' Eppie said. 'You've bet on me, Constable Banks bet on me, Inspector Crellin's bet on me. But Wetherall must have bet *against* me.' And that conversation he'd had with Wetherall in the shop the day before he died, when Wetherall had been so solicitous about his health – presumably Wetherall had just been seeing how the land lay. Maybe he'd hoped to gain some information he could use against Eppie.

Amos patted Eppie on the arm as he had patted the lad. 'Just think about it, Eppie, my lad. Everyone thinks you're going to win, so believe me, the odds are shortening. But you'd get very good odds indeed on someone else winning. However, to get the money, anyone betting that way would have to make sure you couldn't win. The best method of doing that is to remove you from the race altogether. They tried to scare you into leaving town by burgling your shop and home. The attempt to frame you for the murder serves a dual purpose, because, of course, it would get you out of the race *and* deflect suspicion from the real murderer. And even if they couldn't get you out of the race entirely, they could still ruin your chances. Remember the slashing of your tyres? They thought you wouldn't have money to get a new set, so you'd be at a disadvantage even if you did take the start line.'

Eppie tried to make sense of it all. 'Wetherall knew he was going to lose all his money when he told the London lawyer he wasn't entitled to his inheritance, so he was trying to get some money from elsewhere. But for heaven's sake, he wouldn't have got much betting on the five-mile race at the Maryport Easter Sports! It's not as if it's the Derby!'

Though Wetherall's bets were reputed to be very large …

'Suppose it wasn't just you he was betting on. Suppose he had one of those bets where several races are involved – say, the five-mile here at Easter, the latest twelve-hour record attempt by a member of the Catford Club, the two o'clock horse race at Newmarket. And maybe, just maybe, there's something *really* big going on. Maybe he has a bet that doesn't involve money. A wager with a London crony, for instance – those fellows of leisure bet the most amazing things on inconsequential races. You know, something like "my entire Wiltshire estate is yours if Eppie Epford doesn't win on Easter Monday in Maryport."'

Eppie didn't know whether to believe him or not. But hadn't Wetherall said something the day before his death about sometimes having to take big risks to get what you want? And he *had* just come back from London. Goodness, perhaps people did tell their barbers secrets after all. Or at least, significant information. But honestly, wouldn't it just have been easier to keep quiet about his parents' awkwardly premature wedding?

'Ridiculous! What on earth do you get out of betting, Amos?'

'Fun!' Amos beamed. 'That's the point, Eppie. Wetherall would probably have carried on betting regardless of the inheritance thing. Once you have the bug, it doesn't go away. You bet for the sake of betting, for the chance to win. Excitement! What do you get out of racing?'

'With any luck – a gentleman's dressing case worth three guineas, a medal and bragging rights over Dick Sibson and all the others.'

'See. Same thing. The excitement of winning. The feeling of superiority. I bet the bet on you had nothing to do with whether he was going to give up his inheritance or not.'

'I still can't believe a man would do that. Why not simply keep quiet about his parents' marriage?'

Amos tut-tutted. 'Hardly moral behaviour, my dear fellow.'

'Wetherall didn't strike me as a moral man. Think of all those affairs.' And giving his wife's jewellery to the woman he wanted as his mistress. Though he didn't say that aloud.

Did he hear his name? He glanced up and saw Alma hurrying down the hill towards him. She was wearing one of her eminently sensible skirts with a stylish blouse and was waving a parasol over her head. The very picture of femininity, apart from the sling that comforted her left arm. Actually, Eppie wasn't particularly interested in displays of fine femininity – give him Alma on her bicycle in her knickerbockers any day.

She was almost breathless when she came up to them. 'I went to your shop but Harry said you'd come down here.' She glanced at Amos, a trifle self-consciously. 'I want you to know, Mr Danson, that I don't regret for one minute what Eppie and I did in confronting your wife. It had to be done. Eppie's life is at stake, to say nothing of his livelihood and his racing career.'

She lifted her head and presented her chin to them, with an obstinate twist to her mouth. Eppie held his breath and looked at Amos.

Amos burst out laughing. 'My dear Miss Gains, I understand the situation perfectly. You did, in short, exactly what I would have done in defence of Belle. And in any case, as I've just told Eppie, Belle did know something worth knowing. Why don't we all go and have a nice cup of tea and talk this over?'

'There's not a great deal to talk over,' Alma said high-handedly.

'Certainly there is. We need to work out a way to make the murderer confess, don't we?'

Half the ladies of the town seemed to be gathered in the tea-rooms. Eppie had brought Alma up to date with what they knew as they strolled back up the hill from the harbour into town.

'Wetherall was plainly completely mad – he had a bad conscience about owning money that wasn't rightfully his because of his parents' marriage but he had no scruples whatsoever about making bets of doubtful morality and employing someone to dispose of me!'

Alma seated herself in the chair Eppie had just pulled out for her. She glanced around to see if there was anyone she knew. Eppie sat down in his own chair.

'According to what you say this lad Smythe heard, Mr Wetherall had been promised you wouldn't ride in the sports. Maybe he'd been told you could be scared off, or given a minor injury that would have prevented you riding. He may not have intended to harm you.'

'It's an improvement over trying to get me in the condemned cell for murder, I suppose.'

'Well, obviously Wetherall had nothing to do with that! Given that he was the one doomed to die.'

Amos waved imperiously at the waitress. 'If only you two would let me finish! One of my cronies tells me that Maitland has put a large bet on you, Eppie.'

'To win?' Alma raised an eyebrow as Amos nodded.

The waitress came up and they ordered – Amos demanding a plate of cakes big enough for six, on the principle presumably that he himself could probably eat them all on his own.

'Wetherall and Maitland were not in the best of charity with each other – we know that,' Alma said. 'Suppose Maitland provoked Wetherall into a bet. Maitland says you'll win – Wetherall must therefore say that you won't. Wetherall would like the idea of getting the better of his despised future son-in-law.'

'And then?' Eppie asked cautiously.

'And then Maitland employs this mysterious man. He sends him to get Wetherall's confidence by cooking up a plan to get you out of the race. If Wetherall was conspiring with this man, then he'd hardly have been alarmed when the man came up to him in the alley on the day of the murder. He'd simply have said something like "We can't meet now! Not in daylight!" and turned his back on the man. Who would then have been able to hit him over the head and kill him.'

'That sounds reasonable,' Eppie said cautiously. He could see something like that happening.

Amos was eying the plate of cakes the waitress had just put down on the table.

'Why are cakes always so small? I could eat one of those in a single bite.'

He offered the plate to Alma and she took a piece of chocolate cake. Eppie shook his head. 'You can have mine. I'm in training.'

'What I want to know,' Amos said, 'is where the cigars come in.'

Alma sipped tea. 'It was obviously a negotiation of some kind. The number of cigars corresponds to amounts of money. One cigar for ten pounds, two means twenty, three means thirty.'

'Yes, yes, but ten pounds for what?' Amos took two cakes at once – one presumably for himself and one for Eppie.

'I got those meetings with Wetherall and the mysterious man the wrong way round,' Eppie said. 'The man wasn't trying to blackmail Wetherall. Wetherall was paying him to have a go at me and take me out of the race. Manufacture a nice collar bone injury maybe. The cigars signified the amount of money he was willing to pay for the man's services. He offered one pound, the man said no. Two cigars doubled the offer, three tripled it. That's when the man said yes. Or, as you suggested, it was more probably ten, twenty and thirty pounds.'

'I'd want three *hundred*.'

'But of course this man was planning to kill Wetherall on Maitland's orders so he'd never have to carry out the attack on me.'

Alma nodded. 'Which means he could promise to do whatever Wetherall asked, in the sure and certain knowledge he wouldn't have to act on it. And you can guarantee that he made sure that Wetherall paid him the money that night.'

Amos gulped down a butterfly cake. 'In short, he took money from Maitland to kill Wetherall, and money from Wetherall to remove Eppie from the race. Obviously a man who knows the value of his services. But look on the bright side, my dear fellow – it means that in practice there was never any danger to you, because the man never intended to do anything. Except have you arrested for murder of course.'

'Which still,' Alma said, picking apart the chocolate cake, 'leaves us with the critical question: who *is* this mysterious man?'

'We need to set a trap for him,' Amos said, gobbling up the second butterfly cake.

'A trap!' Eppie cleared his throat. 'No, no, I don't like the sound of that. We don't need a trap.'

'Yes, we do, dear boy. Because as you pointed out before, he's hardly going to confess, is he? We need to *make* him confess.'

'I didn't say that, you did.'

'Will you please stop bickering,' Alma said sternly. 'We can't make anyone confess if we don't know who he is! And will one of you pour the tea, because I can't do it with one hand.'

There were a few moments of ruminative silence as Eppie stirred the tea and poured the milk into the cups. Amos presented Alma with the depleted plate of cakes and she took a vanilla slice.

'So *you're* not in training?' he said sympathetically. 'Do I take it the arm won't be healed in time for the sports?'

'I'm afraid not. The doctor has said quite categorically that I need to wear this sling for another two weeks. And I must admit, it does hurt rather.'

Eppie frowned and pushed a cup of tea across the table to her. 'Will you stay with your aunt then?'

'I can't. Not much more than a day or so, at any rate. The headmaster has sent me a letter asking me to return as a matter of urgency.' She smiled slightly. 'He does tend to panic when things aren't exactly the same as they usually are. He likes his routine.'

'What we need to work out,' Amos said, eyeing the last cake – a wedge of apple cake – 'is who would win if you were out of the race. Are you sure you don't want a piece of cake, my dear fellow?'

'Absolutely certain. Why does it matter who'd win if I was out of it?'

'Because the person in question will be the one Wetherall bet on. And very possibly the mysterious man has bet on the same man too, because he knows that with any luck you'll be in prison awaiting trial when the race comes round and therefore not able to compete. How could he resist putting on a bet? If we can identify the likely winner, then I can go off, and try and find out who's bet heavily on him.'

'Oh Lord, this sounds almost as mad as Wetherall's plot to remove me from the running.'

'And you have a better plan, my dear fellow?'

'Well, *you* won't win,' Eppie retorted. 'Not with all that cake you've just eaten!'

'There are half a dozen people who might win,' Alma said. 'Dick Sibson, of course. And I've heard that William Brookes and Alec Howie from Carlisle are planning to come down here and race.'

Amos frowned. 'Don't they have their own Easter Sports? And why are you so sure I have no chance?'

'There's a dispute between the Conservative Cycling Club and the Liberal Cycling Club as to which one the judges for the Carlisle Sports should come from. So the Liberal Cycling Club has decided not to support the event.'

'Oh, really!' Amos said irritably, signalling to the waitress. 'Anyone else want another cake? How petty can you get!'

'That's what happens when you let politics into cycling,' Eppie said. 'Anyway, the Carlisle cyclists won't be here. Because when I was talking to the vicar this morning, who as you know is on the committee for the Sports despite the fact that he hates all things cycling, he told me that the entry forms from the Carlisle cyclists arrived after the closing date.' He sighed. 'He said, and I quote, "which should ensure you win".'

'He's bet on you too!' Amos said. 'I thought clergymen weren't supposed to bet.'

Alma pursed her lips. 'Which leaves only the local men. Dick Sibson, Tom Gill, William White.'

'Yes,' Eppie said, slowly. 'That's all I can think of too.'

'It'll be Dick Sibson,' Amos said. 'The other two aren't bad, but they're better at the short distances.'

Eppie raised an eyebrow. 'So *you* don't think you've any chance of winning either.'

'I'm going for the one mile, my dear fellow.' Amos ordered another plate of cakes. 'I'm going to win that too. I did last year.'

Alma asked Eppie to pour her another cup of tea. 'Supposing Mr Danson does manage to identify someone who has put large sums of money on Mr Sibson to win, what do we do then?'

'Set a trap for the villain!' Amos said with relish.

Eppie sighed. 'One thing at a time. Let's see what we can find out before we dash into plans to set traps. After all, the sort of trap we need to set will depend on who we suspect, doesn't it?'

'It could be argued,' Alma said, 'that we need to set a trap for Maitland. After all, he might give us the name of the mysterious man just to avoid the charge of murder himself.'

Amos shook his head. 'Maitland's an idiot but he'd see through a plan in no time. How about the ladies? Not Mrs Wetherall – Mrs Maitland, I mean. She's old enough to be careful and keep out of trouble – look at the way she's stayed in the background throughout this business. But *Miss* Wetherall – she'd give the man away, I bet.' He preened himself a little and helped himself to one of the new butterfly cakes. 'I could get her to talk.'

Alma cast Eppie an impish little smile.

Eppie thought of Violet Daisy Rose Wetherall sitting here in this tea-room, telling him a pack of lies about herself.

'She certainly thinks she has *my* measure.' He looked at Alma and Amos. Amos waggled his eyebrows at him. 'Well, what can it hurt? Amos, you go off and see what you can find out about the bets against me. We'll go our separate ways and think about the situation, see what ideas we can come up with. Then we can meet here again tomorrow and exchange ideas. What do you say?'

Alma shook her head. 'We ought to move as quickly as possible. That man is still out there – he may try and do you some harm.'

'No, I don't think so.' He saw the scepticism in her face, added, 'There's plenty of time. There's still a chance Crellin might arrest me for Wetherall's murder and take me out of action that way.'

Looking at them, he thought they accepted this, a little reluctantly perhaps. Amos would go round his contacts and try and uncover suspicious betting, and

Alma would stay indoors and rack her brains for what best to do.

Which gave him an evening to sort this whole business out while they were both safe and sound.

40

He had to wait a long time before Dick answered the door and he didn't like standing in the dark street much. The nearest street lamp was out and he was uncomfortably aware that half a dozen women in the terraced street had lifted the corners of their curtains to see who was visiting. Mrs McCormack probably had relatives in these houses. And to cap it all, it was beginning to rain.

Dick opened the door a fraction of an inch and peered suspiciously out.

'Oh, it's you.' He opened the door wider. 'Come on in and make it quick. There's a damn wild dog around that keeps trying to get in houses.'

The poor thing probably wanted a bit of comfort. Not that Eppie minded – he wasn't a dog person. A nice independent cat would be another matter. He'd often thought of getting a cat. One of those no-nonsense black and white ones.

The hallway was narrow, the house dark and smelling of cabbage. Dick must have been conscious of that; he said, 'I've just had my dinner.' He took Eppie straight into the kitchen which was half the size of Eppie's though that was small enough. Dirty dishes stood on the kitchen table, with a bicycle pump and other tools sharing the space and a smudge or two of oil. The only welcoming sound was the kettle boiling and even that seemed to hiss rather than to bubble cheerfully.

'What's this all about then?'

'I was hoping you could lend me a hand.'

Dick poured water into an unwarmed pot. 'With this Wetherall business?'

Eppie nodded. 'I don't want to go to the police, because they'd probably just arrest me, and I don't want to get Amos Danson involved in it because, quite frankly, he's got a habit of messing things up.'

'There's always your lady friend,' Dick said sourly.

Eppie was indignant. 'I think I know better than to get a *lady* mixed up in villainy of this sort! Anyway, if you want that bill of yours paid promptly – and let me tell you it's quite outrageously high despite what we agreed! – you'll have to hope I do well in the Sports. Which means helping me get these men, whoever they are, off my back.'

Dick looked at him sharply and got two chipped cups out of the cupboard. 'So I'm supposed to help get you out of trouble, even though it might mean I lose the races?'

'Or you could look on it as helping a friend out.'

'I'm not helping with anything until I know what's going on.'

Eppie was ready for this. He launched into an explanation of his theory: how Maitland, Mrs Wetherall and Miss Wetherall were all in on the plot, how they'd been desperate to stop Wetherall having his fit of conscience, how they'd hired someone to do the actual killing. And how that certain someone had done a deal on the side with Wetherall – or been encouraged to do so by Maitland.

'And do you know who this someone is?' Dick handed the cup to Eppie. The brew was the strongest Eppie had ever tasted – Dick must have put at least ten spoonsful of tea in the pot.

'I wish I did. But I know who *does* know – Miss Wetherall.' He recounted their encounter in the tea shop. 'She wanted me to believe she was still walking out with young Smith, the chandler's boy. Crellin told me that was over an age ago. Smith himself said he knew she'd found herself someone new – someone a bit rough, he said, though he didn't have the slightest idea who. He said he'd never seen them together, only heard about them. Don't you see – that's the murderer. He's either doing it for love …'

Dick made a derisive noise.

'Or he's doing it for a share of the young lady's dowry. Or for a portion of Wetherall's estate.'

'Money's much more likely,' Dick said, gulping down his tea. '*I* wouldn't do it for love.'

'I wouldn't do it at all,' Eppie said. 'But some people aren't particularly scrupulous. Will you help me?'

'So you don't want to get your lady friend in trouble and you don't want to risk that journalist fellow, but you don't mind putting me in the way of danger.'

'Come on, Dick – you can deal with anything!'

Dick finished his tea. 'Yes, I can. And I know how to look after myself. Which in this case means I don't get involved at all.'

'Then you won't come to the track with me?'

Dick paused in the act of pouring himself more tea. The smell of cabbage and oil was becoming almost overwhelming. He looked sideways at Eppie. 'Why the track?'

'Because that's where I've arranged to meet Miss Wetherall. In about half an hour from now. At least, if she comes in response to the note I sent her ten minutes ago.'

Dick contemplated Eppie thoughtfully. 'I get it – you're going to try and trap her into revealing the name of her lover?'

'I'm going to offer her a deal. She's young and naïve, Dick! She can't know what she was getting herself into. And even if she did, she can't have imagined she could be facing the hangman's noose.'

'Sounds like it'll be easy to get her to talk. So why do you want me there?'

'Because I think she might tell her lover that I've asked to meet her, and he's obviously going to be a totally different kettle of fish. I think he'll tell her to meet me then follow her and hope for a chance to dispose of me. And if that happens I'll need someone strong to lend me a hand.'

Dick sighed. 'Eppie, you're an idiot! The fellow could have a gun – he could simply fire at you from the shelter of the pavilion and there'd be nothing you could do about it.'

Eppie shook his head. 'No. If he kills me, it has to look like an accident, or possibly suicide. If it looks like murder, he'll spark another investigation and there'll be no one convenient left to take the blame. I suspect he'll try to arrange it so it looks as if I fell off my machine. He'll probably be planning to break my neck.' He could see the odd look on Dick's face, laughed wryly. 'You think this is completely mad …'

'I do.' Dick heaved himself off the sink and put his cup down. 'But for what it's worth, I can't think of a better plan. And it would be better to sort this matter out sooner rather than later. Then you can leave me alone to get on with training to beat you on Easter Monday. If you've arranged to meet the lady in half an hour, we'd better be going.'

It had started to rain in earnest, a thin miserable drizzle that dampened more than it seemed to and made the road beneath the bicycle wheels wet and slick. Dick nearly skidded several times, taking corners too quickly. Eppie pedalled along behind him, from the pool of light cast by one street lamp, into darkness, into light again. Feeling curiously content. As Dick had said, if you had to have a confrontation, better to get it over with, so you could concentrate on more interesting things. Like the Sports. And how much he could save, over what period of time, so he and Alma could marry. Also sooner rather than later. A pity he'd have to spend it on a new pair of pneumatic tyres for his racing bike, but without them, he'd never be able to win. And with any luck, once he was revealed as being entirely innocent of murder, the customers would come back. He might do well to put his prices down for a week or two …

The high wall of the cricket field loomed up ahead. Dick took the last few corners much too fast and got ahead of Eppie by a couple of hundred yards. By the time Eppie got there, the narrow gate was swinging open and there was no sign of Dick. Eppie dismounted and shouldered through the gate – after a moment's thought, he shut it carefully. The cricket field was faintly lit by the orange glow from the lamps in the streets around the perimeter – enough to see by though it wasn't exactly easy.

The slope down from the gate was slippery with rain and he slithered a bit before coming onto the hard-pressed grass of the track. Across the other side of the track, he could see Dick, hurrying round to the back of the pavilion, presumably trying to get out of sight before Miss Wetherall turned up.

Eppie took his time crossing the track, checking his watch for the time. Miss Wetherall ought to be here by now, although young ladies in his experience had an imprecise understanding of time. Across the track, he heard the second gate, the larger one behind the pavilion, clang shut. Was that Dick? Maybe he'd just looked out to see if he could spot Miss Wetherall …

He leant his machine against the pavilion wall and settled down on a dry patch on one of the steps to wait. Dick poked his head round the end wall, his face blurred and indistinct.

'She's not here. I'm lying low at the back.'

'Good,' Eppie said.

Dick disappeared again. Eppie looked up at the door into the pavilion at the top of the steps. It was pretty dark up there under the veranda but he couldn't see the padlock on the latch and the door looked fractionally ajar. Well, if the rain got any worse, he'd forgo his distaste of the smell in there and they could go inside. Though he suspected Miss Wetherall was tougher than she looked.

She was a long time in coming but at last the gate at the top of the slope opened and he saw a ghostly white figure slip through. She was wearing white? Surely it should have been mourning? Was that a hint she was putting off pretence? Surely she would rather have lulled him into complacency, put on the dutiful daughter act for him again.

She came down the wet slope of the grass carefully, picking her way down the stone steps put there for the purpose, lifting her skirts to keep them dry. Then she walked across the grass towards him. She was taking her time, nothing hurried about her, though his note should rightly have put her in a panic. In an odd way, Eppie admired that – she was a cool piece, that was for certain. He'd have to find exactly the right words to trip her up.

As she came closer, he saw she was smiling. A hard smile masquerading as demureness. He could almost hear what she was thinking – that she could wrap him round her little finger.

'You've made a mistake,' he said, going straight on the attack, as if it was the last bend of a race. 'If you think that dress is going to make me swoon at the sight of you and bend to your every whim, you're wrong.'

It was a remarkable dress in its own way, rather more revealing than he ever hoped to see on Alma, at least in public. Very thin – sunlight would have revealed every curve of her body beneath it. She stopped, staring at him. Her mouth set in a hard line that was no more attractive than the smile.

'Very well,' she said. 'Let's not shilly-shally. We both know why you wanted to see me so let's get straight to the point of this meeting.' She set her head on one side, considering him. Her blonde ringlets cascaded over one shoulder. 'How much do you want?'

41

WELL, THAT WASN'T a surprising conclusion for her to come to – in fact he'd hoped she'd make that assumption.

'Money, Miss Wetherall? Whatever makes you think I want money from you? By the way, would that be the money your new stepfather is going to give you for your part in the plot to kill your father?'

Miss Wetherall sighed heavily. 'I prefer to call it my dowry. Oh, *please*, Mr Epford, don't tell me you're going to lecture me on filial duty! My father was a complete idiot and you know it. Giving his money back! As if that could ever do any good. *Dear* Papa was going to give up everything for no reason at all, leaving Mama and I paupers.'

Eppie nodded. 'I think you're right, he had no conscience at all. I wonder if when we investigate this whole matter thoroughly, we'll discover he hadn't decided to hand the inheritance back at all.'

She frowned at him. He explained, 'We assumed your father had summoned his London lawyer here to tell him the truth about the inheritance. You know, the lawyer you and your co-conspirators killed? I suspect it may have been the other way round. When we contact the lawyer's London associates, we may well discover *he* had discovered the truth and informed your father of the situation. Knowing there was nothing he could do to escape the situation, your father chose to pose as a man of conscience to make himself look good. A man who's prepared to plot to remove someone from a race in order to win a bet isn't the sort of man who will worry too much about whether the money he bets with is rightfully his or not.'

She shrugged. The revealing dress fluttered so much that Eppie had to resolutely stare at her face.

'What practical difference does it make?'

'Well, I suspect that whatever condition you and your mother found yourselves in, your father would have made sure he would not have been a pauper. I suspect he put a good proportion of his inheritance in places where it couldn't be found by the lawyers. And he certainly indulged in betting what was probably a considerable amount at various races, including the five-mile bicycle race at the Easter Sports. I assume you, or your lover, have a bet or two on that race as well?'

'Using Father's money,' she said limpidly.

But there was a muscle ticking at the side of her mouth, as if she was angry, or afraid. He began to think that if she'd been a bicyclist she would have been a real scorcher. Always riding a little too fast, a little too close to the kerb, a little too high on the banking, always taking the other riders' lines, or forcing them out of the sprint.

'Very well,' Eppie said. 'To practicalities. To what actually happened. Your father hired someone to ensure I didn't race. A simple business transaction. But you and your step-papa, and your lover and your mother, were orchestrating everything. You're all as bad as one another. The man your father hired is your lover and the plan was that he'd kill your father and you'd then use me as a scapegoat, which would obviously take me out of the race. You and your mother would get your inheritance and the added bonus of the money on bets. Maitland would get his wealthy bride and you would take a dowry and marry your working man. Who would of course be very happy to get his hands on both you and your money, even if he had to do some dirty work to get it.'

At least she was listening to him even if she still had that mocking little smile on her lips.

'The money, of course, is essential because you have no intention of finding yourself impoverished, living in a tiny terraced house in a poor area of town. The dowry would buy you and your lover a comfortable life though how long the money will last is hard to say. Not long, I suspect.'

He took a deep breath. Was that smile just a trifle annoyed now?

'And I suspect I even put part of the plot at least into your heads by being so eager to view the body and insist it was murder.'

She smiled sweetly.

'The burglary in the shop was intended to plant evidence on me and implicate me in that break-in at your home – which I'd lay odds never happened.'

'Oh but it did!' she protested, with one of her unpleasant smirks. 'There was a small amount of money taken. But we'd already left the papers in your shop the previous weekend. We thought you'd report the burglary and that Inspector Crellin would discover the papers when investigating and assume that you'd forced Father to give you them. But that didn't happen, so when we discovered the burglary that happened during the funeral, we thought we might as well make use of it. It seemed too good an opportunity to miss. Why didn't you report your burglary?'

'Because,' Eppie said, realizing that he had done at least one thing right, 'when I found the papers, I thought they were relevant to your father's death – as indeed they were – so I kept them to myself. And, I admit, I didn't trust the inspector to come to the right conclusions. Why on earth did you leave papers that were so significant?'

She sighed. 'We had to use some papers that were clearly Papa's and I just picked up the first ones I came across in his desk. They were together with some bills and accounts, and I assumed they were simply financial matters. I hardly looked at them.'

Really, she was a complete fool – to hand him a clue like that!

Even if he had been a bit dilatory in realizing what the papers meant.

The rain came down harder. Miss Wetherall didn't seem to notice. Or perhaps she was glad of it. The thin material of her dress was beginning to cling to her shoulders and to her bosom and to lay a sheen of moisture on the exposed curve of her breasts. And she didn't even seem to be shivering!

Eppie resolutely moved on. 'The burglary at my house on the other hand was intended to try and scare me into leaving town. You and your mother both encouraged me to flee on various occasions. If I ran off, everyone would have assumed I was guilty of the murder. Though how you planned to get around the problem of my being in my shop shaving several constables at the time of your father's death, I can't imagine.'

She looked up at him coyly. 'I'm sure something would have occurred. In any case, Inspector Crellin is hardly the most intelligent man in town.'

'Oh, he's not that bad. And there'd have been a jury to convince too.'

'Who would have heard all the rumours and stories and have it firmly fixed in their minds that you were guilty.'

He was curious. 'Could you have watched me hanged for a crime you knew I hadn't committed?'

'Oh yes,' she said. 'When the alternative was suffering the same fate myself, certainly.'

He mimed astonishment. '*You* were the one who killed your father?'

She sighed. 'You and the inspector are much of a piece, are you not? How could I possibly have hit a man over the head when he was so much taller than me?'

That disposed of the theory that she'd dropped something which Wetherall had bent to pick up. It had never been particularly attractive.

'Well, it couldn't have been your mother – for the same reason – or Maitland – he was in a council meeting. So it was your lover?'

She said nothing.

'You don't want to give me his name? Fair enough. Shall I give you it instead?'

Did a shade of alarm cross her face? He smiled on her. 'You see, there were a number of clues that gave the game away, though I admit I didn't put them all together until quite recently. The so-called burglary at my shop is easy enough to explain – the shop has my name on the window and on the fascia above. But how did your lover know where I lived? And when he burgled the house, he slashed the tyres on all my machines – that was a *big* hint as to his identity.'

'We wanted to stop you entering the race,' she said tightly. 'If you didn't have tyres you couldn't compete.'

He shook his head. 'Every cyclist has spares and the burglar knows that. Oh, they're not as good but no good racer ought to be entirely dependent on his equipment. I ought to be able to put in a decent performance even on inferior tyres.' Well, he ought – even if it would injure his chances of winning. 'No, slashing the tyres was a piece of sheer vindictiveness. Which was a strong indication that the burglar – your lover – has a personal grudge against me. Which in turn indicates that it's someone I know. And he knew too about my friend, Miss Gains—'

She smiled sweetly again and he lost his temper.

'Will you *please* stop smirking! It's a very unpleasant habit, you know. As a matter of fact, Miss Gains is central to this matter. I don't like what you and your family have been doing to me, but in attacking Miss Gains you have gone utterly beyond the pale.'

She opened her mouth to speak but he took hold of her arm, gripping so tightly that she winced and tried to pull back. The bare flesh of her arm was chill and damp with rain.

'No, I haven't finished yet. I want to talk about the death of that poor lawyer from London whose only crime was to be doing his job conscientiously. You believed your father had summoned him here to tell him the truth about the inheritance and decided he had to be done away with before they could meet. Of course, if I'm right, and he was the originator of the information, then his associates in London probably also know all about the matter. They certainly will not let it lie. You may lose that money yet.'

She snarled at him.

'The poor man was lured out to Maitland's house where he was killed by your lover. Since the place is totally deserted and no one is likely to go there for years, it must have seemed an ideal place to commit murder. Even when the body was eventually discovered, Maitland could have convincingly claimed ignorance: "But Inspector, I haven't been to the place for years ... It must have been a vagrant attacking the man for his valuables." You choose your murder sites outrageously, don't you? One incredibly public, the other empty and lonely. And after the lawyer was killed, his murderer went on to attack me. And I was completely idiotic and overlooked the obvious.'

She still had that lifting smirk on her lips, but the lines of her jaw were tense and he saw the fear in her eyes.

He raised his voice. 'It's all right, you can come out now. We can talk this out face to face.'

And he turned towards the pavilion.

42

DICK STROLLED ROUND the side of the pavilion, lounged against the wall. He was smiling. Eppie looked at him as if he was seeing him for the first time. A thin man but tallish, dark-faced, dark-eyed, dark-haired. How could he not have recognized him in Mrs Cartwright's description? And wearing that devil-may-care look that so attracted the ladies.

'Really, Eppie.' Dick sounded amused. 'What bee have you got in your bonnet now? You're blaming me for all this?' He gestured towards Miss Wetherall. 'Look at the lady – why should you think she'd give me a second glance?'

That would have carried more conviction if Miss Wetherall had not been smiling at Dick at the very moment he spoke. A look of smiling complicity.

'You've always known how to handle the ladies, Dick.'

Miss Wetherall began to protest. Eppie unceremoniously cut her off. If she was going to abandon her modesty, her manners, her reputation, and her morals, then he didn't see why he needed to be polite to her any more.

'It was just a little too obvious that you were up to something, Dick – when you rode on ahead so you could get here first. You met Miss Wetherall behind the pavilion, told her what was going on, and suggested she should go out of the gate behind the pavilion then walk round the outside of the ground and come in by the other gate to make it look as if she'd just arrived. While she was distracting me with all this talk, you planned to come out of the shelter of the pavilion and knock me over the top of the head like you did Wetherall. Then, no doubt, you'd have arranged the scene to make it look as if I'd fallen off my bike and hit my head on something. You'd have said you were here and saw it all. Which incidentally makes a change from last night at Maitland's house, when you went to the trouble of pretending to leave then doubling back to attack me.'

Dick said nothing.

'Then you'd have gone off, claiming you were never there and left me to be found alongside our friend the lawyer, whom you had also killed. Or possibly never found at all. Was all that farrago about your encounter with Maitland at the pit just made up, by the way? To gain my confidence, I presume. You were a bit worried when I said how hard up he was, weren't you? Hadn't you realized? Did you worry he might renege on his agreement to give your wife her "dowry"?'

He stopped talking. He looked from Dick to Miss Wetherall and knew that the situation was bad. Neither of them was even bothering to deny his accusations. He'd got himself into a nasty situation and he rather wished he hadn't. Dick had taken hold of the young lady's arm and was standing possessively close to her. Eppie tried sarcasm, in the hope of needling one or the other of them into admitting their guilt.

'When's the wedding?'

'Last week,' Dick said. 'We're off to London immediately after the Easter Sports. Which I'm going to win.'

Well, if in trouble, keep talking. Even if you're making it up as you go along.

'As a matter of interest, Wetherall only asked you to injure me, didn't he? Not to kill me. He wasn't a vicious man, just a selfish one. And Maitland wanted a live suspect, didn't he? He may be unscrupulous but he does have a little bit of sense – he knew my death would simply remove me as a suspect and throw all the suspicion on you all. But you decided to dispose of me more permanently.'

Dick grinned. 'I did, indeed. You're an argumentative fellow, Eppie, and an obstinate one. If you were unjustly accused, you'd never let the matter alone. Not till your last breath. You're a racer – and racers never give up. You'd be in that five-mile race even if you had to tie yourself to the machine. And you'd be in that courtroom till the last possible moment, earnestly trying to convince people of your innocence. And you might just have said something that gave someone pause. Crellin's not a *complete* idiot. But you can have the consolation of knowing I'd forever regret your passing.'

Was all that an admission? Probably not good enough to convince a jury.

'Rubbish! You'd have made hay at the Easter Sports. You wouldn't have regretted it at all.'

'But I would have remembered you fondly.'

'I'm delighted to hear it. Humour my curiosity, Dick, how exactly did you kill Wetherall? A hammer, was it? Or—'

He stopped, heart in mouth. Dick had let go of his wife's arm and stepped back. Eppie blinked. There was a knife in Dick's hand. The blade glinted orange in the faint light of the street lamps.

'Careful,' Eppie said, and was horrified to hear his voice crack. He cleared his throat. 'You can't explain away a knife wound by a bicycle crash.'

'I can blame it on a robbery gone wrong.' Dick put on the air of making up a story. 'We agreed to do a bit of late night training together, a good ride around the quiet streets and out onto the Silloth road.'

'In the dark?'

'I said I'd meet you here but when I got here, you were lying on the ground dead and your watch and money were missing.' Dick frowned. 'We'd better take your bicycle too. A thief would get a good sum for that.'

'Really?' Eppie said mockingly. 'You can hide a watch and money easily enough but what are you going to do about a bicycle?'

'Put it with mine,' Dick said. 'Do you think Crellin would recognize one bicycle from another?' He grinned. 'Taking a bit of a risk, I know, but why not? What else is life for? There's something else I'm going to have to deal with too. Someone else. That lady friend of yours.'

Eppie started forward. Dick raised the knife and waggled it at him. 'You really shouldn't have got her involved in this, Eppie.'

Eppie launched himself at Dick. Taken by surprise, Dick took a step back. Miss Wetherall – *Mrs Sibson* – jerked away from them both. Eppie cannoned into Dick. Dick staggered. Didn't fall. He slashed the knife in Eppie's direction. Eppie leapt back and heard cloth rip. Dick came at him. He ducked.

Slipped on the wet grass, waved his arms for balance. Fell.

He scrambled for purchase on the hard track, trying to get up, failed. Dick was standing over him, smirking. 'I really am sorry, Eppie …'

'The devil you are!'

The knife glistened with drizzle, swung lower …

A tremendous crash. Alma shouted, 'I'm armed! Drop the knife!'

Everyone froze. Dick hung over Eppie, knife poised. Eppie held his breath. So that's where the pavilion's padlock had gone.

'Step back,' Alma called. Where was she? Inside the pavilion? The door had been ajar, hadn't it? 'I warn you, I *will* fire.'

Dick didn't move.

'Who can move fastest?' Alma called. 'Can you hurt Eppie with that knife more quickly than I can fire this gun?'

Eppie started praying: *Please let Dick believe Alma has a gun. Please let Dick believe Alma has a gun …*

'Throw the knife down,' Alma called. 'Toss it to your left. Away from Eppie and your wife.'

Dick hesitated.

Alma shouted, '*Do it!*'

He snarled and tossed the knife away.

Eppie was looking at his face as he did it and he didn't like Dick's expression one little bit. He scrambled up and took several steps back. Now what? When Alma came out of the pavilion, Dick would see she had no gun.

'Eppie! Pick the knife up, please.'

He edged round towards the knife.

Miss Wetherall took flight. She jerked into action, hitched up her skirt and sprinted for the side of the pavilion, stumbling and then jerking herself upright again. Dick roared in fury, started after her, slipped, went headlong in the wet grass. Eppie swooped for the knife, grabbed it, ran towards Dick.

'Don't move!'

'What a good idea,' Inspector Crellin said.

He emerged from behind the pavilion, the other end to where Dick had been hiding, stood beaming at Miss Wetherall, who'd stumbled to a halt. Behind him, Constables Banks and Tinnion loomed like two of the local mountains, high helmets and rain capes making them look like giants.

'Why didn't you come out before?' Eppie protested. 'I was waiting for you to arrest them!'

Crellin shook his head. 'You never got him to actually admit it. He never actually said the words, "Yes, I killed Wetherall."'

'Oh for heaven's sake!'

'But it's all right now he's tried to kill you. Ah ha!'

Miss Wetherall had tried to make another bolt for it. Crellin caught her by the arm. She cried out in pain. He pushed her into Banks' huge arms.

'Constable Tinnion. Arrest Mr Sibson, will you?'

The constable sauntered across and took the knife out of Eppie's hand.

'I'll take that if you don't mind, sir.' He aimed a sharp kick at Dick on the ground. 'Right, you. Get up. And take it carefully!'

Dick gave in without even a scuffle. That was the trouble with scorchers, Eppie thought – they got discouraged easily. Crellin raised a hand to Eppie in thanks then the whole party was trudging off towards the gate. Dick had his head down, Miss Wetherall was uttering language entirely unbecoming a young lady. But then she was a married woman now and presumably thought she was allowed a little more latitude.

Eppie looked back at the pavilion. Alma was standing on the steps, her arm still in its sling. She looked totally unruffled, her red hair an odd glinting orange shade in the light of the street lamps.

'I know,' she said. 'I should have gone home to my aunt's. You wanted to keep me out of danger.'

She started down the steps towards him, came up to him, and straightened his collar, brushed down his coat.

'There are mud and grass stains all over your clothes. Eppie Epford, if we're going to get married …'

'If?' he said, horrified.

'Which we are, you're going to have to accept one thing.'

He was relieved. 'Just one?'

'But an important one. There is no part of your life that I am going to be excluded from, dangerous or otherwise.' She smoothed down the collar. 'Understand?'

'Yes,' he said. 'Please.'